Middle-earth Minstrel

Middle-earth Minstrel

Essays on Music in Tolkien

Edited by
Bradford Lee Eden

McFarland & Company, Inc., Publishers
Jefferson, North Carolina, and London

LIBRARY OF CONGRESS ONLINE CATALOG DATA

Middle-earth minstrel : essays on music in Tolkien / edited by Bradford Lee Eden.
    p.   cm.
Includes bibliographical references and index.

ISBN 978-0-7864-4814-2
softcover : 50# alkaline paper ∞

1. Tolkien, J.R.R. (John Ronald Reuel), 1892–1973 — Criticism and interpretation.   2. Tolkien, J.R.R. (John Ronald Reuel), 1892–1973 — Knowledge — Music.   3. Tolkien, J.R.R. (John Ronald Reuel), 1892–1973 — Knowledge — Middle Ages.   4. Music in literature.   5. Fantasy fiction, English — Medieval influences.   6. Middle Earth (Imaginary place)   I. Eden, Bradford Lee.   II. Title: Music in Tolkien.
PR6039.O32Z6964   2010
823'.912 — dc22   2010006922

British Library cataloguing data are available

©2010 Bradford Lee Eden. All rights reserved

No part of this book may be reproduced or transmitted in any form or by any means, electronic or mechanical, including photocopying or recording, or by any information storage and retrieval system, without permission in writing from the publisher.

On the cover: (top) Detail from the *Codex Manesse*, f. 399r, Meister Heinrich Frauenlob, early 14th century; (bottom) Portion of *Sumer is icumen in,* British Library MS Harley 978, f. 11v, mid–13th century; (background 2010 Shutterstock)

Manufactured in the United States of America

McFarland & Company, Inc., Publishers
Box 611, Jefferson, North Carolina 28640
www.mcfarlandpub.com

This book is dedicated to those people who have had the most influence in my life, and those whom I love the most:

To Boo and Tar, my best friends and fellow Tar-babies, who helped form a literary and scholarly fellowship early in my life, and have since moved on into the next existence.

To Crystal, whose presence in my life as a daughter has helped me to grow and learn, whom I love deeply and continue to be exceptionally proud of.

To my wife Sonja and daughter Noëlle, the loves of my life, who lift me up daily from the rigors of work and my own inadequacies, to celebrate every moment of every day as precious and wonderful with their smiles and their laughter.

Table of Contents

Introduction
    BRADFORD LEE EDEN   1

Horns of Dawn: The Tradition of Alliterative Verse in Rohan
    JASON FISHER   7

"Inside a Song": Tolkien's Phonaesthetics
    JOHN R. HOLMES   26

Æfre me strongode longað: Songs of Exile in the Mortal Realms
    PETER WILKIN   47

J.R.R. Tolkien: A Fortunate Rhythm
    DARIELLE RICHARDS   61

Tolkien's Unfinished "Lay of Lúthien" and the Middle English *Sir Orfeo*
    DEANNA DELMAR EVANS   75

Strains of Elvish Song and Voices: Victorian Medievalism, Music, and Tolkien
    BRADFORD LEE EDEN   85

Dissonance in the Divine Theme: The Issue of Free Will in Tolkien's *Silmarillion*
    KEITH W. JENSEN   102

"Worthy of a Song": Memory, Mortality and Music
    AMY M. AMENDT-RADUEGE   114

Table of Contents

"Tolkien is the Wind and the Way": The Educational Value of
Tolkien-Inspired World Music
    AMY H. STURGIS   126

Liquid Tolkien: Music, Tolkien, Middle-earth, and More Music
    DAVID BRATMAN   140

Performance Art in a Tunnel: A Musical Sub-Creator in the
Tradition of Tolkien
    ANTHONY S. BURDGE   171

Contributors   201
Index   205

Introduction
Bradford Lee Eden

It is with great pleasure that I offer up this book of essays to Tolkien scholars and enthusiasts. It is the culmination of thirty years of personal interest, a discovery not unlike many others that happened during my teenage years and has progressively and inevitably led to advanced education, career directions and choices, and ultimately to this book.

In 2003, I received a grant from the University of Nevada, Las Vegas, to visit the two major archives containing Tolkien-related materials, at Marquette University in Milwaukee, Wisconsin, and the Bodleian Library at the University of Oxford in England, to explore writing a book on musical allusions in Tolkien's works. Having visited the Marquette archives in 1981 as an undergraduate student writing an honors religion paper on Tolkien's views regarding subcreation, it was a wonderful experience to go back again a little older and more knowledgeable and re-examine Tolkien's materials. But the ultimate experience was my three-week visit to the Bodleian Library in April 2003, something that many Tolkien enthusiasts have dreamed of but have never been able to do. Having gone through the extensive process of applying for a reader's pass, then scheduling my visit with the librarian in charge of the Tolkien archives, I can say that my visit was truly enlightening. Not only did I get to touch and study manuscripts, notes, lectures, and various miscellanea that Tolkien himself wrote, but I got to explore the city of Oxford as well, visiting all of the sites associated with Tolkien, including his gravesite and his various homes.

As I examined the materials in the Bodleian, I came across Tolkien's various drafts of a lecture entitled "The Tradition of Versification in Old English, with special reference to the 'Battle of Maldon' and its allitera-

Introduction

tion." All three versions of this lecture refer to some type of musical allusion in their introductions, and Tolkien muses on the recorder/writer of the "Battle of Maldon" poem. Tolkien compares the "Battle of Maldon" poet with other surviving writings of the time, indicating that the "Battle of Maldon" is recorded in a more hasty, less formal manner than earlier poetry. Tolkien indicates that this poem has been more or less constructed by a "minstrel turned scholar," one whose purpose as bard was to document the details of the battle for his listeners, yet in the process becoming an historical observer for those reading the surviving manuscripts. I was struck by this reference, given the close analogy between the sounds of speech and those of music, and how Tolkien would refer to the "Battle of Maldon" poet in this way. Tolkien often referred to himself as a man out of his time, one who felt more comfortable living in the medieval world and its languages than in this modern world. In a twist of his own words from this draft, Tolkien himself could be construed as a "scholar turned minstrel," a modern-day academic whose love and power of storytelling has brought to life an entire mythology that has captured the imagination of young and old alike. One can almost imagine Tolkien thinking of himself in this way, and that his love of languages and mythology helped to sing or compose Middle-earth into existence. And that is what he did, incorporating music into the creation and ultimately the history of that fascinating world that all of us have come to know and love.

I first wrote about these musical allusions in the chapter "The Music of the Spheres: Relationships between Tolkien's *Silmarillion* and Medieval Cosmological and Religious Theory" in the book *Tolkien the Medievalist* (edited by Jane Chance, Routledge, 2004). Since then, many others have commented on the similarities between music and speech in Tolkien's works, and that Tolkien often interchanged and wove his stories and his characters into and around musical allusions. Was all of this a conscious or a subconscious effort on Tolkien's part? Did he base his entire mythology on the "music of the spheres" concept, one where the eventual decay or debasement of the original creation music by time and space would occur, along with the power associated with that music? And when one really looks at Middle-earth, the Elves *are* the music, they are the embodiment of all that is beautiful and good, and they represent the original music of creation throughout Middle-earth's history.

I noticed the close relationships between music and language early in

Introduction (Eden)

my discovery of Tolkien's writings. As a teenager (not unlike many other Tolkien enthusiasts), I reveled in the power of storytelling and drama imbued in *The Hobbit* (especially the dragon Smaug, which started my fascination and study of dragons) and *The Lord of the Rings* with the extensive historical allusions provided in the appendices of *The Return of the King*. But it wasn't until the publication of *The Silmarillion* in 1977 that I realized and understood the depth and breadth of Middle-earth, and how this book was Tolkien's *magnum opus*, the work that he truly loved and wished to have published during his lifetime but was never able to achieve. Tolkien's work was so influential on me that early on I wanted to focus my career on medievalism, which culminated in a Ph.D. in medieval musicology. As each volume of *The History of Middle-earth* appeared during the 1980s and 1990s, I marveled and studied how the different versions, tales, and subsequent drafts of Tolkien's massive writings began to illustrate strong musical allusions, especially in many of his earliest stories and the many early versions of *Ainulindalë*. I took it upon myself to go through all of Tolkien's writings that I could, in order to count and record the number of times words were used that were associated with music. Just in *The Hobbit* and *Lord of the Rings*, the numbers are significant. But when one examines Tolkien's early poetry and early writings related to the mythology, the amount of musical references are astounding; indeed, the use of music as a power in and of itself in the mythology is an overall theme of great importance.

And much of this importance has yet to be researched. In my contribution to this book, I indicate some of the many musical allusions in Tolkien's early versions of his mythology. Some of the characters with great musical ability disappear, morph into something else, or sometimes combine together; there are numerous "songs" that apparently were never written down but Tolkien imagined as being part and parcel of his world; and there is an overall joy and exuberance concerning music in the early writings, particularly in his poetry. There is a marvelous book on Tolkien called *Secret Fire: The Spiritual Vision of J.R.R. Tolkien* by Stratford Caldecott (Darton, Longman and Todd, 2003), that I discovered in a little bookstore off the cathedral square in York, England. It not only examines, quite objectively, the influence of Catholicism in Tolkien's works, but also points out and references many of the musical allusions in Tolkien's writings as well as the importance of music in his own life, especially related to the

Introduction

Catholic liturgy. Humphrey Carpenter's biography of Tolkien includes many of these references to music (given that Carpenter was a well-known biographer of musical composers). The first book to discuss music in Tolkien's works was *The Song of Middle-Earth: J.R.R. Tolkien's Themes, Symbols and Myths* by David Harvey (George Allen and Unwin, 1985), and Verlyn Flieger has published two books that touch on this subject as well: *A Question of Time: J.R.R. Tolkien's Road to Faerie* (Kent State University Press, 1997) and *Interrupted Music: The Making of Tolkien's Mythology* (Kent State University Press, 2005).

But I digress. This book examines the impact and uses of music in Tolkien's works, relationships between linguistics and music, and even the biography of an individual who has taken Tolkien's subcreation philosophy as the basis for his life and work.

To begin, Jason Fisher explores the musical-literary analogies between the Kingdom of Rohan and the Anglo-Saxon kingdom of Mercia, along with musical references to the Vala Oromë the Hunter, the Ents, and the Woses.

John R. Holmes examines how the rhythms, phrasings, and sounds of philology, phonology, and music are intertwined. He illustrates these relationships through numerous examples from historical English literature and provides indications of Tolkien's use of word meanings and sounds to create a kind of *Sprechstimme* sing-song throughout his works.

The themes of longing and exile are the basis for Peter Wilkin's contribution as he researches the "Cottage of Lost Play" texts and their subsequent replacements in "The Lost Road" and "The Notion Club Papers," especially the central character Eriol. The music of the otherworld in literature and in Tolkien is compared as well.

Darielle Richards looks at the literary process Tolkien used to craft his stories, along with interesting references to psychology and philosophy.

Deanna Delmar Evans explores the relationships between the Middle English *Sir Orfeo* and Tolkien's construction of his Beren and Lúthien tale, mentioning some of the musical connections between the two tales.

I have already mentioned my contribution to the book, which examines the Victorian leanings towards musical allusion, Tolkien's place among the Victorian medievalist writers, and a listing of some of the many unresearched musical-literary themes in Tolkien's early writings.

Introduction (Eden)

The issue of dissonance as a theme in Middle-earth is discussed by Keith W. Jensen, as are how this theme developed from the creation myth in *Ainulindalë* and morphs into the issue of free will in the *Silmarillion*.

The concepts of memory and mortality as they relate to music are examined by Amy M. Amendt-Raduege. I think her comment, "although we as readers first encounter songs of Middle-earth as poetry, Tolkien is always careful to remind us that we are, in fact, reading a song, even if we cannot hear the music," is both profound and fundamentally true, as she discusses the many elegies and lays of Middle-earth.

On a more practical level, Amy H. Sturgis recounts her educational uses of Tolkien-inspired world music, listing some of the more recent sub-creational musical compositions that have found their basis in Tolkien's mythology.

David Bratman looks at the role of music in Tolkien's *legendarium*, listing some of Tolkien's musical contemporaries and their influence on him, and then recounting recent classical, heavy metal, jazz, pop, and New Age compositions and composers whose works try to musically depict many of Tolkien's themes, characters, and dramatic encounters.

The book ends with a biography of S.K. Thoth, a visionary whose life work has its basis in Tolkien's concept of subcreation, and whose musical performances in New York City's Central Park have become legendary. Much of what Anthony S. Burdge describes in his biography of Thoth's work is similar in concept to nirvana or enlightenment in Buddhism with elements of new age philosophies, and relates readily to concepts developed by Joseph Campbell in relation to comparative mythology and religion, as well as Campbell's succinct philosophy of "follow your bliss." While this contribution would not necessarily be considered scholarly, I have included it because it illustrates the influence and power that Tolkien's works have had on many individuals, not the least of whom is Thoth.

It is my sincere hope that the information contained in this book will inspire others to enjoy and marvel at the conscious and subconscious musical associations that permeate Tolkien's works, and while Tolkien readily indicated in interviews and his letters that he was not a musical person (at least in the performance of music), I think that many of us who have been influenced by Tolkien's musical-literary style can agree that his reference to the "scholar as minstrel" is an adequate and indeed justified description of himself and his life's work.

Horns of Dawn: The Tradition of Alliterative Verse in Rohan

Jason Fisher

By this point in Tolkien studies, approaching forty years since the Professor's death, it is well-known that Tolkien took as a rough model for his Kingdom of Rohan the genuine Anglo-Saxon Kingdom of Mercia.[1] While there are certainly clear distinctions between them, there are many more similarities than differences. A common language — rendered by Tolkien not just as Old English (Tolkien *Lord of the Rings* 1136), but more specifically, as the Mercian dialect of Old English[2] — goes to the heart of their common characterization. This tongue, with "a strong music in it," "rich and rolling in part, and else hard and stern as the mountains" (Tolkien *Lord of the Rings* 508), is bodied forth through the importance of song and oral tradition in both cultures. The Rohirrim sing and chant using an alliterative verse structure which is strikingly similar to that found in *Beowulf*, *The Battle of Maldon*, indeed the greater portion of the surviving Old English poetry. And like the Mercians, the Rohirrim were also known to give their music another voice through the winding of their horns before battle. Finally, Oromë the Hunter, the Vala whom the Rohirrim revere, provides a direct link backward from the martial and elegiac music of Rohan to the very Music of Creation itself, the Ainulindalë.

I will examine in detail the evidence linking Rohan with Mercia and the significance of their shared alliterative oral and musical traditions, teasing out the connections between alliterative verse, the blowing of war-horns, and key etymologies in the genuine Old Mercian and fictive Sindarin and Quenya languages. Furthermore, we will see that Tolkien had personal as well as scholarly reasons for choosing Mercia as his model. Then, as we explore the Kingdom of Rohan, I will argue further that the alliterative verses and musical culture of the Ents and the Woses — Rohan's neighbors to the north and southeast, respectively — share some of the same features. "There is a kinship," Tolkien wrote,

> in spite of all the remoteness and the strangeness, in Old English verse with Modern English: it is definitely part of the history of the mind and mood of England and the English. The men who made it walked this soil and under this sky. All the immense changes of life here in more than a thousand years have not made the end entirely foreign to the beginning [Tolkien A38, folio 3, quoted in Lee and Solopova 19].

To locate the origins of Anglo-Saxon oral and musical culture, we have to travel back in time to the very dawn of the recorded history of the British Isles. The bulk of the surviving literary corpus in Old English dates from no earlier than the tenth century CE.[3] This beats the oldest surviving Norse texts by several hundred years, but the date is still relatively late in several respects. For one, Roman, Greek, Egyptian, Sumerian, and Sanskrit texts antedate the oldest Old English texts by *many* centuries, in some cases by millennia, indicating a very long swath of the history of man on which the Old English texts are silent. For another, nearly all of the surviving Old English texts come after the Christianization of the Anglo-Saxons (circa, the seventh century), which presents difficulties in discovering the nature of their own pre–Christian religious beliefs, *ab antiquo*. But in spite of these challenges, the surviving Old English corpus offers some truly remarkable specimens of a uniquely Germanic species of literature, as sharply contrasted with the literary traditions of the Mediterranean. I refer to alliterative verse, meant to be chanted or sung, with the accompaniment of the harp.

Alliterative verse, here, is a rather broad term for what is actually a quite complex and often abstruse topic. Indeed, the second half of Snorri Sturluson's great work, the Prose Edda, called the Skáldskaparmál ("the language of Skaldic poetry"), is itself a substantial work, describing in enormous detail the many intricate forms in which the skalds — the Norse equivalent to the English scops or Celtic bards — made their heroic and elegiac verses. I will have a little more to say about the Norse tradition below, but I mention Sturluson's work here to make the point that alliterative verse is not a topic easily potted in a paragraph. There were innumerable varieties of it, each verse form with its own particular (and generally speaking, inflexible) rules. A full rehearsal of the subject would be well beyond the scope of this essay.[4]

Tolkien was an expert in the Germanic alliterative tradition, not just in the many varieties of Old Norse verse, but also the alliterative forms in Old English, as exemplified in *Beowulf*; Old Saxon, primarily in the ninth-century ecclesiastical work, the *Heliand*; roughly contemporary with this, the Old High German *Hildebrandslied*—not to mention the proliferation of Middle English alliterative forms, to which I will return in due course. To offer the simplest possible explanation for alliterative verse in the Germanic languages—a gross injustice, but necessary for the sake of brevity: "a line divided into two halves, two stressed syllables in each, the third of the four always carrying alliteration, to be matched by one or both of the first two, the fourth never (or the second half-line would become identical to the first and the sense of the line itself would disappear)" (Shippey "Tolkien out–Wagners Wagner"). Alliteration, simply defined, is the repetition of similar initial consonant sounds (e.g., from Shakespeare's *A Midsummer Night's Dream*, "Whereat, with blade, with bloody blameful blade, / He bravely broach'd his boiling bloody breast"). Another, more general literary term, *assonance*, is often used nowadays to describe the repetition of *vowel* sounds, but in the Germanic tradition, vowels as well as consonants alliterate with one another; moreover, *any* vowel alliterates with any other. Let me elucidate with an example from the opening lines of *Beowulf*. Here, the alliterating syllables are shown in bold-face type, with the governing syllable also underlined:

> Hwæt, wé **Gár**-Dena   in **géar**dagum
> þéodcyninga   **þrym** gefrúnon,
> hú ðá æþelingas   **el**len fremedon! [*Beowulf*, ℓℓ. 1–3]
>
> ("Lo, we Spear-Danes in days or yore
> have heard of the glory of the kings of our people,
> how the princes did valorous deeds.")[5]

While *Beowulf*, *The Battle of Maldon*, Cynewulf's *Elene*, and the many other works in verse of the Old English corpus are usually thought of as poems by today's literary standards, they were really closer to *songs*, meant to be performed, chanted or sung, accompanied by the Anglo-Saxon harp

(Pope 88–95).⁶ Archaeological evidence has shown that various Anglo-Saxon musical instruments existed — harps, whistles, horns, bells, drums, and so on (Arnold 97–8, Lapidge 328–9, see also Crowest). Furthermore, textual evidence attests musical notation as early as the tenth century (Rankin 97), but for evidence that the Anglo-Saxons had a musical culture at all, we need look no further than those sibling rivals, Lit. and Lang.,⁷ in this case, the language of the Anglo-Saxons and the literature through which it is attested.

First, the language. Old English contains a number of words used to describe musical culture, including words for musical instruments, verbs to describe playing or singing, and words for the kinds of people responsible for the entertainment in mead-halls in every corner of the island. Just to give a few of them, for instruments and other musical nouns we have: *hearpe* "harp" (more properly, a kind of lyre), *hwistle* "a pipe, flute, whistle," *béme* "trumpet," *horn* "horn" (animal, potatory, as well as musical; analogous to Latin *cornū* "horn" → English *cornet*), *gléo-cræft* "glee-craft, the art of music" (whence the modern English "glee club")⁸, and *sang* "song." For verbs of music-making: *hearpian* "to play the harp," *hwistlian* "to whistle," *singan* "to sing." For performers: *hearpere* "harper," *hwistlere* "whistler," *bémere* "trumpeter," *gléoman* "a gleeman, minstrel," and the most well-known, *scop* "a poet, singer" (literally, a *shaper*).

Now, let's have a look at the literature. Again, a mere few of the surviving examples will suffice. From *Beowulf*, "þǽr wæs hearpan swég, / swutol sang scopes" (*ll.* 89–90: "there were harps sounded, the singer's clear song"), and "leóð wæs ásungen, gleómannes gyd" (*ll.* 1159–60: "the lay was sung, the gleeman's song"). From laws laid down by King Wihtræd,⁹ a rather dire intimation that the failure to sound a horn might cost a man his life:

> Gif feorran cumen man oððe fræmde búton wege gange and hé ðonne náwþer ne hrýme ne hé horn ne bláwe for ðeóf hé bið tó prófianne: oþþe to sleánne oþþe to alýsenne [Sedgefield 324].

> ("If from a distance comes a man or a stranger, and goes out of the highway, and he then neither shouts nor blows the horn, he is to be regarded [and tried] as a thief: either to slay [him] or to let [him] go.")

And finally, from the Old English *Exodus*, of which Tolkien himself produced an edition, published posthumously in 1981: "Æfter þam wordum werod wæs on salum, / sungon sigebyman" (*ll.* 564–5), which Tolkien translates: "After these words the host rejoiced; the victorious trumpets sang a music fair" (Tolkien *Exodus* 32).

We have seen how the Germanic tradition of alliterative verse was a professional focus, and a personal interest, of Tolkien's. As I hinted above, this is no less true of the Middle English literature than of the Old. Scholars often refer to the renaissance of alliterative verse in the fourteenth through sixteenth centuries as the Alliterative Revival,[10] and this broad movement includes three key works of literature of which Tolkien made very close study: *Sir Gawain and the Green Knight*, *Pearl*, and *Sir Orfeo*. With E.V. Gordon, Tolkien published an edition of *Sir Gawain and the Green Knight* in 1925. The two scholars planned to collaborate on an edition of *Pearl* as well, but in the end, it was not to be.[11] In 1944, Tolkien produced his own edition of *Sir Orfeo*, printed privately by the Academic Copying Office of Oxford University.[12] Two years after Tolkien's death, his own translations of all three poems were finally published.

It is a matter of some debate whether the practice of writing alliterative verse in the Middle English period follows directly from that in the Old English period, or stands more or less independent from it. "Was late medieval alliterative verse," asks Christine Chism,

> an antiquarian revival of past poetic forms, or were those half-lost forms freely reinvented for contemporary purposes? Or, to cut closer to Tolkien's quick, is the Alliterative Revival a nativizing invention of twentieth-century scholars with an investment in rescuing the ancient English past from the encroachments of other cultural traditions? The debate continues [Chism 9–10].

One must imagine Tolkien would be sympathetic to such a vested interest.[13] On the other hand, Tolkien himself was one of those who believed that Middle English alliterative verse was "descended [from Old English] through an unbroken oral tradition" (Tolkien and Gordon 118). To make his case, he invokes the authority of the *Gawain* poet, who describes his own story as "stad and stoken [...], / With lel letteres loken, / In londe so hatȝ ben longe" (Tolkien and Gordon 2). This Tolkien renders in his own translation, "fixed and fettered [...], / thus linked and truly lettered, / as was loved in this land of old" (Tolkien *Sir Gawain* 25–6). Whichever is true — that the Middle English Alliterative Revival was or was not the direct descendent of the Old English tradition, Tolkien's use of alliterative forms for his own original poetry should properly be regarded as the terminus of a continuum from the Old and Middle English alliterative styles, whether genuine or merely scholarly, and beyond.

Examples of Tolkien's own alliterative poems are numerous.[14] These, normally composed in Modern English but occasionally in Old English and once in Gothic, "were quite various in date, intention, and even literary model" (Shippey "Alliterative Verse" 10). One of the most substantial is the *Lay of the Children of Húrin*, published in *The Lays of Beleriand*, which runs to more than three thousand lines. But the best-known are naturally the poems of *The Lord of the Rings*, and most of the alliterative verses in that work are associated with Rohan. Therefore, in addition to the language, on which I have touched above and will have more to say below, this shared heritage of verse forms — and hence, shared musical culture — represents another bridge between the people of Rohan and those of Anglo-Saxon England.

To be sure, there are differences between the Anglo-Saxons and the Rohirrim, foremost among them the reverence of horses.[15] However, Tolkien wrote to Rhona Beare in 1958 that, although not strictly "medieval," the Rohirrim match the Anglo-Saxons portrayed in the Bayeux Tapestry "well enough" (Tolkien *Letters* 281). Tolkien does not say so explicitly, but in many of the scenes in the Bayeux Tapestry (particularly in the depiction of the Battle of Hastings), figures in the tapestry are shown on horseback. Indeed, the tapestry depicts more than two hundred horses, one for every three human figures, though one must allow that the greater part of these were associated with the Normans, not the Anglo-Saxons.[16] It also bears remembering that Hengest and Horsa, the two legendary figures associated with the *adventus saxonum*, had equine names (meaning, respectively, "stallion" and "horse"). Tolkien constructed a parallel on this in the Hobbit names, Marcho and Blanco, both of which also mean "horse" (Shippey *Road* 102), but of more relevance to the present discussion, many Rohirric words and names likewise contain the element *eoh* "horse" — e.g., Éomer, Éowyn, Éomund, Éothéod, *éored*.

Tom Shippey has taken the argument that the Rohirrim are like the Anglo-Saxons much further, saying (*pace* Martinez):

> You remember, no doubt, the footnote, in one of the Appendices, where Tolkien says you mustn't think that the Riders [of Rohan] resemble the ancient English in any except accidental respects. Absolutely untrue! Tolkien cover-

ing his tracks yet again! The Riders of Rohan resemble the Old English down to minute detail. Their names are all Old English [...] but they also behave that way. All the habits which he talks about like [...] piling arms outside, not being allowed in to see the king with weapons in your hand, the counsellor sitting at the feet of the king, all these come straight out of *Beowulf*, down to minute detail. The actual things they say are said by characters in *Beowulf*, very often ["Tolkien Society Annual Dinner" 15].

So let us take as a given (recognizing there is still debate in some quarters) that Tolkien modeled his Riders of Rohan, to the greater extent, on the early Anglo-Saxons. Having granted this, it is possible to be even more specific, and I have indeed already tipped my hand above: the Rohirrim were meant to reflect one particular kingdom of Anglo-Saxons, the Mercians. I am not the first to suggest it. I take my the cue from the preeminent Tolkien scholar, Tom Shippey, who made this observation more than twenty-five years ago. Shippey explains that "[a]ll the Riders' names and language are Old English, as many have noted [...]"[17]; however,

> Not many have noted that they are not in the "standard" or "classical" West Saxon dialect of Old English, but in what is thought to have been its Mercian parallel; so Saruman, Hasufel, Herugrim for "standard" Searuman, Heasufel, Heorugrim, and cp. *Mearc* and **Marc* [*Road* 123].

Tom Shippey has demonstrated, too, how the name the Rohirrim gave to their own land, the Mark, is demonstrably the Mercian form (unattested, as shown by the asterisk in the quotation above) for the West Saxon *Mearc*, which is "Mercia" itself.[18] In surviving texts, the people of Wessex called their neighbors in the Midlands to the north the Myrce (*Author of the Century* 91–2), which is "Mercians." The word was sometimes recorded as Mirce or Mierce, and meant "border-people" (from the common West Saxon word *mearc* "limit, border"). It signified a land bordered on all sides: by the English Kingdom of Wessex to the south, and the Welsh Kingdom of Powys to the west, by the Kingdom of Northumbria to the north, and by the lesser Kingdoms of East Anglia and Essex to the east. The region in question, particularly the western half of it, corresponded to the home of the West Midland dialects of Middle English, which Tolkien studied and whose works he translated, as well as the West Midland counties where Tolkien himself grew up.[19] And let us take a moment to consider perhaps the strongest physical intimation of a parallel between Mercia and Rohan: Offa's Dike.

Offa was king of the Mercians over the latter half of the eighth century, during the height of the ascendancy of Mercia over its neighbors. A particularly vexatious neighbor was the Welsh Kingdom of Powys, with its tendency to raid villages of the western Midlands.[20] During the second half of Offa's reign and probably under his direct supervision (as near as we can tell from English and Welsh documentary evidence), an earthwork more than one hundred miles in length was constructed in western Mercia, along the border between the two kingdoms (Stenton 211–3). Can it be coincidence that Tolkien places a similar dike in the western part of Rohan, to keep at bay the incursions of the wild, one might even say *Celtic*, inhabitants of Dunland?[21] In Éomer's words: "[n]ot far ahead now lies Helm's Dike, an ancient trench and rampart scored across the coomb, two furlongs below Helm's Gate. There we can turn and give battle" (Tolkien *Lord of the Rings* 530). Offa's Dike is considerably the more impressive of the two; however, a defensive dike buffering a hostile and pagan region to the immediate west of both Mercia and Rohan seems to be more than mere coincidence.

Beyond Tolkien's personal connection to the soil of Mercia, there are very practical reasons why Tolkien might have chosen that land for his model. Almost all of the surviving Old English texts of any literary interest — and indeed, the vast majority of all the surviving texts, *irrespective* of their interest — are recorded in the West Saxon dialect, not the Mercian. Why is there no significant body of Mercian literature? No one knows the whole story, but this would have represented the kind of loss Tolkien would feel anxious to redress, a literary and linguistic lacuna he would wish to fill if he could. It would have been an even more highly localized loss than the destruction of pre–Christian, and later pre–Norman, Anglo-Saxon literature as a whole. Yet, though literary Old English is almost entirely West Saxon, it is from the Mercian dialect through the Midland dialects of Middle English (eastern and western), that Modern English in large part has developed. This makes understanding the Mercian dialect all the more important, but the acute insufficiency of its corpus all the more difficult to bear.

Of course, a few valuable Mercian texts do survive. Perhaps the most important is the so-called Vespasian Psalter (British Museum Cotton Vespasian A. 1), a text Tolkien is known to have studied and taught (Scull and Hammond *Chronology* 162, 167, 177, sqq.). It was probably from the Vespasian Psalter that Tolkien borrowed many of the Mercian forms of Old English words he used in his *legendarium* (Scull and Hammond *Chronology* 380, Tolkien *Shaping of Middle-earth* 290). In 1942, while engaged in writing *The Lord of the Rings*, Tolkien produced an intricate diagram of the "Normal Development of 'A' in Vespasian Ps[alter] & Ancrene Wisse," bridging the gap between Mercian Old English and West Midland Middle English (*Life and Legend* 75, 78).

Moving from linguistic, historical, and archaeological connections, let us turn now to a discussion of the similarities in the Rohirric and Mercian musical cultures. As I see it, there are five major types of music, *sensu lato*, represented in the surviving Anglo-Saxon corpus: heroic, martial, elegiac, gnomic, and ecclesiastic. All but the last are mirrored in *The Lord of the Rings*. Heroic verse, comprising ballads, epics, and historical works such as *Beowulf* and *The Battle of Maldon*, find echoes in Tolkien in poems such as "Eärendil was a mariner," but the style is represented much better by Tolkien's moving and musical prose (as in "The Ride of the Rohirrim" and "The Battle of Pelennor Fields," on which more below). Martial music is not necessarily recorded in plain words, but rather consists in the winding of horns before and during battle, the beating of drums (or of spears on shields), the sounds of marching boots, and the war-cries of thanes. Such music is not attested but *described* in the surviving literature. Of elegiac verses, there are many examples from *The Lord of the Rings*; a beautiful, alliterative specimen may be found in the lament for King Théoden, made by his minstrel, Gléowine.[22] And finally, gnomic verse comprises riddles, maxims, and recorded wisdom. The Anglo-Saxon Exeter Book contains much of this material, but there is also another important work, "Maxims II," which finds an echo in *The Lord of the Rings* in Treebeard's alliterative bestiary poem, "Learn now the lore of Living Creatures" (Lee and Solopova 183–93).[23]

Given that the War of the Ring is the tapestry on which Tolkien's finer plot elements are embroidered, it should come as no surprise to find within its pages many instances of martial verse and music. I would like to examine a few of these more closely now, most especially in examples taken from Rohan and its immediate neighbors. Let me begin with a passage from *Beowulf*:

> [...] Frófor eft gelamp
> sárigmódum   somod aér dæge
> syððan híe Hygeláces   horn ond býman
> gealdor ongéaton   þá se góda cóm,
> léoda dugoðe   on lást faran [*Beowulf*, *ll.* 2941–4].
>
> ("[...] Rescue came again
> To those sorrow-hearted men with the dawn
> when they Hygelac's horn and trumpet
> and his battle-song[24] they heard, then the good king came
> with the power of his people on the track marching.")

This selection from the poem's fortieth fitt should remind the reader of Rohan's "in the nick of time" succor of Gondor. And in these lines, we can discern another illuminating point of contact with the larger backcloth of Tolkien's *legendarium*. In one of the relatively few explicit references to the Valar in *The Lord of the Rings*, readers learn that the Rohirrim revered Oromë the Hunter, whom they credited with bringing the original sire of the *mearas* (simply, "horses") to Middle-earth from Valinor (Tolkien *Lord of the Rings* 1065). In Rohirric, they gave Oromë the name Béma, from an Old Mercian word meaning "horn, trumpet." The West Saxon form of this word, *býma*, occurs in the passage above.

That the Rohirrim would name Oromë Béma is quite logical, as he is identified with the Valaróma, "the Horn of the Vala." Indeed, though Tolkien waffled a little on this point,[25] the putative etymology of the name Oromë is "horn-blowing," from the Primitive Eldarin root, √ROM "loud noise, horn-blast." Deriving from this root are Quenya *romba* "horn, trumpet" and *róma* "loud sound, trumpet-sound" (Tolkien *Lost Road* 384). The relationship to Oromë and his Valaróma is obvious. Moreover, it is elsewhere made clear that the Quenya *róma* can also mean "horn," and refers to the musical instrument and not to the horn of an animal (Tolkien *War of the Jewels* 368). This makes Old English *béma* "trumpet" the correct choice for representing Oromë in the Rohirric language, as opposed to Old English *horn* "(1) horn of an animal; (2) drinking horn; (3) horn, trumpet," though indeed, there is a Rider of Rohan with the name Horn, who perished in the battle before Minas Tirith and is remembered in one of Tolkien's more eloquent alliterative elegies (Tolkien, *Lord of the Rings*, 849).

It seems, then, that we may trace the origins of the Rohirrim's martial music — horns and drums and marching feet — back to Oromë and to the music of battle and the hunt. This, in turn, would seem to have been Oromë's own contribution to the Ainulindalë, the Music of the Ainur. Is there an analogue to this divine transmission in the Germanic tradition? Indeed, "[t]he origin of the art of the scóp or scald [Anglo-Saxon and Norse, respectively] was attributed to Odin or Wodin [Norse and Anglo-Saxon, respectively], the father of the Saxon gods," writes Crowest (84). But because of the loss of all but a few vestigial traces of England's own pre–Christian (i.e., pagan) belief system, we must turn to the Anglo-Saxons' northern neighbors to fully appreciate the significance of the mythological origins of this music.[26]

In the Old Norse tradition, the *skáldskapar mjaðar* "the mead of poetry"[27] (also, *Suttungmjaðar* "Suttungr's Mead") was a mythological nectar — a rather unappetizing amalgam of spittle, blood, and honey — that conveyed to any who drank it a mastery of skaldic poetry and music. In the Prose Edda, Snorri Sturluson recounts the wonderfully pagan story of how Odin connived to swallow all of the giant Suttungr's mead in three great swallows, then fleeing the giant (both of them taking the form of eagles), to regurgitate it into three jars once safely back in the abode of the gods, Asgard. From that point on, Odin shared the mead with those who wished to master the arts of the skald.[28] While there are no simple one-to-one relationships in Tolkien's complex manipulation of source material, it seems defensible to argue that Oromë's part in the Ainulindalë inspired the martial music and verse of Middle-earth in an analogous fashion (though differing in the details), just as others of the Valar may have been responsible for other aspects of the musical culture of Middle-earth.[29]

As scholars of Tolkien know very well by now, where we find one connection, we're likely to find another — sometimes many others. There exists another Eldarin root, √RŌ "rise," from which derives Quenya *rómen* "east." Of course, the similarity of √RŌ to √ROM could be entirely coincidental, yet there are reasons to suppose it is not. In another of the few references to the Valar in *The Lord of the Rings*, recall that the storied horn of Boromir was made from the horn of "the wild kine of Araw in the far fields of Rhûn" (Tolkien *Lord of the Rings* 755; see also 1039n1). There are three important points here: (1) once again, we have a horn, winded before battle; (2) Araw is the Sindarin form of the name, Oromë; and (3) Rhûn is simply the Sindarin word for "east" (cognate to Quenya *rómen*). Recall, too, that it was Oromë who first discovered the Elves in Cuiviénen, in the extreme *east* of Middle-earth (Tolkien *Silmarillion* 48–50). Clearly, though never spelled out explicitly, readers are meant to infer a connection between Oromë and the furthest reaches of the east. It is of course from the east that dawn comes, traditionally heralded by the cock, but one might as well imagine the horn in its place.[30]

Returning to the passage from *Beowulf* cited above, the proximity of two key phrases—*aér dæge* "dawn" (literally, "before day"), followed by *Hygeláces horn ond býman* "Hygelac's horn and trumpet"—is echoed by Tolkien through a corresponding link between Oromë, the Rohirrim, dawn in the east, and the music of the horn. We see all of these elements brought together in a single scene in Tolkien's description of Théoden's arrival at Minas Tirith:

> [H]e seized a great horn from Guthláf his banner-bearer, and he blew such a blast upon it that it burst asunder. And straightway all the horns in the host were lifted up in music, and the blowing of the horns in Rohan in that hour was like a storm upon the plain and a thunder in the mountains. [...] [Théoden] was borne up on Snowmane like a god of old, even as Oromë the Great in the battle of the Valar when the world was young. His golden shield was uncovered, and lo! it shone like an image of the Sun, and the grass flamed into green about the white feet of his steed. For morning came, morning and a wind from the sea; and the darkness was removed [...] [Tolkien *Lord of the Rings* 838].

In this passage, attentive readers will notice a third explicit reference to Oromë (by three different names) in *The Lord of the Rings*.[31]

I would like to close with a cursory look at the music of the Woses and the Ents, Rohan's neighbors to the southeast and the north, respectively. Their musical and poetic cultures, it transpires, share much in common with that of the Riddermark. The Woses are much the simpler of the two, wild men and wary, who communicate with one another over great distances through the beating of drums. We know very little about the Drúedain, and it is probably not quite right to call this tympanic communication *music*, in the strictest sense; nevertheless, the drum is the traditional instrument accompanying martial and hunting songs. The choice cannot be accidental.

The Ents present a clearer case.[32] The chapter "Treebeard" contains five separate poems, more than any other chapter in *The Lord of the Rings*, and they are all pretty clearly meant to be sung, chanted, or even hummed. Even the Ents' voices are musical (likened to woodwind instruments) and their language tonal and polyphonic. More to the point of the present study, their verses are broadly representative of several of the categories of Anglo-Saxon verse discussed above — from the alliterative gnomic verse, "Learn now the lore of Living Creatures," to the elegiac songs of Treebeard and Quickbeam, to the rousing and bellicose marching song that closes the chapter, "To Isengard!" This last, moreover, is a genuine song with a musical accompaniment of horn and percussion: "a marching music began like solemn drums, and above the rolling beats and booms there welled voices singing high and strong [...] beating time with their hands upon their flanks" (Tolkien *Lord of the Rings* 484–5).

Whether deliberate or merely fortuitous, it is quite appropriate that the largest concentration of medieval Germanic verse-forms and musical types should occur in Rohan and its two nearest neighbors — to a lesser extent in neighbors further afield, such as in the Shire and Bree. In this way, the events in Rohan and its environs are the heartwood of Tolkien's novel, where the histories of the Elves, Sauron, and the Ring are its roots, and the Hobbits' experiences before and after the War of the Ring are its blossoming branches.[33] That an Old English undercurrent should be detectable in both roots and branches is logical. "So-called Anglo-Saxon cannot be regarded merely as a root," writes Tolkien, "it is already in flower. But it is a root, for it exhibits qualities and characteristics that have remained ever since a steadfast ingredient in English" (Tolkien "Valedictory Address" 22). And moreover, I think Tolkien captured exactly what these should be in his essay, "On Translating Beowulf." Here, *mutatis mutandis*, Tolkien's words apply equally well to *The Lord of the Rings*:

> And therein lies the unrecapturable magic of ancient English verse for those who have ears to hear: profound feeling, and poignant vision, filled with the beauty and mortality of the world, are aroused by brief phrases, light touches, short words resounding like harp-strings sharply plucked [Tolkien *Monsters* 60].

To typify this profound feeling, poignant vision, beauty, and mortality, it is quite a masterstroke for Tolkien to link the blowing of martial horns with the profoundly moving image of dawn (and hope) returning, to link the Riders of Rohan with the knights of Anglo-Saxon Mercia, and to recall the Vala, Oromë, like his sometime antecedent, Odin, from the dimly preserved mythology of a remote, and shared, past.

Notes

1. For a good introduction to the Kingdom of Mercia, see Chapter VII "The Ascendancy of the Mercian Kings" in Stenton's *Anglo-Saxon England*.

2. Tom Shippey discusses the use of the Mercian dialect in *The Road to Middle-earth* (123) and *Author of the Century* (91–2, 169). Apart from this, the subject has been almost completely overlooked. Christopher Tolkien mentions his father's use of Mercian in *The History of Middle-earth* (*passim*), but not in connection with the Riders of Rohan. To address this gap in the scholarship, I am preparing an extended study, of which the evidence of the dialect presented below is an abridgement.

3. There are isolated survivors from earlier centuries, such as the eighth-century *Cædmon's Hymn*.

4. For those interested in learning more, a good place to begin is Chapter 6 "Alliteration" of Geoffrey Russom's *Beowulf and the Old Germanic Meter*. Or for still more, the entirety of Tom Cable's *The English Alliterative Tradition*. For Tolkien's own description of the medieval Germanic alliterative tradition and its mechanics, see his essay, "On Translating Beowulf" (in *The Monsters and the Critics*), as well as Christopher Tolkien's further elucidation in the introduction to *The Legend of Sigurd and Gudrún* (45–50) and Lee and Solopova's introduction to *The Keys of Middle-earth* (38–42).

5. All translations are mine, unless otherwise noted. It bears pointing out that the initial consonants in *Gár-Dena* and *géardagum* are not sounded alike (rather, in *géardagum*, the initial sound matches that in English *year*); but this qualifies as alliteration according to the rules of the *scop*. For further discussion, see Minkova, particularly 3.2 "The alliterative conundrum" (72–77) and 3.6 "Alliterating voiced velars in early Old English" (113–20).

6. For a very thorough look at the evidence of the Anglo-Saxon harp — exactly what kind of instrument it was, how it was played, and an exhaustive survey of Anglo-Saxon literary references to it — see Boenig.

7. See Tolkien's "Valedictory Address to the University of Oxford," published in *The Monsters and the Critics*.

8. Though *gléo* (and variously, *gleow, gliw, glig*) actually means "glee, joy," it is most often used, particularly in compound forms, with a musical connotation. It is also distinctly English. The word does not occur in any of the other Germanic languages, with the exception of Old Norse *gleði*. Even there, the word is rare (Kershaw 164n52).

9. King of Kent from the final decade of the seventh century through the first quarter of the eighth.

10. For more information on the Alliterative Revival, see Dorothy Everett's *Essays on Middle English Literature*, especially chapters 2–3. And see Thorlac Turville-Petre's *The Alliterative Revival*. Thorlac Turville-Peter himself has a distant connection to Tolkien. His mother, Joan, edited Tolkien's posthumous edition of the Old English Exodus (1981).

Horns of Dawn (Fisher)

His father Gabriel, published in 1957 an edition of *Hervarar Saga ok Heiðreks*, for which Christopher Tolkien wrote the introduction.

11. Tolkien was ultimately unable to commit the necessary time to the project. When E.V. Gordon died in 1938, the project languished for some years before his widow, Ida, completed the edition in 1953, with "valuable notes and corrections" ([iii]) from Tolkien.

12. This edition was reprinted, with an introduction and notes by Carl Hostetter, in *Tolkien Studies*, Volume 1 (2004).

13. I will not digress into a full discussion of Tolkien's wish to restore to England its lost native mythology, destroyed over a period of centuries by invasion and conquest. The term "Mythology for England" has become a commonplace in Tolkien studies, and it is both too well-known and too far outside my present scope to spill further ink here. For those seeking a concise introduction to the concept, see Fisher.

14. For examples, see (*inter alia*) *The Lays of Beleriand*, *The Legend of Sigurd and Gudrún*, and of course, *The Lord of the Rings*. It bears pointing out that Tolkien also wrote an alliterative verse *drama*, "The Homecoming of Beorhtnoth Beorhthelm's Son," designed to accompany his essay on *The Battle of Maldon*.

15. For discussion of many other differences, see Chapter 7 "Things You Might Not Have Known about the Northmen," in fan-scholar Michael Martinez's *Parma Endorion: Essays on Middle-Earth*.

16. "Depicted along its length are 626 human figures, 202 horses, 55 dogs, [etc.]" (Bridgeford 5). Of the tapestry's fifty-nine scenes, thirty-two of them include horses. In one particular case (scene 36: "HIC EXEVNT CABALLI DENVAVIBVS"), "[t]he tapestry's artist was impressed by the novelty of so many horses travelling by sea, for he shows us the horses, rather than the men, leaving ship. One horse has a hind leg still on the boat as he clambers into the shallow water. There must have been hundreds, and perhaps thousands, of such horses being led off the ships that day" (Ibid. 128).

17. A few examples from the years before the appearance of Shippey's seminal book: John Tinkler's "Old English in Rohan" (1968) and Jim Allan's "The Giving of Names: Names of the Rohirrim" (1978); and, for all their flaws, Lin Carter's *A Look Behind "The Lord of the Rings"* (1969) and Ruth Noel's *The Languages of Tolkien's Middle-Earth* (originally published in 1974). However, as far as I am aware, Tom Shippey was the first scholar to note the Mercian forms of the Rohirric nomenclature, and very few have noted it since.

18. The longer form of the name, Riddermark, is meant to be a modernization of *riddena-mearc (= "riders' mark"), so Tolkien indicates in the index to the second edition of *The Lord of the Rings*.

19. See Tolkien's letter to W.H. Auden, 7 June 1955, for his own thoughts of the West Midlands (*Letters* 213). See also two letters to his son, Christopher, 9 December 1943 and 18 January 1945, where Tolkien makes plain his connections to and fondness for Mercian (*Letters* 65, 108).

20. "Offa's Dyke was a defensive earthwork rather than [I would say, in addition to] simply a boundary marker. By providing a linear frontier for Mercia it acted as a deterrent to Welsh raiders, whose horses did not relish scaling its 25-foot bank" (Jenkins 37).

21. Of course, this characterization of the Welsh is from a distinctly Mercian vantage; the Welsh undoubtedly has similar feelings about the Mercians. The whole region which Tolkien called "the counties upon the Welsh Marches" (Tolkien *Letters* 218) was

hotly and repeatedly contested by the Welsh and English throughout the period of Mercia's ascendancy and only fully resolved from a state of "perennial conflict" (Lloyd 325) when Mercia bowed to the emerging dominance of Wessex in the ninth century. See also Lloyd, *passim*.

22. The name is apt: Gléowine is an Old English compound meaning "minstrel" (*gléo* "music" + *wine* "friend").

23. The word *gnomic* derives from the Greek γνώμη "intelligence;" whence, also the word *gnome*, originally a Paracelsian sprite, which Tolkien used to describe the Noldoli, the Second Kindred of the Elves, during his earliest myth-making (Tolkien *Lost Tales I* 43–4). Tolkien's own word, *noldo*, had a similar etymology (though in Elvish, not Greek), and it can be no coincidence that Tolkien chose Nóm, homophonic with *gnome* and indeed meaning "wisdom," for the name the first Men gave to the Noldo, Finrod Felagund.

24. The Old English word *gealdor, galdor* generally refers to a spell, charm, or incantation (cp. *gealdor-cræft* "sorcery"), though it is related directly to the verb *galan* "to sing." The connection between spell-craft and music is an old one, quite apparent also in the English *enchantment* (Latin *incatātio*), but I have thought it most sensible to translate the word as "battle-song," rather than "spell" or "enchantment." Benjamin Thorpe agrees in spirit, having amended the line to read *galan* for *gealdor* in his edition of the poem.

25. In a relatively late essay, "Quendi and Eldar," Tolkien decided that Oromë = "horn-blowing" was merely Elvish folk-etymology, by association with Quenya *romba* "horn, trumpet." The original Valarin name, he says in the essay, "had no such meaning" (Tolkien *War of the Jewels* 400). One gets the feeling, however, that this is rather a straw-man line of reasoning, imposed by Tolkien long after the fact.

26. Tolkien was not at all uncomfortable with the substitution of Norse myths for those lost in England. In his 1936 lecture on *Beowulf*, Tolkien explained: "Of English pre–Christian mythology we know practically nothing. But the fundamentally similar heroic temper of ancient England and Scandinavia cannot have been founded on (or perhaps rather, cannot have generated) mythologies divergent on this essential point" (Tolkien *Monsters* 21). See also Tom Shippey, "Tolkien and Iceland: The Philology of Envy."

27. More accurate — but less poetic — might be "poetry of mead" (consisting of *skáld-skapr* "skaldship, poetry" together with *mjaðar* "of mead," the genitive of *mjöðr*).

28. This is, of course, only the merest summary of the story. For the complete tale, readers may consult any convenient edition of the Prose Edda, specifically, the opening chapter of the Skáldskaparmál. Or for a fuller and better summary than I have given here, see Grimm 902–4, 1581–2; and for a thorough accounting of the divine source(s) of poetry and song, ranging across the mythological spectrum, refer to all of Grimm's Chapter XXX "Poetry."

29. In *The Silmarillion* it is said that the Elves received the gift of song and poetry from Manwë (40), who is also a kind of Odinic figure (as are aspects of Oromë, Gandalf, and other characters). Also, for example, Ulmo's great horns (shell, not animal horn), the Ulumúri, betoken the music of the waters. And even the clamorous music of Melkor, itself clearly martial, reached the ears of Men.

30. Hildórien, the birthplace of Men, was also somewhere in the extreme east of Middle-earth.

31. Including appendices and notes along with the main text, there are six total references to Oromë: three by the name Oromë, two by the name Araw; and one by the

name Béma. Looking at just the main text, there are two references to Oromë, three to the Valar as a single divine body, one to Morgoth, and a stunning twenty-five to Varda (however, most of these occur in poems and invocations). None of the other Valar are named in the main body of *The Lord of the Rings*.

    32. The Ents are, without a doubt, the most musical inhabitants of Middle-earth, unmatched by the Elves, and perhaps even more musical than the tuneful Tom Bombadil. The words *music, song, drum, horn*, and their variations and synonyms occur more than fifty times in this single chapter!

    33. For a discussion of Anglo-Saxon connections among the oldest legends of the Elves, see Hostetter and Smith as well as Flieger; for links between the lost Anglo-Saxon mythology and the world of the Hobbits, see Goldberg and Honegger.

Works Cited

Allan, Jim. "The Giving of Names: Names of the Rohirrim." *An Introduction to Elvish*. Ed. Jim Allan. Hayes, England: Bran's Head, 1978, 212–20.
Arnold, C.J. *An Archaeology of the Early Anglo-Saxon Kingdoms*. London: Routledge, 1988.
Boenig, Robert. "The Anglo-Saxon Harp." *Speculum* 71.2 (April 1996): 290–320.
Cable, Tom. *The English Alliterative Tradition*. Philadelphia: University of Pennsylvania Press, 1991.
Carter, Lin. *A Look Behind "The Lord of the Rings."* New York: Ballantine, 1969.
Chism, Christine. "Alliterative Revival." In Drout, 9–10.
Crowest, Frederick James. *The Story of British Music: From the Earliest Times to the Tudor Period*. New York: Charles Scribner's Sons, 1896.
Drout, Michael D.C., ed. *J.R.R. Tolkien Encyclopedia: Scholarship and Critical Assessment*. New York: Routledge, 2006.
Everett, Dorothy. *Essays on Middle English Literature*. Ed. Patricia Kean. Oxford: Clarendon, 1955.
Fisher, Jason. "Mythology for England." In Drout, 445–7.
Flieger, Verlyn. "The Footsteps of Ælfwine." *Tolkien's Legendarium: Essays on the History of Middle-earth*. Eds. Verlyn Flieger and Carl F. Hostetter. Westport, CT: Greenwood, 2000, 183–98.
Goldberg, Robert. "Frodo as Beowulf: Tolkien Reshapes the Anglo-Saxon Heroic Ideal." *Mallorn* 44 (August 2006): 29–34.
Gordon, E.V., ed. *Pearl*. The Rev. Ida Gordon, with the assistance of J.R.R. Tolkien. Oxford: Clarendon, 1953.
Grimm, Jacob. *Teutonic Mythology, Volumes I–IV*. 4th ed. Trans., with notes and appendix, James Steven Stallybrass. Mineola, NY: Dover, 1966.
Honegger, Thomas. "A Mythology for England? Looking a Gift Horse in the Mouth." *Myth and Magic: Art According to the Inklings*. Eds. Eduardo Segura and Thomas Honegger. Cormarë Series 14. Zurich and Berne: Walking Tree, 2007, 109–130.
Hostetter, Carl, and Arden Smith. "A Mythology for England." *Proceedings of the J.R.R. Tolkien Centenary Conference*. Eds. Patricia Reynolds and Glen GoodKnight. Milton Keynes, England: Tolkien Society, 1995, 281–90.
Jenkins, Geraint H. *A Concise History of Wales*. Cambridge Concise Histories. Cambridge: Cambridge University Press, 2007.

J.R.R. Tolkien, Life and Legend: an Exhibition to Commemorate the Centenary of the Birth of J.R.R. Tolkien (1892–1973). Oxford: Bodleian Library, 1992.

Kershaw, Nora, ed. and trans. *Anglo-Saxon and Norse Poems*. Cambridge: Cambridge University Press, 1922.

Lapidge, Michael, et al., eds. *The Blackwell Encyclopaedia of Anglo-Saxon England*. Oxford: Blackwell, 1999.

Lee, Stuart D., and Elizabeth Solopova. *The Keys of Middle-earth: Discovering Medieval Literature Through the Fiction of J.R.R. Tolkien*. Houndmills, Basingstoke, Hampshire, UK: Palgrave Macmillan, 2005.

Lloyd, John Edward. *A History of Wales from the Earliest Times to the Edwardian Conquest, Vol. I*. 2nd ed. London: Longman, Green, 1912.

Martinez, Michael. *Parma Endorion: Essays on Middle-earth*. <http://www.michael-martinez.com/books/parma_endorion.html>, accessed September 17, 2009.

Minkova, Donka. *Alliteration and Sound Change in Early English*. Cambridge: Cambridge University Press, 2003.

Noel, Ruth S. *The Languages of Tolkien's Middle-earth*. Boston: Houghton Mifflin, 1980.

Pope, John Collins. *The Rhythm of Beowulf: An Interpretation of the Normal and Hypermetric Verse-Forms in Old English Poetry*. Rev. ed. New Haven, CT: Yale University Press, 1966.

Rankin, Susan. "From Memory to Record: Musical Notations in Manuscripts from Exeter." *Anglo-Saxon England 13*. Cambridge: Cambridge University Press, 2007. 97–112.

Russom, Geoffrey. *Beowulf and Old Germanic Metre*. Cambridge Studies in Anglo-Saxon England. Cambridge: Cambridge University Press, 2009.

Scull, Christina, and Wayne G. Hammond. *The J.R.R. Tolkien Companion and Guide: Chronology*. Boston: Houghton Mifflin, 2006.

Sedgefield, Walter John. *An Anglo-Saxon Prose-Book*. English Series, No. 16. Manchester: University Press, 1928.

Shippey, Tom. "Alliterative Verse by Tolkien." In Drout, 10–11.

_____. *J.R.R. Tolkien: Author of the Century*. Boston: Houghton Mifflin, 2000.

_____. *The Road to Middle-earth: How J.R.R. Tolkien Created a New Mythology*. 3rd rev. and expanded ed. Boston: Houghton Mifflin, 2003.

_____. "Tolkien and Iceland: The Philology of Envy." Roots and Branches: Selected Papers on Tolkien. Zurich: Walking Tree, 2007, 187–202.

_____. "Tolkien Out–Wagners Wagner." *The Times Literary Supplement*. May 6, 2009. http://entertainment.timesonline.co.uk/tol/arts_and_entertainment/the_tls/article6232731.ece, accessed September 16, 2009.

_____. "Tom Shippey Speaks at the Tolkien Society Annual Dinner, York, April 19, 1980." *Digging Potatoes, Growing Trees: A Selection from 25 Years of Speeches at the Tolkien Society's Annual Dinners, Volume 1*. Swindon, England: Tolkien Society, 1997, 6–30.

Stenton, F.M. *Anglo-Saxon England*. The Oxford History of England. Gen. ed. G.N. Clark. Oxford: Clarendon, 1943.

Tinkler, John. "Old English in Rohan." *Tolkien and the Critics: Essays on J.R.R. Tolkien's The Lord of the Rings*. Eds. Neil D. Isaacs and Rose A. Zimbardo. Notre Dame, IN: University of Notre Dame Press, 1968, 164–9.

Tolkien, J.R.R. *The Book of Lost Tales, Part I*. Ed. Christopher Tolkien. Boston: Houghton Mifflin, 1984.

_____. "The Homecoming of Beorhtnoth Beorhthelm's Son." *The Tolkien Reader*. New York: Ballantine, 1966, 1–27.

_____. *The Lays of Beleriand*. Ed. Christopher Tolkien. Boston: Houghton Mifflin, 1985.
_____. *The Legend of Sigurd and Gudrún*. Ed. Christopher Tolkien. Boston: Houghton Mifflin Harcourt, 2009.
_____. *The Lord of the Rings*. Fiftieth anniversary ed. Boston: Houghton Mifflin, 2004.
_____. *The Lost Road and Other Writings: Language and Legend Before "The Lord of the Rings."* Ed. Christopher Tolkien. Boston: Houghton Mifflin, 1987.
_____. *The Monsters and the Critics and Other Essays*. Ed. Christopher Tolkien. Boston: Houghton Mifflin, 1983.
_____. *The Old English Exodus: Text, Translation, and Commentary*. Ed. Joan Turville-Petre. Oxford: Clarendon, 1981.
_____. *The Shaping of Middle-earth: The Quenta, the Ambarkanta, and the Annals*. Ed. Christopher Tolkien. Boston: Houghton Mifflin, 1986.
_____. *The Silmarillion*. Ed. Christopher Tolkien. Boston: Houghton Mifflin, 1977.
_____. *Sir Gawain and the Green Knight, Pearl and Sir Orfeo*. Ed. Christopher Tolkien. London: George Allen and Unwin, 1975.
_____. "Sir Orfeo: A Middle English Version by J.R.R. Tolkien." Ed., with introduction and notes, Carl Hostetter. *Tolkien Studies* 1 (2004): 85–123.
_____. "Valedictory Address to the University of Oxford, 5 June 1959." *J.R.R. Tolkien, Scholar and Storyteller: Essays in Memoriam*. Ed. Mary Salu and Robert T. Farrell. Ithaca, NY: Cornell University Press, 1979.
_____. *The War of the Jewels: The Later Silmarillion, Part Two*. Ed. Christopher Tolkien. Boston: Houghton Mifflin, 1994.
_____, and E.V. Gordon, eds. *Sir Gawain and the Green Knight*. Oxford: Clarendon, 1925. Reprinted with corrections, 1946.
Turville-Petre, Thorlac. *The Alliterative Revival*. Cambridge: D.S. Brewer, 1977.

"Inside a Song": Tolkien's Phonaesthetics

John R. Holmes

I wonder if C.S. Lewis was thinking of Sam Gamgee when he wrote this haunting phrase in his London *Times* obituary for Tolkien: "He had been inside language." Sam had described the experience of entering the realm of the elves in Lothlórien the same way: "I feel as if I was *inside* a song, if you take my meaning" (*Lord of the Rings* Book Two, Chapter VI, p. 342). In fact, Sam's anxiety about having his meaning taken (and that phrase is something of a mantra for him, if you get my drift) might be part of the *meaning* of music in Tolkien's fiction. Like the Elvish language, music conveys meaning (sometimes) without apparently engaging the semantic mechanism of the brain. The Platonic dream of a language that conveys meaning directly, because the word is not a counter for the thing itself but somehow the essence of that thing in sound, is all the more credible because we know of a phenomenon that does something like that. The phenomenon is *music*.

In a letter to his Jesuit friend Fr. Robert Murray, Tolkien called anyone who can play a stringed instrument "a wizard worthy of deep respect" (*Letters* 173). But if Tolkien's modesty in the presence of the true wizards — those who play strings — would forbid him to say so, I hope that a less modest literary critic (with, no doubt, even less aptitude for music than Tolkien had) might be permitted to assert that Tolkien's chosen profession, philology, has its own music, and that Tolkien was perhaps its most accomplished wizard. Furthermore, Tolkien's nearly unique approach to philology did not isolate that discipline from poetry, whose aspirations to music are more widely admitted. All three disciplines, music, poetry, and philology, share at least two elements: the medium of *sound* and the phenomenon of *rhythm*. As the neo–Thomist philosopher Peter Kreeft put it in *The Philosophy of Tolkien*: "Music is not ornamented poetry, and poetry is not ornamented prose. Poetry is fallen music, and prose is fallen poetry." Poetry, he elaborates, "is music made speakable" (162). No wonder Sam felt he was inside a song.

Connecting *poetry* with music is one thing — the essence of poetry is the lyric impulse, and "lyric" means "of the lyre" (a stringed instrument requiring a wizard to play it; we will look at Tolkien's comments on the lyre below). But *philology*? I can hear the skeptics turning the pages. Even those who are still here are saying, "Is he kidding? What in the world is musical, or even lyrical, about Grimm's Law? Who could pipe a tune to 'The Semi-vocalization of Post-liquid palato-velars in Middle English'?" Well, Tolkien could, for one, and what's more, he could do it in a prose that sings, prose that is "music made speakable."

The non-philologist hears jargon like "semi-vocalization" and "post-liquid" and "palato-velar," and thinks we couldn't be farther from the beauties of language. But consider: the non-musician might react the same way to a discussion of "Homotonality and the Tonic Minor in Mozart's Italian Overtures"— and yet appreciate the beauty of that homotonality upon hearing the overtures, blissfully indifferent to the jargon. Let's just listen to what Tolkien does with the semi-vocalization of post-liquid palato-velar, and then decide how far it is from music.

First we need to take some of the sting out of that philological jargon. Let's start with the phonological term *liquid*. Many phonologists today don't use the term: they prefer the term *approximant*. But though the name has changed, the concept has not: it is a sound produced by placing the tongue near, but not touching, the roof of the mouth, as in the letter *r*; or lightly touching and directing voiced air around the sides of the tongue, as in the letter *l*. Already, in this description, the connection with music should be dawning on us. For the whole science of phonology, a major branch of what used to be called philology (indeed, Thomas Shippey argued in a 1991 MLA paper that one cause of the demise of philology was its overemphasis on phonology)— that whole science, I say, is the human branch of a science crucial to music: acoustics. In fact, what we study when we look at the phonology of vowels is merely a specialized version of the acoustics of wind instruments. Just as the clarinetist determines what note she plays by changing the shape and volume of the air passing through her instrument, the speaker (or singer) determines the vowel by changing the shape and volume of air passing through her mouth. The clarinetist uses valves to affect those changes; the singer uses a valve called the tongue.[1] And it is the position of the tongue that determines the liquids: pointed at the alveolar ridge, that bump in back of the teeth, to form the *r* (straight out if you're from the West Midlands of England like Tolkien, bent backwards if you're a Yank like me); touching that ridge lightly to form the *l*.

But there's more to philology than phonology. What fascinated Tolkien was the historical development of letters and words. Again, the non-philologist can look at a consonant chart illustrating Grimm's Law and see only a linear progression of letters. But if we remember that what that sequence of letters represents is a change in *sounds*, we're back on the trail of music again. To make sure we stay there, let's look at the particular historical sound change we have picked out: the semi-vocalization of post-liquid palato-velars. Now that we know that liquids are *l*'s and *r*'s, that phrase makes a little more sense: it's something about what happens to palato-velars when they come after liquids in a word.

What happened, late in the Old English period and early in Middle English — the process had already begun when Beorhtnoth Beorhthelm's son fell at the Battle of Maldon — was that the palato-velars changed. The sound of our particular palato-velar — what is a palato-velar? I suppose palato-velars need some description nowadays, since they have become rare and shy of the "Lit. People" as they call us. They are (or were) sounds caused by stopping the flow of air with the back of the tongue pressed against the roof of the mouth — either the hard part toward the center (the palate) or the softer part toward the back (the velum). In some languages the exact position would make a difference, but in modern English it doesn't: to me, a modern Yank, the first sound in *Gandalf* sounds identical to the first sound in *Gollum*, even though the philologist, whose ear should be as finely trained as that of a good piano tuner, could tell you that *Gandalf* begins with a voiced palatal stop and *Gollum* with a voiced velar stop. (Repeat the first syllable of each name in rapid succession and you will feel the very slight shift in tongue position: *Gæ / Gah*.) For speakers of English it doesn't matter whether a *g* is palatal or velar, just as a

"Inside a Song" (Holmes)

Gondorian couldn't tell a Stoor from a Fallohide, and just called them all hobbits. Let's just call all the *g* sounds palato-velar stops.

Only they weren't all stops. Sometimes, instead of *stopping* the flow of air by pressing the tongue against the palate or velum, the vocal musician can just slow it down a little, causing not an explosion like the *g* in *Gandalf*, but a friction like the *g* in the *aagh* Charlie Brown makes when he's frustrated, or the sound the rest of us make when we're gargling. That's the palato-velar fricative, no longer used in English except for the unvoiced form in Scots words like *loch*.

So what happens when Old English *g* and *h*, the palatovelar stop and fricative, respectively, follow a liquid, *l* or *r*? Well, the previous sentence sports a word that results from that sequence: *follow*. In Old English the ancestor of the word *follow* was *folgian*. It was spelled with a *g*, but that *g* was probably pronounced as a fricative unless it preceded a back vowel, as it did in the herald's description of the feud of Ongenðio at the end of fitt 40 of *Beowulf*: *ond ðā folgode / feorhgeniðlan* "and then he followed his life-enemies." In the very earliest Middle English which Tolkien made his special study early in his career (the 13th-century West Midlands English for which Tolkien coined the name "AB dialect" in 1929), the palato-velar is still a fricative, though spelled with an *h*.

In Tolkien's edition of *Ancrene Wisse* we read "*Sikerliche his folhere mot wið pine of his flesch folhin his pine*"—"His follower must follow his suffering in the suffering of his own flesh" (Tolkien, *Ancrene Wisse* 186; Salu 161). But by the time William Langland, also a West Midlander, had produced his second draft of *Piers Plowman*, the B-text of 1377, he was saying not *folgian* but *folwen*. Interestingly enough, Tolkien's favorite 14th-century poet, the *Gawain*-poet, may have still been using the older pronunciation. The scribes recording the words of the poet who wrote *The Pearl* and *Sir Gawain and the Green Knight* spelled the past tense of *folwen* with a *yogh* (ʒ), that funny-looking cross between a *g* and a *y*. The spelling suggests that the Gawain poet might have said *folʒode* (with the voiced fricative), but his pronunciation was already old-fashioned, and doomed to extinction. Chaucer and Gower and Langland were all saying *folwede*. The stop and the fricative, the *g* and the *h*, had become a semivowel, *w*.

Now, the beauty of this change for a poet is that a whole category of words, words in which *r* and *l* were *followed* by, or *swallowed* up, or *wallowed* in a *g* or an *h* were *mellowed* from a stop or a fricative to a semivowel, the rounded glide between vowels that we spell with a *w*. There is a spell to these words, an attraction for which Tolkien coined the term *phonaesthetic*, a subjective appeal which every speaker of every language has felt, if he has any ear for the music of a language, yet the scientific linguistics of Tolkien's day was bent on denying.

The mystical connection between the spoken word and the "true name" that Plato espoused in *Cratylus* was to most twentieth-century linguists a pre-scientific superstition.[2] Even as he was extending the work of the great nineteenth-century historical philologists, Ferdinand de Saussure was making some of their quaint notions of a language that was "isomorphic with reality" obsolete. In 1913, the year of Tolkien's momentous "change of major" from classical to Germanic languages, de Saussure published his *Cours de linguistique générale* which established the distinction between *signifié*, the *concept*, and *significant*, the "*sound-image*" — the polarities of *signified* and *signifier* that are now taken as axiomatic both by linguistic and literary theorists anywhere Elves are no longer cherished — places like France and Yale. It's bad enough that de Saussure hammered a barrier between the sound and the concept in a linguistic sign: to add insult to injury, as far as Tolkien is concerned, the first example he chose was *arbor*, "tree."

Now, intuition and common sense (as well as anyone who has been to France or Yale) tell us that de Saussure was right: "the linguistic sign is arbitrary." Nor is the observation original with de Saussure: the reversal of the classical assumption of a natural connection between sound and sense was one of the major projects of the so-called Enlightenment. Locke's *Essay Concerning Human Understanding* presented the multiplicity of languages as sufficient proof that it was "not by any natural connexion that there is between particular articulate sounds and certain ideas, for then there would be but one language amongst all men" (3.2.1). The loss of the Platonic confidence in the "rightness" of a *significant* for its *signifié* can be seen in 18th-century treatments of the renaissance rhetorical trope of *hypotoposis*. In its widest usage, this jargon term was used to refer to the narrative or dramatic poet's painting of word pictures, but it also included what the modern critic calls "onomatopoeia." (Indeed, the multiplicity of signifiers for the same signified in the history of classical rhetoric might itself make de Saussure's case: they can't *all* be the "right" word). Alexander Pope's famous "Sound and Sense" passage from *An Essay On Criticism*

(1711; lines 362–383), influenced by a similar passage the neo–Latin *De Arte Poetica* of Marco Girolamo Vida (1527), led Augustan critics to question the very assumption that made such poetry possible: patchworks of words that "sounded like" the ideas they conveyed. "That there is much of imagination in this imitation of the sense by the sound of words," wrote John Walker in *A Rhetorical Grammar* (1785), "must be allowed. A judicious critic has very justly observed, that it most frequently exists only in the fancy of the writer or reader, and that the words we suppose to echo the sense, have no other resemblance than what arises from association" (186–187).[3]

By the Age of Johnson, then, the theoretic rift between signifier and signified was already wide enough for a camel's nose. The rarely-acknowledged pedigree of de Saussure's distinction might be enough to convince the modern reader that he was right. But anyone who has read Tolkien's "Mythopoeia," or has tried to name a child, knows that the Swiss philologist was not *wholly* right. We have all known parents who go into the maternity ward convinced that their final choice is *Alphonse* for a boy and *Belinda* for a girl — only to take one look at the kid and realize she doesn't look *one bit* like a Belinda; he doesn't look *anything* like an Alphonse — in fact, the poor kid looks like a *Sid* or a *Shirley* — and how is *that* going to play at the country club? How can our poor baby expect to get into Yale, let alone France, with a name like *Shirley*?

Tolkien, who understood this mystery, the metaphysical and *not* altogether arbitrary connection between *signifier* and *signified*, put it to use in his extraordinary and Adam-like (or Bombadillian) gift for inventing names. So great was this gift that even Tolkien's detractors acknowledged it. In that same letter to Father Murray in which he called string-players wizards, Tolkien told his friend that he derives aesthetic pleasure "from the *form* of words (and especially from the *fresh* association of word-form with word-sense)" (*Letters* 172). Tolkien's emphasis on the word *fresh* is I think the key to his quarrel with modern linguistics. However divorced signifier and signified are in our fallen world, it *is* a sundering of what God, or at least Adam, had joined — that's the bad news. But the good news is that the sundered connection can be refreshed — by the philologist, who knows the history of the sundering of sound and sense, but also the poet, who knows when the sound is carrying his sense, even if he doesn't know why. In creating his names and his verse, Tolkien was exercising both skills, in pursuit of what he called "phonaesthetic pleasure" (*Letters* 176).

To illustrate, let's turn back to our abandoned palato-velars. The phonaesthetics of the post-liquid palato-velar is a thing of beauty. It captured the heart of a young Texas poet with the unlikely name of Tom Jones when he was in college, and he filled a whole song with them, which became the opening song of *The Fantasticks*, the longest-running musical in the history of the New York stage. The song was called "Try To Remember." The refrain was the single word we have looked at in its transformation from Old to Modern English: *follow, follow, follow*. In each stanza Jones crammed as many of the mutated-liquid words he could: first *mellow, yellow, fellow*, then *willow, pillow, billow*, and then *follow* and *hollow*, finally ending where the song began with *mellow*. Two-thirds of these words began life in Old English with post-liquid palato-velars: "fellow" from *fēolaga*, "willow" from *welig*, "billow" from Old Norse *bylgja*, hollow from *holh*.

Tolkien does not incorporate quite so many of these mutated palato-velar words in any one place, but the mention of the word *willow* should signal to any Tolkien reader where I am going next: to the old Willow-man of *The Adventures of Tom Bombadil* and "The Old Forest" chapter of *The Lord of the Rings*. In the "Tom Bombadil" poem, which first appeared in the *Oxford Magazine* in February of 1934, we encounter several of these liquid-mutated palato-velars as rhyme words: *fellow, willow,* and *swallow*. As soon as they appear as rhyming words in a poem — the poetic term in fact is itself one of our mutated palatovelar words: pairs of words that rhyme in a structurally meaningful way are called *rhyming fellows* — as soon as they appear in a poem, we are forced to notice a secondary effect of the mutation that turns *g* and *h* into *w*: all of the words are trochees, two-syllable words with the stress on the first syllable. In the poem *The Adventures of Tom Bombadil* we have ten rhyme-words created by the semi-vocalization of *g* or *h: fellow, berry, wallowing, swallowing, hollow, follow, willow, burrow, sorrow, bellows*. Using these words as rhyming fellow forces a two-syllable rhyme known as feminine rhyme. Not only does each of the 134 lines of *The Adventures of Tom Bombadil* have a feminine ending, but the characteristic rhythm of all of Tom Bombadil's dialogue in *The Lord of the Rings* is built on the falling cadence of feminine endings.

Yet the word *willow* has other rhythmic implications. In Old English words like *folgian* and *holh*, we have the palato-velar immediately following the liquid. But in the Old English ancestor of "willow," *welig*, we have a vowel in between, a vowel that is lost in the mutation. The loss is obscured by the fact that both the Old English word *welig* and the Modern English word *willow* are trochees, but if we look at the root form, we see two consonants come together by dropping a syllable, in a rhythmic process that both musicologists and phonologists call *syncopation* (*welig* → *welg*, which will later fill out to *wilwe* and then *willow*).

All of this, however, still touches only the "word form" part of Tolkien's phonaesthetics: how does it associate with the "word meaning" part which Tolkien wants to make fresh? In the case of the imagery of the willow on the bank of a stream, Tom Shippey has given us a hint in his discussion of Tom Bombadil, both in *The Road to Middle-earth* and *Author of the Century*. Shippey points out that the name Tolkien coins for the river along which Tom Bombadil lives combines the elements of the real-life Oxford landscape Tolkien is trying to evoke, the willow breaks along the river Cherwell. The Cherwell is a stream which flows past Addison's Walk, where Tolkien and C.S. Lewis hammered out their differences not only on the momentous implications of Christian myth, but also on the connection between signifier and signified in words like *Tree* and *Leaf* (*Author* 63, *Road* 108). Tolkien called Tom Bombadil's river the Withywindle, *withy* being a West Midlands word for willow, and *windle* a word meaning "winding river"—which is exactly what the *Cher* in Cherwell means.

But something that Shippey does not examine is the fact that by giving us a *fresh* name for willow and winding, Tolkien has revitalized an image that has largely disappeared from the word *willow*. He is engaged in precisely the act which he told Fr. Murray gives him aesthetic pleasure: "the *fresh* association of word-form with word-sense." The name *Withywindle* is what is called a doublet: both parts of the compound originally conveyed the idea of bending, or — and here's where the sense of danger comes from — enclosing, wrapping around. For that matter, the name *Cherwell* is also a doublet, with both of its roots also bearing the concept of bending or turning: *cierran*, "to turn," and *weallan*, "to bubble," originally from the same idea of turning. That original sense still survives in the idiom "to well up," and its Latin cognate gives us the word *valley*, something riven by the welling waters of a river (as in Rivendell). It is this imagery of winding and turning and above all else being wreathed in willows that Tolkien invokes in the two sentences with which he introduces the Withywindle in Book One, Chapter VI of *The Lord of the Rings*.

"In the midst of it there wound lazily a dark river of brown water" (115). The anastrophe in this clause — the reversal in word order forced by the expletive use of "there"—is puzzling. Modernists (including friends like Hugh Brogan, with whom Tolkien engaged the issue of word order in September of 1955), assume that such an "inversion" (Tolkien objected to that term) is a facile attempt at archaism. But this wording (whether it be "In the midst of it there wound," or "In a hole in the ground there lived") is in fact exclusively modern, since the expletive use of *there* was not a feature of Old English. In this case, Tolkien is clearly risking the near-passive construction in order to produce the rhythmic echo of *dark river* and *brown water*. What follows is a string of four parallel participial phrases, each participle linked by the preposition *with* to the word *willow*: "bordered with ancient willows, arched over with willows, blocked with fallen willows, and flecked with thousands of faded willow-leaves."

Here the rhythmical pattern is a bit more complex, and its music must be appreciated not in terms of the meters we know from Modern and Middle English poetry, stressed and unstressed syllables alternating in predictable patterns, but in the metrical patterns of Old English verse. In Old English poetry, each line (in fact, each half-line) must have the same number of stresses, but may vary in the number and position of unstressed syllables, or syllables of secondary stress. When Tolkien explained his understanding of Old English prosody — which he did quite succinctly in his preface to Hall's translation in Wrenn's edition of *Beowulf* (1940) — he touched on his theory of *phonaesthetics* without using the word (which he had perhaps not yet coined). After outlining the six possible patterns in the OE half-line according to the system devised by Eduard Sievers, Tolkien almost imperceptibly flung down a gauntlet to those who disguised their tin ear for the music of OE verse behind a sneer for its "foreign" sound. Tolkien knew bloody well that the "foreign" note in English verse came from imported metrical schemes from Romance languages; that the rhythms of OE verse still lived not only in Modern English poetry, but modern English prose, and even everyday conversation. In "On Translating Beowulf" he argued that the six patterns of stress that Sievers identified can be found in any randomly-chosen passage of English, whether prose or poetry; Old, Middle or Modern ("On Translating" 62). The implication that Old English meter arose from the natural language of Old English speech expresses a linguistic principle of metrical analysis formulated by linguist Roman Jakobson and applied to Tolkien's verse by Geoffrey Russom: "Units of metrical form (metrical positions, feet, verses) are projected from units of natural language (syllables, words, phrases, clauses, sentences)" (Russom 53).

If Tolkien was confident that any passage in Modern English would demonstrate the rhythmic patterns of Old English, then surely the passage we have chosen, the mature work of a man who had spent his life teaching that ancient language, whose ear was attuned to them, would betray those rhythms. And it does — not only in the programmatic way that Tolkien was talking about in the essay on translating *Beowulf*,[4] but in the more general way that the metrical weight of a phrase is heard and felt in native English verse. I emphasize "native," because the traditional system employed since the renaissance to designate English verse patterns was borrowed from the Greeks via the Romans via the French and Italians, and involves recurring patterns of stressed and unstressed syllables (or in Greek and Latin verse, long and short).

By such neoclassical measure, the rhythms we can manifestly hear in Tolkien's description of the River Withywindle have no clear pattern. Each phrase is different. The first, "bórdered with áncient wíllows," is roughly trochaic trimeter, but with an extra unaccented syllable, "with." The second, "árched óver with wíllows" begins with what the neoclassics would call a spondee (or a pyrrhic substitution; see Russom 56), but Tolkien, again using Sievers's language, called a "clash": two stressed syllables coming together. The double stress of the clash (árched ó-) causes a corresponding doubling of the unstressed syllable, heard as a dactyl in "óver with." It is still a falling meter, however, starting on the stress (or "lift" as Tolkien called it, translating Sievers's *Hebung*) and falling off to one or more unstressed syllables (or "dips," translating *Senkung*). And although the first phrase has one syllable more than the second (bordered with ancient willows, 7; arched over with willows, 6), each has only three stressed syllables. They would have to be considered metrically equal.

And the third phrase is equal to the other two. In neoclassic terms it is perfect trochaic trimeter: "blócked with fállen wíllows." But then the last phrase reminds us that we are hearing prose, not verse: it does not resolve into three stressed beats: "and flécked with thóusands of fáded wíllow-léaves"—five stresses in all. Yet surely the added beats are intentional, even if by the idea of "intention" we are invoking not Tolkien's prodigious intellect, but his ear for rhythm. In European prose rhythms, there is abundant precedent for this pattern. The master of prose rhythm for the ancient world was Cicero, and his prose was marked by a rhythmic device the Romans called the *clausula*, sort of a prose-rhythm version of the resolution of a chord in a piano sonata. When we hear the satisfying completion of the chord, we know that the piece is over. When we reach the specific patterned ending of a sentence in Cicero, we know the sentence has concluded. Tolkien prepares us for the ending by postponing it with the extra syllables. The three successive three-beat phrases create the expectation of the pattern; we expect closure within three beats. When closure is postponed in the fourth clause, we experience a sense of finality that coincides with the end of the sentence — just as in Cicero's clausula, or in the extra foot of the Alexandrine that ends each stanza in the mostly-pentameter "Spenserian Stanza." We can see it (and hear it) if we stacked the clauses in stanzaic form:

> bordered with ancient willows,
> arched over with willows,
> blocked with fallen willows,
> and flecked with thousands of faded willow-leaves.

The tension of waiting for the other shoe to drop (or in this case, the fourth; this beast is a quadruped) is the essence of the periodic sentence, as well as one of Ogden Nash's favorite comic rhyme techniques. Nash enjoyed setting a severely truncated rhyme against a just-as-severely hypermetric rhyming fellow, as in his poem, "Hypochondriacs."

But the sense of finality in this periodic sentence of Tolkien's is also due to an additional metrical trick, another rhythmical difference between the first three phrases and the last. The three metrically equal phrases all end with an extra unaccented syllable, the so-called "feminine ending." The final clause, however, in addition to bearing additional syllables, ends with the stressed monosyllable "leaves." The chord resolves; the sonata is over. It's safe to applaud now.

Well, we have strayed a bit from the phonological analysis into metrical analysis, but we'll return to the music of phonology in a moment. But note how much more like music metrical analysis is compared to rhetorical analysis, which is also based on patterns of repetition. In terms of rhetorical tropes, Tolkien's winding willow-sentence is a tricolon (pattern of three) of epistrophe (clauses ending with the same words, "with willows"). Yet even here there is considerable variation in the rhetorical analysis: the repeated "with willows" appears in the first and third clauses with intervening adjectives, "ancient" and "fallen." Identifying the part of speech (adjective) suggests yet another type of pattern, with which we began our study: grammatical. In grammatical analysis, the pattern of this passage becomes much more absolute. Each clause resolves to a single pattern:

[past participle] + *with* + *[adjective]* + *willows*	
bordered	ancient
arched over	fallen
blocked	[no adj.]
flecked [variation]	faded [variation]

Variations include the null adjective in the third clause, the insertion of a further modifier "thousands of" in the fourth, and the substitution of "willow leaves" for "willows" at the end.

After this fourfold repetition of the key semivocalized palato-velar in "willow," the next sentence only uses the word "willow" once, but is sprinkled with other *l*-sounds, *fluttering, yellow, gentle, softly, rustling, valley*— the last of which, as we noted above, conveys etymologically the image of twisting and curving. But so does "fluttering," a word which at first glance seems to be onomatopoetic or hypotopical in the Alexander-Pope-sense noted earlier. With the softness of a sound like "fluttering," we are convinced that Shippey's assessment of this passage (*Author* 63, *Road* 108) applies here, too: surely something that "flutters" cannot be as menacing as the sound-sensical monosyllables *clap, snap, clash, crash, crush, smash, pound, swish, smack* of the horrible goblin song in Chapter 4 of *The Hobbit*. But as with the seemingly harmless *willow*, a glance at the philological history of the word refreshes the "fresh association" of *fluttering* with reeling and writhing (if not the last of the 3 R's, *rhythmatic*) — and an archetypal connection between such wavelike undulation and menacing evil.

The skeptic of "inherent meaning" would find the onomatopoetic nature of the word *flutter* (historical linguists prefer the term "echoic" or "imitative" for such etymologies) merely an illusion. It is simply an iterative form of the word *float*, another word for rolling water such as we have seen in the etymologies of Middle-earth's *Withywindle* and Oxford's *Cherwell*. The Latin cognate *pluere* means "to rain," and the Greek *plein* "to swim." Nothing too ominous there. But the back-and-forth imagery of the iterative suffix-*erian* that gives us the Old English ancestor of *flutter* excites the primitive association between snakelike movements of water and the lurkers below such as the sea-monsters Beowulf stirred up in his swimming contest with Breca. The passage is awash with cognates for the wriggle-words we have been examining.

*flōdȳ*þum feor

wado *weallende*...

Nō hē wiht fram mē
flēotan meahte...
...oþ þæt unc *flōd* tōdrāf,

[Not a whit could he
far in the *flood*waves *swim* from me...
...until the *flood* parted us,
the *welling* waters...] (541–546).

The best-known association in Tolkien between wriggling and the monstrous is of course *wraith*, which as Shippey has demonstrated was connected with OE *wriðan*, "to twist," is in the modern English *wreath* (*Road* 148–150).

Shippey assumes that C.S. Lewis's iconography of evil as "bent" in his space novel *Out of the Silent Planet* was influenced by Tolkien's philological understanding of *wraiths*, and that may be so. But it need not be. The imagery of bending that we see in the deceptively menacing willow and in the twisted souls of the Ringwraiths was standard medieval iconography that Lewis certainly would have known had he never met Tolkien. Medieval theologians, long before anthropologists re-invented the term, called unfallen man *homo erectus*— that is, not only upright, but righteous (the etymologies of both words suggesting "straight, not curved"; we call a 90° angle "right" because in early Modern English a straight line was called a "right line"). But fallen man became *homo incurvatus*, bent over like an animal, closer to the ground (the lowest and most curved animal being the serpent), and closed in on himself, self-centered. The iconography is immediately recognizable from Genesis, but the principle is also spelled out by Ecclesiastes: "God made mankind straight, but men have had recourse to many calculations" (7:29).[5]

In addition to Genesis and Ecclesiastes, the Old Testament had its own writhing menace beyond the serpent of Eden. In Job it is called *Leviathan*, but etymologically it is a wraith or a writhing wreath: the name is conjectured to come from the Hebrew verb לויתד, *livyatan*, "coiled," and the related noun *livyd^h*, "wreath, garland."[6] Etymological and mythological speculations in Hebrew, however, are generally dead ends in Tolkien studies, and we do need to return to the main topic of philological music. But the connection with the languages and mythologies Tolkien taught should occur to the reader with "Northern" sensibilities. To the student of the *Eddas*, Leviathan evokes thoughts of *Jörmungandr*, the *Miðgarðsormr* or "World-worm," the evil spawn of Loki, whom Thor is destined to slay at the end of the world. That monster definitely twines around the world, yet unlike Leviathan, its name does not apparently originate in any word for twisting. Yet its Norwegian descendent, the *kraken*, does. Recent exposure in *The Pirates of the Caribbean* has limited philological discussion of this monster's name to debates about its pronunciation — whether it rhymes with *bracken* or *bacon*. But its etymology is an exact match with that of *leviathan*: the Norwegian dialect word *krake* means "a twisted thing," and is cognate with a number of words beginning *kr-* in Germanic languages, including the English words *crooked* and *creep*.

And it is with such words that we creep our crooked way back to the *sounds* of words, and thence back to music. Our discussion of the connection between evil, fear, and crookedness or bentness has so far escaped the context of the sounds of those words. But a consideration of the multitude of words in English alone cognate with *kraken* might shake our enlightened conviction that any link between a sound and an idea is arbitrary. If we trace their etymologies there is some connection with the idea of curving and the onset *cr-* : *cramp* (German *krampf*), *crumpet*, *crumple*, *crummie* (German *krumm*), *cringe*, *creep* (German *kriechen*), *crawl*, *crinkle*, *creek*, *cruller*, *croup*, *cradle* (think of the curved rockers, and of the related words *crèche* and *crib*; see Marchand 326). Even the word *curl* itself was originally a *cr-* word, as Chaucerians will recall when they think of the Squire's "lokkes crulle as they were leyd in presse" (General Prologue 81). Is there then a mysterious connection between the phonemes [k] and [r]? Surely the gathering of so many sounds cannot be mere coincidence?

As it turns out, there is a linguistic *via media* between "inherent meaning" and sheer coincidence in this collocation of *cr-* words — a compromise very close to the phenomenon Tolkien dubbed "phonaesthetics." In 1930, linguist J.R. Firth coined the term "phonaestheme" for a phonological unit which conveys a specific idea seemingly independent of meaning (211). As early as 1836, Wilhelm von Humboldt had considered a similar concept under the name *iconism*, a term revived in the twentieth century.[7] English philologists at the end of the nineteenth century borrowed a French coinage from Greek, *apophonie*, for the bearing of meaning by sound. To say that [kr] is a phonaestheme, a "sound image," for the concept of bending or twisting, is not to say that the connection is inherent or natural. But it is not altogether arbitrary: it is indeed dependent on the phonetic tastes of the inventor of the word. And Tolkien's references to phonaesthetics were always in the context of the sub-creation of words.

In the Willow-man scenes of *The Lord of the Rings*, and the earlier poem on which they were based, "The Adventures of Tom Bombadil," there is no proliferation of *cr-* words, and the *lw* pattern that is prevalent — the result, as we have seen, of the semivocalized post-liquid palatovelar — may not meet the criterion of a phonaestheme. But the consistency of a consonant sound is not the only kind of phonaestheme. There is also the variability of vowel sounds known as ablaut phonaesthesia, and Tolkien uses it to create a unique musical effect in his "Tom Bombadil" poem.

In *ablaut* we have another philological term which reminds us of the approximation of phonology to music. Variations in vowels are achieved, as we have seen, by moving the tongue to change the shape and volume of the vocal space within the mouth. The changes in vowels which signal grammatical changes in Germanic verbs are what Jacob Grimm and his disciples called *ablaut*, such as modern English *ride, rode, ridden* or *sing, sang, song, sung*. But though words of similar meaning can cluster around a phonaestheme such as *cr-*, they can also radiate out, away from the phonaestheme, in one of two ways. Either they can rhyme, as *crash, smash* or *crack, smack*, so that *smash* and *smack* are alienated from the *cr-* phonaestheme (though notice the tendency to cluster around a new phonaestheme, *sm-*); or they can keep the initial (and sometimes final) root consonants but alter the vowel in a way that tends to follow the ablaut patterns of English. Thus *chitter / chatter, jiggle / joggle, snip / snap*.

"Inside a Song" (Holmes)

In "The Adventures of Tom Bombadil," the poem in which Tolkien first introduced the character in 1934, not only are many of the rhymes (all feminine) involved with our friends the semi-vocalized palato-velars (fellow/yellow, wallowing, swallowing, hollow/follow, willow/pillow, burrow/sorrow, dwellers/bellows), but each succeeding threat or enemy (none, alas, beginning with *cr-*) advances the ablaut series of ejaculations that announces the confrontation between each successive threat (Goldberry, Willow-man, Badger-brock, Barrow-wight), and the prey, Tom Bombadil.

Even that "enemies list" is musical in invention: in a poem in which all rhymes are feminine (two-syllable, with emphasis on the first), each of the antagonists has a name in roughly the same rhythmic pattern. I say "roughly," because Tolkien might have taken issue with Sir Philip Sidney's adoption of the Italian term *sdrucciola* for this kind of dactyl. Sidney, in *The Defense of Poesy* (1595), argues for the metrical versatility of English compared to Italian, which has only feminine rhyme and *sdrucciola* (long-short-short, as *femina/semina*), but not masculine; or compared to French, which has masculine and feminine, but not *sdrucciola*. Sidney, like any modern poet, would consider each of Tom Bombadil's antagonists to be possible rhyming-fellows for a *sdrucciola*, rendering them in accentual verse as dactyls (in Siever's terms as translated by Tolkien, lift-dip-dip). But Tolkien's ear for the music of poetic rhythm was subtler than that — and it was subtler undoubtedly because his training in metrical analysis was not just a matter of Lit., but Lang. as well.

In his "Prefatory Remarks" to Wrenn's 1940 edition of the Clark Hall translation of *Beowulf*, Tolkien observed that a pure dactyl, which he illustrated with the modern English words *handily* and *instantly*, are, as Sidney observed, quite common in modern English, but did not exist in Old English ("On Translating" 64). The Lit.-trained ear, rendered a mite tone-deaf by a pedagogy that forces Germanic rhythms into Greek molds, might object, "Not exist! The dactyl not exist in Old English? What about *gūð-sēaro* (battle-armor) or *famig-heals* (foamy-necked) or *ðancedon* (thanked)? Ain't they dactyls?" Well, no, as we can see by Tolkien's Sieverean analysis of those words in the "Prefatory Remarks" ("On Translating" 68), they ain't. Germanic metrics cannot do with a binary pattern borrowed from Greek through Latin (which in any event was designed to measure quantitative, not accentual verse: *long-short* rather than *lift-dip*). What classical metrics describes as a single pattern, whether you call it dactyl or sdrucciola, is two distinct patterns in Old English verse: Sievers type D*a* (which Tolkien calls "falling by stages"), and D*b* (which he calls "broken fall"; see Tolkien's Chart, "On Translating" 62), because Old English metrical analysis requires a third term between stressed and unstressed, a secondary, or as Tolkien called it, "subordinate stress." Using the acute accent (´) for a strong stress and the grave accent (`) for a subordinate stress, and no mark for an unaccented syllable, we would mark *Góldbèrry* as the "falling by stages" type (D*a*) and the other three—*Wíllow-màn, Bádger-bròck*, and *Bárrow-wìght*—as "broken fall" (D*b*).

So now that we have four antagonists with similar but distinct rhythms to their names, what about this ablaut series? In the poem, each antagonist hails Tom with an ejaculatory syllable which moves progressively backward in the mouth as the ablaut progresses. Each syllable is a nonsense syllable, ostensibly a greeting or the semantically-empty utterance which linguist Bronislaw Malinowski called "phatic communion" (Malinowski 315). Goldberry says "Hey, Tom Bombadil!" but the colloquial friendliness of "hey!" is ironically undercut by the fact that she expresses it while attempting to drown Tom. Similarly, the syllable "ha!" which Willow-man blasts at Tom is to the English ear a phonaestheme for laughter. Yet laughter can be the bloodthirsty "ha-ha!" of the predator in cornering its prey, as Grendel laughed at the prospect of Beowulf's men (*þā his mōd āhlōg,* "then his mind laughed," *Beowulf* 730). Willow-man's "ha!" is definitely a "gotcha!" Badger-Brock's exclamation is "ho!," which can also express the predator's delight in the prey; and Barrow-wight's "hoo!" is a ghoulish (or owlish) shout. The ablaut series makes a circuit of the vocal chamber in which vowel-music is played: beginning in the middle portion of the front third (mid-front): *hey*, dropping down and back to the lowest portion of the central third (low-central): *ha*, rising up and yet further back (mid-back): *ho*, and then rising again to the highest back position (high-back): *hu*. There are numerous ways of distinguishing vowel positions, and the division of both axes into three positions is arbitrary, but the position of each of these vowels in the mouth could be fairly represented by the chart on the following page.

This brief discussion of Tolkien's wizardry with the music of phonology is only a sketch, and perhaps even a stretch in connecting Tolkien's

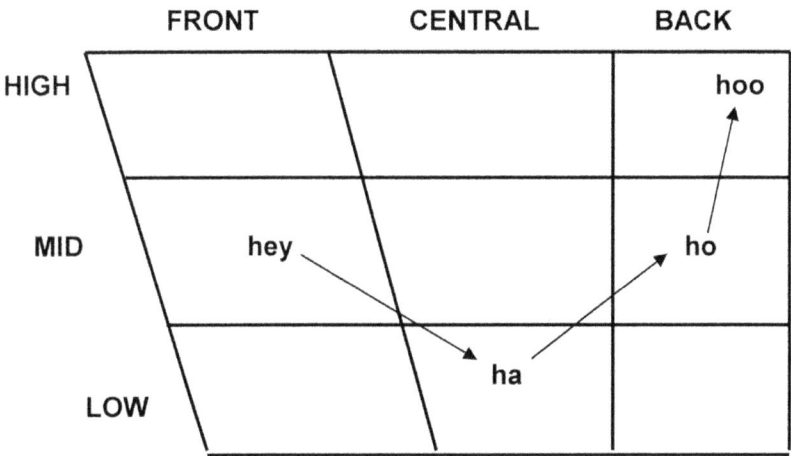

art with music as a discipline, but there is one point of contact with musicology in Tolkien's research, and I have alluded to it once already. For if the connection of Old English metrics with music is a stretch, it is a stretch that Tolkien himself made, though with some apology. On the one occasion he was pressed to address a group of musicians — in this case, the Lincoln Musical Society — Tolkien, in awe of all who play stringed instruments, connected Old English poetry with the one most associated with it: the harp. "I never imagined that it could ever be my fate —" Tolkien told his audience, "or fortune — to address a Musical society. A man little endowed by nature and less instructed by study in such matters would be hard to find." Yet, he continues, "If I do address this society then, it is chiefly to address a question to it: what function can it be imagined that the *harp* played in the recitation of verse composed in the ancient English manner?" (MS. A 30/1, fol. 96).

As he develops his theme, Tolkien's argument reveals how much philology can contribute to musical knowledge, because, though he acknowledges his ignorance of the history of harps or harp music (though one did survive as part of the Sutton Hoo archaeological find), the history of the word tells us that the Romance languages borrowed it from Germanic, not the other way around. "The *name* at least is Germanic, beyond doubt," says Tolkien, and is "ancient in all the northern Gmc tongues of Iceland, Norway, Sweden, Denmark, North Germany, England, and when the name appears elsewhere (as in the Romance languages) it is borrowed from the North Southwards: not the reverse" (fol. 96).

The rest of the lecture is a talk on Old English metrics that largely parallels his "Prefatory Remarks" for the Clark Hall *Beowulf*, offering "something about the nature and structure of this verse — from a harpist and *whistler's* point of view" (fol. 96). Like Themistocles, Tolkien could not fiddle, nor could he harp. But the English whistling tradition is quite intricate musically, so even "a whistler's point of view" might tempt the cellists or violinists from Lincoln in his audience — maybe even, if they were lucky, leave them feeling as if they were, like Sam Gamgee, "inside a Song."

Notes

1. It could be argued that the human vocal instrument does involve one other valve: the uvula, which pulls forward from the throat to produce nasal sounds (*m*, *n*, and *ng*), or presses back against the throat to produce non-nasal sounds (every other consonant).

2. Identifying the theory of sound-symbolism with Plato, as I do throughout this essay, is a bit disingenuous, as in the dialogue *Cratylus* Plato has Socrates back away from the theory when presented with evidence to the contrary by Hermogenes. The fact that what I herein call the "enlightenment" attack on supposedly "classical" notions of language was already inherent in Plato demonstrates either my own hypocrisy or the enlightenment's genius for re-inventing the wheel. For the fairy-story motif of the "true name," see the entry under that name in John Clute and John Grant, eds., *The Encyclopedia of Fantasy* (New York: St. Martin's, 1997), 966.

3. The "judicious critic" was Samuel Johnson. Walker cites *The Rambler* No. 93, but that essay has only a peripheral relation to the issue of sound and sense; Walker must have had in mind *Rambler* 92, where Johnson illustrates the phenomenon of sound echoing sense in Homer, taking examples first cited by the first-century B.C.E. rhetorician Dionysius of Halicarnassus.

4. The passage quoted does, however, reveal many of the typical patterns of Old English verse Tolkien specifies in his essay: Sievers type A, falling-falling: *blócked with | fállen*; type B, rising-rising: *the áir | was thíck*; type C, clashing: *of brówn | wáter*; type D, broken fall: *wóund | lázily*. Type E does not appear in this brief passage, nor does the variation on type D that Tolkien calls "falling by stages," but I hope that the appearance of four of the six types in the space of thirty-two words is enough to prove Tolkien's point.

5. In a recent study of Luther's use of these terms, Matt Jenson has argued that the idea behind them stems from Augustine, but the term *homo incurvatus* seems to belong to Bernard, *Sermones in Cantica*, Sermo LXXX, 2, *Patrologia Latinae* 183, 1166–1167; see Bernard of Clairvaux, *On the Song of Songs IV*, trans. Irene Edmonds (Kalamazoo, MI: Cistercian, 1980), 146–147. See also St. Bonaventure, *Itinerarium Mentis in Deum* 1.7, and especially Philotheus Boehner's commentary in his edition (St. Bonaventure, NY: Fran-

ciscan Institute, 1956), 112–113, n. 12. Jenson's study is *The Gravity of Sin: Augustine, Luther, and Barth on "Homo incurvatus in se."* London and New York: T&T Clark, 2006.

6. The standard Biblical references to Leviathan are Job 41, Psalm 74: 14, and Isaiah 27:1. The noun *livyd^h* appears only twice, in Proverbs 1:9, in which the instructions of one's father are described as "a garland to grace your head," and Proverbs 4:9 where Wisdom is personified as a "supreme" woman who will "set a garland of grace on your head" (New International Version, www.biblegaeway.com). See William L. Holladay, ed., *A Concise Hebrew and Aramaic Lexicon of the Old Testament.* Grand Rapids, MI: Eerdmans, 1971, 174.

7. Literary critics will think of the phrase "verbal icon" in relation to an influential book of that name by the formalist critic and literary theorist W. K. Wimsatt, Jr., *The Verbal Icon: Studies in the Meaning of Poetry* (Lexington: University of Kentucky Press, 1954); in its linguistic sense, however, the term *iconism* was revived in the first decade of the twentieth century in Charles Saunders Pierce's theory of signs.

Works Cited

De Saussure, Ferdinand. *Cours de linguistique générale.* Paris: Payot, 1916; *Course in General Linguistics.* Ed. Charles Bally and Albert Reidlinger, trans. Wade Baskin. New York: Philosophical Library, 1959.
Firth J.R. *The Tongues of Men, and Speech.* London: Oxford University Press, 1930.
Locke, John. *An Essay Concerning Human Understanding.* In Robert Maynard Hutchins, ed. *Great Books of the Western World.* Chicago: Encyclopædia Britannica, 1952, Vol. 35.
Malinowski, B. "The Problem of Meaning in Primitive Languages." Supplement I to C.K. Ogden and I.A. Richards, *The Meaning of Meaning.* Eighth Ed. New York: Harcourt, Brace, and World, 1946, 296–336.
Marchand, Hans. *The Categories and Types of Present-day English Word-Formation: A Synchronic-Diachronic Approach.* Alabama Linguistic and Philological Series #13. Tuscaloosa: University of Alabama Press, 1966.
Nash, Ogden. "Oh to Be Odd!" *Free Wheeling.* New York: Simon and Schuster, 1931, 97.
Russom, Geoffrey. "Tolkien's Versecraft in *The Hobbit* and *The Lord of the Rings.*" In George Clark and Daniel Timmons, *J.R.R. Tolkien and His Literary Resonances.* London: Greenwood, 2000, 53–69.
Salu, Mary, trans. *Ancrene Riwle.* London: Burns and Oates, 1955.
Shippey, Tom. *Author of the Century.* New York: Houghton Mifflin, 2000.
_____. "Recent Writings on Old English." A paper read at the 107th Convention of the Modern Language Association, San Francisco, December 28, 1991. Accessed from *http://members.aol.com/mcnelis/AEstell/Shippey1.html* August 10, 2004.
_____. *The Road to Middle-earth.* Rev. and Expanded Ed. New York: Houghton Mifflin, 2003.
Sievers, Eduard. *Altgermanische Metrik.* Halle: M. Niemeyer, 1893.
Tolkien, J.R.R. *Ancrene Wisse: The English Text of the Ancrene Riwle,* edited from MS. Corpus Christi College Cambridge 402, Early English Text Society No. 249, introduction by N.R. Ker. London: Oxford University Press, 1962.

———. "*Ancrene Wisse* and *Hali Meiðhad*." In H.W. Garrod, ed., *Essays and Studies by Members of the English Association*, Vol. XIV (Oxford: Clarendon, 1929), 104–126.
———. *The Lord of the Rings*. New York: Houghton Mifflin, 2004.
———. "On Translating Beowulf." In *The Monsters & the Critics and Other Essays*. London: HarperCollins, 1997.
Ullman, B.L. *Ancient Writing and Its Influence*. New York: Cooper Square, 1963.
von Humboldt, Wilhelm. *Über die Verschiedenheit des menschlichen Sprachbaues und ihren Einfluß auf die geistige Entwickelung des Menschengeschlechts*. Bonn: F. Dümmler, 1960 [photoreproduction of first edition, 1836].

Æfre me strongode longað: Songs of Exile in the Mortal Realms[1]

Peter Wilkin

Tolkien remained consistently preoccupied with the idea of longing throughout the long and complex development of his *legendarium*. Eriol, the central mariner figure in one of his earliest mythological conceptions, *The Cottage of Lost Play*, is driven to the land of the Elves by an intense sea-longing where he later hears and records the history of the first age of Middle-earth. While this story was ultimately abandoned, the mariner figure haunted by a longing for the West remained present in both *The Lost Road* of the 1930s and *The Notion Club Papers* some fifteen years later. In *The Lord of the Rings*, Frodo, and to a lesser extent Bilbo, may be considered as representative of this central figure. Both desire the company of the Elves and eventually find themselves sailing West. In Tolkien's later poems such as "Sea-bell" and "The Last Ship," published in *The Adventures of Tom Bombadil* in 1961, the idea of longing takes on a more somber tone. If we may generalize for a moment on the basis of the examples above, the idea of longing manifests itself as an intense, restless desire to sail over the western seas and, ultimately, to reach the deathless lands beyond. What is also significant, however, is the close association between this idea of longing and the concept of poetry.

In Tolkien's mythology, those mortals who are troubled by sea-longing are frequently poets. They are also close friends with the Elves, who themselves are strongly associated both with poetry and the idea of longing for the West, as I will show.[2] At another level, however, it is possible to see a deeper significance attached to this theme. There are several indications that Tolkien located the fundamental source of Art, that is, human creativity in its various manifestations, in the natural human desire for and corresponding inability to attain eternal life. The evidence for this argument will be reserved for the second and final section of this discussion.

The first encounters between mortals and Elves that occur in *The Hobbit*, *The Lord of the Rings* and *The Silmarillion* are all initiated by the hearing of poetry and music.[3] The most significant example of such an encounter occurs in *The Silmarillion*, in the chapter entitled "Of the Coming of Men into the West" when Finrod first comes across a group of Men sleeping around a campfire. Hiding in the woods, he waits for them to fall asleep and then, taking up one of their rude harps, begins to play. The stories in his song, of the making of the world and the paradise of Valinor, come "as clear visions before their eyes" and confer deep wisdom on those who are especially moved.[4] This tribe of Men, the House of Bëor, eventually produces the greatest mortal heroes of *The Silmarillion*, including, most notably, Eärendil, the only mortal in the First Age to reach Aman.

In *The Fellowship of the Ring*, the first encounter between Elves and mortals makes more explicit the Elves' particular association with the longing for the West. As in *The Silmarillion* and *The Hobbit*, the hobbits hear the sound of Gildor's hymn to Elbereth before they actually catch sight of the Elves. This time, however, we see most clearly the Elves' own yearning to make the journey over the sea. The emphasis in the last stanza of Gildor's song is placed on the separation of Valinor and Middle-earth and the consequent sundering of the High Elves. Despite their lingering "in this far land beneath the trees," they "remember" Elbereth's "starlight on the Western seas."[5] The longing of the Elves for the West is reiterated in several other instances where we hear the Elves sing. In Rivendell another poem about Elbereth is sung in Sindarin in the Hall of Fire.[6] In Lothlórien Galadriel recalls the exile of the Noldor in Middle-earth and her desire to sail back West in two songs she sings to the Fellowship as they leave Caras Galadon.[7] On the Fields of Cormallen, Legolas sings a song expressing a similar desire. Despite the differences between the various Elves the hobbits encounter on their journey, whether from Lothlórien or Mirkwood, the same restless longing stirs them.

Æfre me strongode longað (Wilkin)

Interestingly, the same cannot generally be said of the Elves' counterparts, Men. With notable exceptions such as Aragorn, Bilbo, Frodo, Sam, Merry, Pippin and a few strange hobbits who are said to have gone away with the Elves,[8] neither the Men of Gondor and Rohan, nor the hobbits of Hobbiton and Bree seem to feel the strange disquiet that takes Bilbo over the mountains to Rivendell a second time. On the other hand, those peculiar hobbits mentioned above are indeed stirred by a longing comparable to that of the Elves. The poem most recited by Bilbo and Frodo, "The Road Goes Ever On," also deals with a kind of yearning, not explicitly for the West perhaps, but for a (very hobbit-like) "lighted inn." Most significantly, in the last chapter of *The Return of the King*, Frodo's recital of the "Road Goes Ever On" is replied to by the Elves with the last stanza of Gildor's song mentioned above. This instance would seem to suggest some kind of connection between the yearnings expressed in the two songs.

The Exile and Return of the Elves

The desire of the Elves to return to the West is mentioned explicitly at several points in *The Lord of the Rings*. After his hymn to Elbereth, Gildor says to Frodo that he and his companions are exiles and that they are only lingering a short time before returning to the West beyond the sea.[9] The Elves' association with exile is subsequently reinforced throughout *The Lord of the Rings*, particularly in Rivendell and Lothlórien.[10] The story of the Elves' return into the West focuses especially on Legolas, however, who represents a very different tradition from other important Elves in the story such as Gildor, Elrond and Galadriel. Whereas the latter were part of the tragic history of the Exile of the Noldor from Valinor in the First Age, Legolas and his kindred, the Sindar, remained in Mirkwood at a distance from the larger politics of the Noldorin princes. While Elves such as Gildor and Galadriel retain a memory of the bliss of Valinor, Legolas' own people never undertook the great journey to the West in the first place.[11]

Nevertheless, in spite of this major difference, Legolas clearly shares the innate Elvish desire to return to the West. Galadriel's warning, passed on to Legolas by Gandalf in Fangorn Forest, implies that once he hears the sound of the gulls, his longing for the sea will be awakened and he will no longer be able to live contentedly in Mirkwood.[12] It is interesting in this regard that Legolas has never experienced the sea before, yet he accepts without question its powerful effect.

The Elves as a whole are thus united in their innate and natural desire to return West; they are aware, as Galadriel herself makes very clear, that the world is changing and the age of Men is at hand.[13] Their yearning to sail into the West is something that is familiar if not inevitable, even if they, like Legolas, have never been to Eressëa before. Legolas emphasizes this point in his song to the sea which he sings on the Fields of Cormallen where he refers to Eressëa as "elvenhome" and "land of my people."[14] His longing and, conversely, the restlessness he feels in Middle-earth, is really a desire to return to his true home.

Mortals

Whereas all Elves share the desire for the West, the mortals of Middle-earth, Men, dwarves and hobbits, possess a more ambivalent attitude. Those mortals who do possess such a desire, however, are often marked out by their reaction to the sea. Sam, arguably the most rustic and conservative of the hobbits, is deeply moved when he first hears the waves breaking on the shores of Middle-earth.[15] The overwhelming effect the sea has on Sam is particularly striking when compared to his strong, characteristically hobbit-like aversion to boats and water.[16] There is also an interesting similarity between Sam and Legolas, both of whom attach a deep significance to the sea despite never having experienced it before.

Curiously, special emphasis is placed on sound rather than sight. Galadriel tells Legolas to beware of the cry of the gulls, while Sam is moved by the particular sound of the waves. Why is the sound of the sea so significant? One answer lies in a statement in the "Ainulindalë" of the *Silmarillion*. The "Ainulindalë" is an account of the creation of the world by God (Ilúvatar) and his arch-angelic spirits (Ainur) who sing three mighty themes of music as a creative act. Water is mentioned specifically as the "most greatly praised" element created for it contains, more than any other element, an "echo" of the Music of the Ainur. The Children of Ilúvatar, "hearken still unsated to the voices of the Sea, and yet know not for what they listen."[17] Sam's experience of the sea at the Grey Havens is surely related to this innate power of water, which quietly echoes the Music of the Ainur. The precise effect the sound of the music has on the Children of Ilúvatar is not explained; indeed, the passage expresses a paradox: on the one hand the Children have an "unsated" desire for the sound of the sea; on the other, they "know not for what they listen." This ambiguity is realized in Sam's case where it is clearly implied that the sea has a profound effect on him, yet it is unclear how it changes him or what his experience means.[18]

Unlike the Elves, the desire of mortals for the West is fraught with uncertainty. While the yearning for the West is evident enough in some mortals, it is not at all clear whether it can ever be fulfilled. One of Tolkien's earliest mariner characters, Eriol,[19] exhibits this point clearly. Details about Eriol's life differ according to the stages of his conception: in one instance he is led to the sea after his parents are killed in the Viking incursion into Anglo-Saxon England, while in another, he inherits the sea-longing from his father who had mysteriously vanished while on a voyage. The most important detail, however, is that Eriol is an exile with an inherent sea-longing which ultimately leads him to Eressëa. Once there he eventually finds the Cottage of Lost Play, where he is told the history of the Elder Days. Tolkien wrote a number of poems that he attributed to Eriol concerning his wanderings and his desire for the West. One of the most notable of these is the "Song of Eriol" where Eriol describes his journey to Eressëa. He recalls how he broke free from his bonds when he heard the "calling" of the "great seas' flood" and wandered about the isles and capes on the Western shores.[20]

Like the Elves, Eriol feels the strong call of the sea, but it is notable that the object of his desire, "the dark western shores," is very different in tone from the homely Eressëa which Legolas refers to in his song. The shores that Eriol refers to are, for one thing, not only ambiguous but dangerous, especially so if we consider the importance of light and dark imagery to Tolkien's works. The waves are "unknown," the capes are not lit by day but are in "twilight," the sounds of the sea are "perilous." One of the most important questions Eriol's poem prompts us to ask is whether this longing could be fulfilled, if indeed a mortal *could* set foot in the immortal realms of Eressëa and Valinor. It is highly significant in this case that Tolkien's answer appeared to be in the negative. In "The Song of Eriol," the mariner does indeed find the land of the Elves, referred to in the poem as "this isle of magic," but he does not appear to find any contentment there; the poem ends ambiguously with his continued wandering.[21]

With these considerations in mind, it is possible to characterize the differences between the longing of Elves and mortals in more depth.[22] Whereas the Elves as a whole appear to possess a desire for the West, only special individual mortals such as Sam and Frodo are conscious of such a desire. The Elves' longing for Eressëa and Valinor is a familiar longing for home, whereas the West is only barely remembered by mortals and shrouded in mystery and peril. Most decisively, where the Elves are able to return to the West along the Straight Road, the way is effectively blocked for mortals.[23]

Valinor and Eden

The longing of Elves and those certain mortals for Valinor takes on a deeper meaning when considered in relation to the biblical fall of man.[24] There are two major indications that the West can be associated with Eden before the fall. First, Valinor and Eressëa have strong resonances with the biblical Eden through the use of tree-symbolism. Second, there appear to be strong connections between the fall of man and the exiles of the Noldor from Valinor and the Númenóreans from Númenor.

In the *Silmarillion* there is a close equation between Valinor and Eressëa with trees. In Valinor, Yavanna planted the Two Trees, Laurelin and Telperion, in order to provide light for the world before the coming of the Elves. Despite their destruction by Melkor and Ungoliant, the Two Trees nevertheless retained their significance in the poetry of the Elves. Galadriel's first song in Lothlórien, which she sings to the Fellowship as they are about to leave, makes clear the symbolic significance of the Two Trees. She sings of "leaves of gold" which may refer either to the "golden tree" that grows in Eldamar or the mallorn trees that grow in Lothlórien.[25] Whichever the case, the very ambiguity in the lines sets up a comparison between the mallorn trees and Laurelin, the golden tree, which in turn allows us to compare Lothlórien with Eldamar itself. Such a comparison, however, reveals an important difference between these two places, as Galadriel sings in the following lines: "Winter," the "bare and leafless Day" comes to Lórien.[26] But, by implication, in Eldamar there is no decay.

The leaves of the trees in this respect serve to symbolize change. While the shedding of leaves naturally heralds the passing of seasons, it seems that something more is meant by "Winter" than just a season. Rather, "Winter" denotes the fading of the Elves in Middle-earth, as the Third Age closes and the dominion of men grows. Even Lothlórien, despite its strong links with the timeless memory of the Elder days, is nevertheless a place of change and thus a place of decay. It is significant then that Eldamar is characterized in contradistinction to Lothlórien as a place that is changeless. The same imagery is used to emphasize this point in Legolas' song of the sea, where he describes Eressëa as a place "where the leaves fall not."[27] Unlike Lothlórien, the leaves do not fall in Eldamar. If Eldamar is a place of changelessness then it is also a place of deathlessness, and this quality endows the lands of the West with a powerful significance that recalls the changelessness of the pre-fallen biblical Eden.

The tree symbolism in the song of praise on the Fields of Cormallen makes the connection between the West and Eden in a stronger manner.[28] The "King," referring on the surface level to Aragorn, has an obvious resonance with Christ and the Resurrection, and indeed the song itself resembles a psalm in both its form and language.[29] It is especially notable how closely the tree is connected with the fact that the city "shall be blessed." The "withered Tree" referred to in the song indicates the spiritual decay of Gondor under the rule of the stewards, and the replanting of the tree by Aragorn (who finds it miraculously growing on the side of the mountain) symbolizes the spiritual renewal of the city under the true king.[30] The connection between blessing and trees is offered again in a parallel to the white tree. When Saruman attempts to take control of the Shire and corrupt it through industry, his most decisive act is to chop down the Party Tree. The tree, however, is replaced by Sam with a mallorn seed, which takes root and successfully grows into a healthy mallorn. Afterwards, when Sam meets Galadriel in the havens, she remarks that he has used her gift well, for the Shire "shall now be more than ever blessed and beloved."[31]

The link between trees and the spiritual state of the land and people it is associated with adds a new dimension to the comparison that is made between falling leaves in Lothlórien and the trees in Valinor. If Valinor is characterized as a place of deathlessness, it poses as a sharp contrast to the spiritual corruption of Middle-earth under Sauron. At a further level, Valinor as a heavenly paradise on Earth takes on the strong resemblance of a biblical Eden. This allows us to characterize the longing of the Children of Ilúvatar in a new light: the desire of both mortals and Elves for the West may be considered as a longing to return to a paradise on Earth. Yet, as we have established previously, one of the most decisive differences between Elves and mortals is that the latter do not belong in Valinor or Eressëa.

The Fall

The differences between the longing of mortals and Elves for the West are reflected in the different natures of their falls. The fall of the Noldor may be regarded as a "sub-creative fall."[32] Angered by the theft of the Silmarilli, Fëanor leads a great host of Elves out of Valinor against the will of the Valar with the intent of taking up war against Morgoth in Middle-earth. In their haste to set sail, a host of the Noldor under the leadership of Fëanor slays a number of the Teleri, their kindred, who refused to relinquish their ships. The blood-spilling of Elf by Elf, an act which resembles the Cain and Abel story, provokes the Valar to curse the Noldor and bar them from Valinor.[33]

The exile of the Noldor is thus made explicit, and the subsequent history of the First Age is characterized by the fulfillment of the curse of Mandos. Despite the allusion to the Cain and Abel story, however, the fall of the Elves is not a complete fall in the same sense. To begin with, it is not a fall which extends over the entire race of Elves; only the Noldor and those Elves which took part in Fëanor's rebellion are subject to the curse of exile. Otherwise, the Teleri and the Quendi who remained in the West are exempt from the doom of the Valar and maintain their "unfallen" state. Second, Fëanor's sin, as Tolkien makes clear in his letter to Milton Waldman, is to succumb to the elvish temptation of "possessiveness" over the Silmarilli which he created with the light of the Two Trees.[34] The fall of the Noldor is thus a "sub-creative" one in their jealousy to preserve their own works and arrest change. Finally and most decisively, the Elves are able to return to Valinor once Fëanor's oath is brought to its final conclusion. Consequently, the elvish yearning to return to the Edenic West is able to be fulfilled once they receive pardon, as indeed Galadriel demonstrates in *The Lord of the Rings*.

The contrasting inability of mortals to reach the West and their apparent exiled state thus implies a complete fall that extends beyond the "subcreative" fall of the Elves. Any reference to this fall in *The Silmarillion*, however, appears to be highly elusive. In his letter to Milton Waldman Tolkien stated that "there cannot be any 'story' without a fall," yet proceeded to assert a paragraph later that in his mythology, "The first fall of Man, for reasons explained, nowhere appears."[35] Undoubtedly, the apparent contradiction is solved if we take Tolkien's statements to mean that the fall does not appear explicitly in the mythology, leaving the possibility of its implicit occurrence. One of the most revealing passages in this regard occurs in the description of Men's arrival into the West in *The Silmarillion*:

> Of his (Morgoth's) dealings with Men the Eldar indeed knew nothing, at that time, and learnt but little afterwards; but that a darkness lay upon the hearts of Men (as the shadow of the Kinslaying and the Doom of Mandos lay upon the Noldor) they perceived clearly even in the people of the Elf-friends whom they first knew.[36]

No fall is stated explicitly in this passage, but it is surely implied. While the nature of the "darkness" that resides in the "hearts" of men is left unexplained, there is certainly an allusion to some kind of spiritual corruption. A clue is given in the reference to the Kinslaying of the Noldor, which, as mentioned earlier, resembles the Cain and Abel story. Such an allusion brings with it a marked biblical overtone. Moreover, in contrast to the fall of the Noldor, which applied only in part to the race of Elves, this darkness extends to *all* Men, including the Elf-friends.

The comparison to the biblical fall of man in this passage is not complete, however, for there is no mention, even in an implied sense, of an original Eden in the awakening of Men. If mortals' desire for the sea is emblematic of a return to paradise, surely there once existed an original paradise, equivalent to Eden. There is, however, another instance in *The Silmarillion* which offers a more detailed parallel to the first mysterious "fall" mentioned above.

The downfall of Númenor in the Second Age resembles the original Fall of Man more fully than the previous passage.[37] The account of the slow spiritual corruption of Númenor describes the Númenóreans yearning more than ever for the "undying city that they saw from afar" and "everlasting life." Their restlessness increases and they murmur against the restriction the Valar imposed on them that they should never set foot in Eressëa or Valinor.[38] At the height of their power, a "shadow" descends upon the Númenóreans which is specifically attributed to the "will of Morgoth." Thus, in both the passage describing the corruption of the Númenóreans and the passage hinting at the original fall of Men in the East, the presence of Morgoth, the "shadow," is referred to as the source of Men's corruption. From the Númenor passage, we can infer the nature of Morgoth's corrupting influence: instilling in Men the fear of death and stirring up the corresponding hope that they can overcome death by their own efforts. This hope and this fear constitute the ultimate hubris on the part of men, since death is the ordained and natural fate of mankind.[39]

The Downfall of Númenor also offers an explanation for the loss of an Edenic paradise after the fall of man. Númenor itself bears a striking resemblance to Eden, particularly when it is placed in comparison with Middle-earth itself. Geographically, this similarity is emphasized by its close proximity to Eressëa which is stated to be within sight of the westernmost haven of Númenor.[40] Before the arrival of Sauron, the land itself is described as a place of longevity and the Númenóreans resemble the Elves even more than they do the other Men of the East.[41] After the destruction of Númenor, Valinor and Eressëa are removed from the Earth and can no longer be reached except via the Straight Road which is physically impassable for mortals. Consequently, the complete destruction of Númenor by Ilúvatar himself represents on this level the loss of Eden as a result of the fall of man and, unlike the fall of the Elves, Men are unable to return in spite of their longing to do so. This idea of a deep longing for the West that we have seen thus takes on a thoroughly biblical dimension.

How do poetry and music fit in with this conception? The source of poetic inspiration derives precisely from this intense longing for a deathless paradise and the frustration of its fulfillment as a result of the fall. Poetry, in this sense, is a reaction to the problem of death, a way of articulating or giving vent to the restlessness it inspires in those mortals who are marked out by their special friendship with the Elves.[42] Thus it is no accident that mortals such as Eriol, Bilbo and Frodo are the transmitters of the tales which give us the legends of *The Silmarillion*, and the stories of *The Hobbit* and *The Lord of the Rings*.[43] Tolkien's point about poetic inspiration reaches out beyond his secondary world; it stands as a possible explanation for the nature of poetry itself in our own, primary world.[44] It also allows us to see with greater clarity Tolkien's rationale for his own creativity.

It is clear, then, that despite the futility of attempting to restore the paradise of Eden, mankind's longing for the deathless lands in the West is the crucial catalyst for the poetic process. Nevertheless, with the blessings that poetry brings, Tolkien adds a serious warning. As the story of Númenor's downfall illustrates, the longing for the West can easily be corrupted and perverted into an impious and hubristic obsession for acquiring eternal life and divine power through mankind's own technological efforts—the other, more perilous alternative to poetic sub-creation.

Notes

1. This Old English quotation is taken from one of Tolkien's "asterisk poems" printed in Tom Shippey's *The Road to Middle-earth* (Boston and New York: Houghton Mifflin, 2003), 356–357.
2. See also Tolkien's statement about Elvish "magic" being Art, "delivered from many of its human limitations." J.R.R. Tolkien, *The Letters of J.R.R. Tolkien*, ed. Humphrey Carpenter (Boston and New York: Houghton Mifflin, 2000), 146.
3. In *The Hobbit*, the party first hears the light-hearted Elf-song as they enter Rivendell. J.R.R. Tolkien, *The Hobbit* (London: HarperCollins, 1993), 45–47.
4. J.R.R. Tolkien, *The Silmarillion*, ed. Christopher Tolkien (London: HarperCollins, 1999), 163.
5. J.R.R. Tolkien, *The Fellowship of the Ring* (London: HarperCollins, 1993), 114.
6. Ibid., 311.
7. Ibid., 484 and 490–1.
8. J.R.R. Tolkien, *The Hobbit*, 7.
9. J.R.R. Tolkien, *The Fellowship of the Ring*, 115.
10. Ibid., 311 and 484.
11. After their awakening in Middle-earth, the Elves migrated West to Valinor under the leadership of Oromë. A number of the Elves remained, for various reasons, in Middle-earth and refused to make the journey West over the Sea. See the chapter "The Coming of the Elves" in J.R.R. Tolkien, *The Silmarillion*, 43–53.
12. J.R.R. Tolkien, *The Two Towers* (London: HarperCollins, 1993), 130.
13. J.R.R. Tolkien, *The Fellowship of the Ring*, 488.
14. J.R.R. Tolkien, *The Return of the King* (London: HarperCollins, 1993), 283.
15. Ibid., 378.
16. It is noteworthy that the Fellowship does not trust Sam with an oar, when they leave by boat out of Lothlórien. See also the Gaffer's discussion about Frodo's parents in J.R.R. Tolkien, *The Fellowship of the Ring*, 41.
17. J.R.R. Tolkien, *The Silmarillion*, 8.
18. There are at least two more direct connections between water and music in *The Fellowship of the Ring*. In Rivendell Frodo drifts off into a "dream of music" which ends

in "running water." Again, when crossing the Nimrodel Frodo thinks he can hear the sound of singing "mingled" in the stream. J.R.R. Tolkien, *The Fellowship of the Ring*, 306 and 440 respectively.

19. J.R.R. Tolkien, *The Book of Lost Tales 1*, ed. Christopher Tolkien (London: HarperCollins, 1994), 14.

20. J.R.R. Tolkien, *The Book of Lost Tales 2*, ed. Christopher Tolkien (London: HarperCollins, 1995), 299.

21. Related to this idea is the much later poem "The Last Ship" where Fíriel, a mortal woman, cannot sail off with the Elves. See J.R.R. Tolkien, *The Adventures of Tom Bombadil* (London: Unwin, 1975), 141–144.

22. See also Verlyn Flieger's discussion on the discrepancy between the Elvish and mortal point of view on death. Verlyn Flieger, *Interrupted Music: The Making of Tolkien's Mythology* (Kent and London: Kent State University Press, 2005), 45–54.

23. With the exception of those of the fellowship who sail with Gandalf to the West.

24. For a discussion on the fall of man in Tolkien's mythology see, Jonathan Evans, "The Anthropology of Arda" in *Tolkien the Medievalist*, ed. Jane Chance (London and New York: Routledge, 2000), 194–224.

25. J.R.R. Tolkien, *The Fellowship of the Ring*, 484.

26. Ibid., 488.

27. J.R.R. Tolkien, *The Return of the King*, 283.

28. Ibid., 292.

29. Shippey notes in *The Road to Middle-earth* that the song strongly echoes Psalms 24 and 33. See Tom Shippey, *The Road to Middle-earth* (Boston and New York: Houghton Mifflin, 2003), 200.

30. It is of further note that Aragorn's name may be translated as "tree-king" in Sindarin.

31. J.R.R. Tolkien, *The Return of the King*, 375. Cf. Tolkien, J.R.R., *The Silmarillion*, 314. Further instances of this pattern are found in *The Silmarillion*. In Númenor, the white tree Nimloth is cut down by Sauron once he succeeds in corrupting the Númenóreans for the desire of eternal life. A sapling is planted by Elendil when the new kingdoms are founded in Middle-earth. These examples serve as a reminder of the first tree slaying, when Morgoth destroys the two Trees of Valinor.

32. Tolkien states this explicitly in his letter to Milton Waldman. See J.R.R. Tolkien, *The Letters of J.R.R. Tolkien*, 145.

33. J.R.R. Tolkien, *The Silmarillion*, 94.

34. J.R.R. Tolkien, *The Letters of J.R.R. Tolkien*, 148. A parallel instance of this point is seen with the creation of the three elven rings (resembling the three Silmarills) which were intended to arrest change and preserve the work of the Elves.

35. Ibid., 147–8. Tolkien's reason for not including an explicit reference to the fall of man is that it would compromise the integrity of his secondary world.

36. J.R.R. Tolkien, *The Silmarillion*, 164.

37. In one letter, Tolkien referred to the Númenor story as the "second fall of man." J.R.R. Tolkien, *The Letters of J.R.R. Tolkien*, 154.

38. J.R.R. Tolkien, *The Silmarillion*, 315.

39. There is of course a fundamental difference between Tolkien's conception of the fall of man in *The Silmarillion* and the account in Genesis. Whereas death is a punishment for transgression in Genesis, it is said to be the most important gift of Ilúvatar to

Men in *The Silmarillion*. Morgoth's corruption of Men, precipitating their fall, seems to consist of instilling in them a *fear* of death. Tolkien did not regard this interpretation of Genesis to be incompatible with Christian doctrine. See J.R.R. Tolkien, *The Letters of J.R.R. Tolkien*, 285–6.

40. J.R.R. Tolkien, 313.
41. Ibid., 311.
42. The strong connection between the fall and poetic inspiration is also reflected in the Elves' case. In the account of the exile of the Noldor in chapter 9 of *The Silmarillion*, Fëanor replies to Mandos' dreadful curse, saying that the deeds of the exiles 'shall be the matter of song until the last days of Arda.' See J.R.R. Tolkien, *The Silmarillion*, 95. It is of further note that a comparison seems to be implied between Fëanor's stubborn refusal to heed the Valar and Ar-Pharazôn's blasphemous invasion of Valinor. In both cases, each "hardened his heart." See J.R.R. Tolkien, *The Silmarillion*, 95 and 333.
43. In the terms of Tolkien's secondary world, *The Hobbit* and *The Lord of the Rings* are actually stories taken from "The Red Book of Westmarch" composed by various authors, but chiefly Bilbo, Frodo and Sam. See the "Note on Shire Records" in J.R.R. Tolkien, *The Fellowship of the Ring*, 34–36. *The Silmarillion* is a more complex case because it was never properly completed. It is clear, at least on the basis of Tolkien's earlier versions of the *legendarium* that he intended to give it a frame and a textual history like he did with *The Hobbit* and *The Lord of the Rings*. Eriol in "The Cottage of Lost Play" stories, Auboin and Audoin in "The Lost Road" and Alwin Arundel Lowdham and Wilfred Trewin Jeremy in "The Notion Club Papers" were, at various stages, intended to be the transmitters of the tales of the first age. All of these characters were troubled by sea-longing. See J.R.R. Tolkien, *The Book of Lost Tales I*, 13–44, J.R.R. Tolkien, *The Lost Road and Other Writings*, ed. Christopher Tolkien (London: HarperCollins, 1993), 36–104 and J.R.R. Tolkien, *Sauron Defeated*, ed. Christopher Tolkien (London: HarperCollins, 2002), 145–327 respectively.
44. Tolkien's statement that "all stories are ultimately about the fall" in his letter to Sir Stanley Unwin may be understood precisely in regards to this point. Tolkien also hinted at his rationale in his letter to Michael Straight where he says that his Elves and Men are really just different aspects of the "Humane" and represent "the problem of Death." J.R.R. Tolkien, *The Letters of J.R.R. Tolkien*, 147 and 236 respectively.

Works Cited

Eden, Bradford Lee. "The "Music of the Spheres:" Relationships Between Tolkien's *The Silmarillion* and Medieval Cosmological and Religious Theory." In *Tolkien the Medievalist*, ed. Jane Chance. London: Routledge, 2003, 183–193.

Flieger, Verlyn. *Interrupted Music: The Making of Tolkien Mythology*. Kent and London: Kent State University Press, 2005.

Gordon, I.L., ed. *The Seafarer*. London: Methuen, 1966.

Shippey, Tom. *The Road to Middle-earth*. Boston and New York: Houghton Mifflin, 2003.

Tolkien, J.R.R. *The Adventures of Tom Bombadil*. London: George Allen and Unwin, 1975.

―――. *The Book of Lost Tales 1*. Ed. Christopher Tolkien. London: HarperCollins, 1994.

―――. *The Book of Lost Tales 2*. Ed. Christopher Tolkien. London: HarperCollins, 1995.

_____. *The Fellowship of the Ring.* London: HarperCollins, 1993.
_____. *The Hobbit.* London: HarperCollins, 1993.
_____. *The Letters of J.R.R. Tolkien.* Ed. Humphrey Carpenter. Boston and New York: Houghton Mifflin, 2000.
_____. *The Lost Road and Other Writings.* Ed. Christopher Tolkien. London: HarperCollins, 1993.
_____. *Morgoth's Ring.* Ed. Christopher Tolkien. London: HarperCollins, 2002.
_____. *The Return of the King.* London: HarperCollins, 1993.
_____. *Sauron Defeated.* Ed Christopher Tolkien. London: HarperCollins, 2002.
_____. *The Silmarillion.* Ed. Christopher Tolkien. London: HarperCollins, 1999.
_____. *Tree and Leaf.* London: HarperCollins, 2001.
_____. *The Two Towers.* London: HarperCollins, London: 1993.
Wilcox, Miranda. "Exilic Imagining in *The Seafarer* and *The Lord of the Rings.*" In *Tolkien the Medievalist.* Ed. Jane Chance. London: Routledge, 2003, 133–154.

J.R.R. Tolkien:
A Fortunate Rhythm

Darielle Richards

Now we are a conversation, soon we shall be a song. — Hölderlin

"I don't like it, and no one else does either!" came one of the many review statements in reaction to J.R.R. Tolkien's book *The Lord of the Rings*.[1] Tolkien's critics were quick to point out his unconventional literary approach with exasperation. "Why couldn't he just follow the normal story structure and end it in the usual way?" Amidst the outcry from his numerous detractors and pressures to finish *The Lord of the Rings,* Tolkien managed to remain true to his own literary nature and to his desire to craft enchantment. Such an imaginative mode, which is the subject of this chapter, surely tested his patience and that of his publishers, who in the end had to wait twelve years for the book that would follow the very successful *Hobbit*. It was not his indomitable (though mostly well-mannered) temperament that was foreign to the literary critics, but Tolkien's willingness to allow the material to arise from levels not accessible by the analytical mind, a mode which baffled them. Those critics might have found it puzzling that Tolkien's writings continue to touch the deepest reaches of the collective psyche over a half of a century later. But there are other writers who have walked this way before Tolkien.

There is indeed a well-established though hidden tradition of visionary temperament and thought — a "fellowship" of another kind — with which Tolkien earns his association through his literary approach. This long lineage of illustrious individuals who preceded him, poets and artists from antiquity to the modern era, seeks the truth of the imagination, along with the knowledge of the intellect.

These innovative individuals share a constellation of values and principles, and speak through diverse schools of thought in almost every age. One knows them by their creative works — works filled with symbols, metaphors, as well as invisible but felt dimensions, works expressing a sense of unity with all life. Something in their expression changes us. We are initiated, and are called to birth something new

Each scholar, writer, artist, and healer of this tradition seeks a *poesis* or a creative process which stems from a participatory and transformative threshold innate to the heart, not the reasoning mind. Why does anyone seek this creative threshold but that it provides a finer lens of perception, one that enables us to see past the merely personal, opening to a more conscious and compassionate relationship with the world outside ourselves. This perception includes the greater story of the living epiphanic creation and our relationship with it. Gareth Knight, biographer of the Inklings — Tolkien's literary brotherhood at Oxford — described their work of creating magical worlds: "By a 'magical work,' we mean a way of evoking the creative imagination of the reader to participate through story and landscape and characters in a deeper level of truth or reality."[2]

It was only after years of struggling against the tide of a reductionist, Cartesian hegemony, that Kathleen Raine, poet and scholar of the works of Blake and Yeats, discovered the discredited and neglected writings that constitute what she called the learning of the imagination.[3] She found that this learning, expressed through "the human breast," is the perennial wisdom, an ageless philosophy that can be known "in the nature of things, verified and re-experienced again and again."[4] She recognized that this philosophy was reflected in the works of the Romantic poets and C. G. Jung. The tide she fought against in the sixties and seventies was (and is) the same tide that Tolkien faced as he began his writings of fairy-story in the early twentieth century.

Without doubt the *literati* and other critics of Tolkien's time would have been less perplexed by his books had they understood his literary tradition. A closer look at the writing and purposes of Tolkien and the Inklings would have revealed a connection with antiquity among the group of friends who inspired and supported one another through their love of ideas and of the imagination.

J.R.R. Tolkien (Richards)

Interestingly, another literary friendship in the late eighteenth century between Samuel Taylor Coleridge and William Wordsworth produced the *Lyrical Ballads*, a body of work which opens to other worlds, worlds created in part by the level or intensity of consciousness. This work is said to have begun the Romantic movement with its own new vistas of inspiration, its belief in the spiritual truth of feelings and nature, beauty, oracular knowing, creativity, and compassion — a poetic movement which in turn clearly contributed to the founding of the Inklings over a hundred years later. Thus one can observe how this imaginative legacy continues to inspire those who follow.

For Tolkien and his literary friends, whose educational and religious backgrounds varied greatly, a shared purpose was to celebrate friendship, but friendship with something remarkable about it. The entire company of Inklings shared in Tolkien's belief that as offsprings of a Maker, they each carried the power of a maker in his (or her) soul. "We make still in the law in which we're made."[5] It is this sense of creative divinity alive in each person that seeded another literary renaissance, this time in high fantasy. And yet we can trace this new genre and find its beginnings deep in antiquity.

Christopher Bamford, Neoplatonist and Hermetic scholar, writes of some of the earliest thought of this tradition and its perennial wisdom from 600 B.C. Persia, "it places humanity as the crucial partner, companion, fellow-worker and even friend of divinity."[6] This core belief in the divinity of humanity and of the imagination echoes through all time; it can be found embodied in other small world-changing groups such as that of Pythagoras' community in fifth-century B.C. Crotona, Italy; Plotinus' Neoplatonic school in third-century Rome; Rumi's *Mevlevi* (the Whirling Dervishes) community of thirteenth-century Persia; Dante's *Fedele D'amor* fellowship in thirteenth-century Italy; and in the Medici Platonic Academy at Careggi headed by Marsilio Ficino in the fifteenth century, the gathering place and birthplace of the Florentine Renaissance. Each such gathering of artist/thinker/healers demonstrated an overcoming of cultural bias against their deep vision and participation in an on-going Creation.

As Tolkien's letters reveal, it appears that he intended to open a way for others to follow after him in the perceiving of and "subcreation" of worlds,[7] not only as a refreshment to the soul, but as a natural literary mode and inherited right for each of us as the creative offspring of a Maker. All this was to be accomplished while valuing the freedom and well-being of others, and while holding sacred this world and its biosphere.

An Elvish Love of Enchantment

When a fortunate rhythm has been struck by the artist, you experience a radiance. — Joseph Campbell

Rayner Unwin, son of publisher Stanley Unwin, was the ten-year-old boy whose enthusiastic response to reading a draft of *The Hobbit* inspired his father to publish it. In the 1992 documentary, *J.R.R. Tolkien, A Film Portrait,* Rayner describes Tolkien as an unbelievably loyal friend, but he also notes, "He tried not to make me feel embarrassed, but I was often embarrassed, because he was after all a ferocious intellect."[8]

In the face of this memorable insight into the power of Tolkien's intellect, and even though he had already established himself as a scholar and highly respected literary theorist — still being the recognized authority on *Beowulf* today — Tolkien sought not the life of the intellect alone but aspired to create the kind of enchantment expressed in "elvish craft."[9] This would be the kind of "food" he needed, a thing basic to his survival, nourishment to fuel his ability to bring the wonder of Other Worlds onto the page. He did not seek more sustenance for his powers of reason, which were already robust.[10]

Fortunately, Tolkien wrote a great deal about his literary process through his lectures and letters. His was a quick-silver mind capable of multiple paths at once. This mercurial quality contributed to his sometimes talking too fast to be understood. Carpenter explains, "his poor articulation was really due to having too much to say rather than to experiencing any physical difficulty in saying it. He could and did recite poetry with the greatest clarity."[11] In his letter to Stanley Unwin in December of 1937, he asked for more patience on their part, and explained that not only was his mind occupied with many aspects of his fantasy, but he was also intensely emotionally engaged as well, and admitted that the "stories tend to get out of hand."[12] He was well aware of his own creative tension in the creation of his fairy-stories: "An absorbing, though continually interrupted labour (especially since, even apart from the necessities of life, the mind would wing to the other pole and spend itself on the linguistics)...."[13] Surprisingly, what emerges from his letters on what might be called a dual focus is the image of a balanced if intense process, one that allows for the mind to engage its intellect through a philological precision without neglecting the deep desires of the heart with its imaginative encounters. He would develop a mode of allowing for both modes of cognition.

We find Tolkien following clearly in the footsteps of Wordsworth, who wrote of poetry in his preface to the *Lyrical Ballads*, "all good poetry is the spontaneous overflow of powerful feelings," yet he writes, for the writing to have value, these emotions must be recollected in tranquility through "thought long and deep."[14] Writing in the familiar terms of the garden, Tolkien translated this understanding into a paradoxical metaphor, whereby an author can be both a seed and a gardener.[15] In the seed state, one waits silently in the dark soil for the new thing, for the transformation. In spite of the fiery intellect which drove part of his process, he respectfully practiced the gentle art of letting go, holding to the knowledge that he was not consciously in control of what was unfolding in the mythology. In his letters, he assures us that making only comes through grace after all.[16]

In *The Two Towers*, not unlike Tolkien himself, Gandalf had been contemplating what the Ents might do to Isengard: As the others watched Gandalf, they saw rays of sunlight falling upon his hands "which lay now upturned on his lap. They seemed to be filled with light as a cup is with water."[17] This image is quite apropos to Tolkien's process, for amidst his great activity, it appears he held in reserve the place of the "cupped hand."

In the Middle Ages, such a receptive mode of creation was known as the *via negativa,* a method of perception through deep contemplation and inner sight that looks to the guiding truths of "not this" and "not that." This place reserved is a "negative" capability of which the Romantic poet Keats speaks wherein one seeks "verisimilitudes" or likenesses (images) of the truth as the raw material of poetry or the arts.[18] Here we find a camaraderie of thought with Tolkien, who often wrote of the glimpses or hints of those other dimensions that allow us to see a glimmer coming through into this world, ennobling it and gladdening it.

To be sure, part of Tolkien's natural talent for receptivity, with its willingness to allow the truth to reveal itself over time, was born of his philological experiences and temperament. Through his linguistic research,

Tolkien developed a passion for looking beyond the ancient words, and he admits to having a fascination for the "vanished past."[19] Humphrey Carpenter reports one of the most dramatic examples of Tolkien's seeking into the unknown past; he writes that when Tolkien first found the Anglo Saxon poem of Cynewulf, which contained an Old English line "*Éala Éarendel engla beorhtast*," (Hail Earendel, brightest of angels), he was exceptionally moved. Of this encounter Tolkien wrote, "There was something very remote and strange and beautiful behind those words, if I could grasp it, far beyond ancient English."[20] His dedication to this phrase of deep antiquity — and his desire to create the world in which it could be spoken — never waned. The charmed greeting finally came home to Middle-earth in *The Fellowship of the Ring* over twenty-five years later.

Devoted to metaphor, Tolkien lets Elrond express the understanding that one does not try to look directly at the hidden images with the eye of the intellect. Elrond knew that Moon-letters are actually runes, but that one cannot see them directly. He explains in *The Hobbit*, "They can only be seen when the moon shines behind them."[21] In spite of the fact that his publishers George Allen and Unwin were pressing for the book, Tolkien knew the inner vision reveals itself only through its own "magic" and cannot be forced.

Jung once wrote that "The autonomous activity of the psyche is the source of myths and fairy tales."[22] Jung refers here to the work of the psyche that goes on without interference by the conscious mind, work that allows the greater universal and mythic patterns and archetypal images of life to arise. Reflections of this activity come to the conscious mind in visions and dreams. Tolkien knew this premise to be true and, in 1939, referred to the unconscious work prerequisite to fairy-stories in his lecture for St. Andrews "Of Fairy-Stories," explaining that it is "realization independent of the conceiving mind, of imagined wonder" that fulfills the primal desire of Faërie.[23] The wonder comes through a "direct appreciation" by the mind without the "chain of argument" typically experienced through reasoning.[24]

Tolkien found his stories developing quite without his participation, with much of the work taking place "when one is saying how-do-you-do," or even while one is sleeping.[25] He wrote in his letters that he planned very little.[26] It was the very process of something going on in the "unconscious," that made him believe he was not inventing the mythology at all, but that he was only reporting on what had truly taken place. It was in his times of greatest pressure to finish and not being able to go on that he realized he had to wait until "What really happened" came through.[27] He found a large margin of error in the process, and admitted to being only 75 percent satisfied by the results.[28] But then Art does not seek perfection. To those who have read his books, Verlyn Flieger's insight on his art is surely appropriate, "His vision is not perfect, it is just unforgettable."[29]

Putting in his time, he wrote story outlines, though his mode was clearly one of inquiry not strategic planning. "The story unfolded itself as it were."[30] By the end of 1939, Tolkien had fully written and polished the story all the way to Rivendell, but as Christopher Tolkien writes, "yet at this time my father was without any clear conception of what lay before him"[31] At times, a year or more would pass before he could go forward with the writing. He hit moments of despair, and said so. The questions he had about the tales remained unanswered.[32] The project had grown so vast, that as Christopher Tolkien writes, "any attempt to trace in 'linear' fashion the history of the writing of LOR cannot at the same time take full account of the great constructions that were rising behind the onward movement of the tale."[33] The whole of *The Silmarillion* would be moved by the events that took place in the *Lord of the Rings*. All this while Tolkien had the sense of the tale "pressing towards unforeseen goals" when all he wanted to do was finish the book for the waiting publisher.[34]

It is humorous to note that Tolkien's creative approach mystifies those who are not familiar with (or in philosophical agreement with) its guiding principles. They are in fact driven to make comments like, "He just made it up!" and he wanders lost like his characters, the only stable thing about his creative process being "that it is *un*stable."[35] We simply need to review the great literature to find Tolkien has had a wealth of good company, an entire lineage in fact, that practices Tolkien's way of literary creation. Jung, whose work took place contemporaneously with Tolkien's, is an excellent example of this tradition of the imagination in another arena. While Tolkien sought myth and fairy-story to find answers to his deepest questions, Jung pioneered in psychology seeking answers in the images he found in dreams and visions. His autobiography *Memories, Dreams,*

Reflections is filled with numinous events from his life, none of which were conjured by conscious willing. Honoring both reason and the dreaming psyche, he wrote (it seems somewhat tongue-in-cheek) in his Commentary to Richard Wilhelm's translation of the *Secret of the Golden Flower* that "consciousness is forever interfering."[36]

In "Horses With Wings," Denise Levertov describes the gift of imagination by comparing the poet to the flying horse — both being animal, but above all, she tells us the poet must treasure the gift of intuition which transcends the limitations of deductive reasoning. "The imagination is the horses' wings, a form of grace, unmerited, unattainable, amazing, and freely given."[37] Because Tolkien treasured "the wings," he was willing to endure the disciplines required to harmonize all the creative forces within himself, keeping a special hand on the intellectual reigns.

A fortunate balance of intellect and imagination was struck on that fateful day he was grading student exams. "On a blank leaf I scrawled 'In a hole in the ground there lived a hobbit.' I did not and do not know why."[38] Tolkien's mind had been fruitfully employed with the grading process, freeing his imagination to make use of the unanticipated blank page. Ira Progoff, protégé of Jung, discussed situations where the mental activity is "lowered," in this case fully occupied, allowing for the emotions and intuitive, imaginative side to intensify.[39]

In his lecture, "The Heart of Archetypal Psychology," Robert Sardello, archetypal psychologist, describes this same function as a principle of life that we have all experienced — that whenever an activity is restrained, the very act of that harnessing will awaken a higher activity. It is because a child is constrained as an infant that the desire for (and capacity for) standing awakens. Consequently, one can progress from speaking to thinking to imagination to inspiration to conscious on-going intuition. Joseph Campbell, mythologist and storyteller, confirms these findings in *The Flight of the Wild Gander*, writing that the imagination is released when the busy brain is lulled to sleep. "The phenomena of dreams commonly impresses us more strongly than those of waking life just because in sleep the brain is off guard."[40] In a sense then, Tolkien's creative process involves the proverbial "one hand tied behind the back." In this case, however, his "hand" behind is engaged in multiple other constructive but more analytic endeavors.

J.R.R. Tolkien (Richards)

An Orchestration of Powers

Poetry, Painting, and Music, the three powers in man of conversing with Paradise. — William Blake

Confirming what scholar-psychologist Roberts Avens has written, "Myths are not invented, they are experienced."[41] Tolkien drew on his own life experiences and observations as the "leaf mould" of the mind. In seeking the mythic level, he transformed these personal events into "unfamiliar embodiments."[42] Notice of course that these "embodiments" will not carry a message or be planned out in the conventional sense of the word. What came forth from the story maker's "compost pile" of personal memories — keep in mind especially "volunteer plants" — Tolkien found to be the most vital, fresh and sturdy of new plants (his stories), yet he told us their source is primarily the *prima materia* of memories that have gone "under," beneath the conscious level. Similarly, he drew from the brew of the collective imagination, or what he called the "Cauldron of Story"[43] where "so many potent things lie simmering age long on the fire...." Like a pot of soup containing the history of stories and fairy-tales always boiling, where tasty morsels "have continually been added, dainty and undainty,"[44] Tolkien writes that the great Pot has been stewing for millennia and that it is the repository of the raw materials that provides access to a hardy soup for all.

With the exception of *Leaf By Niggle,* which Tolkien says was fully present in his mind when he woke one morning and needed only to be written down,[45] he put a lot of plain hard work into the writing of his mythology, sometimes "niggling" over words and writing pages over as many as eighteen times.[46] Tolkien began the work in earnest in the early years of World War I, often writing upon scraps of paper. Christopher Tolkien explains that these little notes would continue to be characteristic of his process, which often began in a rapid jotting down of ideas for the tales.[47]

His writing first came in broad strokes, and then with each next revision, more clarity came. Such iteration is a problem-solving method, each next step building on the one proceeding it toward more accuracy. Finally for Tolkien, after enough re-visiting, the chapter would seem to "write itself."[48]

One of Tolkien's writing practices took him back repeatedly to earlier parts of his mythology, working on multiple subjects and themes and interlacing it all anew, "The tying-up was achieved, so far as it is achieved, by constant re-writing backwards."[49] To literary theorist William Franke, this reflexive doubling back is the "circling back" of the hermeneutic process. He writes in *Dante's Interpretive Journey* that the creative doubling back is a return upon the "literal" with a "willingness to be guided."[50] Indeed, Christopher Tolkien has often admitted to wrestling with seemingly endless "final" versions of the same pages from his father's writing.[51]

Twentieth-century French philosopher and mathematician Gaston Bachelard suggests that this kind of back and forth writing allows the words to dream.[52] Just as Jung allowed dream and vision images to unfold from within in a process he called "Active Imagination,"[53] so Tolkien allowed the words and the images to open like seeds each time he revisited them.

Then there was the mechanics of map making, and the many-columned calendar with dates that tracked where all the characters or groups were at any one time.[54] "Geography, chronology, and nomenclature all had to be entirely consistent."[55] This extensive graphing included many elements — dates and time, phases of the moon, and sometimes even the direction of the wind. All of this activity was coordinated to be consistent within the whole, while Tolkien practiced the time-honored art of weaving into a narrative form the images and stories that arose in his mind.

Finally, once all the elements of the stories for *The Lord of the Rings* had been found satisfactory and in their truest form, a new quality came into his process. On the nature of Tolkien's later writing, Christopher explains, he "tended to compose in this way, driving several subjects abreast by means of interlaced notes."[56] There was a gathering of the threads, the synchronizing of the times, and the interweaving of the narrative that had been so long on Tolkien's mind — until at last, there came the bringing together and orchestrating of the whole mythology.

Tolkien's creative process brings to mind the way in which another of his lineage listened inwardly and then brought the pieces together — writing the whole staff (for each instrument) all at once. Though the artists are centuries apart, the parallels are stirring. It was Amadeus Mozart, who describes his intuitive and humble habits of work:

> What, you ask, is my method in writing and elaborating my large and lumbering things? I can, in fact say nothing more about it than this: I do not know

myself and can never find out. When I am in particularly good condition — perhaps riding in a carriage, or on a walk after a good meal — or during a sleepless night, then the thought comes to me in a rush, and best of all. Whence and how — that I do not know and cannot learn. Those which please me I retain in my head, and hum them perhaps also to myself — at least, so others have told me ... (farther on he describes how the "crumbs" spontaneously join one another into a whole, grow, and finally assume a finished form in his head). All the finding and the making only goes on in me as in a very vivid dream."[57]

The kind of creation Tolkien sought came just so — from a dreaming psyche just below the surface, personal and collective. His master strokes often arose written in "Moon Letters" to be transcribed. The kind of stories he sought, and sought to create, were composed of living images that move the reader with a kind of music arising in the heart.

The figures that exemplify for Tolkien that special kind of creation are the elf bards, who in *The Lord of the Rings* can make appear before the listener's eyes the visions of which they sing. We can see this artistry too in the timeless Tom Bombadil.[58] While dining at Tom Bombadil's house, the hobbits are given food in abundance and many merry songs from their hosts. As the evening progresses, they realized they were singing "as if it was easier and more natural than talking."[59] Though they could not understand Bombadil's ancient words — filled with "wonder and delight" — the hobbits experienced an unfolding vision as he spoke, "like a vast shadowy plain over which there strode shapes of Men, tall and grim with bright swords, and last came one with a star on his brow."[60] These images caught the hobbits up in a kind of reverie or dream, touching those Other Worlds within each of them. This is the gift Tolkien sought to give, and this is the legacy he leaves for the next generation of scribes and dreamers.

Notes

1. Tom Shippey interview, *A Film Portrait of J.R.R. Tolkien*, Dir. Helen Dickenson (Princeton, N.J., 1992).
2. Gareth Knight, *The Magical World of the Inklings* (Dorset: Element, 1990), 4.
3. Kathleen Raine, *Defending Ancient Springs* (London: Oxford University Press, 1967), 107.
4. Ibid., 110.
5. J.R.R. Tolkien, *Tree and Leaf* (Boston: Houghton Mifflin 1965), 54. From Tolkien's poem for his close friend and fellow Inkling C.S. Lewis, "Mythopoeia."
6. Christopher Bamford, "The Dream of Gemistos Plethon" (*Sphinx* 6 1994), 58.

7. J.R.R. Tolkien, *The Letters of J.R.R. Tolkien,* Ed. C. Tolkien (London: George Allen and Unwin, 1981), 146. Tolkien explains that "subcreation" is not about domination and power or a "tyrannous reforming of creation," it is instead Art and what we might call "co-creation" especially of "Other Worlds" within the greater Creation.
8. Rayner Unwin interview, *A Film Portrait of J.R.R. Tolkien.*
9. J.R.R. Tolkien, *Tree and Leaf,* 49.
10. J.R.R. Tolkien, *The Letters of J.R.R. Tolkien,* 214.
11. Humphrey Carpenter, *J.R.R. Tolkien: A Biography* (London: George Allen and Unwin, 1977), 48.
12. J.R.R. Tolkien, *The Letters of J.R.R. Tolkien,* 34.
13. Ibid., 145.
14. William Wordsworth, *Lyrical Ballads,* ed. Schofield (Hertfordshire, Great Britain: Wordsworth, 2003), 8.
15. J.R.R. Tolkien, *The Letters of J.R.R. Tolkien,* 240.
16. Ibid., 126.
17. J.R.R. Tolkien, *The Two Towers* (London, 1954), 126.
18. Christopher Bamford, "Negative Capability" *Parabola* (May 2005), 14–20.
19. J.R.R. Tolkien, *The Letters of J.R.R. Tolkien,* 110.
20. Humphrey Carpenter, *J.R.R. Tolkien: A Biography,* 64.
21. J.R.R. Tolkien, *The Hobbit* (Boston: Houghton Mifflin, 1966), 48.
22. Robert Avens, *Imagination Is Reality* (Dallas: Spring, 1980), 41.
23. J.R.R. Tolkien, *Tree and Leaf,* 14.
24. _____. *The Letters of J.R.R. Tolkien,* 101.
25. Ibid., 231.
26. Ibid., 172.
27. Ibid., 212.
28. Ibid., 221.
29. Verlyn Flieger, *A Question of Time: J.R.R. Tolkien's Road to Faërie* (Kent, OH: Kent State University Press, 1997), 253.
30. J.R.R. Tolkien, *The Letters of J.R.R. Tolkien,* 258.
31. _____. *The Treason of Isengard: The History of the Lord of the Rings Part II,* ed. C. Tolkien (Boston: Houghton Mifflin 1989), 18.
32. _____. *Tree and Leaf,* vii.
33. _____. *The Treason of Isengard,* ed. C. Tolkien, 29.
34. _____. *The Letters of J.R.R. Tolkien,* 40.
35. Tom Shippey, *The Road to Middle-earth: How J.R.R. Tolkien Created a New Mythology* (New York: Houghton Mifflin, 2003), 304.
36. Richard Wilhelm, *The Secret of the Golden Flower* (New York, 1962), 93.
37. Denise Levertov, "Horses with Wings" (*Spring,* 1985): 83.
38. Humphrey Carpenter, *J.R.R. Tolkien: A Biography,* 177.
39. Ira Progoff, *Jung, Synchronicity, and Human Destiny* (New York: Dell, 1973), 115.
40. Joseph Campbell, *The Flight of the Wild Gander* (New York: Viking, 1969), 186.
41. Robert Avens, *Imagination Is Reality,* 141.
42. J.R.R. Tolkien, *The Letters of J.R.R. Tolkien,* 194.
43. J.R.R. Tolkien, *Tree and Leaf,* 26.
44. Ibid., 27.
45. J.R.R. Tolkien, *The Letters of J.R.R. Tolkien,* 257.

46. Humphrey Carpenter, *J.R.R. Tolkien: A Biography*, 196.
47. J.R.R. Tolkien, *The Book of Lost Tales*, ed. C. Tolkien (Boston, 1983), 11.
48. J.R.R. Tolkien, *The Letters of J.R.R. Tolkien*, 231.
49. Ibid., 258.
50. William Franke, *Dante's Interpretive Journey* (Chicago: University of Chicago Press, 1996), 108.
51. J.R.R. Tolkien, *The Treason of Isengard*, 5.
52. Gaston Bachelard, *The Poetics of Reverie: Childhood, Language and the Cosmos* (Boston: Beacon, 1960), 16.
53. Ira Progoff, *Jung, Synchronicity and Human Destiny*, 32.
54. J.R.R. Tolkien, *The Letters of J.R.R. Tolkien*, 258.
55. Humphrey Carpenter, *J.R.R. Tolkien: A Biography*, 194.
56. J.R.R. Tolkien, *Unfinished Tales: Of Numenor and Middle-earth*. Ed C. Tolkien (New York: Houghton Mifflin, 1980), 4.
57. Pitirim Sorokin, *The Crisis of Our Age* (Oxford: Oneworld, 1992), 110.
58. J.R.R. Tolkien, *The Letters of J.R.R. Tolkien*, 26.
59. J.R.R. Tolkien, *The Fellowship of the Rings* (London, 1954), 173.
60. Ibid., 199.

Works Cited

Avens, Roberts. *Imagination is Reality: Western Nirvana in Jung, Hillman, Barfield and Cassirer*. Dallas, TX: Spring, 1980.
Bachelard, Gaston. *The Poetics of Reverie: Childhood, Language and the Cosmos*. Boston: Beacon, 1960.
Bamford, Christopher. "The Dream of Gemistos Plethon." *Sphinx 6* (1994): 48–73.
_____. "Negative Capability: How the Heart Knows." *Parabola* vol. 30, no. 2 (May 2005): 14–20.
Campbell, Joseph. *The Flight of the Wild Gander*. New York: Viking, 1969.
Carpenter, Humphrey. *J.R.R. Tolkien: A Biography*. London: George Allen and Unwin, 1977.
Dickenson, Helen. *J.R.R.T.: A Film Portrait of J.R.R. Tolkien*. Documentary Film. Princeton, NJ: Films for the Humanities and Sciences, 1992.
Flieger, Verlyn. *A Question of Time: J.R.R. Tolkien's Road to Faërie*. Kent, OH: Kent State University Press, 1997.
Franke, William. *Dante's Interpretive Journey*. Chicago: University of Chicago Press, 1996.
Jung, C.G. *The Collected Works of C. G. Jung, CW 16: The Practice of Psychotherapy*. 2nd ed. Princeton, NJ: Princeton University Press, 1982.
Knight, Gareth. *The Magical World of the Inklings*. Dorset, England: Element, 1990.
Levertov, Denise. "Horses with Wings." *Spring* (1985): 74–83.
Progoff, Ira. *Jung, Synchronicity, and Human Destiny*. New York: Dell, 1973.
Raine, Kathleen. *Defending Ancient Springs*. London: Oxford University Press, 1967.
Sardello, Robert. "The Heart of Archetypal Psychology." Lecture. Psychology on the Threshold Conference. Santa Barbara, CA: Pacifica Graduate Institute. 2 September 2000.
Shippey, Thomas. *The Road to Middle-earth: How J.R.R. Tolkien Created a New Mythology*. New York: Houghton Mifflin, 2003.

Sorokin, Pitirim. *The Crisis of Our Age*. Oxford: Oneworld, 1992.
Tolkien, J.R.R. *The Book of Lost Tales*. Ed. Christopher Tolkien. Boston: Houghton Mifflin, 1983.
———. *The Hobbit*. Boston: Houghton Mifflin, 1966.
———. *The Letters of J.R.R. Tolkien*. Ed. Humphrey Carpenter. London: George Allen and Unwin, 1981.
———. *The Lord of the Rings: The Fellowship of the Ring*. London: HarperCollins, 1993.
———. *The Lord of the Rings: The Two Towers*. London: HarperCollins, 1993.
———. *The Treason of Isengard: The History of the Lord of the Rings Part Two*. Ed. Christopher Tolkien. Boston: Houghton Mifflin, 1989.
———. *Tree and Leaf*. Boston: Houghton Mifflin, 1965.
———. *Unfinished Tales of Númenor and Middle-earth*. Ed. Christopher Tolkien. New York: Houghton Mifflin, 1980.
Wordsworth, William. *Lyrical Ballads*. Ed. Martin Schofield. Hertfordshire, Great Britain: Wordsworth. 2003.

Tolkien's Unfinished "Lay of Lúthien" and the Middle English *Sir Orfeo*

Deanna Delmar Evans

"The definition of a fairy-story — what it is, or what it should be — does not, then, depend on any definition or historical account of elf or fairy, but upon the nature of *Faerie*: the Perilous Realm itself, and the air that blows in that country." So states J.R.R. Tolkien in his famous essay, "On Fairy-Stories" (32). Although he portrays himself in that essay as "a wandering explorer (or trespasser) in the land, full of wonder but not information" (27), Tolkien obviously succeeded brilliantly in creating fantasy fiction set in what he deemed the perilous realm. After reading Tolkien's fiction, readers tend to feel refreshed, and Verlyn Flieger explains why: "Experiencing the fantastic, we recover a fresh view of the unfantastic, a view too long dulled by familiarity" (25). Indeed, in the best of his fiction, Tolkien could be said to provide readers with all four of the benefits he says derive from the reading of successful fairy-stories: "Fantasy, Recovery, Escape, Consolation" (59).

It is hardly surprising that some satisfied readers have wondered about where the author found inspiration for his elaborate secondary world of Middle-earth. As Humphrey Carpenter, author of Tolkien's "authorized" biography, asks: "Where did it come from, this imagination that peopled Middle-earth with elves, orcs, and hobbits?" (293). Some of Tolkien's most astute and dedicated critics have attempted to supply some answers. Looking to Tolkien's profession, Tom Shippey believes "Tolkien's fiction is certainly rooted in philology" (*Author*, xiii) and explains Tolkien believed "philology could take you back even beyond the ancient texts it studied" (*Author*, xiv). Jane Chance looks to Tolkien's scholarship: "If Tolkien wished to develop a 'mythology for England' akin to the Northern mythologies

... what better way than to use those Old and Middle English works native to his country in fashioning his own work?" (3). Interestingly Shippey inadvertently validates Chance's hypothesis, for he claims he has found a probable source of inspiration for Tolkien's elfin realm in one such Middle English work.

In *The Road to Middle-earth*, Shippey offers the opinion that "for the elves, their fusion or kindling-point would seem to be some twenty or thirty lines from the centre of the medieval poem of *Sir Orfeo*" (63). Characteristics of that medieval lay Shippey believes to have impacted Tolkien's imagination are that "the land of the dead has become elf-land" and that the character of Sir Orfeo "is successful in his quest and bears his wife away, overcoming the elf-king by the mingled powers of music and honour" (63). In a later study, Shippey more assertively repeats that idea and, in fact, makes a specific claim: "Tolkien drew his immediate inspiration for the Wood-elves of *The Hobbit* from ... a single passage from the Middle English romance *Sir Orfeo*" (*Author* 34). Criticism of *Sir Orfeo* supports and complements Shippey's claim. John Block Friedman, in *Orpheus in the Middle Ages*, explains that the medieval writer or writers of *Sir Orfeo*, "medievalized Orpheus ... not only in his ideals and behavior, but also in his dress, his dwelling place, and his customary pursuits" (160). He further notes that "the land of the fairies in *Sir Orfeo* is neither an afterworld nor an underworld [but] ... actually a counter world that exists side by side with the world of man" (190). The elfin realm within Tolkien's Middle-earth may be similarly described, especially the world of the Wood-elves whose dwelling place like that of *Orfeo's* fairy king co-exists in an ancient forest.

There is no question that Tolkien was well acquainted with the Middle English *Sir Orfeo*. He worked on an edition published in 1921 as part of Kenneth Sisam's anthology, *Fourteenth Century Verse and Prose* (Chance 3). In a way, Tolkien could be credited with having "created" the Middle English lay of *Sir Orfeo* as it is known to modern readers, for he based his edition on three different manuscript sources and shaped them, with all their variations, into a coherent whole. He also made a Modern English poetic translation of *Sir Orfeo*, but apparently completed it many years later; Humphrey indicates the translation was prepared for a wartime cadets' course at Oxford (158). Prior to publishing the edition, Tolkien began composing fantasy narratives, and shortly after its completion,

Tolkien began composing a verse romance of his own set in a fairy-tale world.

Christopher Tolkien, his youngest son, has edited the extant fragments as the *Gest of Beren and Lúthien* in the volume, *The Lays of Beleriand* (1985); elsewhere he indicates his father composed the basic tale in 1917 ("Preface," *Children* 9). Initially Tolkien called his romance *Tinúviel*, but on the cover of a set of revised drafts, he wrote the following title: "The/ Gest/ of Beren son of Barahir/ and/ Lúthien the Fay/ called/ Tinúviel the Nightingale/ or the Lay of Leithian/ Release from Bondage" (*Lays* 188). Brian Rosebury provides a basic plot summary of the fragmented poem:

> The hero (Beren, a mortal man) falls in love with a heroine of superior "status" (Lúthien, an immortal Elf). Her father (Thingol, King of the Elvish realm of Doriath) opposes their union, and sets the hero a seemingly impossible task as the price of her hand (to bring a Silmaril from the iron crown of Morgoth, alias Melkor). The hero succeeds in the task, but dies as a result [98].

As revealed in Rosebury's summary, the *Gest* essentially is based on the same story line Tolkien used in the prose "Tale of Tinúviel" included in the *Lost Tales II* and the prose tale of Beren and Lúthien constituting Chapter 19 of *The Silmarillion*.

The *Gest* is written in octosyllabic couplets, the verse form of the Middle English *Sir Orfeo* in the Auchinleck manuscript, Tolkien's primary manuscript source for his edition (Sisam 13). The *Gest* remains fragmented and incomplete, but Tolkien returned to the story again around 1950, after completing *The Lord of the Rings* (*Lays* viii); there the tale is both alluded to and also woven into Elrond's family history.

Christopher Tolkien provides valuable information for dating the fragments of his father's poetic *Gest*. In introducing the early alliterative *Lay of the Children of Húrin,* he indicates that on an envelope containing a twenty-eight-page manuscript entitled a "Sketch of the Mythology with especial reference to 'The Children of Húrin,'" his father had written: "Original 'Silmarillion' ... to explain background of Túrin [later Húrin] and the Dragon ... begun c. 1918" (*Lays* 1). He theorizes that his father had completed the earliest drafts of *Húrin* before taking his first teaching post at Oxford in 1925, but discontinued that work in order to give more attention to the new verse romance he was calling *Tinúviel* (2). He indicates that the "rough workings" for the entire poem are extant (183), and labels the earliest as the A text while those his father rewrote and revised constitute the B text. The earliest fragment is dated August 23, 1925, and the last, September 17, 1931 (183). He notes, however, that the dates refer to Tolkien's "copying of verses out fair in the manuscript, not to their actual composition" (183).

Before the end of 1929, Tolkien had given a copy of what he had written up to that point to his friend C. S. Lewis, and a letter from Lewis, written in December 1929, indicates a most positive response: "I can honestly say that it is ages since I have had an evening of such delight.... The two things that come out clearly are the sense of reality in the background and the mythical value: the essence of myth being that it should have no taint of allegory to the maker and yet should suggest incipient allegories to the reader" (qtd. in C. Tolkien, *Lays* 184). Lewis sent Tolkien fourteen pages of commentary on the poem, some of which Tolkien used in making subsequent revisions (185).

In the Auchinleck ms. of *Sir Orfeo*, the classical myth has been transformed into English legend: Orfeo "was a king of old,/ In England ... (*Sir Orfeo*, trans. Tolkien, lines 25–26). In the preface to his edition, Tolkien calls attention to that transformation: "An amusing instance is the attempt in the Auchinleck ms. to give the poem an English interest by the unconvincing assurance that Traciens ... was the old name of Winchester" (Sisam 13). A brief comparison of the *Gest of Beren* fragments against the lay of *Sir Orfeo* indicates that Tolkien apparently adapted some elements of the Middle English lay for his own narrative. This is not to say that Tolkien deliberately set out to imitate or to "re-create" the medieval work; the influence is less tangible and perhaps was best described by Tolkien himself when he named *Beowulf* as his "most valued" source for *The Hobbit*; in that instance Tolkien acknowledged he had been influenced by the Old English epic but added, "it was not consciously present to the mind in the process of writing" (qtd. in Chance 3).

Tolkien's *Gest of Beren* is like *Sir Orfeo* in that it centers on the adventure of a human hero in *Elfinesse* (*Lays* 189, line 21), a realm populated by elves and ruled by an elf king. The narrative voice in the *Gest* states that the elves "dwelt amid Beleriand,/ while Elfin power yet held the land, / in the woven woods of Doriath" (*Lays* 190, lines 41–43). (The setting indicates they are Wood-elves, adding support for Shippey's theory that *Sir Orfeo* contains the seeds of influence for Tolkien's elves.) Although he does not explore the similarities between *Sir Orfeo* and the *Gest,* Shippey notes that *The Lay of Leithian* "is full of motifs taken from earlier story," and remarks, "Rash Promises between mortals and the inhabitants of Faerie are an old tradition, as in *Sir Orfeo*" (*Author* 255). The mortal heroes also have something in common: Sir Orfeo is a king who voluntarily became a beggar and went to live in the forest among the animals. Beren is the son of the leader of a robber band living in the forest, but he is descended from nobility. His father, Barahir the robber baron, "a prince of Men was born" (*Lays* 198, line 130).

The plots of both the *Gest* and *Sir Orfeo* revolve around the enmity between supernatural beings and mortals. In *Sir Orfeo,* the fairy king initiates the action, for in a dream he tells Heurodis, Orfeo's mortal wife, she must go away with him or literally be torn to pieces:

> If let or hindrance thou doest make,
> where'er thou be, we shall thee take,
> and all thy limbs shall rend and tear [Trans. Tolkien, lines 169–171].

In spite of the dire warning, King Orfeo bravely arms himself and calls for "full ten hundred knights with him,/ all stoutly armed" (lines 183–84). But men and arms all prove useless when the fairy king comes for Heurodis:

> yet from midst of that array
> the queen was sudden snatched away;
> by magic was she from them caught,
> and none knew whither she was brought [lines 191–94].

The hostility of the fairy king toward humans is again evident when Sir Orfeo enters his hall; Orfeo sees "folk ... mourned as dead, but were no so" (lines 389–90). Yet possessed of manly courage and motivated by love for his wife, Sir Orfeo continues to seek his enemy in spite of the grotesque sights he encounters along the way:

> For some there stood who had no head,
> and some no arms, nor feet; some bled
> and through their bodies wounds were set [lines 391–93].

Orfeo rescues Heurodis in the end, but part of his success owes to a vestige of honor embedded in the character of the fairy king; he will not renege on a promise he had made to Orfeo while enthralled by the mortal's music.

Middle-earth Minstrel

In designing his *Gest*, Tolkien surpasses the medieval writer's description of enmity between the fairy king and Sir Orfeo by creating not one but several non-human enemies for Beren. One is the elfin minstrel Daeron, who plays his flute for Lúthien the night Beren first sees her and falls in love; Daeron's hostility is rooted in jealousy because he loves Lúthien himself and hates that she eventually gives her heart to the mortal. Another is the elf King Thingol of Doriath, Lúthien's father; he is the closest counterpart of *Orfeo's* fairy king in Tolkien's *Gest*. Thingol strongly opposes his daughter's union with a mortal and so assigns Beren an impossible task: If Beren wants to win Lúthien's hand, Thingol tells him, he must steal one *silmaril* from the crown of the evil King Morgoth. (In *The Silmarillion, the Silmarilli* were the three great jewels of the elves stolen by Morgoth.) Thingol, knowing the power of Morgoth, assumes that Beren will die in the process. However, the worst enemy Beren encounters is King Morgoth; he is a primordial monstrous being who has taken over the land and represents the incarnation of pure evil:

> There sat a king: no Elfin race
> nor mortal blood, nor kindly grace
> of earth or heaven might he own,
> far older, stronger than the stone
> the world is built of, than the fire
> that burns within more fierce and dire;
> and thoughts profound were in his heart:
> a gloomy power that dwelt apart [*Lays,* 197, lines 107–114].

Clearly Morgoth is a satanic figure in the *Gest* (as he will be in the future *Slimarillion*.) Tolkien did not need to find a model for him in the medieval lay of *Sir Orfeo* even if, as J. B. Friedman indicates, the medieval author "quite pointedly" draws a connection between the fairy king with Satan (190). Tolkien needed only to look back to his own recent war experiences: he had served as an infantry subaltern on the Somme in 1916 and had lost two of his closest friends (Shippey *Author* x). Tolkien had learned first hand that evil existed in the world, and no doubt was convinced that the Satan he had heard about in his boyhood catechism classes was real. Morgoth's evil nature was central to the development of Tolkien's plot, just as the fairy king's evil actions were crucial to the plot in *Sir Orfeo*. Morgoth revealed his animosity toward humans before the initial meeting of Beren and Lúthien. He had forced Beren's father Barahir to abandon his kingdom and throne. Barahir and ten faithful retainers had taken refuge in the forest to hide from Morgoth. But Morgoth, intent on finding them, coerces one member of the band, a retainer named Gorlim, into betraying the others.

Gorlim's situation exploited by Morgoth has parallels with Sir Orfeo's. Gorlim, like Sir Orfeo, had lost his wife, "Eilenel the fair" (*Lays 200, line 217*), to Morgoth, but Morgoth convinces Gorlim that he can rescue Eilenel if he will tell where Barahir and the others are dwelling. To convince Gorlim that Eilenel is alive, Morgoth provides Gorlim with a glimpse of Eilenel looking sad. This incident parallels Sir Orfeo's glimpse of his wife on a hunting expedition with the fairy king. Gorlim, like Sir Orfeo, wants to rescue his wife, and so agrees to Morgoth's plan. But Morgoth, like the devil, is ever the liar and so deliberately had deceived Gorlim. As soon as Gorlim betrays Barahir and the other men, Morgoth boasts to the terrified man that Eilenel already walks among the dead and it is time for him to join her. Gorlim "dies a bitter death /and cursed himself with dying breath" (lines 233–234). His rueful ghost visits Beren in a nightmare and urges Beren, who was away at the time of the attack, to warn his father and the others of Morgoth's plans. But Beren arrives too late and finds them all dead. After burying his father, Beren flees into the woods, becoming "grey in his hair, his youth turned old" (line 552). His sudden physical transformation also has a parallel in *Sir Orfeo*. Sorrow over the loss of his wife causes Sir Orfeo to age prematurely although his physical change in appearance occurs less dramatically. After the heartbroken king abdicated his throne, he wandered aimlessly in the forest and became an old man with a gray beard.

Yet it is while they are mourning in their respective forests that the heroes each experience a reversal of fortune. It is in the forest that Sir Orfeo serendipitously catches a glimpse of his wife and the fairy king out on a hunting trip. Now convinced she is alive, Orfeo sets out to follow the fairy king to his castle in order to rescue Heurodis. In Tolkien's *Gest*, Beren experiences a similar reversal of fortune while riding in the forest. Prematurely gray and depressed over the deaths of his father and his father's men, Beren hears beautiful music as he rides through the forest; lured by the music, he is drawn to the grove where he sees Lúthien; she is dancing in a lonely woodland clearing to music played by Daeron, minstrel to her father. In this instance Tolkien creatively inverts portions of the *Orfeo* plot: the mortal Beren goes to live in the woods, as does Sir Orfeo, but while Sir Orfeo is saved in the woods by his ability to create music and thereby experience the friendship of birds and beasts, Beren finds solace in the woods not by his ability to make music but by hearing fairy music that draws him to Lúthien.

In spite of the parallels noted, the *Gest* differs significantly from the Middle English *Sir Orfeo* in one crucial respect — the absence of a happy ending, what Tolkien calls *Eucatastrophe* ("Fairy-stories" 68). Tolkien believed *Eucatastrophe* (the opposite of *catastrophe*) was an important element of a successful fairy-story, and indeed *Sir Orfeo* provides two: Sir Orfeo rescues his wife and he reclaims his throne from his faithful steward. Yet Tolkien does not provide a happy ending for Beren's tale. The reason for its absence perhaps stems from Tolkien's need to be true to his subject matter, some of which had sprung from his own life experience; indeed, there is a strong personal element in the tale of Beren and Lúthien.

Not only does the name *Lúthien* appear under Edith Bratt Tolkien's name on their shared tombstone, but the name *Beren* is inscribed under Tolkien's own (Carpenter 293). As Jane Chance observes, "Beren the man, linked with the Elf Lúthien, together a couple in whom Tolkien recognized himself and his wife Edith" (199). Lúthien, as described in the *Gest*, is not unlike Tolkien's 1917 description of his wife whom he described as follows: "Her hair was raven, her skin clear, her eyes bright, and she could sing — and *dance*" (qtd. in Carpenter 109). At that time, as Carpenter notes, Tolkien was enjoying a brief military leave with her and their newborn, first son (109). But it was also during this year, as his youngest son maintains, that he devised the basic plan for *Tinúviel* ("Preface," *Children* 9). After Edith's death, Tolkien explained in a letter to his youngest son why he wanted to include the name *Lúthien* on her tombstone: "She was (and knew she was) my Lúthien" (qtd. in Carpenter 110).

It seems most likely that while composing his poetic *Gest* so many years earlier, Tolkien had already identified with his protagonist, the "robber" Beren (intentionally punning on the epithet "Robber Baron") who dared to trespass into the realm of *elfinesse* and won Lúthien for his bride. The marriage of Edith Bratt and J.R.R. Tolkien had met with considerable opposition (Carpenter 88–89), not unlike the wedding of their elfin counterparts. Tolkien, serving as an officer in a devastating war, knew that in his world, where the presence of evil was as strong as Morgoth in Beren's, there could be no happy-ever-after ending. Any *Eucatastrophe* for Tolkien and his bride could take place only at the Last Judgment.

The impossibility of the *Gest* ending happily is evident from the beginning. To win his bride, Beren must do the impossible, steal a *Silmaril* from Morgoth. When Tolkien began composing the *Gest*, he faced an uncertain future as a young philologist and academic, and had set for himself a seemingly impossible task in his desire to recover the lost mythology of England. Shippey comments that early in his career Tolkien had felt "that a consistency and a sense lay beneath the chaotic ruin of the old poetry of the North — if only someone would dig it out" (*Road*, 64). As young scholar and fledgling writer of fantasy, Tolkien was trying to do just that. No wonder he identified with the robber Beren in this early poetic work and some years later, with Bilbo Baggins in *The Hobbit,* whose stated profession was *burglar.*

Yet in the *Gest*, Beren is more than a robber born a prince; he is Tolkien's rendition of Orpheus, the mythic hero who in the modern era had become an icon for poets and musicians. Venerated in ancient Greece as the son of Apollo and the muse Calliope, Orpheus was believed capable of soothing savage beasts with his music and song, and when his beloved bride Eurydice died from a snake bite, he followed her into the underworld where he charmed Hades with his music ("Orpheus," *Oxford Dictionary of Classical Myth & Religion*, 394). If Beren is Tolkien's reconstruction of Sir Orfeo, an anonymous medieval poet's reconstruction of the mythic hero Orpheus, Beren then becomes Tolkien's reconstructed post-war Orpheus, one twice removed from the mythic original. Created after the Great War had transformed the world, Tolkien's Beren could never be more than an imperfect reflection of the mythic hero. Beren is not a musician but only a lover of music. He is not a composer of music but a robber assigned a robber's task. While the singing and dancing of the superior Lúthien bring solace to her mortal lover, she cannot protect him or their world from monstrous evil. Lúthien can and does ease Beren's pain, but for her effort, she will share his human destiny.

In *Orpheus: The Myth of the Poet*, Charles Segal discusses several twentieth-century writers (not Tolkien) who chose to retell the Orpheus myth. Segal explains that modern writers are drawn to the Orpheus myth for various reasons, from reflecting "on the banalization of art and feeling in modern society" to seeing "Orpheus as a voice of hope and renewal amid brutalization and fragmentation" (197). If Tolkien is drawing upon the Orpheus myth in his *Gest* of Beren and Lúthien, as is being suggested, his reasons for doing so seem to belong to both categories, but especially the latter. In the fragments of his unfinished poetic romance, Lúthien, not Orpheus, may be seen as Tolkien's symbol of hope and renewal in a world that he personally had seen brutalized and fragmented by the Great War. It is hardly surprising, then, that Tolkien returned to this story some twenty years later, after having lived through yet another, even more devastating war, one that enlisted the services of two sons and caused the physical destruction of significant portions of his beloved England. Surely he sensed the presence of Morgoth in the midst of such horrors.

Works Cited

Carpenter, Humphrey. *Tolkien: A Biography*. New York: Ballantine, 1978.
Chance, Jane. *Tolkien's Art*, rev. ed. Louisville: University of Kentucky Press, 2001.
Flieger, Verlyn. *Splintered Light: Logos and Language in Tolkien's World*. Kent, OH: Kent State University Press, 2002.
Friedman, John Block. *Orpheus in the Middle Ages*. Cambridge, MA: Harvard University Press, 1970.
"Orpheus." *The Oxford Dictionary of Classical Myth & Religion*. Ed. Simon Price and Emily Kearns. Oxford and New York: Oxford University Press, 2003.
Rosebury, Brian. *Tolkien: A Cultural Phenomenon*. New York: Palgrave Macmillan, 2003.
Segal, Charles. *Orpheus: The Myth of the Poet*. Baltimore: Johns Hopkins University Press, 1993.
Shippey, Tom. *J.R.R. Tolkien: Author of the Century*. Boston: Houghton Mifflin, 2000.
_____. *The Road to Middle-earth: How J.R.R. Tolkien Created a New Mythology*. Rev. ed. Boston: Houghton Mifflin, 2003.
Sisam, Kenneth, ed. *Fourteenth Century Verse & Prose*. Oxford: Clarendon, 1921; rev. ed. 1959.
Tolkien, J.R.R. *The Book of Lost Tales, Part II*. Ed. Christopher Tolkien. New York: Ballantine, 1992.
_____. *The Children of Húrin*. Ed. Christopher Tolkien. Boston: Houghton Mifflin, 2007.
_____. *The Lays of Beleriand*. Ed. Christopher Tolkien. New York: Ballantine, 1994.
_____. "On Fairy-Stories," 1947. Rpt. in *Tolkien on Fairy-stories*. Ed. Verlyn Flieger and Douglas A. Anderson. London: HarperCollins, 2008.
_____. *The Silmarillion*. 2nd ed. Ed. Christopher Tolkien. Boston: Houghton Mifflin, 2001.
_____, trans. *Sir Gawain and the Green Knight, Pearl, Sir Orfeo*. London: George Allen and Unwin, 1975; rpt. New York: Ballantine, 1980–1992.

Strains of Elvish Song and Voices: Victorian Medievalism, Music, and Tolkien

Bradford Lee Eden

> Rise, my true knight. As children learn, be thou
> Wiser for falling! walk with me, and move
> To music with thine Order and the King.[1]
>
> In hawthorn-time the heart grows light,
> The world is sweet in sound and sight...
> And all his life of blood and breath
> Sang out within him: time and death.[2]
>
> ...I must follow in their train
> Down the crooked fairy lane
> Where the coney-rabbits long ago have gone,
> And where silvery they sing
> In a moving moonlit ring...
> O! the warmth! O! the hum! O! the colors in the dark!
> O! the gauzy wings of golden honey-flies!
> O! the music of their feet — of their dancing goblin feet!
> O! the magic O! the sorrow when it dies.[3]

These poetic lines of Tennyson, Swinburne, and Tolkien, while encompassing about a 60-year period (1842, 1896, and 1915, respectively), all refer to some type of musical allusions throughout not only these works, but many of these authors' other poetic and prose writings. Tennyson often uses the musical harmony/disharmony theme in his Arthurian works. Swinburne, often compared to and in competition with Tennyson and his writings during his lifetime, also incorporated musical themes and phrases throughout his works. And in his first published poetry, Tolkien also picked up the idea (consciously or unconsciously) of music, song, and dance as an important structural element.

This essay will focus on the influence of English Victorian fiction on Tolkien's writing style, particularly in relation to musical-literary symbolism. There are obviously many tangents and influences to follow when speaking of musical influence on Tolkien's writing style, including the romantic compositions of Richard Wagner, the influence of medieval philosophers such as Plotinus and Augustine, parallels to the theosophical writings current in the nineteenth century, the singing/enchantment/ ancient origin tales such as the Finnish *Kalevala* (which we know had a strong early influence on Tolkien) and Icelandic sagas, just to name a few. One cannot discuss all of these influences in a single article; the author is currently researching and writing a book that will examine the conscious and subconscious musical influences on Tolkien's writings. For this article, the writings of three major English Victorian fictionists are examined, and parallels between their use of musical-literary language and Tolkien's are illustrated.

Although Tolkien has been quoted that he never imitated anyone's writing style nor ever used current literature or events as analogies or metaphors in his writings, careful study of Tolkien's writings show an extensive predilection and use of musical language similar to the Victorian writers. The resurgence of Arthurian literature during the Victorian period, the rise of philology and the study of ancient and medieval languages as a discipline, and the incorporation of rhyme and prosody into Victorian fiction, all had an influence on Tolkien's writing style, whether he chose to admit it or not. Many of the great Victorian scholars and philologists were also contributors to the wealth of Victorian fiction and fantasy that arose in the nineteenth century (in fact, Tolkien was the last in a long line of Victorian philologist/fiction writers). The interest in ancient languages, their sound and pronunciation, along with the discovery and translation of many medieval legends and myths, helped to feed the growth of fictional poetry and prose based on Arthurian legend and medieval myths. Although Tolkien grew up in Edwardian England, his writings indicate a strong predilection, use, and emulation of Victorian concepts and techniques, not the least of which is a strong emphasis on music and its power, music and its relationships, and music as a unifying concept and theme that consciously or unconsciously ebbs and flows throughout his writings, particularly his earlier endeavors to write fiction.

The concept of "medievalism" in the Victorian period comprised a wide range of artistic, cultural, and political pursuits. In religion, the Oxford Movement sought to bring back the ancient liturgical and musical traditions once practiced in English cathedrals prior to the Dissolution. In painting, the works of Dante Gabriel Rossetti and the Pre-Raphaelite Brotherhood, while short-lived, served to inspire styles of painting well into the twentieth century. In historiography, the writings and constitutional work of scholars such as J. R. Green, William Stubbs, and Edward Freeman looked back into the English past. In social and aesthetic criticism, the essays of Victorians such as John Ruskin, William Morris, Thomas Carlyle, A. W. Pugin, and Benjamin Disraeli were constant and politically motivated. Even in their physical environment, the Victorians sought to emulate the Middle Ages. Neo-Gothic law courts and town halls, cathedrals and churches, railway stations and public buildings, were built to contrast dramatically with factory smokestacks and commercial industry. Finally, in literature, Alfred Tennyson, Algernon Charles Swinburne, and William Morris sought to emulate ancient and medieval prose and poetry, as well as use Arthurian romances and themes, to transport their readers into a "heroic age" where things such as honor, virtue, and chivalry were the norm rather than the exception. It was this heritage into which Tolkien was born and grew up, and even the university environment of Oxford itself was reflective of the medieval culture from which it had first emerged. Even Tolkien's profound distaste for all things related to technology, and his love of trees and nature, can trace its source back to the Victorians and their concept of medievalism:

> The association of such ideas as nature, harmony, creativity, and joy with medievalism points up the other major aspect of the medieval revival, its attempt to create a coherent world view. As we have seen, medievalism was a response to historic change and to the problems raised by the various revolutions and transformations of the eighteenth and nineteenth centuries. But medievalism was also simultaneously a part of that vast intellectual and emotional response to change which we somewhat fuzzily denominate Romanticism. As such it had links to the renaissance of interest in nature, primitivism,

and the supernatural and to the increasing valuation placed upon the organic, the joyous, and the creative. Just as medievalism was very much a part of the desire to give man a sense of social and political belonging, so it was also an attempt, in the decline of any transcendental order, to naturalize man in the universe and make him feel related to it. It was opposed to the Newtonian and Lockean view of the universe as a vast machine in which man was a subordinate mechanism moved by pleasure and pain. As part of the Romantic contradiction of these concepts, medievalism substituted a picture of man as a dynamic and generous creature, capable of loyal feeling and heroic action. Far from being isolated from nature, medieval man was seen as part of it, and his chivalry mirrored its benevolence. In its hostility to a mechanistic metaphysics, medievalism as a philosophical movement thus paralleled its opposition to machinery on economic and social grounds. Both aspects of medievalism — the political and the metaphysical — saw materialism and mechanization as inimical to the human. The return to the Middle Ages was conceived of as a homecoming.[4]

The three Victorian writers whose works best illustrate the blending of medievalism with musico-literary symbolism were Alfred Tennyson, Algernon Charles Swinburne, and William Morris.[5] All three incorporated musical themes and motives throughout their fiction, especially in relation to their Victorian "resetting" of the medieval Arthurian and French epic tales.

Alfred Tennyson (1809–1892) started writing poetry at a young age, and is best known as the Poet Laureate of England from 1850 until his death, and for his epic tale of King Arthur and the knights of Camelot, *Idylls of the King* (1859–74). Throughout the *Idylls*, Tennyson weaves musical ideas such as harmony and discord into a number of the Arthurian stories, especially the tragic tale *Balin and Balan*, composed in 1885 (the last story in the *Idylls* to be written). In this tale, which is recounted in the Old French *Suite du Merlin* and Malory's *Morte d'Arthur*, the twin brothers Balin and Balan are cursed by fate, and eventually end up killing each other. Balin, in particular, is instrumental in the downfall of Arthur's Camelot. He wounds King Pellam with the sacred spear that pierced the side of Christ, the blow known as the Dolorous Stroke (the Fisher King story in the Grail epic). Balin also wields and will not give up a sword that has been prophesied to him will slay the man he loves most in the world and bring about his own destruction. In the end, Balin fights his own brother, whom he does not recognize, and both are fatally wounded. Tennyson makes Balin an important figure in developing some of the major themes in *The Idylls*

Strains of Elvish Song and Voices (Eden)

of the King. His Balin is known as "the Savage" (Malory called him "Balin Le Savage") and he has a major role in the struggle of Arthur to destroy the bestial both in the realm and in his subjects, and thus to raise themselves to a higher level, the level of the angels.

To illustrate some of Tennyson's use of music and language in his Arthurian epic, it is essential to mention some lines of *Balin and Balan*. For instance, Balan immediately upon introducing himself to Arthur, says:

> They followed; whom when Arthur seeing asked
> "Tell me your names; why sat ye by the well?"
> Balin the stillness of a minute broke
> Saying "An unmelodious name to thee,
> Balin, 'the Savage'—that addition thine—
> My brother and my better, this man here,
> Balan...."[6]

There are constant references to music in the court at Camelot, music that is harmonious and orderly, just like Arthur's lofty goals and dreams for his realm:

> Thereafter, when Sir Balin entered hall,
> The Lost one Found was greeted as in Heaven
> With joy that blazed itself in woodland wealth
> Of leaf, and gayest garlandage of flowers,
> Along the walls and down the board; they sat,
> And cup clashed cup; they drank and some one sang,
> Sweet-voiced, a song of welcome, whereupon
> Their common shout in chorus, mounting, made
> Those banners of twelve battles overhead
> Stir, as they stirred of old, when Arthur's host
> Proclaimed him Victor, and the day was won.

Even after Balin is granted the boon of bearing the Queen's crown-royal upon his shield, the power of music is weaved into Balin's personality at that moment, both in his achievement and in his ultimate fate:

> So Balin bare the crown, and all the knights
> Approved him, and the Queen, and all the world
> Made music, and he felt his being move
> In music with his Order, and the King.

> The nightingale, full-toned in middle May,
> Hath ever and anon a note so thin
> It seems another voice in other groves;
> Thus, after some quick burst of sudden wrath,
> The music in him seemed to change, and grow
> Faint and far-off.

As Balin begins to lose his sanity, especially after discovering the Queen and Lancelot in a secret tryst, the musical language used to describe him becomes more discordant and twisted. Balin's personality begins to turn into that of a raging beast, aptly described by Tennyson, as Balin attacks and wounds King Pellam, and fights the anonymous knight that he eventually discovers is his own brother. The tenderness and emotion as the two brothers die in each other's arms has a considerable effect on the reader:

> "O brother" answered Balin "Woe is me!
> My madness all thy life has been thy doom,
> Thy curse, and darkened all thy day; and now
> The night has come. I scarce can see thee now.
> Goodnight! for we shall never bid again
> Goodmorrow — Dark my doom was here, and dark
> It will be there. I see thee now no more.
> I would not mine again should darken thine,
> Goodnight, true brother."
> Balan answered low
> "Goodnight, true brother here! goodmorrow there!
> We two were born together, and we die
> Together by one doom:" and while he spoke
> Closed his death-drowsing eyes, and slept the sleep
> With Balin, either locked in either's arm.

Algernon Charles Swinburne (1837–1909) was born into the British aristocracy, and early on was trained by his grandfather and mother in the French and Italian languages. As a student at Oxford, he acquired a detailed knowledge of religion and the Bible, and established friendships with Dante Gabriel Rossetti, William Morris, and Edward Burne-Jones. Swinburne was in frail health most of his life and of slight build (he was under 5 feet tall), and throughout the 1860s and 1870s was in an alcoholic stupor.

Strains of Elvish Song and Voices (Eden)

Finally, in 1879, he was able to give up alcoholism, but was always sick for the remainder of his life. He was quite the personality within Victorian society. He challenged all of the norms and conventions of his time. He openly flaunted his homosexuality and his masochistic tendencies, and these appeared often in his writings. He introduced Victorian society to medieval French troubadour poetry and contemporary French literature (especially Bautier, Baudelaire, and Hugo), and even promoted the works of American writers such as Edgar Allan Poe and Walt Whitman. His poems are on tragic love and heroism, dominated by strife and frustrated love, by fickle men and women who are victims of a malevolent fate. He was a scholar in the truest sense; he revived medieval forms such as the rondel, the alba, and the ballad.

In 1896, Swinburne published his own version of the Arthurian tale of Balin and Balan, called *The Tale of Balen*. This poem was written in direct opposition to Tennyson's recent version of this Arthurian tale. Far from portraying the Victorian's obsession with medievalism as an idyllic or "golden age," Swinburne actively wrote on the desperate passions and hatreds of the human psyche that were contained in the Arthurian legends. As such, his use of musical imagery is even more vivid and dramatic than Tennyson's.

Again, examination of the work itself is essential to understanding the extensive use of imagery that Swinburne incorporates throughout this work. The opening of *The Tale of Balen* is provided at the beginning of this article, and seeks to symbolize the musical harmony inherent in the Arthurian realm prior to the tragedy of Balen. Balen contains the "Northern" spirit, that which is full of the sea and the wild:

> And all his life of blood and breath
> Sang out within him: time and death
> Were even as words a dreamer saith
> When sleep within him slackeneth,
>   And light and life and spring were one.
> The steed between his knees that sprang,
> The moors and woods that shone and sang,
> The hours wherethrough the spring's breath rang,
>   Seemed ageless as the sun.

When confronted by a knight who debased his Northern heritage at

Arthur's court, Balen strikes him down and is cast from Arthur's court. The whole world of Balen is truly dolorous and strange, and no matter how virtuous his motives are, his actions inevitably generate suffering, if not tragedy. As a central symbol of fate, Balen obtains the sword that no one else in Camelot's court can conquer, and must accept the fate that he will slay that which he loves the most. By the end of the tale, Balen has killed the Lady of the Lake, Launceor, Garlon, and eventually his own brother Balan. The use of nature, sea, and musical imagery is very reminiscent of Tolkien's early mythological writings. Here is just a small sample of Swinburne's musical symbolism[7]:

> But bright and dark as night or noon
> And lowering as a storm-flushed moon
> When clouds and thwarting winds distune
> The music of the midnight, soon
>   To die from darkening star to star
> And leave a silence in the skies
> That yearns till dawn find voice and rise,
> Shone strange as fate Morgause, with eyes
>   That dwelt on days afar.
>
>   As morning hears before it run
> The music of the mounting sun,
> And laughs to watch his trophies won
> From darkness, and her hosts undone,
>   And all the night become a breath,
> Nor dreams that fear should hear and flee
> The summer menace of the sea,
> So hears our hope what life may be,
>   And knows it not for death.
>
>   From choral earth and quiring air
> Rang memories winged like songs that bear
> Sweet gifts for spirit and sense to share:
> For no man's life knows love more fair
>   And fruitful of memorial things
> Than this the deep dear love that breaks
> With sense of life on life, and makes
> The sundawn sunnier as it wakes
>   Where morning round it rings.

Strains of Elvish Song and Voices (Eden)

 And there they laid their dead to sleep
Royally, lying where wild winds keep
Keen watch and wail more soft and deep
Than where men's choirs bid music weep
 And song like incense heave and swell.
And forth again they rode, and found
Before them, dire in sight and sound,
A castle girt about and bound
 With sorrow like a spell.

 In winter, when the year burns low
As fire wherein no firebrands glow,
And winds dishevel as they blow
The lovely stormy wings of snow,
 The hearts of northern men burn bright
With joy that mocks the joy of spring
To hear all heaven's keen clarions ring
Music that bids the spirit sing
 And day give thanks for night.

 As toward a royal hart's death rang
That note, whence all the loud wood sang
With winged and living sound that sprang
Like fire, and keen as fire's own fang
 Pierced the sweet silence that it slew.
But nought like death or strife was here:
Fair semblance and most goodly cheer
They made him, they whose troop drew near
 As death among them drew.

 And Balen rose again from swoon
First, and went toward him: all too soon
He too then rose, and the evil boon
Of strength came back, and the evil tune
 Of battle unnatural made again
Mad music as for death's wide ear
Listening and hungering toward the near
Last sigh that life or death might hear
 At last from dying men.

William Morris (1834–96), in stark contrast to Swinburne, was the ideal Victorian medievalist. He was raised in a fantasy world in his home, Woodford Hall, which was a moated grange where medieval festivities were still actually observed. His parents presented him with a tiny suit of armor to wear about the family estate as a child. As a youth he became a devotee of Pugin and a disciple of Ruskin, whose work on medieval craftsmanship inspired Morris to base his life on that ideal. Morris designed all types of medieval materials in the nineteenth century, from architecture to painting to furniture to gardens, as well as carpets, poetry, calligraphy, and the translation of Icelandic sagas. His *News from Nowhere* (1890) is a story of a dream by a time-traveler who sees an England of the future — a future similar to the fourteenth century, after a violent revolution. The only difference is that there are no churches, no Christianity. Morris's influence on Victorian medievalism was profound and unique; his craftsmanship still survives today in various museums and galleries around the world.

Morris also used poetry as his preferred device to depict the Arthurian romances. Through a number of poems, such as *The Defence of Guenevere, In Arthur's House, King Arthur's Tomb,* and *Sir Galahad: A Christmas Mystery,* Morris uses musical and sea imagery to great effect. Here are just a few samples of his musical symbolism[8]:

> "Nay Dame," he said, "I am but young;
> A little have I lived and sung
> And seen thy face this happy noon."
> (*In Arthur's House*)

> It chanced upon a day that Launcelot came
> To dwell at Arthur's court: at Christmas-time
> This happened; when the heralds sung his name,
>   Son of King Ban of Benwick, seemed to chime
> Along with all the bells that rang that day,
> O'er the white roofs, with little change of rhyme.
> (*The Defence of Guenevere*)

> For no man cares now to know why I sigh;
> And no man comes to sing me pleasant songs,
> Nor any brings me the sweet flowers that lie
> (*The Defence of Guenevere*)

> That very evening in their scarlet sleeves

Strains of Elvish Song and Voices (Eden)

> The gay-dress'd minstrels sing; no maid will talk
> Of sitting on my tomb, until the leaves,
> Grown big upon the bushes of the walk,
> (*Sir Galahad: A Christmas Mystery*)

J.R.R. Tolkien's writings, especially his early mythological and poetic endeavors, were strongly influenced by the musico-literary symbolism of Victorian fictionists. The conscious/subconscious use of musical language and symbolism arises not only from the Victorian tradition, but from Tolkien's own personal background. His grandfather was a piano maker, and in his *Letters*, Tolkien refers to the fact that his family has musical talent, but that this predilection had unfortunately not surfaced in him. Carpenter's biography of Tolkien often makes reference to musical influences in Tolkien's life, especially his wife Edith's talent in piano playing (a prerequisite for all women in Victorian society), and how much Tolkien himself enjoyed the sound of music throughout his home.

An examination of Tolkien's early poetic endeavors reveals this predilection for musical symbolism. The poetry quoted at the beginning of the article was Tolkien's first published work at the age of 23. Cursory research of Tolkien's early published poetry illustrates the strong Victorian tendencies towards music symbolism:

> And songs long silent once more awake[9]
>
> Or shrill in sudden singing sheer...
> There melodies of music spill.[10]
>
> In mighty music from his monstrous head...
> Do neighbors musical in western lands.[11]
>
> a sudden music came to her...
> Flutes there were, and harps were wrung, and there
>   was sound of singing...
> They sang their song, while minstrels played on
>   harp and flute slowly.[12]
>
> I'll sit and sing till the moon comes, as they sing
>   beyond the mountains...
> and he sang a dirge for Higgins...
> A sad song... a dragon's song or colour.[13]

These are only a few of the musical allusions that are prevalent in

Middle-earth Minstrel

Tolkien's early published poetry. Tolkien's early mythological works continue these musical associations. Obviously, "Ainulindalë" in *The Silmarillion* was written early in Tolkien's career, and the musical nature of the creation of Middle-earth has been commented upon before.[14] *The Book of Lost Tales*, begun between 1916–17, contains not only the earliest versions of "Ainulindalë," but also much of the foundation upon which Middle-earth would later be built. In addition, these early stories illustrate the broad influence of the Victorian period upon Tolkien's writing style, despite his comments to the contrary. Tolkien was influenced early on by the concept of chivalry and the idea of "loving from afar" which was very much a part of the trouvere/troubadour tradition in medieval music. Almost all of Tolkien's early work is done in the context of tales/stories as related or sung to a listener or listeners. What we are reading is the documentation of that experience by the listener, again another strong indication that Tolkien was trying to portray the way medieval audiences would have heard and listened to the great stories of their past. In any event, the use of, presence of, and reference to music in Tolkien's earlier versions of his mythology are so strong, that reading the published versions does not do justice to his imaginative power and both conscious and subconscious references to music. Here are a few of these examples:

Tinfang Warble: Tinfang Warble is the greatest minstrel in Middle-earth. His early appearance is in relation to the telling of the tales in the *Book of Lost Tales*, where he recounts some of the stories of the Valar that would eventually find their way into *The Silmarillion*. Tinfang does not appear in any published stories, but his early influence on Tolkien is profound. In the list of the greatest minstrels ever, Tinfang takes first place above Maglor and Dairon. Part of his history is told in the *Book of Lost Tales* p. 107, but he appears in various other stories, particularly stories related to the Beren and Lúthien lay.

Dairon: In the first versions of the Beren and Lúthien saga, Dairon is Lúthien's brother, one whose power and use of music is even more profound than the published version of the story indicates. What is interesting is Tolkien's gradual diminishing of Dairon's musical role and power in the story, such that he eventually becomes a lover of Lúthien from afar, and not her brother. While his power as a musician is great, and is attested to by Tolkien in his listing of the three greatest musicians ever in Middle-earth, it is a fascinating personal account to follow the development of

Strains of Elvish Song and Voices (Eden)

Dairon as a character in Tolkien's writings. In fact, the metered version of the lay of Beren and Lúthien contains some very powerful references to Dairon's power as a musician and his use of music to affect change in environment and circumstances.

Names of songs: More than any other topic, Tolkien names songs in his earlier writings, songs that he then proceeds to compose either in verse or prose. A list of some of these songs includes: Song of the Valar, Song of Aryador, Song of Light, Song of the Sleeper, Flight of the Gnomes, Song of the Sun and Moon, The Siege of Angband, The Bowman's Friendship, Song of the Great Bow, the Song of Tuor for Earendel (which is in 3 versions and 5 different texts), and Light as Leaf on Lindentree (which Aragorn quotes from and sings on Weathertop). These are just a few of the titles. In addition, in the Lays of Beleriand, the verse versions of the Beren and Lúthien story are filled with some of the most powerful language this author has ever encountered in mythological literature on the use and power of music. Three of these musical/dramatic events, which are much more powerful here than in the published *The Silmarillion*, are the battle of music and song between Finrod Felagund and Thû, the description of Lúthien's song to rescue Beren from Thu and destroy the prison where Beren is being held, and finally the description of Beren's song of farewell to earth and light after leaving Lúthien and Huan as he starts to enter Morgoth's domain. These are powerful, evocative, musical events in which drama and music are interwoven and recited, similar to a musical composer using all the resources at his or her disposal to present a symphonic masterpiece, including melody, harmony, instrumentation, texture, and volume. Indeed, Carpenter's and even Tolkien's references to powerful links between linguistics and music in his life are very apparent in these early writings.

One major story that does not appear in *The Silmarillion*, but for which Tolkien spent a lot of time writing and rewriting, was the legend of the making of the Sun and Moon. There is a long, detailed account in his early writings of the construction, launching, personalities involved, and even the end of days regarding the Sun and Moon. This legend, while I have not had sufficient time to examine and research it, also holds many links to the philosophy of Plotinus, especially in regards to the Vision vs. Reality model of Neoplatonism. The published version in *The Silmarillion* does little justice to Tolkien's early efforts in writing this story.

Finally, the character of Túrin deserves mention. Tolkien's earlier stories and accounts of Túrin are powerful and do little justice to his character in *The Silmarillion*. Not only are musical links extensive and vast, but Túrin's power as a musician and his training in Gondolin as a minstrel are truly dramatic in both the verse and prose versions of the Fall of Gondolin story, much of which never made it into the *The Silmarillion*. Indeed, the song of Tuor for Earendel, as stated previously, exists in 3 versions and 5 texts. Túrin's abilities as a minstrel and musician made him probably the greatest musician among Men, and most of his training was from the elves in Gondolin, from meeting Ulmo and hearing his many-faceted musical instrument, and from the Music of the Ainur such as it still existed in the sound of the sea, where it is still felt and heard the strongest amongst the elves.

In conclusion, the Victorian predilection towards medievalism, and for musical symbolism in particular, had a strong influence on Tolkien's writing style. Whether he chose to admit it or not, he was influenced by Victorian writers. As for his musical leanings, Tolkien often referred in his *Letters* and other correspondence of the close relationship between linguistics and music, between philology and musical composition, between the sound and construction of words and the timbres and pitches of music. As Tolkien well knew, music was studied and respected as part of the quadrivium along with geometry, astronomy and arithmetic in the Middle Ages. It was such a common understanding that music guided and directed everything, that the discipline itself was studied as a scholarly pursuit rather than a practical application. Just as the medieval world saw music both consciously and subconsciously apparent in both the practical and the divine, so in Tolkien's writings the idea of music underlies yet intertwines all of the early verse and prose versions of his mythological world, much more so than is apparent in *The Silmarillion*. One passage in particular illustrates Tolkien's views on his early compositional process:

> This leads to the matter of "external history," the actual way in which I came to light on or choose certain sequences of sound to use as names, *before* they were given a place inside the story. I think, as I said, this is unimportant: the labour involved in my setting out what I know and remember of the process, or in the guess-work of others, would be far greater than the worth of the results. The spoken forms would simply be mere audible forms, and when transferred to the prepared linguistic situation in my story would receive meaning and significance according to that situation, and to the nature of the story

told. It would be entirely delusory to refer to the sources of the sound-combination to discover any meanings overt or hidden.[15]

What is wonderful about this statement is not just Tolkien's opinion on how he created words in his languages, but the implication in the quotation of himself as a "composer of words," which is an apt analogy. Whether or not Tolkien thought of himself as a true composer in the musical sense, he certainly can be described as a composer of words, and in his own way his mythology and his stories are true symphonic works in the linguistic sense. Music was certainly part of his heritage, part of his personal, professional, and religious life, and to be sure it was a strong influence on his writing style, as it appeared in its many and varied guises throughout his mythology. The Victorian medieval/musical-literary heritage helped to inspire Tolkien's compositional process, his musical roots helped to nurture his interest in philology and the sound of words, and his own love of both music and linguistics combined to produce one of the greatest mythologies ever written.

Notes

1. John D. Rosenberg, *The Fall of Camelot: A Study of Tennyson's "Idylls of the King"* (Cambridge, MA: Belknap Press of Harvard University Press, 1973), p. 78. Lines 72–74 from Tennyson's *Idylls of the King*. "The interpolation serves to stress the motif of music versus discord that is especially prominent in "Balin and Balan" and that runs throughout the *Idylls*" (footnote).

2. Algernon Charles Swinburne, *The Complete Works of Algernon Charles Swinburne. Vol. IV: Poetical Works,* ed. Sir Edmund Gosse and Thomas James Wise (New York: Russell and Russell, 1968), p. 171. (The beginning stanzas of *The Fall of Balin*, 1896.)

3. J.R.R. Tolkien, "Goblin Feet," *Oxford Poetry* (Oxford: B.H. Blackwell, 1915), p. 65.

4. Alice Chandler, *A Dream of Order: The Medieval Ideal in Nineteenth-Century English Literature* (Lincoln: University of Nebraska Press, 1970), pp. 7–8.

5. Douglas A. Anderson, in *Tales before Tolkien* (New York: Ballantine, 2003), comments on the many writers whose influence on Tolkien is both recorded or implied, especially George MacDonald. MacDonald's influence on Tolkien's writings can be specifically attributed to Tolkien's concept of children's literature and especially the production of *The Hobbit*, but I can find no direct influence of MacDonald on Tolkien's early mythological writings.

6. Quotes from *Balin and Balan* are taken from The Camelot Project, available at http://www.lib.rochester.edu/camelot/idyl-bal.htm.

7. Quotes from *The Tale of Balen* are taken from The Camelot Project, available at http://www.lib.rochester.edu/camelot/swinbal.htm.

8. All quotes are taken from The Camelot Project, available at *http://www.lib.rochester.edu/camelot/cphome.stm*.
9. J.R.R. Tolkien, "Iumonna Gold Galdre Bewunden," *The Gryphon*, New Series, January 1923 (v. 4, no. 4), p. 130. Last line.
10. J.R.R. Tolkien, "The Nameless Land," *Realities: An Anthology of Verse*, edited by G.S. Tancred (London: Gay and Hancock, 1927), pp. 24–25.
11. J.R.R. Tolkien, "Iumbo, or ye Kinde of ye Oliphaunt," signed Fisiologus, *The Stapeldon Magazine*, June 1927 (v. 7, no. 40), pp. 123–27.
12. J.R.R. Tolkien, "Firiel," *The Chronicle*, Convent of the Sacred Heart, Roehampton, 1934, pp. 30–32.
13. J.R.R. Tolkien, "The Dragon's Visit," *The Oxford Magazine*, February 4, 1937 (v. 55, no. 11): 342.
14. Brad Eden, "The Music of the Spheres: Relationships Between Tolkien's *Silmarillion* and Medieval Cosmological and Religious Theory." In *Tolkien the Medievalist*. Ed. Jane Chance (New York: Routledge, 2004).
15. J.R.R. Tolkien, The *Letters of J.R.R. Tolkien*. Ed. Humphrey Carpenter with assistance from Christopher Tolkien (London: George Allen and Unwin, 1981), pp. 383–84.

Works Cited

Anderson, Douglas A., ed. *Tales Before Tolkien: the Roots of Modern Fantasy*. New York: Ballantine, 2003.
Boos, Florence S., ed. *History and Community: Essays in Victorian Medievalism*. New York: Garland, 1992.
The Camelot Project. Available at http://www.lib.rochester.edu/camelot/mainmenu.htm
Carruthers, Gerard, and Alan Rawes, eds. *English Romanticism and the Celtic World*. Cambridge: Cambridge University Press, 2003.
Chandler, Alice. *A Dream of Order: The Medieval Ideal in Nineteenth-Century English Literature*. Lincoln: University of Nebraska Press, 1970.
Chapman, Raymond. *The Sense of the Past in Victorian Literature*. New York: St. Martin's, 1986.
Eden, Brad. "The Music of the Spheres: Relationships Between Tolkien's *Silmarillion* and Medieval Cosmological and Religious Theory." In *Tolkien the Medievalist*. Ed. Jane Chance. New York: Routledge, 2003.
Fay, Elizabeth. *Romantic Medievalism: History and the Romantic Literary Ideal*. New York: Palgrave, 2002.
Filmer, Kath, ed. *Twentieth-Century Fantasists: Essays on Culture, Society and Belief in Twentieth-Century Mythopoetic Literature*. New York: St. Martin's, 1992.
Gervais, David. *Literary Englands: Versions of "Englishness" in Modern Writing*. Cambridge: Cambridge University Press, 1993.
Harrison, Anthony H. *Swinburne's Medievalism: A Study of Victorian Love Poetry*. Baton Rouge: Louisiana State University Press, 1988.
Larrington, Carolyne. "The Fairy Mistress in Medieval Literary Fantasy." In *Writing and Fantasy*. Ed. Ceri Sullivan and Barbara White. London: Longman, 1999.
McSweeney, Kerry. *Tennyson and Swinburne as Romantic Naturalists*. Toronto: University of Toronto Press, 1981.
Picker, John M. *Victorian Soundscapes*. Oxford: Oxford University Press, 2003.

Prickett, Stephen. *Victorian Fantasy*. Bloomington: University of Indiana Press, 1979.
Rose, Jonathan. *The Edwardian Temperament, 1895–1919*. Athens: Ohio University Press, 1986.
Rosenberg, John D. *The Fall of Camelot: A Study of Tennyson's "Idylls of the King."* Cambridge, MA: Belknap Press of Harvard University Press, 1973.
Shippey, T.A. "The Undeveloped Image: Anglo-Saxon in Popular Consciousness from Turner to Tolkien." In *Literary Appropriations of the Anglo-Saxons from the Thirteenth to the Twentieth Century*. Ed. Donald Scragg and Carole Weinberg. Cambridge: Cambridge University Press, 2000.
Simons, John, ed. *From Medieval to Medievalism*. New York: St. Martin's, 1992.
Sussman, Herbert L. *Victorians and the Machine: The Literary Response to Technology*. Cambridge, MA: Harvard University Press, 1968.
Swinburne, Algernon Charles. *The Complete Works of Algernon Charles Swinburne. Vol. IV: Poetical Works*. Ed. Sir Edmund Gosse and Thomas James Wise. New York: Russell and Russell, 1968.
Tolkien, J.R.R. *The Book of Lost Tales, Part I*. Vol. 1 of *The History of Middle-earth*. Ed. Christopher Tolkien. London: George Allen and Unwin, 1983.
_____. *The Book of Lost Tales, Part II*. Vol. 2 of *The History of Middle-earth*. Ed. Christopher Tolkien. London: George Allen and Unwin, 1984.
_____. "The Dragon's Visit." *The Oxford Magazine*, vol. 55, no. 11 (February 4, 1937), 342.
_____. "Firiel," *The Chronicle*, Convent of the Sacred Heart, Roehampton (1934): 30–32.
_____. "Goblin Feet." *Oxford Poetry*. Oxford: B.H. Blackwell, 1915, 64–65.
_____. "Iumbo, or ye Kinde of ye Oliphaunt," signed Fisiologus. *The Stapeldon Magazine*, vol. 7, no. 40, (June 1927): 123–27.
_____. "Iumonna Gold Galdre Bewunden." *The Gryphon*, New Series, vol. 4, no. 4 (January 1923): 130.
_____. *The Letters of J.R.R. Tolkien*. Ed. Humphrey Carpenter with assistance from Christopher Tolkien. London: George Allen and Unwin, 1981.
_____. "The Nameless Land." In *Realities: An Anthology of Verse*, ed. G.S. Tancred, London: Gay and Hancock, 1927, 24–25.
_____. *The Silmarillion*. Ed. Christopher Tolkien. London: George Allen and Unwin, 1977.
Wade, Stephen. *In My Own Shire: Region and Belonging in British Writing, 1840–1970*. Westport, CT: Praeger, 2002.
Wawn, Andrew. *The Vikings and the Victorians: Inventing the Old North in Nineteenth-Century Britain*. Woodbridge, Suffolk, England: D.S. Brewer, 2000.

Dissonance in the Divine Theme: The Issue of Free Will in Tolkien's *Silmarillion*[1]

Keith W. Jensen

As one reads "The Ainulindalë" chapter from J.R.R. Tolkien's *The Silmarillion* carefully, an odd event occurs. Melkor, Tolkien's equivalent on many levels to the biblical Lucifer, has created a dissonance in the Divine Music that Ilúvatar conducts. The dissonance is not surprising, considering that Melkor is the embodiment of evil in *The Silmarillion*, but what is odd is that not only does Ilúvatar allow it, but he announces that Melkor's dissonance is part of his divine plan to begin with. Does such a statement by Ilúvatar hint at malice on his part? Can Ilúvatar, the ultimate force for good,[2] readily embrace the evil suggested by the dissonance? His action raises a still more puzzling question: Why does Ilúvatar allow evil to enter the world?

Allowing evil into the world is a problem that Christians have puzzled over for centuries. How can a divine creator, who can do anything, allow evil to happen?[3] Saint Augustine posited in *The Confessions* that God gave us choices, and that it is our choices, our free will, that allows evil to happen: "when I willed or did not will something, I was utterly certain that none other than myself was willing or not willing" (Chadwick 114), so any wrongdoing was his own choice. His theory stems from his dissatisfaction with Manichean notions that both good and evil existed in opposition to one another in a corporeal form; furthermore, he notes this "erroneous" point when he writes, "[a]s a result, I believed that there was some such substance of evil which possessed its own foul and formless mass...: [the Manicheans] pictured it as a malignant mind creeping over the earth" (Bourke 121).[4] The problem, Augustine would discover, is that, because of this Manichean belief, he had difficulty accepting the Incarnation because he could not accept that it was possible for Christ to exist without the possibility of defilement of the flesh (Bourke 122). Yet he ultimately came to believe that God is "incorruptible and inviolable and immutable" (Bourke 162).

Augustine's issue with corporeality leads to another conundrum, which is that if evil is corporeal, it could in some way fight with God, perhaps even injure or defeat Him, making him "capable of violation and corruptible" (Bourke 164). If such an event is possible, it casts doubt on God's omnipotence, which is not an acceptable answer to Augustine. In his search, then, for the cause of evil, he has to look for an answer by which he would "not be forced to believe that the immutable God is mutable" (Bourke 165). Ultimately, he came to a Neo-Platonic conclusion that evil has no reality of its own and is simply the loss of good (Deane 15). The only way evil can exist is for a being to move away from good, to turn away from God: "the choice is left to man, but, as we shall see, the consequences of the choice are eternally fixed and determined by God" (Deane 16). The issue with this notion of free will is that free will is not the same after the Fall as it was before the Fall. According to Herbert Deane's interpretation of Augustine, in Genesis the choice in Eden was between doing good or doing evil (17–18). After the expulsion from the Garden, "his freedom was reduced to the choice between one or another sin" (Deane 19).

Deane's discussion is helpful in explaining Augustinian thought, but even a careful reading of *The Confessions* raises more questions than it actually answers. He hasn't solved the issue of where evil comes from, and it begs the question that if God can create a whole world, couldn't he stop people from making poor choices or correct the poor choices they make? Yet He doesn't. Why? Perhaps the answer lies in the fact that we would then no longer be human, and there would be no story. This answer may then explain Ilúvatar permitting Melkor's dissonance. Tolkien was a storyteller at heart, and stories need conflict, just as humanity does. So the creation of dissonance is necessary for there to be the conflict needed to allow humans to learn from their mistakes and to grow. This chapter will explore the concepts of dissonance and free will,[5] how they apply to the Divine Theme of Ilúvatar through a careful reading of "The Ainulindalë," and how free will can lead both to tragedy and Eucatastrophe, which explains its necessity in our world and the world of Middle-earth.

Dissonance

According to *The New Grove Dictionary of Music and Musicians*, dissonance is "an antonym to consonance, hence a discordant sounding together of two or more notes perceived as having 'roughness' or 'tonal tension'" (*s.v.* 7:380). While words such as "unpleasant" and "grating" are often used to explain what dissonance sounds like, all music incorporates dissonance in some way ("Consonance and Dissonance"). "The buildup and release of tension (dissonance and resolution) ... is to a great degree responsible for what many listeners perceive as beauty, emotion, and expressiveness in music" ("Consonance and Dissonance"). Essentially, dissonant chords or notes are necessary to fill out and complete a musical selection, and such dissonance can only be created through individuality. Using a musical metaphor from Judy Kaplow (a colleague), if someone sings a solo, there can be no dissonance. The person is working alone. In a choir, if everyone sings the exact same melodic line, a monophony, the music sounds the same. It may sound pretty, but it is simple and often uninteresting. What adds interest, the spice if you will, is the act of an individual choosing to sing something different within a community of singers, which causes the dissonance.

At the beginning of "The Ainulindalë," Ilúvatar tells the Ainur to harmonize a "Great Music," but because he has kindled within them the Flame Imperishable, they will be able to adorn the Music with "his own thoughts and devices" (Tolkien 15). Ilúvatar's intent is to create a harmonious, in-sync music that would bring forth great beauty; however, he has already allowed for each member of the Ainur to bring his own "spice" to the music, which would indicate that he is already allotting them free will. Of course, Melkor, who has the greatest of the gifts given to the Ainur, decides to literally take Ilúvatar up on his offer, and begins to weave his own ideas into the music, and, because he seeks to "bring into Being things of his own" (Tolkien 16) against the music conceived by Ilúvatar, his music creates dissonance in the Divine Theme. In many ways, Melkor resembles Lucifer, God's brightest angel who falls from Grace, so anyone with a background in Judeo-Christian theology might assume that Melkor will be punished for creating discord. Ilúvatar does not punish him, however, but patiently suffers through two themes in the divine music, changing them and adding to them to counterbalance Melkor's dissonance, and then he makes use of the dissonance to create a powerful third theme that interweaves the "most triumphant notes" into its own "solemn pattern" (Tolkien 17).

In itself, Ilúvatar's patience and his willingness to incorporate Melkor's dissonance into the Divine Theme seems oddly discomfiting, but then he says to Melkor that "no theme may be played that hath not its uttermost source in me, nor can any alter the music in my despite" (Tolkien 17). In this passage, Tolkien's "God" figure frankly admits that although Melkor has exercised free will, the source of that free will comes from Ilúvatar himself. No one can change the music, make it dark and evil, unless He allows it. Such a statement emphasizes the initial question raised in this paper: Can there be malice in the Divine Theme? As Verlyn Flieger points out in *Splintered Light: Logos and Language in Tolkien's World*,

> The Children [of Ilúvatar] come *with*, not (as might be expected) *in* the third theme, which is not just the direct result of Melkor's rebellion, but also Ilúvatar's acceptance of it and decision to work with it. Nevertheless, for all their directness of origin, Elves and Men will find their lives complicated and profoundly affected by the Music, which accompanies their placement in the world. After Melkor — and certainly to some degree because of him — Elves and Men will live in a world of immeasurable sorrow as part of a pattern that can take the most triumphant of the discordant notes and weave them into the whole [128, emphasis Flieger's].

Because Ilúvatar chooses to work with Melkor's dissonance, Elves and Men, and for that matter, Dwarves and Hobbits, will have to live with sorrow, tragedy, and other difficulties. They are not the cause of it, because they do not bring it about as Adam and Eve do by their disobedience in chapter 3 of Genesis. Instead, the inhabitants of Middle-earth will have to live with the marring Melkor brings about and decide what to do with it. Ilúvatar has granted his peoples the choice to make what they will of their lives. As Flieger also points out, this is an important departure from the Christian mythos with which Tolkien's work is so often "compared and associated" (128), and such a decision could possibly be seen as malicious, particularly since Ilúvatar fades into the background after the creation of Arda and does not directly interfere with its affairs. The only exception is when the Valar lay down their authority, and he changes the shape of the world in the Akallabêth.

Paul Kocher would argue that Ilúvatar's actions are not malicious. Instead, as he points out in *A Reader's Guide to* The Silmarillion, "Ilúvatar would permit selfish, rebellious Evil to exist but would always transmute it so as to serve the ends of his divine Providence" (16), and while he has indeed allowed the discord, he does not necessarily allow it limitlessly, which is evidenced by the fact that the Creator abruptly ends the third theme in wrath (Kocher 16). He would eventually see that Melkor's crimes would be punished through the various battles he has with the Valar. So, why is the dissonance necessary, why does Ilúvatar sanction Melkor's rebellion, and, in addition, is dissonance really such as bad thing?

To take the third question first, dissonance is not necessarily bad, or at least good can come from it, and as is shown through the various tales he presents, Tolkien quite possibly felt the same way. Melkor is an individual who makes a choice, and Ilúvatar sanctions his choice because Ilúvatar (or Tolkien) wants to make free will part of his world, to flesh it out, to make it interesting. Yes, Melkor is evil, and does evil things to mar the world, but the world wouldn't be what it becomes without it. Arda would be beautiful and carefree, almost Eden-like, but there would be no growth and no reason to grow. Life would be boring. If one looks at it from a Neo-Platonic perspective, Humans, Elves, Dwarves, and later Hobbits in *The Hobbit* and *The Lord of the Rings* have the capacity to grow or regress, and it is through dissonance, adversity, that the peoples can choose these options. But for humans, choice is even more important, because as Flieger also points out, "Men can change the Music," which is like fate to the Elves, and it is through the actions of men the world shall be "fulfilled" or brought into "actuality" (129). Flieger's comments are based on pages forty-one and forty-two of *The Silmarillion* in which Ilúvatar decides that the hearts of Men "should seek beyond the Music of the Ainur." The dissonance of Melkor is an ingredient in Ilúvatar's overall plan to allow Humans, and arguably the other peoples of Middle-earth, to grow.

Free Will

The necessity of "free will" will be explored through a discussion of two additional chapters from *The Silmarillion*: "Of Beren and Lúthien" and "Of Túrin Turambar." "Of Beren and Lúthien" is Tolkien's great love story, and it is an important example of the value of free will for a number of reasons, perhaps most notably because it is the one tale in which a female figure exercises it. Tolkien has long been noted for his delight in male companionship through the various societies he belonged to, including the TCBS (Tea Club Barrovian Society), the Kolbítar (Coalbiters), and the Inklings. His relationship with his wife, whom he called his Lúthien, never revolved around intellectual activity, and he expected her to play the conventional role of wife and mother (Carpenter IV.5). Women also generally played very conventional roles in his works: Éowyn, the bane of the Lord of the Nazgûl, gave up her role as a "shield-maiden" to marry Faramir and become, one assumes, a conventional wife.

Lúthien, on the other hand, is the strongest character in a tale of strong characters. She is an Elf who falls in love with the mortal Beren, who is himself a fine hero. Both suffer personal tragedies in this tale. Beren loses his father and his group of men. Lúthien suffers separation from Beren. At first, one could easily assume that Lúthien is not that strong because she remains silent at the beginning of her relationship with Beren. When he is given the task Thingol sets for him, to retrieve one of the Silmarils from Morgoth's crown, she says nothing as he says goodbye to her and refuses to sing while he is gone (Tolkien 168). However, Lúthien is not a weak character willing to wait for her lover to win her hand through heroic deeds. She *chooses* to find Beren and help him, despite obstacles placed before her by her father, who locks her in a tree-house; by Celegorm and Curufin, who waylay her on her way to find Beren; and by Sauron, who attempts to hinder her rescue of Beren with many dark creatures, including himself as a werewolf (Tolkien 172–175). Granted, she accepts the help of the Valinorean hound, Huan, in the last two cases, but it is her determination to save Beren that counts. She lets her hair grow to make a ladder to escape the tree-house prison built by her father,[6] and she has the presence of mind to cast a part of her dark cloak over Sauron to blind him so that Huan could get his fangs into Sauron. She could opt to stay put, but she knows that Beren will need her help, and only together can they hope to retrieve the Silmaril from the Iron Crown.

Beren, himself, becomes an obstacle to Lúthien's choice. He does not want her to face the danger with him, and he attempts to leave her so that she will remain safe. But she tells him that he has to choose between relinquishing the quest and facing Morgoth, "[but] on either road I shall go with you, and our doom shall be alike" (Tolkien 177). He, too, has a choice to make, and of course he opts for the second choice, but he still does not want Lúthien to accompany him, and, after Celegorm and Curufin attempt to waylay them again, and he rescues her from capture, he leaves her while she sleeps. But Lúthien takes Huan with her and follows him, determined to help and guide him. Finally, when they catch up with Beren, Huan informs him that he can no longer save Lúthien from "the shadow of death" (Tolkien 179). They must either go into exile together seeking a vain peace or face Morgoth, a difficult but not impossible task; but, if Beren leaves Lúthien, she will still die because her love for Beren ties her to death (Tolkien 179). At this point, Beren recognizes the wisdom of Huan's advice, or at the very least accepts that Lúthien will not leave him, and allows her to accompany him on his journey.

Beren's choice is a good one, for it takes both him and Lúthien together to steal the Silmaril from Morgoth. Lúthien, in the form of a vampire bat, sings Morgoth to sleep, and Beren, in the form of a wolf, cuts the gem from the crown. But the victory is not without sorrow. Beren loses his hand to Carcharoth the wolf, and although he reconciles with Thingol, who gives him permission to marry Lúthien, he is mortally wounded in a final battle he and the Elf-king lead against the wolf. At this point comes the greatest, and yet in some ways, most sorrowful choice of all. Lúthien willingly dies and goes to the Halls of Mandos. There she sings of her sorrow to the Keeper of the Houses of the Dead, and for the first and only time in Arda's long history, he is moved to pity.

This event illustrates an interesting point, for Lúthien uses musical themes, weaving them sorrowfully yet triumphantly together, as Ilúvatar weaves his theme with Melkor's dissonance to make a triumphant world. The parallel is significant. Mandos is never moved to pity, but the song is so beautiful that he changes his own long-term frame of mind and speaks on behalf of Beren and Lúthien to Manwë, who grants Lúthien a last choice: to be released from Mandos and dwell in Valimar until the world's end, or to return to Middle-earth with Beren as a mortal and live a life "without certitude of life or joy" (Tolkien 187). She chooses mortality, and while to the Elves this would become a great grief, she has a second chance at happiness with the man she loves. There are some griefs that she faces, the death of her father for one, but still she leads a happier life with Beren than without him. In any case, her choice ultimately has a happy consequence for the future residents of Middle-earth, for from her and her husband eventually spring Aragorn and Arwen, who make the same choice as Lúthien. They will become the new King and Queen of the Golden Age of Men. Without the freedom of choice, and the ability to make good choices, the doom of Beren and Lúthien would have been quite different.

The story of Túrin Turambar, however, tells a very different story. Túrin is one of the two children of Húrin, captured and punished by Morgoth for attacking him, and he creates some profound tragedies, including his responsibility in the deaths of Saeros and Beleg and his disastrous decision to marry his sister. None of these tragedies are entirely his fault. Saeros makes a snide remark about the women of Túrin's tribe, and Túrin punishes the Elf by making him run naked in the forest. In his terror, Saeros falls into a chasm, and his body is broken (Tolkien 199–200). It is not his fault that Saeros falls, but Túrin does inspire the fear, so the other Elves, particularly Mablung, ask Túrin to return to face the judgment of Thingol. Túrin refuses because he considers himself an outlaw, but the king would have pardoned him had he sought mercy and forgiveness. Túrin causes Beleg's death when the latter tries to rescue Túrin from a band of orcs, and Túrin is startled from sleep and follows the old adage, strike first and ask questions later (Tolkien 208). Beleg dies, and Túrin holds on to the grief from that event for the rest of his life. He cannot forgive himself for what he has done, and his choices force him to live as an exile even among friends. He names himself at Nargothrond "Agarwaen the son of Úmarth (which is the Bloodstained, son of Ill-fate)" (Tolkien 210). His attitude throughout the rest of his life is that he is a doomed man, fated to suffer. He has no hope, and it is this lack of hope which forces him to make bad choices. Gwindor points this out when Túrin is angered by the betrayal of his right name: "[t]he doom lies in yourself, not in your name" (Tolkien 211). This statement strongly suggests that Túrin creates his own doom because of his choices.

The greatest tragedy of this tale is his ill-fated marriage with Nienor, his sister. In this case, fate does seem to conspire against him, but that fate at least in part is brought about by a creature of Morgoth, Glaurung the dragon. Glaurung first places a spell on Túrin that makes him think of himself as worthless and as a deserter to his mother and sister, whom he has never seen, and this feeling forces him to go find them. In his search he has a series of adventures that bring him both renown and shame for killing in pride and wrath, most particularly the death of Brodda, which seems rash and unnecessary because Túrin kills him when he realizes that he has been duped, but by Glaurung and not by Brodda (Tolkien 215). Brodda clearly did nothing wrong towards Túrin. Glaurung is to blame for lying to Túrin and tricking him into believing the lie, but the murder of Brodda is Túrin's own fault.

    Nienor, who wanders long distances searching for Túrin, is put under a spell by Glaurung in which she forgets who she is and whom she is looking for. Túrin finds her, names her Níniel, and takes her to his new home in Brethil. She ultimately marries Túrin, not knowing who he is, despite misgivings in her mind. She makes a mistake here in not listening to her misgivings, but she can't be blamed because she wants to keep Túrin from war, and he vows to return to war if they do not marry (Tolkien 220). Up to this point, Glaurung can truly be blamed for much of what has happened, but it is still the choices that both Nienor and Túrin make that lead to their downfall. Ultimately Glaurung, in his dying throes, removes his spell from Nienor, and she realizes that she has committed incest and then commits suicide without a second's thought (Tolkien 223). Túrin, who slays the dragon, wakes from a swoon, returns to his home, and is told by Brandir what Glaurung had said to Nienor (Tolkien 224). Túrin, in wrath, slays Brandir because he believes that Brandir is a liar and only wants to ruin the relationship between Túrin and his wife. Of course, he ultimately finds out the truth, and kills himself for what he considers his unlucky fate and his poor choices (Tolkien 225). Much of his misfortune could have been avoided if he had not trusted so much to fate. Túrin never understands that humans make their own choices and can decide their own fate. He has no hope of redemption, and that lack of hope causes him to make poor, and often rash, choices. Nevertheless, they are choices, and while the life of this man ends in tragedy, he is the one who ultimately causes it. One can blame Glaurung and other outside sources for leading him astray, but his final decisions are his own.

    What separates these two tales of free will is the idea of hope. Through the music of the Divine Theme, dissonance and all, Ilúvatar and the Ainur have created a world that will contain sorrow, pain, and anguish. They have left it to its inhabitants to decide what to do with it, and the ability to hope is an important part of that decision. Beren and Lúthien had the hope that they would be able to take the Silmaril from Morgoth's crown to live a life together. Without that hope, they would not have worked so hard to achieve the quest and to ultimately succeed. If Lúthien had no hope that Mandos might listen to her, she would not have tried to save Beren, and the paths of the two lovers would have been sundered forever.[7] Túrin Turambar had the same choices to make, but he lacks hope. He sees himself as ill-starred to begin with, so he often acts impulsively and never waits to find out if there is an alternative that could lead to a better life.

Choice is necessary. We could have a perfect world, but it would be boring. It is often the bumps, the dissonance if you will, of life's happenings and the choices we make that help us to grow the most. A perfect world offers no challenge, no growth. In similar fashion, Tolkien the storyteller cannot have a story of depth, power, or meaning without conflict. So Melkor's dissonance in the making of Arda may have made for an imperfect world, but it is a world that offers challenge, conflict, and the possibility of joy. Theologically, Tolkien still hasn't really solved the problem of evil, sin, and free will for the confused or the skeptical, but he has at least answered it for himself.

Notes

1. This chapter was first presented at the "Music and Language in Tolkien" session of the 42nd International Congress on Medieval Studies on May 11, 2007.

2. The interpretation of Ilúvatar as the ultimate force for good is a personal one, for Tolkien himself never refers to Ilúvatar as good. However, the reference raised such an interesting debate at the conference that the author decided to include it in the final version of this essay.

3. This question, of course, begs a relativistic argument that God can be judged in human terms, but it is nevertheless a question that is often asked, and so the author has included it in reference to Augustine's argument.

4. As Vernon Bourke explains in his translation notes, "Still under the influence of Manichaeanism, Augustine pictured God as limited only on one side, by the opposing Principle of Evil. He thought that the Catholic teaching required one to picture God as limited on all sides by the shape of the human body of Christ. The Manichaeans regarded the Incarnation as anthropomorphism" (121).

5. Some scholars, such as Kathleen Dubs, have argued elsewhere about Boethian notions of free will in the works of Tolkien. Dubs' argument, as outlined in "Providence, Fate, and Chance: Boethian Philosophy in *The Lord of the Rings*," explores the complex relationships between fate, providence, and chance and their relationships with free will and choice as they relate to Boethius' *Consolation of Philosophy* and *The Lord of the Rings*

(Chance 8). She ultimately argues that the seeming contradictions that arise among these concepts can be resolved "by following Boethius in distinguishing providence, which orders the universe; fate, the temporal manifestation of that order; chance, of which we are unaware; and of course, freedom of will, which operates as part of this providential order" (Dubs 141). Such an argument is interesting and would be worth pursuing in an analysis of *The Silmarillion*, but is too large for the scope of this essay.

    6. Tolkien often borrowed stories from fairy tales and mythology and wove them into his work. The reference to Lúthien's long hair is similar to the tale of Rapunzel by the Brothers Grimm.

    7. Interestingly, hope is also what separates Beren and Lúthien from two classical tales that may have partly influenced Tolkien in the writing of his great love story: "Pyramus and Thisbe" and "Orpheus and Eurydice," both of which Ovid recounted in his *Metamorphoses*. Pyramus and Thisbe were two lovers forbidden to see each other by their parents, so they spoke with each other secretly through chinks in the wall separating the family properties. They decide to meet secretly and run away together. While Thisbe waits for Pyramus, a lioness arrives, and Thisbe flees. The lioness, who has just been hunting, tears at Thisbe's veil, which has been left behind, with her bloody mouth. When Pyramus later arrives, he sees the bloody veil, assumes that Thisbe is dead, and kills himself (Ovid 76–79). Pyramus had no hope that Thisbe might be alive, and he had no hope that he might find love again with another, so he killed himself, which of course took away Thisbe's hope as well. Thisbe shows up and kills herself after seeing his corpse. In the story of Orpheus and Eurydice, Eurydice dies of a snake bite and goes to the underworld. Orpheus, inconsolable, follows her with the hope that his beautiful singing might sway Pluto and Proserpina, the King and Queen of the Underworld to let her live again. Much like Mandos, Pluto and Proserpina are moved to pity, and grant his wish, but leave him with the admonition that he must not look at her until they return to the surface. Orpheus fails in this task and Eurydice returns to the Underworld forever (Ovid 225–228). Although Ovid does not indicate it, other versions of the myth imply that Orpheus does not entirely trust Pluto and Proserpina, and this lack of trust, and perhaps the lack of hope that he will have his wish come true, ultimately causes his quest to fail, and he loses Eurydice a second time.

Works Cited

Bourke, Vernon J., trans. *Saint Augustine: The Confessions*. The Fathers of the Church Series. Washington, DC: Catholic University of America Press, 1953.

Carpenter, Humphrey. *Tolkien: A Biography*. Boston: Houghton Mifflin, 1977.

Chadwick, Henry, trans. *The Confessions of Saint Augustine*. Oxford: Oxford University Press, 1991.

Chance, Jane. "Introduction: A 'Mythology for England?'" In *Tolkien and the Invention of Myth*. Ed. Jane Chance. Lexington: University Press of Kentucky, 2004, 1–16.

"Consonance and Dissonance." Wikipedia. 29 April 2007. http://en.wikipedia.org/wiki/Consonance_and_dissonance.

Deane, Herbert A. *The Political and Social Ideas of St. Augustine*. New York: Columbia University Press, 1963.

"Dissonance." *The New Grove Dictionary of Music and Musicians. Volume VII: Dan tranh to Eques*. 2nd ed. Ed. Stanley Sadie. New York: Macmillan, 2001, 380.

Dubs, Kathleen E. "Providence, Fate, and Chance: Boethian Philosophy in *The Lord of the Rings.*" In *Tolkien and the Invention of Myth*. Ed. Jane Chance. Lexington: University Press of Kentucky, 2004, 133–142.

Flieger, Verlyn. *Splintered Light: Logos and Language in Tolkien's World*. Kent, OH: Kent State University Press, 2002.

Genesis. *The Holy Bible*. Revised Standard Version. New York: American Bible Society, 1970.

Kocher, Paul M. *A Reader's Guide to* The Silmarillion. Boston: Houghton Mifflin, 1980.

Ovid. *The Metamorphoses*. Trans. A.D. Melville with an introduction and notes by E.J. Kenney. Oxford: Oxford University Press, 1986, 76–79, 225–228.

Tolkien, J.R.R. *The Silmarillion*. Ed. Christopher Tolkien. Boston: Houghton Mifflin, 1977, 15–22, 162–187, 198–226.

"Worthy of a Song": Memory, Mortality and Music

Amy M. Amendt-Raduege

The moment Gollum and the Ring fall into the fires of Orodruin marks a profound change in the tone of *The Lord of the Rings*. Obviously, the Ring's destruction signals the end of Sauron's reign and heralds the dawn of the Age of Men, but the repercussions of these changes extend well beyond sociopolitical connotations. Until the Ring is destroyed, the peoples of Middle-earth have been primarily backward-looking, remembering the great exploits of heroes past and lamenting what has been lost or must be sacrificed in the long war against Sauron. But when Frodo's task is completed, the emphasis shifts. No longer are the songs and stories focused on preventing further decay, but on preserving memories of the present for the future. The characters, especially Sam, shift from seeing themselves as participants in an historical event to being historical figures in their own right. Increasingly, they see the songs that will be made of their deeds as the means by which their memories will be transmitted to future generations. Because they link past, present, and future, songs free their subjects from the restraints of time, and thus become another vehicle for the discussion of what Tolkien himself described as the real theme of *The Lord of the Rings*: death and immortality.[1] Although much has been said regarding the physical immortality of some of the races of Middle-earth, there has been remarkably little on the symbolic immortality achieved in song. The songs and stories of Middle-earth, however, promote immortality in a different form: they serve as foci for communal commemoration, and thus locate immortality within culture itself.

Of course, such an idea is nothing new. One of the earliest and most instinctive ways of commemorating the dead is simply by telling stories about them. Many of the earliest texts of Western literature, beginning with the *Epic of Gilgamesh*, represent this ancient belief, transmitting the deeds of ancient heroes first in oral form, and then later through writing. Thus, "literature is culture's memory, not as a simple recording device but as a body of commemorative actions."[2] Some scholars have even argued that all literature is commemorative, recording the memory of departed heroes, lost cultures, and eras of human history that have otherwise faded into oblivion. But songs and stories of the past, especially in pre-literate cultures, keep the dead always present, always available, always living. For centuries, history was transmitted not through written records — though written records and oral histories often functioned in parallel — but through songs and stories, spread throughout Europe by *scops* and bards who kept the memories of the past alive. The poets of the past, according to their own testimony, served as "the custodians of folk-memory," keeping the histories of heroes and of peoples of the past alive.[3] In *Widsith*, the poet makes this function clear:

> Forþon ic mæg singan ond secgan spell,
> mænan fore mengo in meoduhealle
> hu me cynegode cystum dohten.[4]
>
> ["Therefore I will sing, and tell my tale, sing before
> the company in the meadhall how noble men honored
> me with their gifts."]

Clearly, the poet's function is not only to tell clever stories or repeat old tales: he also determines whose stories will be told. It was necessary, therefore, for warriors to accomplish something significant enough to be worthy of a song: it was their best hope for immortality.

Almost all warrior societies put emphasis on the value of deeds and honor, but in the post-conversion recording of Germanic stories in particular, the question of the afterlife became increasingly important. Because the heroes commemorated in these stories were pre–Christian, their ultimate fate in the afterlife was uncertain. Would God welcome even pagan heroes into Heaven? If not, then surely the best hope of immortality for their pagan ancestors was to ensure that their deeds would be remembered — a sentiment made clear by Beowulf himself:

> "Ure æghwylc sceal ende gebidan
> worolde lifes; Wyrce se þe mote

domes ær deaþe;   þæt bið drihtguman
unlifgendum   æfter selest" [*Beowulf ll.* 1386–1389].

["Each one of us must live to see the end of life of the world; he who may might achieve glory before death; that is best for a man after he is dead."]

    The monks and scribes of medieval England, then, must have understood that speaking and writing the stories down preserved them, allowing the memories of past generations to be transmitted to the future, so that the deeds of their ancestors need not be completely forgotten. They carried on the work of the *scops* and bards before them, albeit in a different form. Much of the old heroic tradition was already fading by the time of the *Beowulf*-poet, as Tolkien himself pointed out,[5] replaced by other forms of storytelling and other preferred genres of writing. The anonymous poets of the Anglo-Saxon corpus seem to have felt, as Tolkien thought the *Beowulf*-poet did, that their heathen ancestors were not *automatically* worthy of perdition. If nothing else, the raw courage with which the heroes of old faced their deaths was worthy of commemoration, and if the poets could not assure such heroes their place in heaven, they could at least assure them of their place in history.

    The same sentiment appears throughout the Anglo-Saxon corpus as we now have it. The narrators of the poems themselves often speak of winning *lof* and *dom* (commonly translated as "fame" and "glory") as necessary for ensuring some form of immortality. But as Tolkien pointed out, *lof* became associated with the ideas of heaven and the celestial choirs, while *dom* flowed into ideas of judgment, especially over judgments of the dead[6] (as in our modern word "doomsday"). Both *lof* and *dom* thus carry within them overtones of the afterlife, especially an afterlife determined by what glories can be achieved in this life. The necessity of *lof* and *dom* is particularly prevalent in *Beowulf*, but frequently appears in other poems, especially the Exeter Book elegies: *The Wanderer, The Seafarer, Widsith,* and *Deor.* Typically, an elegy is defined in relation to the past, a song or poem which is marked by "a contemplation of a satisfying and favourable past now lost to a speaker who is exiled or dislocated within an unhappy present,"[7] quite often with the tacit anticipation of an equally unhappy future. The elegies are also concerned with mortality itself, with the transience of life and the inevitability of death, and the hope that one's own

"Worthy of a Song" (Amendt-Raduege)

life might be esteemed by future generations. *The Seafarer,* for instance, repeats the same sentiment found in Beowulf, that

> Forþon bið eorla gehwam æftercweþendra
> lof lifgendra lastworda betst [*ll.* 72–3].

> ["Therefore for every man praise from those who speak of him afterwards, from the living, is the best memorial."]

The famous poet Cynewulf was even more direct. He knew quite well that writing such poems could ensure his name would be remembered, and says so directly in *The Fates of the Apostles*:

> Her mæg findan foreþances gleaw,
> se ðe hine lysteð leoðgiddunga,
> hwa þas fitte fegde

> ["here the one wise in thought, the one who enjoys the recitation of poems, may discover who wrote this song"]

Just to be sure future readers of his poem get the point, he then proceeds to hedge his bets by spelling out his name in runes, becoming one of the earliest English authors to ensure his own immortality by signing his work.

So it is that remembering the names and deeds of those who died remains important, to us as to the Anglo-Saxons before us. If "memory was the sign of a good name" in the Middle Ages, as Paul Binski suggests,[8] it is scarcely less so today. As the heirs of this great tradition, we still "sing the praises" of people we admire, or lament the sacrifice of the "unsung heroes" who fell nameless in battle. And we still speak of being "immortalized in song" or "famed in song and story." We even long for the "glory days" of youth, when life was fresh and the strength of youth still made unlikely events seem possible. Nowadays, the terms "song" and "story" have bifurcated, but this distinction is a modern one: songs are but poems set to music, and music and poetry did not become separate entities until the advent of sixteenth-century print culture.[9] Certainly the Anglo-Saxons seem to have made no such distinction; words such as *leoð* and *fit*— which appeared in the verses given earlier—can be translated as "song" *and* "story." It is a commonplace among singers that all songs tell a story, and a commonplace of storytelling to underscore important parts of the story with music—a technique used by Anglo-Saxons *scops* and modern movie-makers, and one employed by Tolkien as well. In *The Lord of the Rings*, "glory" and "fame" repeatedly appear in association with song and story. Although we as readers first encounter the songs of Middle-earth as poetry, Tolkien is always careful to remind us that we are, in fact, reading a song, even if we cannot hear the music.

The songs and stories of Middle-earth, then, tell us something significant about its themes, both about what is remembered and what is worth remembering. Each of the races of Middle-earth sing songs, and the songs they sing reveal vital elements about their cultures. Hobbits sing of home and comfort; Dwarves sing of treasure and mighty cities under mountains; and Elves, intriguingly, sing of loss and memory. A significant number of the elegies we hear in *The Lord of the Rings* are Elvish in origin, even though the Elves are meant to be immortal within the confines of the world. But their longevity is the very cause of their grief: since they are not meant to die, when death actually does occur, the anguish and agony of those left behind is both heightened and prolonged. Mortals recognize that death is a natural if unwelcome consequence of life; Elves do not. Death and loss thus form an unlikely link between the various peoples of Middle-earth; everyone, even the Elves, can understand what it's like to lose someone. The songs thus provide access to a communal memory of a heroic but vanished past, and the excerpts we hear amplify this theme. Just as in *Beowulf*, where "*dom* and the stories that bestow, preserve and transmit it are depicted as the threads that stitch together the fabric of society,"[10] the songs of Middle-earth hold *its* story together, connecting all the seemingly disparate events into a coherent whole: all stories, every story, are but echoes of the vast history of Middle-earth, of which *The Lord of the Rings* itself is only a part. So we hear of the fall of the Elven king Gil-galad from a hobbit and the loss of Nimrodel from an Elf, the glories of Khazad-dûm in Durin's Day from a Dwarf and the accomplishments of Beren and Lúthien from a Man. These songs, representing the various kindreds of Middle-earth, thus serve the trifold purpose of commemoration, consolation and communion, and their subjects cross all barriers of culture, race, and even time itself.

But if one's name is going to be remembered in song, one must first accomplish something commendable. For "no matter how bravely men die, they do not achieve heroic stature unless they sacrifice themselves for some purpose which readers can recognize as significant and worthy."[11] Fortunately, whatever other obstacles Frodo and Sam must overcome, *that* is not one of them. Everyone knows that the hobbits' quest is heroic — except, perhaps, the hobbits themselves. What the others see as a noble undertaking, the hobbits see as bare necessity — to do what they must, because no one else is able. They have at the outset no real conception that their undertaking might win them lasting fame, no ideas of winning *lof* or *dom*. That will come later. Like the narrators of the elegies, they see themselves primarily as exiles, increasingly cut off by bitter circumstance from home, comfort and fellowship. Much of their journey recalls the attitude of the narrator of *The Wanderer* or *The Seafarer*: looking back on brighter days, and viewing all heroic deeds as being behind them. For Frodo and Sam, memories of home and comfort and fellowship lie more or less literally behind them: their backs are to Gondor and Rohan.

And it is in Rohan that the ideals of the heroic elegy are most clearly expressed. Perhaps this is not surprising; the Riders of Rohan bear a strong resemblance to Anglo-Saxon culture, although as Tom Shippey notes the Rohirrim "are not to be equated with the Anglo-Saxons of history, but with those of poetry, or legend."[12] Even before we meet them, the intense connection between the culture of the Rohirrim and their songs is accented. Aragorn describes them as a culture that preserves its culture entirely in songs, which are often sung, but never written.[13] Songs serve a vital role in the culture of Rohan: they transmit cultural memory, call warriors to action, inspire courage, pose riddles, and mourn the fallen — all roles also fulfilled by surviving Anglo-Saxon texts. In fact, the opening stanzas of the Lament of the Rohirrim, sung when the diminished company of Aragorn, Legolas, Gimli and Gandalf approaches Edoras, famously parallels strophe 92 from *The Wanderer*:

Hwær cwom mearg? Hwær cwom mago? Hwær cwom maþþumgyfa?
Hwær cwom symbla gesetu? Hwær sindon seledreamas? [*ll*. 92–93].

[Where has gone the horse? Where has gone the warrior? Where has gone the giver of treasures?
Where has gone the banquet-place? Where have gone the joys of the hall?]

The "Lament for the Rohirrim" begins much the same way, recalling the glories of warrior-life now long past:

Middle-earth Minstrel

Where now the horse and the rider? Where is the horn that was blowing?
Where is the helm and the hauberk, and the bright hair flowing?
Where is the hand on the harpstring, and the red fire glowing?[14]

This song is a clear indication of the oral tradition whereby the Rohirrim transmit their history; the Lament commemorates Eorl the Young, the great hero of ancient Rohan and the founder of their royal house. The poet of Rohan who composed these lines, unlike Cynewulf, has long been forgotten, but because of his song, the memory of Eorl is alive and well: men still sing of him in the evening.[15] Like Beren and Lúthien, Nimrodel, Gil-galad or Durin, Eorl has achieved "that immortality which belongs to elegy."[16] Not for nothing is it a poet of *Rohan* who, long after the battle, composes the elegy which mourns the fallen of Pelennor Fields, listing fourteen of the most notable dead by name.

Perhaps because he is an old man and close to death, Théoden in particular recognizes the importance of song to his people. It is he, for instance, who gives voice to the realization that when the songs fade, knowledge passes also. When he hears of the Ents, he reacts not with scorn or disbelief, but with wonder and with sorrow. He realizes at once that there are songs that tell of such marvels as walking, talking trees, but they are slowly being lost, relegated to the nursery instead of regarded as necessary.[17] He grieves that things he thought existed only in song might soon be extinguished except in song. But he also voices the hope that, perhaps, his deeds will be significant enough to be cast into verse. During the Battle of Helm's Deep, he asks Aragorn to ride with him against the Orcs, saying that they will either cleave a path, or "make such an end as will be worth a song."[18] Théoden does not die in that battle, of course, but goes on to lead his people to their victory in Gondor, and winds up with not one song, but three.

For the Rohirrim, then, singing is a serious business, and they quite clearly recognize songs as an appropriate means of sharing and preserving communal memory. The hobbits, however, apparently have no such tradition, no elegies. We are told of walking-songs and supper-songs, adventure songs and bath-songs, but if they sing funeral songs or histories, Tolkien does not mention them. Pippin tells Denethor that hobbits rarely sing of anything more terrible than foul weather; most of their songs, he says, are about things that make them laugh, or about food and drink.[19]

"Worthy of a Song" (Amendt-Raduege)

So it takes them quite some time to start thinking of the events of their own times as being worthy of a song, and even longer before they begin to express the hope that their own actions might be deemed worthy of remembrance.

Not surprisingly, it is Sam, the lover of songs and tales, who first makes the connection between song and memory. In his slow, methodical way, he first realizes that the adventures of the tales that really matter are not sought, but destined. What wins a hero *lof* or *dom* is perseverance, even (or perhaps especially) in the face of overwhelming odds, even when the end is in doubt, even when death itself is all but certain. And finally, Sam realizes that what he and Frodo are doing is significant enough in itself to be worthy of a song, and consoles himself with the thought that they, too, might be remembered.[20]

Once Sam has given voice to this idea, it stays with him. From that point forward, he repeatedly notes parts of their journey that might be dubbed worthy of a song. So when Frodo defeats Shelob, albeit temporarily, Sam's comment is that the Elves would make a song of it, if they ever heard the tale.[21] He likewise wonders if the Elves might make a song of his battle with the Orcs just outside Cirith Ungol, though he dubs the escape from the Tower "too long to make a song about."[22] And he consoles himself, at the end of it all, with the wish that perhaps future generations will listen to the tale of Nine-Fingered Frodo and the Ring of Doom.

But Sam also realizes that, if Sauron wins, there will be no more songs.[23] If, as George Jellinek said, "The history of a people is found in its songs," Sauron's victory represents an annihilation more thorough than mortality itself. For whatever one's personal beliefs might be, there is a kind of comfort in the notion that, at the very least, one's memory will be sustained. But if Sauron wins, that avenue too will be cut off. Especially if the purpose of such songs is to convey a kind of immortality, then the absence of such songs implies another kind of death, a death more horrible even than physical death, because it destroys all hope of a continued existence. Sauron's victory means utter abnegation, not just of freedom or civilization, but of even the *memory* of freedom and civilization. It consigns the great heroes of the past to oblivion, and the great accomplishments of the present to insignificance. Communal memory will be destroyed. There will be no more songs, no more remembering: it will be as if history itself had never been.

Middle-earth Minstrel

So it is natural that, with Sauron's defeat, the peoples of Middle-earth commit themselves to ensuring that the accomplishments of their times will not be forgotten. The text becomes a kind of inverted elegy: no longer lamenting the losses of the past, but concerned with preserving the record of present events for future generations. The glory of the present is captured in song, word and stone, to live on in days yet to come. The music of mortality and transient glory gives way to the music of mirth and abiding hope; from the moment Frodo wakes up in Ithilien, songs of rejoicing fill the air. In the fulfillment of Sam's wish, he and Frodo actually hear a minstrel sing "Nine-Fingered Frodo and the Ring of Doom." Back in Minas Tirith, Faramir tells Éowyn that she has won fame that will not be forgotten,[24] and Ioreth gossips that Gandalf promised her that men would long remember her words.[25] And during Aragorn's reign, the city itself is made even more beautiful than it has ever been, so lovely that even after the end of the Third Age "it preserved the memory and the *glory* of the years that were gone"[26] (emphasis mine). For a time, the story is suffused with joy, and the thought of all that has gone by falls away.

For a time. But an inverted elegy is still an elegy, filled with the sense that *lif is læne* and all things in this world must past away. The Ents, the Elves, and the Dwarves all know that their time on Middle-earth is ending; a new age has begun. Aragorn's marriage to Arwen, for instance, marks the reunification of the two branches of Eärendil's house, but it also signals the end of the Elves' time in Middle-earth. Éomer becomes King of the Mark in the shadow of Théoden's death, and Frodo himself, having suffered so greatly, can no longer find peace or comfort on Middle-earth. More poignantly still, the characters all recognize that no matter how great or significant their actions might be, the time will come when the music will falter and the tales will fall silent. Against that time, they take every precaution to ensure that some part of their legacy will remain. Thus, in addition to the minstrel's song, the momentous events of the Third Age are carefully recorded. It is not without purpose that Frodo and Bilbo set their memories, including the songs, down in a book, hoping against hope that writing them down will preserve them, untarnished, farther into the future. The last thing Frodo says to Sam is both prophetic and prescriptive, reminding his former gardener to read the Red Book, and so keep alive the memory of the past so that the hobbits might love their beloved home all the more. And then, because their part in the song is over, he and the

"Worthy of a Song" (Amendt-Raduege)

Elves and Gandalf depart forever over the Sea. "For the Third Age was over, and the Days of the Rings were passed, and an end was come of the story and song of those times."[27]

But the story does not end there. Sam, Merry, and Pippin return to the Shire, and we know that they did keep alive the memory of the events that ended the Third Age, telling the tales and singing the songs, and passing them on to their children. The story was also preserved in the Red Book of Westmarch, wherein the old songs were so carefully set, until Tolkien "discovered" them ages later. And for the millions of us who have read and loved *The Lord of the Rings*, the memory of Frodo's adventures stays with us long after we have set the physical text aside. It is even possible, through Donald Swann's collection, to hear the music of Middle-earth. Through song and story, we ourselves keep alive the history and memory of these times that never were alive—as long as our part of the story goes on.

Notes

1. J.R.R. Tolkien, *The Letters of J.R.R. Tolkien,* ed. Humphrey Carter (Boston: Houghton Mifflin, 2000), p. 246.

2. Renate Lachmann, "Cultural Memory and the Role of Literature," *European Review* 12 (2004): 165–178.

3. William Nash, "The Poetry Business," *A Departed Music: Old English Poetry* (Norfolk, England: Anglo-Saxon, 2006), p. 9–26.

4. "Widsith." The Labyrinth: Resources for Medieval Studies. Georgetown University. 4 June 2009. *byrinth/library/oe/texts/a3.11.html.*

5. J.R.R. Tolkien, "Beowulf: The Monsters and the Critics," *The Monsters & The Critics and Other Essays.* Ed. Christopher Tolkien. (New York: HarperCollins, 1988), p. 51.

6. *The Monsters and the Critics*, p. 37.

7. Melanie Heyworth. "Nostalgic Evocation and Social Privilege in the Old English Elegies." *Studia Neophilologica* 76 (2004): 3–11. 22 April 2006, from , 3.

8. Paul Binski, "Introduction: The Roots of Medieval Death Culture," *Medieval Death: Ritual and Representation.* (Ithaca, NY: Cornell University Press, 1996), p. 22.

9. Jody Enders, "Music, Delivery, and the Rhetoric of Memory in Guillaume de Mauchat's Enders Remedie de Fortune." *PMLA* 107.3 Special Topic: Performance (May 1992), p. 450.

10. Roy M. Liuzza, "Beowulf: Monuments, Memory, History," *Readings in Medieval Texts: Interpreting Old and Middle English Literature.* Ed. David Johnson and Elaine Treharne (Oxford: Oxford University Press, 2005), p. 95.

11. Fred C. Robinson, "God, Death and Loyalty in the Battle of Maldon." *J.R.R. Tolkien, Scholar and Storyteller: Essays in Memoriam.* Ed. Mary Salu and Robert T. Farrell (Ithaca, NY: Cornell University Press, 1979), p. 89.

12. Tom Shippey, *The Road to Middle-earth: How J.R.R. Tolkien Created a New Mythology.* Rev. and expanded edition (Boston: Houghton Mifflin, 2003), p. 124.

13. J.R.R. Tolkien, *The Lord of the Rings* (Boston: Houghton Mifflin, 1994), p. 420.
14. Ibid., p. 497.
15. Ibid.
16. Raymond Grant, "Beowulf and the World of Heroic Elegy," *Leeds Studies in English* 8 (1975), p. 68.
17. Tolkien, *Lord of the Rings*, p. 537.
18. Ibid., p. 527.
19. Ibid., pp. 788–9.
20. Ibid., p. 697.
21. Ibid., p. 705.
22. Ibid., p. 890.
23. Ibid., p. 718
24. Ibid., p. 943.
25. Ibid., p. 945.
26. Ibid., p. 947
27. Ibid.,. 1006.

Works Cited

Beowulf: An Edition with Relevant Shorter Texts. Eds. Bruce Mitchell and Fred C. Robinson. Malden, MA: Blackwell, 1998.

Binski, Paul. "Introduction: The Roots of Medieval Death Culture." *Medieval Death: Ritual and Representation*. Ithaca, NY: Cornell University Press, 1996, 8–28.

Cynewulf. *The Fates of the Apostles*. In *Old and Middle English c. 890–c. 1400: An Anthology*. 2nd ed. Ed. Elaine Treharne. Malden, MA: Blackwell, 2004, 90–97.

Enders, Jody. "Music, Delivery, and the Rhetoric of Memory in Guillaume de Mauchat's Remedie de Fortune." *PMLA* 107.3 Special Topic: Performance (May 1992): 450–464.

Grant, Raymond. "Beowulf and the World of Heroic Elegy." *Leeds Studies in English* 8 (1975): 45–75.

Heyworth, Melanie. "Nostalgic Evocation and Social Privilege in the Old English Elegies." *Studia Neophilologica* 76 (2004): 3–11. Accessed 22 April 2006, www.jstor.org.

Jellinek, George. "The History of a People Is Found in Its Songs." Music Quotes. William S. Carson. 28 June 2006. 2 June 2009, http://www.public.coe.edu/~wcarson/music quotes.htm

Lachmann, Renate. "Cultural Memory and the Role of Literature." *European Review* 12 (2004): 165–178.

Luizza, Roy M. "Beowulf: Monuments, Memory, History." *Readings in Medieval Texts: Interpreting Old and Middle English Literature*. Ed. David Johnson and Elaine Treharne. Oxford: Oxford University Press, 2005, 91–108.

Nash, William. "The Poetry Business." *A Departed Music: Old English Poetry*. Norfolk, England: Anglo-Saxon, 2006, 9–26.

Robinson, Fred C. "God, Death and Loyalty in the Battle of Maldon." In *J.R.R. Tolkien, Scholar and Storyteller: Essays in Memoriam*. Ed. Mary Salu and Robert T. Farrell. Ithaca, NY: Cornell University Press, 1979, 76–98.

The Seafarer. In *A Guide to Old English*. 6th ed. Eds. Bruce Mitchell and Fred C. Robinson. Malden, MA: Blackwell, 2002, 276–282.

Shippey, T.A. *The Road to Middle-earth: How J.R.R. Tolkien Created a New Mythology.* Rev. and expanded edition. Boston: Houghton Mifflin, 2003.
Tolkien, J.R.R. "Beowulf: The Monsters and the Critics." In *The Monsters & the Critics and Other Essays.* Ed. Christopher Tolkien. New York: HarperCollins, 1988, 5–48.
_____. *The Letters of J.R.R. Tolkien.* Ed. Humphrey Carter. Boston: Houghton Mifflin, 2000.
_____. *The Lord of the Rings.* New York: Houghton Mifflin, 1994.
The Wanderer. In *A Guide to Old English.* 6th ed. Eds. Bruce Mitchell and Fred C. Robinson. Malden, MA: Blackwell, 2002, 268–275.
Widsith. The Labyrinth: Resources for Medieval Studies. Georgetown University. 4 June 2009. http://www8.georgetown.edu/departments/medieval/labyrinth/library/oe/texts/a3.11.html

"Tolkien Is the Wind and the Way": The Educational Value of Tolkien-Inspired World Music
Amy H. Sturgis

If musicians across the world have entered Middle-earth and made themselves comfortable in its landscape, this is because creator J.R.R. Tolkien, by exciting their imaginations and stirring their spirits, invited them into his world. Such an invitation was not altogether unintentional. In a letter to Milton Waldman probably written in 1951, Tolkien described the dream that he once had cherished for his Middle-earth literature as a loosely-connected cycle of storytelling. "I would draw some of the great tales in fullness, and leave many only placed in scheme, and sketched," he wrote. Those parts that he created would support the greater vision as a whole, he explained, "and yet leave scope for other minds and hands, wielding paint and music and drama" (Tolkien *Letters*).

Musicians ranked equally with painters and dramatists were among those he hoped would join him in fleshing out and populating Middle-earth. Although Tolkien later abandoned as ludicrous the dream of others joining him in such participatory storytelling, we can see from our later vantage point that it was inevitable that others would be moved by Tolkien's fiction to become, to use his terminology in his 1947 essay "On Fairy-Stories, "sub-creators" in their own right, exemplifying what was highest and noblest — perhaps even most sacred — in human nature via their personal acts of creativity. If Tolkien did not anticipate that such sub-creations would eventually take the forms of folksy country/western tunes, vehement power metal anthems, complex progressive rock epics, and defiant rap music, among others, well, we can hardly blame him.

"Tolkien Is the Wind and the Way" (Sturgis)

Tolkien himself, though not a musician, certainly appreciated the importance of music in building a three-dimensional fictional world. His Middle-earth works are full of descriptions of music and verses reflecting various languages, styles, and cultures. In *The Lord of the Rings*, for instance, he assigned to songs the work of key exposition (Aragorn's tale of Beren and Lúthien, and Bilbo's story of Eärendil, for example), symbolic acts (such as Treebeard's incorporation of Hobbits into the Ent taxonomy), and turning-points in the plotline (Sam's singing in Cirith Ungol and Frodo's reply, for example). We even have an idea of how Tolkien imagined some of these songs to sound; he sang a few of them a capella in his 1952 taped recording (now available from Caedmon) of selections from *The Hobbit* and *The Lord of the Rings*, and Donald Swann's 1967 composition *The Road Goes Ever On: A Song Cycle*, endorsed by Tolkien, incorporates what Swann learned of the author's personal musical inspirations, such as the "Gregorian chant" model for Galadriel's "Namárië."

In an upper-division college course "J.R.R. Tolkien in History, Political Thought, and Literature," developed and taught at Belmont University, the author uses Tolkien's 1952 recordings and Donald Swan's sanctioned compositions to help students analyze Tolkien's understanding of his creations. A stark contrast is evident, for instance, in the rustic tune Tolkien provides for "Sam's Rhyme of the Troll," fit for any working-class pub sing-along, and the somber liturgical sound assigned to the Elves in Donald Swann's "Namárië." One is humble, informal, and cheerful, the other aloof, mysterious, even heavenly. Fruitful discussions about the nature of Hobbits and Middle-earth's Firstborn inevitably follow from juxtaposing the two songs.

Yet Tolkien's word on the subject of music is but the first step in a longer journey involving art, interpretation, and popular culture. Just as one reads scholarship by Tolkien authorities to provide new analytical windows through which to view *The Hobbit*, *The Lord of the Rings*, *The Silmarillion*, *The Adventures of Tom Bombadil*, and "Bilbo's Last Song," so the author and her students listened to selections from the immense and diverse body of Tolkien-inspired world music for fresh insights into Middle-earth. The author does not pretend to be a music scholar, but the goal is not to judge the songs on their individual merits as art, but instead to utilize the different lenses they offer to see Tolkien's writings in new ways. The immensely thorough Tolkien Music List website (www.tolkien-music.com) has proven to be an invaluable resource for exploring Tolkien-inspired world music. Such music not only reflects the importance of the first sub-creator and minstrel himself, but it also serves to assist, illuminate, and challenge experiences of his texts, and thus it is ideal for use in the classroom.

Adaptations

While Tolkien's Middle-earth has inspired a number of compelling instrumental compositions, from Johan de Meij's *The Lord of the Rings: Symphonie No. 1* to David Arkenstone's *Music Inspired by Middle-earth*, the author focused on two particular kinds of music in her course: adaptations, or songs that employ Tolkien's original verses as lyrics; and what one could term "sub-sub-creations," or songs that feature original lyrics based on Tolkien's characters and themes. The fact that these songs include lyrics that can be read and studied both while and after listening to the music makes them especially amenable to class discussions.

If students have been exposed to Tolkien-related music before the class, apart from the random Led Zeppelin song, it is likely that this exposure can be credited to one of the dramatizations of Tolkien's work. Here the survey begins. The first music composed for a successful adaptation of Tolkien's writing appeared in the original soundtrack to the Rankin/Bass animated film *The Hobbit* in 1977. Many of the songs include Tolkien's original verses. Of these, "In the Valley, Ha! Ha!" is perhaps the most interesting from a pedagogical perspective. Performed in a deliberately upbeat, folk-inspired style by singer-songwriter Glenn Yarbrough, the happy-go-lucky, laughing verses present a very different interpretation of the Rivendell Elves than, for example, Ted Nasmith's art or Peter Jackson's films. The playful, childlike humor underscored by the tune communicates a carefree security and easy affection that often surprises students, who expect Elves to be grave, aloof, and dignified. Students' expectations are often founded not on *The Hobbit*, but on *The Lord of the Rings*: this song provides a springboard for discussion of the differences between *The Hobbit* and *The Lord of the Rings*, from their themes and intended audiences, to their narrative structures; moreover, it offers an opportunity to talk about the publication history of how *The Lord of the Rings* followed from *The Hobbit*, and what changes Tolkien made in later editions of *The Hobbit* so it would better fit with its "sequel" books.

The 1981 BBC Radio Drama of *The Lord of the Rings* yielded excellent music composed and conducted by Stephen Oliver. The most exceptional of these is "Bilbo's Last Song," which is particularly significant because most students have not been exposed to its verses, as the poem was published separately from Tolkien's other Middle-earth works. The haunting song, made more ethereal by the voice of Jeremy Vine, the young treble singer, captures the mix of resignation and hope Bilbo feels while leaving Middle-earth for the Undying Lands. His conviction that he will find longed-for peace and respite highlights both the reward he will receive for his heroic act of relinquishing the Ring willingly, and the price he already has paid for being a Ringbearer for so many years. This song inspires talk about the characteristics of Bilbo as a hero (in both *The Hobbit* and *The Lord of the Rings*), the nature of sacrifice and healing depicted in *The Lord of the Rings*, and the meaning of the Grey Havens and the Undying Lands — and, by implication, Tolkien's presentation of mortality and immortality. The wistful lyrics, partnered with the funeral tune, invite a question certain to stir discussion: Does Tolkien's conclusion to *The Lord of the Rings* provide readers with a "happy ending?"

Howard Shore's 2003 score for Peter Jackson's *The Lord of the Rings: The Return of the King* film uproots and reinterprets one of Tolkien's verses from the original *The Fellowship of the Ring* book to create the song "The Steward of Gondor" (www.howardshore.com). In Tolkien's novel, Frodo Baggins, Samwise Gamgee, and Pippin Took sing an innocent walking song as they make their way from Hobbiton. The words seem happy enough. Howard Shore transplants the song to Gondor, however, where Pippin (portrayed by Billy Boyd) sings it at Denethor's command, while the camera contrasts the Hobbit's gentle voice and horrified expression with scenes of Denethor's violent attack of his meal and Faramir's near-suicidal charge against the enemy. Students are likely to be familiar with the visual context of this song in the film. Questioning why Shore chose this song in general, and only certain verses in particular, to pair with his images leads students to consider a number of issues related to cinematic storytelling versus print narrative, while comparing the very different worlds of The Shire and Gondor and what they represented both to Tolkien and to Jackson.

Middle-earth Minstrel

Other adaptations of Tolkien's verses, unrelated to dramatizations, also prove useful in teaching about Middle-earth. Many more exist than can be discussed here, but some deserve special merit. The Tolkien Ensemble, which hails from Denmark, released several single albums before collaborating with special guest Christopher Lee to release their 2006 collection *The Lord of the Rings: Complete Songs and Poems*, a four-CD set interpreting all of Tolkien's unabridged verses from *The Fellowship of the Ring* through *The Return of the King*. Playing excerpts from the various classical pieces provides an excellent opportunity to analyze the different peoples and places of Middle-earth. Why, for example, would The Tolkien Ensemble choose to represent the Hobbits with a guitar and the Elves with a harp, or Treebeard with a bass and Legolas with a tenor? How do such musical "characterizations" fit and amplify Tolkien's descriptions? Contrasting the sound of the original Elvish version of "Song of the Elves Beyond the Sea: Galadiel's Song of Eldamar" with the sound of the English "Song of the Elves Beyond the Sea, Translation: Galadriel's Song of Eldamar" additionally opens the door for dialogue about Tolkien's invented languages, their role in his creation of Middle-earth, and their relevance to the themes of his story.

In 1989, Canadian music scholar James A. Stark released his album *Songs of Middle-Earth*, which includes a classical interpretation of "Song of the Rings." Presented via tenor and harp, the rhyme captures a sense of formal, even ritualized narrative; as one student noted, it sounds like something one would imagine hearing in Elrond's Halls of Fire, where lore is communicated in the most artistic and polished — and Elvish — of ways. This inspires a discussion of how the students imagine Tolkien's cultures and settings, based on the evidence he provides in his texts. How would Rivendell, or Hobbiton, or Mordor sound? The Hobbitons from the Netherlands, by contrast with Stark, offer a rustic and pastoral tone in their 1996 album *Songs from Middle-Earth* (home.wxs.nl/~hobbiton). Their "Old Walking Song (The Road Goes Ever On)" does for Hobbits what Stark does for Elves. The Hobbitons even include sound effects in some of their songs, such as the thoroughly creepy "The Mewlips" from *The Adventures of Tom Bombadil*. Once again, this song exposes students to verses they may not have read; the addition of loathsome dripping, bubbling, and gurgling effectively illustrates the action as the listener encounters the repugnant and deadly creatures in their dank lair.

"Tolkien Is the Wind and the Way" (Sturgis)

Adaptations also underscore how global and multifaceted Tolkien's impact continues to be. "Of Amroth and Nimrodel" by Caprice from the Russian *Elvenmusic* (2001), and "Eärendil" by Andi Grimsditch from the Argentinian *The Tolkien Song Cycle, Vol. I* (2002), for instance, are dually instructive. First, they allow students to revisit key stories from Tolkien's verses in a very entertaining and moving manner. These tales are worth emphasizing; it is not uncommon for some students to skip these lengthy verse passages either because of their unfamiliar format, or the sense that they are distractions from the primary narrative. The stark otherworldliness of Caprice's "Of Amroth and Nimrodel," and the distinct, dramatic movements of Grimsditch's "Eärendil," however, command attention. Second, the significant contrast of these adaptations' musical styles reflects the wide reach (both artistic and geographic) of Tolkien's influence.

Additionally, adaptations can challenge and expand students' reading of a text. For example, some students find the character of Tom Bombadil in *The Lord of the Rings* to be a kind of jester figure, humorous and therefore easily discounted. Musical adaptations sometimes reinforce Bombadil's lunacy by creating bouncy, light tunes that trippingly play along his nonsensical singsong verses. "Tom Bombadil's Song (I)" by The Tolkien Ensemble is one such example. Italian artist Giuseppe Festa, however, focuses on a more serious side of the character and his purpose in "Tom Bombadil" from the 1999 album *Voices from Middle Earth* (www.lingalad.com). Choosing a slow, soothing rhythm and introducing natural sounds, such as the splash of water in a brook, Festa emphasizes the warmth and welcome Bombadil provides as he promises to go ahead of the weary travelers to light candles and open his door for their welcome. Festa's artistic choices focus attention on the safety of Bombadil's home, and by implication the dangers the Hobbits faced and will face on their journey. This Bombadil is wise and reassuring, the kind of character who could offer a safe haven where one could dream deep dreams, the type of creature who would not feel the pull of the Ring. Festa's interpretation of this song serves as a springboard for fruitful debates about who and what Tom Bombadil is, and why the Hobbits' interlude in his home is important to the larger story of *The Lord of the Rings*.

Sub-Sub Creations

Musical sub-sub-creations based on Tolkien's sub-creation of Middle-earth are so numerous that they present a daunting task to anyone who wishes to present a sampling to an audience of students, scholars, and/or fellow fans. One expects a band named The Tolkien Ensemble to perform Tolkien-related music, or an album titled *Voices from Middle-earth* to include songs about Middle-earth, but sub-sub-creators who compose new songs and verses inspired by Tolkien and his Middle-earth often do not advertise themselves so overtly. Only by inspecting Rush's 1975 album *Fly by Night* do we see that the song "Rivendell" is included (www.rush.com); we only learn Led Zeppelin's 1969 song "Ramble On" is an extended Tolkien reference when we listen closely to the second verse and hear about Gollum (see lyrics at www.led-zeppelin.com).

As a rule, because Tolkien-related songs are so numerous, the author focuses on musicians who have created entire theme albums in homage to Middle-earth for this portion of the course. There are a couple of exceptions to this rule, and these come from the category of parody. No class is complete without sampling the dubious delights of Leonard Nimoy's 1968 groovefest "The Ballad of Bilbo Baggins" from *The Two Sides of Leonard Nimoy*, a pop dance tune extolling the virtues of Bilbo's pipe and toes in a humorous fashion, and also pointing to the popularity of Tolkien after the release of *The Lord of the Rings* trilogy in paperback editions. The Great Luke Ski's 2003 "Stealing Like a Hobbit," a pastiche of rapper Eminem's songs "Cleaning Out My Closet" and "Lose Yourself," takes particular aim at fans of Peter Jackson's films: "I really gotta pee,/ Can we please have intermission? ... Will I prevail and survive or will the spider get me?/ I don't know: I haven't read through Book Two and Book Three!" (www.lukeski.com). By combining lyrics that alternately represent the point of view of Frodo, Arwen, Sam, and Gollum, with references to recent fantasy works such as the Harry Potter series and *Shrek*, The Great Luke Ski proves the ongoing relevance and popularity of Tolkien's Middle-earth thirty-five years after Leonard Nimoy first sang Bilbo's praises. The parodies are great fun for the class, and they also serve as an auditory palette cleanser before considering sub-sub-creations in depth.

On the whole, musical sub-sub-creations underscore similar lessons as musical adaptations of Tolkien's verses: specifically, that Tolkien inspired participatory storytelling through music, a global phenomenon that has spanned nearly half a century. Individually, musical sub-sub-creations may serve many of the same functions of fan fiction — that is, fiction written by Tolkien's readers and based on his writings. Some artists want to draw attention to a particular theme of Tolkien's work. Others seek to evoke a feeling, inviting the audience to experience Middle-earth. Some wish to explore the interior landscape of a character in order to uncover his or her motivations and emotions. Others wish to "fill in the gaps" and tell stories that tie together different threads of plot already woven in Tolkien's books.

The 1977 soundtrack to the Rankin/Bass film *The Hobbit* includes a folk-style song performed by Glenn Yarbrough entitled "Old Fat Spider." It relates a story that did not take place in Tolkien's book *The Hobbit*. According to the song, Bilbo, while defending the Dwarves from the spiders, encounters an old, decrepit spider in a tattered web that is nearly blind with age. Rather than attacking this harmless creature, Bilbo spares him, and even helps it obtain food for a meal. By telling an original story, the song underscores Bilbo's mercy, a key theme of *The Hobbit*, and one that proves to have profound reverberations in *The Lord of the Rings*. Listening to this song opens a class discussion about the idea of mercy in both books.

"Mithrandir," from Leonard Roseman's soundtrack to the 1978 Rankin/Bass film *The Lord of the Rings*, offers an interpretation of the song of mourning sung in Lothlórien by the Elves after the fall of Gandalf. The song begins softly, talking about the night and the day to come, and builds to a moving orchestral crescendo. Although they agree that the song stirs the emotions, students often are puzzled as to why "Mithrandir" leads with a children's chorus, because they do not associate small children with the realm of Galadriel and Celeborn. This objection leads to a class dialogue about this artistic choice. Why represent Lothlórien with children's voices? The class considers the range of attributes associated with children's voices: innocence, purity, even heavenliness. How do these relate to the Elves? Might the fact that children are ageless, untainted by time, also play a role in this choice? Why? As the students analyze "Mithrandir," they gain new insights about Tolkien's understanding of the Elves and our own, as well as the creating challenges of communicating the experience and "feeling" of a place like Lothlórien.

Next the class moves to *The Silmarillion* with the German power metal band Blind Guardian and their 1998 album *Nightfall in Middle-Earth* (www.blind-guardian.com). This work retells the tragic story of the theft of the Silmarils, the Oath of Fëanor, and the Kinslaying, to the dawn of the Second Age. The driving energy of power metal, after the classic orchestration of "Mithrandir" and the rustic folk of "Old Fat Spider," offers a powerful contrast in style. Although one can assume that Tolkien was not a headbanger, the author often asks the class if this is nonetheless an appropriate sound to capture these stories from *The Silmarillion*. The students often answer in the affirmative. The music conveys rage and despair, which fits lyrics such as "The doom of the Noldor drew near/ The words of a banished king, 'I swear revenge!'" Not only does the song provide an excellent literacy test for the students, distilling a complex narrative and challenging them to identify all of the actors and actions to which it refers, but "Nightfall" also involves the students with the loss and desolation of the story — it is difficult to ignore the raw cry of "Our hearts full of hate, full of pride,/ How we screamed for revenge!" — and opens the door for additional exploration of Tolkien's understanding of The Fall.

Continuing the chronological survey of sub-sub-creations, next comes Kevin Henry's 2000 American country/western theme album *Bilbo's Great Adventure* (www.thehobbitcd.com). The immediate issue that comes to mind after hearing the song "Dared and Scared" is one of genre; just as one questions why artists would choose power metal to fit the violent action of *The Silmarillion*, one must consider why an artist would use the twang of traditional country/western music to complement the wholesome heroism of *The Hobbit*. Students often mention the rural, "small town" feel of the Shire, and how the country/western sound allows them to inhabit the story from Bilbo's point of view. The lyrics add to the "local boy makes good" message of the album, beginning by portraying Bilbo as an underdog character with whom it is easy to identify and empathize.

"The End of Summer: Galadriel's Song," from Bob Catley's 2001 British rock epic *Middle-earth*, is an excellent example of how a song may illumine Tolkien's texts for students (www.bobcatley.com). In fact, the author finds it difficult to limit herself to one song from *Middle-earth*, as many raise interesting questions of interpretation. "The Return of the Mountain King" compares the return of Thorin Oakenshield to the Lonely Mountain in *The Hobbit* with the return of Aragorn to Gondor in *The Lord of the Rings*, for example, and "The Fields That I Recall/ Stormcrow and Pilgrim" considers how Gandalf is viewed differently by individual characters, from Frodo to Gríma Wormtongue. "The End of Summer: Galadriel's Song," however, is a powerful rock ballad that students seem to especially like. Its lyrics seem to alternate between Celeborn's and Gimli's point of view, and appear to allude to Galadriel's exile as described in *The Silmarillion* as well as her Lothlórien experience as detailed in *The Lord of the Rings*. Galadriel's characterization leads to particularly productive discussions. As students explore these metaphors, they consider what it means in *The Lord of the Rings* for the age of the Elves to be waning, and why it matters that Galadriel knows she and her land will diminish if the Ring is destroyed, and yet she nevertheless chooses to support the Fellowship and their quest. The song invites them to look at Galadriel as a character, even as they consider the overarching theme of sacrifice.

Some sub-sub-creations allow listeners to enter the heads of characters to experience their motivations. "The Grey Havens" from the 2001 album *The Rings Project* by acoustic rock singer-songwriter Alan Horvath, gives students a glimpse of Frodo's emotional struggle as he prepares to leave The Shire for the last time: "Sam, I really hate to go,/ But the time has come for me/... I can sing of glory,/ Knowing that my people are free" (http://www.alanhorvath.com/). "Aníron" from Howard Shore's 2001 soundtrack to the film *The Lord of the Rings: The Fellowship of the Rings* gives insight into Aragorn's love for Arwen. Composed in Tolkien's Sindarin Elvish language, and performed by Enya, "Aníron" communicates Aragorn's enchantment and desire (www.howardshore.com). Such songs can be used effectively as role-playing exercises. If they are persuaded by the song, students usually gain more appreciation for the richness of the characters; if they challenge the songwriters' interpretations, they often are forced to return to the text and marshal evidence in defense of a different reading. Either outcome is productive.

Other sub-sub-creations offer "gap fillers," in that they relate stories that flesh out the narrative spaces where Tolkien remains silent. "Greenwood the Great (Shadowy Glades), from the 2001 album *Music Inspired by the Lord of the Rings* by Canadian band Mostly Autumn, does this by relating the story of how Greenwood the Great became Mirkwood, for example (www.mostly-autumn.com). Although the lyrics suggest Sauron's approach, the bulk of the storytelling is instrumental, as the ethereal, understated melody is overtaken by harsh, ominous disharmony. This leaves the transformation largely to the students' imagination, and they discuss the process by which a realm of Silvan Elves might have fallen under the shadow of Sauron's darkness, as well as what can be learned of Mirkwood's fate at the conclusion of the Third Age in Tolkien's writings.

A particularly stirring piece is "The King's Beer," from 2001's *The Middle-earth Album* by American progressive rockers Glass Hammer (www.glasshammer.com). This is the second of the band's Tolkien theme albums; the first, 1993's *The Journey of the Dunadan* retells *The Lord of the Rings* from Aragorn's perspective, and is noteworthy in particular for its exploration of Aragorn's feelings for Arwen in "The Way to Her Heart." The first half of *The Middle-Earth Album* depicts a live performance from the Prancing Pony pub at Bree, complete with clapping, stamping, and Dwarvish hecklers in the audience. The rowdy drinking song "The King's Beer" suggests what might have happened when Aragorn, no longer Strider, returned to visit his former haunt as King of Gondor. Rather than take revenge on those who treated him as an outcast, or lord his new title over the commoners of Bree, Aragorn proves himself a most egalitarian and humble sovereign, buying a round of drinks and joining in his companions' song: "Some kings may sip from a cup of gold,/ but a wooden mug is all I'll hold./" This puts students in the midst of Bree, as fellow audience members with Men and Hobbits and Dwarves, and allows them to discuss the atmosphere created by the song and how it fits their conceptions of the setting. The song also raises key questions about Aragorn's style of leadership and reign as king, which sends the class back to the texts to consider Gondor and its relationship with other lands in the Fourth Age.

The Brodbingnagian Bards' 2003 Celtic-influenced song "The Psychopathic, Chronic, Schizophrenic Gollum Blues" from *Memories of Middle-earth* would be at home at a Renaissance Faire (www.thebards.net). Written from Frodo's point of view, it describes how the Hobbit feels about being "hunted by a schizo,/ Be it Smeagol or Gollum," noting that the creature "leading me to Mordor,/ Wonders if Sam and I are gay." The many self-conscious anachronisms of the song, which describes the journey to the Undying Lands as an "Elven cruise," not only bring laughs, but also allows the class to discuss how *The Lord of The Rings* speaks to the twenty-first-century reader and translates into modern popular culture.

"Tolkien Is the Wind and the Way" (Sturgis)

Another self-consciously modern, or even postmodern, work is Hobbit's 2003 album *All for the One* (www.hobbitband.com). The American progressive rock band has been making Tolkien-related music since 1977, when their *Two Feet Tall* debuted. Their latest album includes songs that consider events depicted in *The Lord of the Rings* from different characters' points of view ("One More Time" from Bilbo's, "Whispers" from Gollum's, etc.). Nevertheless, in the middle of these interpretive works is a musical "aside" aimed directly at the audience, a song entitled "The Wind and The Way." This piece steps away from the album's larger narrative to encourage readers to let themselves go and enjoy Tolkien's fairy-story: "Go to a place called Middle-earth/ You'll never again be the same./ ... Get lost in the fantasy!/ You and I, comin' up the Greenway/ For Tolkien is the wind and the way...." In effect, the band pauses from the act of channeling the characters in order to exhort fellow fans to abandon themselves to the fantasy. "Please, don't awaken from this dreamin,'" they sing, promising "it waits for you and me/ In the story on the page." A whispered "Open the book!" challenges listeners to become readers. This song provides a perfect place to end the musical tour on which the author takes her class, as it reminds one clearly of the relationship between Tolkien's words and the songs that have been heard.

Conclusion

The author continually updates the playlist used for the class. The most recent additions at the time of this writing include the excellent 2005 album *In Elven Lands* by The Fellowship, a group of artists including Jon Anderson, Caitlin Elizabeth, Adam Pike, and others, and the latest downloads from the first Tolkien-related rappers in cyberspace, the Lords of the Rhymes (www.lordsoftherhymes.com). The constant production of new Tolkien-related albums and songs gives the phenomenon of Middle-earth-related world music a heritage of more than half a century, and proves that the recent celebration of Tolkien in popular culture is not exclusively tied to Peter Jackson's film trilogy. Sharing with students the fact that Tolkien has inspired artists in Italy and Russia and Canada and Argentina, as well as musicians who prefer folk and country/western and progressive rock and power metal, helps to underscore the wide reach and resonance of the

Middle-earth cycle. Using songs to introduce discussions about Tolkien's themes, characters, worlds, and storylines challenges students to think in imaginative and critical ways and bring new analytical tools to their reading of the texts. The author likes to think that Master Tolkien would approve.

Works Cited

Arkenstone, David. *Music Inspired by Middle-earth*. Neo Pacific, 2001.
Blind Guardian. *Nightfall in Middle-Earth*. Century Media, 1998.
Brobdingnagian Bards. *Memories of Middle-earth*. Gunn-McKee, 2003.
Caprice. *Elvenmusic*. Prikosnovenie, 2001.
Catley, Bob. *Middle-earth*. Now and Then Records, 2001.
The Fellowship. *In Elven Lands*. United States of Distribution, 2005.
Festa, Giuseppe. *Voices from Middle-earth*. Pongo Edizioni Musicali, 2001.
Glass Hammer. *Journey of the Dunadan*. Arion, 1993.
_____. *The Middle-earth Album*. Arion, 2001.
Grimsditch, Andi. *The Tolkien Song Cycle, Vol. I*. Andi Grimsditch, 2002.
Henry, Kevin. *Bilbo's Great Adventure*. Warm Weather Music, 2000.
Hobbit. *All for the One*. Midwest, 2003.
The Hobbitons. *Songs from Middle-Earth*. Ron Ploeg, Willem van Wordragen, and Gilles Tuinman, 1996.
Horvath, Alan. *The Rings Project*. Alan Horvath, 2001.
Laws, Maury, and Jules Bass, with Glenn Yarbrough. *The Hobbit* Original Soundtrack, Buena Vista, 1977.
Led Zeppelin. *Led Zeppelin II*. Atlantic, 1969.
Lords of the Rhymes, Official Website. Last visited 16 March, 2007. http://www.lordsoftherhymes.com.
Meij, Johan de. *The Lord of the Rings: Symphonie No. 1*. Atma Classique, 1998.
Mostly Autumn. *Music Inspired by the Lord of the Rings*. Classic Rock Legends, 2001.
Nimoy, Leonard. *The Two Sides of Leonard Nimoy*. Dot, 1968.
Oliver, Stephen. *The Lord of the Rings* Original Soundtrack to the BBC Radio Drama. 1979. Reissue. BBC, 2002.
Roseman, Leonard. *The Lord of the Rings* Original Soundtrack. 1978. Reissue. Fantasy, 1991.
Rush. *Fly By Night*. 1975. Reissue, Island/Mercury, 1997.
Shore, Howard. *The Lord of the Rings: The Fellowship of the Ring* Original Soundtrack. Warner/Reprise, 2001.
_____. *The Lord of the Rings: The Return of the King* Original Soundtrack. Warner/Reprise, 2003.
Ski, The Great Luke. *Worst Album Ever*. Luke Sienkowski, 2003.
Stark, James A. *Songs of Middle-Earth*. Prime Time Productions, 1989.
Swann, Donald. *The Road Goes Ever On and On: A Song Cycle*. New York: Ballantine, 1967.
Tolkien Ensemble, The. *The Lord of the Rings: Complete Songs and Poems*. Premiere Music, 2006.

Tolkien, J.R.R. *The J.R.R. Tolkien Audio Collection.* Caedmon, 2001.
_____. *Letters of J.R.R. Tolkien.* Ed. Humphrey Carpenter. Boston: Houghton Mifflin, 2000: 161.
_____. "On Fairy-Stories." In *The Tolkien Reader.* Ballantine, 1966, 33–99.
Tolkien Music List, Official Website. Last visited 16 March, 2007. http://www.tolkien-music.com

Liquid Tolkien: Music, Tolkien, Middle-earth, and More Music

David Bratman

Music in Tolkien's Life and Legendarium

Much has been written on the role of music in J.R.R. Tolkien's imaginary lands of Middle-earth, but less consideration has been given to the importance of music to Tolkien personally. Some writers even deny that music had any importance to him. Michael White in his biography of Tolkien writes, "He had little interest in music ... [it] seems to have been a blank area in his artistic tastes."[1]

White's book is, regrettably, a landmine of inaccurate and misleading statements, and this one is nonsense. Tolkien loved music; it was vitally important to him. This is obvious from his works alone, as well as from his declared love for music.[2] White bases his statement partly on Tolkien's known antipathy to the popular music of his adulthood[3]; but as Tolkien was equally antipathetic to many other cultural features of his time, the operative phrase is *of his time* and this says nothing about his interest in *music*. White also notes that Tolkien rarely attended concerts. For much of his life Tolkien could afford neither the time nor the money for frequent concerts, but Tolkien was also in his artistic tastes a connoisseur, and White has perhaps mistaken lack of quantity for lack of quality. The Tolkien home had a piano, and while he himself had no aptitude as a performer, his wife Edith was a pianist of considerable talent, so there was the opportunity for fine music-making at home. His tastes in piano music included the often-delicate miniatures of Frédéric Chopin.[4] And he had regular encounters with live music while attending Catholic Mass.

Tolkien's love for music is also reflected in his fiction. Turn to almost any chapter of *The Hobbit* or *The Lord of the Rings* and you will find poetry. And as often as not that poetry is described as being sung. The very first poem in *The Hobbit*, "Far over the misty mountains cold," is described as accompanied by a Dwarf orchestra of flutes, clarinets, fiddles, viols, harp and drum.[5]

If Middle-earth has a prehistoric or even a medieval setting, there are some amazing anachronisms and misfits here, especially the clarinets, an instrument not invented until the 18th century, but as ever in his fiction, Tolkien is more interested in effect than accuracy.[6] From here on, when I allude to the "actual" music of Middle-earth, I mean the music it is "calqued" on, to use Tom Shippey's term[7]; what subcreationally would be called "Middle-earth in translation," the way Tolkien actually imagined it, anachronisms and all; not the music of a hypothetical prehistoric civilization.

Tolkien makes no claims for the quality of the Misty Mountains poem he prints, but says it "is like a fragment of [the Dwarves'] song, if it can be like their song without their music."[8] That last clause makes it seem hopeless to try to reproduce what Tolkien imagined the music of Middle-earth should sound like. But, surprisingly, we do have a very good idea of this — or at least we do for some of it. When Sam stands up before Strider and the hobbits in the Trollshaws to present the tale of the Stone Troll, Tolkien says that he sings it "to an old tune."[9] When Tolkien read selections from *The Lord of the Rings* into George Sayer's tape recorder in 1952, most of the poems he recited in spoken voice, even if the text says the characters sang them. But this one, Tolkien himself sang, in words slightly different from the published version.[10]

Tolkien's voice is rough and untrained, but surely so was Sam's. The tune that Tolkien sings, George Sayer says in his liner notes to the LP release of the tapes, is "an old English folk-tune called The Fox and Hens." This is apparently a Birmingham variant tune — untranscribed in any folk-song field collection books this writer examined — for the folk-song better known as "The Fox and the Goose" or "The Fox Went Out on a Chilly Night." Certainly "The Stone Troll" scans identically to all the texts I have seen for "The Fox and the Goose"— the tale of a fox hunting down and devouring a goose with the same gusto as Sam's troll devotes to its bone — and thus can be sung to any of the various tunes known for it. Tolkien sings a major-key melody, which is thus not in the class usually called modal, but that is true of many traditional English folk tunes, including all of the southern English melodies Cecil Sharp collected for "The Fox and the Goose" from 1908 to 1914, and Tolkien's is very much in their style.[11] And this is appropriate for, as Tolkien observed, "the Shire ... is in fact more or less a Warwickshire village of about the period of the Diamond Jubilee,"[12] that is in 1897, when Tolkien was five and living in Sarehole, at a time when English villagers were still singing the folk songs that were to be collected by Cecil Sharp and his colleagues a few years later.

In various settings of "The Stone Troll" by Tolkien-inspired songwriters, a little American hillbilly twang may creep in, as in the fast, bouncy fiddle and jaws harp accompaniment to Brocelïande's setting of "The Man in the Moon Stayed Up Too Late."[13] This may seem incongruous, but it is not exactly inappropriate, for Appalachian songs are often astonishingly well-preserved variants of the English originals — and they too all have the air of English folk-songs.[14]

So Tolkien meant us to think of the hobbits as English country folk singing English folk songs. Which is why it was so disconcerting to go to Peter Jackson's *Fellowship of the Ring* movie and hear the hobbits depicted by music that is not English at all but neo–Celtic: composer Howard Shore's attempt at copies of Irish whistle and fiddle-and-accordion tunes in lush orchestral arrangements. Tolkien spent a lifetime differentiating English civilization from Celtic. He would have been deeply unhappy, to say the least, to have heard Irish music, and imitation Irish music at that, applied to his hobbits. If orchestral music is wanted for a hobbit film, some apt examples are offered by the actual folk song collectors among English composers, who based many compositions on their findings. Ralph Vaughan Williams's popular *Fantasia on Greensleeves*, whose middle section is a folk melody called "Lovely Joan," or Gustav Holst's *Somerset Rhapsody*, Op. 21 No. 2, employing the same melody for "A Rosebud in June" as used in Steeleye Span's arrangement on their electric-folk album *Below the Salt*, are works that Tolkien might have accepted as orchestral film music for hobbits. Some readers say they cannot hear the ethnic difference between this English music and Shore's neo–Celtic. But Tolkien could.

What about the Elves? There is more elven music in the "Silmarillion" tales than one might expect: in various tellings, Lúthien dances to a pipe unseen, and sings to sleep both Sauron and Morgoth, for instance; but few have attempted to re-create such music. The most prominent music is in the "Ainulindalë," which is discussed below.

For Elves in *The Lord of the Rings*, again we have Tolkien's own evidence, both from Sayer's tape recorder and as reported by Donald Swann, whose song cycle *The Road Goes Ever On* was the first authorized setting of Tolkien's poems to original music. "Professor Tolkien approved five [of my songs]," says Swann, "but bridled at my music for 'Namárië.' He had heard it differently in his mind, he said, and hummed a Gregorian chant."[15]

It was indeed what Tolkien had in mind, and consistently so, for Swann's transcription of Tolkien's hum is astonishingly close, differing only in a few small details, to the chant that Tolkien had intoned into George Sayer's tape recorder some thirteen years earlier. Clearly, then, Tolkien had the same melodic line in mind over that gap in time. Swann has left Tolkien's unaccompanied setting largely *a cappella*, adding only his own instrumental introduction, interlude, and coda. In both versions, this has the feel of plainchant to it: the melodic flow, the a cappella monophony, that is, the lack of harmonic accompaniment. What it lacks is melisma, the characteristic stretching of a syllable over many notes; instead it has the opposite, the holding of a note for many syllables, which also occurs in Gregorian chant, though less commonly.

Why Gregorian chant, though? This type of plainchant was systematized as the standard liturgical music of the Catholic Church by Pope Gregory I about 600 A.D. It may still be heard occasionally today, and was a frequent accompaniment to Catholic masses up until the reforms of the Second Vatican Council. To Tolkien, a conservative Catholic, Gregorian chant would have been the music of holiness and closeness to God. That sense of connection to the divine is part of what Tolkien is trying to show with the Elves and their connection to Valinor, and Catholic symbolism in the Elves has often been noted by critics, so why should not their music be divine Catholic music? This is perhaps not the sound that most readers think of in connection with the Elves; but it is clearly what Tolkien thought fit for Galadriel, at least.[16]

The Dwarf orchestra mentioned in *The Hobbit* is unusual. Most of the songs in *The Lord of the Rings* are unaccompanied or with minimal accompaniment such as a harp. The Rohirrim chant or recite alliterative verse. Some work has been done recently in reconstructing the likely musical styles and accompaniment used by Anglo-Saxon bards, but Tolkien is unlikely to have been deeply familiar with this research. In any case he recited and did not sing or chant the Rohirric poetry into Sayer's tape recorder. The only other poem in the Sayer collection he sang at all was the Ents' marching song on Isengard, which he gives as a very simple, primitive chant.

The most remarkable musical event in all of Tolkien's *legendarium* is the "Ainulindalë," the *Music* of the Creation of Arda. Surely it should not be possible to read a mythological creation story in which the world is created through music, and then write that the art of music meant little to its author.

The account of the Great Music is remarkably detailed, as precise as many a program note description of actual concert music; it could serve as a detailed blueprint for any composer audacious enough to try to create a musical version of this story.[17] Tolkien is describing, with considerable sophistication, a massive structure of counterpoint, in which themes create harmony by being played simultaneously in different voices, and themes evolve one into another. "The voices of the Ainur, like unto harps and lutes, and pipes and trumpets, and viols and organs, and like unto countless choirs singing with words, began to fashion the theme of Ilúvatar to a great music; and a sound arose of endless interchanging melodies woven in harmony that passed beyond hearing…. [It] was deep and wide and beautiful, but slow and blended with an immeasurable sorrow, from which its beauty chiefly came."[18]

What could Tolkien have thought it ought to sound like? Something of unearthly beauty, to be sure, but in the form of music you could actually hear, there is no question in my mind: if the Elves were singing Gregorian chant, the Ainur would be singing sacred choral music. From the slowness and calm Tolkien describes — reminiscent of the "music of the spheres," the constant "hum" of harmony supposed by medieval philosophy to be emitted by the planets — combined with complexity and intricacy, one likely inspiration is the elegant and transparent music of the High Renaissance. Works by Giovanni Palestrina, or the *Vespers of 1610* by Claudio Monteverdi, or the antiphonal motets by the great Venetian, Giovanni Gabrieli, convey the same epic, resonant grandeur as Tolkien's story.

Liquid Tolkien (Bratman)

But from the scale at which this story works, and Tolkien's reference to the sound of many instruments, what comes to my mind's ear when reading the "Ainulindalë" is the mighty choral-orchestral masterworks of the 18th century, when sacred choral music reached its greatest magnificence and sophistication. One might imagine, perhaps, the voices of the Ainur creating a fugue, a musical form in which a single theme is overlaid on top of itself in different voices, creating complexity by interweaving. Something, perhaps, like the fugue concluding George Frideric Handel's oratorio *Messiah,* an enormous four-voice structure of 88 bars whose text is but a single word, "Amen."

Messiah is the centerpiece of the British sacred choral repertoire, and a work Tolkien must have known, even though Handel was a Protestant. But there is Catholic music of the period with the same magnificence. The "Confutatis" from W.A. Mozart's *Requiem,* K. 626, setting the words "Confutatis maledictus, flammis acribus addictis" ("When the wicked are confounded, doomed to flames of woe unbounded") in a fierce *Sturm und Drang,* contrasted with the gentle supplication of the rest of the movement, embodies a conflict akin to that between the discord of Melkor and the harmony of Ilúvatar in the "Ainulindalë." The only problem is that Mozart presents the two styles sequentially, rather than simultaneously as Tolkien describes them. But it might not be possible for the human mind to compose music that would convey both discord and harmony at the same time without sounding like a muddle. Most music, even of the most direct storytelling nature, that tries to present two sides with widely varying music at the same time, tends to present them in turns.

The *Gloria* in D, RV 589, by the Venetian Baroque composer Antonio Vivaldi, is another well-known work of sacred Catholic vocal music that might induce the same sense of excitement and awe as a reading of the "Ainulindalë."

Tolkien always expected, or at least hoped, that music would be written inspired by his writings. Literature has always inspired composers, even of non-vocal music. One thinks of Shakespearean music ranging from Felix Mendelssohn's *Midsummer Night's Dream* incidental music to Serge Prokofiev's *Romeo and Juliet* ballet to Giuseppe Verdi's not one but three Shakespearean operas, *Macbeth, Otello,* and *Falstaff.* And that is just a small sampling of the foreign composers inspired by one great English writer. In his long letter to Milton Waldman describing his *legendarium,*

Middle-earth Minstrel

Tolkien mentions his original ambition to create a mythological cycle of varied legends, that would "leave scope for other minds and hands, wielding paint and music and drama," that is the non-literary arts.[19] To Carey Blyton, as described below, Tolkien wrote that he had "long hoped to ... have inspired a composer," adding plaintively that he "hoped also that [he] might find the result intelligible ... or feel that it was akin to [his] own inspiration."[20]

To gauge the type of music that Tolkien might have hoped would be inspired by his writings, and to get a sense of what the great masters of the previous century or two might have written had they had the chance to be inspired by Tolkien, one might listen to some music inspired by the literature that itself nourished Tolkien's imagination. It is easy enough to have a listening party consisting of music that you personally think would go well with Tolkien, or music that you hope Tolkien might have liked, whether or not he could have heard it; but that runs the risk of being an arbitrary selection. What we want here, though, is something more specific: composers whose work Tolkien could have known, and in one case certainly did; who were, most of them, inspired by literature akin to Tolkien's own works; and who are among the composers who established the musical vocabulary that means epic fantasy today. If the kind of sweeping Romantic score that Howard Shore wrote for Peter Jackson's films feels like the kind of music that ought to go in a film like that, it is because composers like these established the style by writing music like this. Listeners may discover these earlier masters to be better composers than Howard Shore, whose music I found merely serviceable, competent but uninspired hackwork, no match for the quality of the story it tried to tell.

Of all musical works based on medieval literature, one stands monumentally above all others: *Der Ring des Nibelungen*, the four-opera cycle by the 19th century German composer Richard Wagner loosely dramatizing stories from the medieval German *Nibelungenlied* and the Norse *Volsunga Saga*.

Tolkien is well-known to have been antipathetic to Wagner, but misunderstandings of his reaction are common. He was not unwilling to listen to Wagner's music. He once joined his friends, the Lewis brothers, in an evening reading aloud the libretto of *Die Walküre*, part of the *Ring* cycle, in preparation for an anticipated trip to hear the opera staged in London.[21] His crossness on the subject was due to the assumption by ignorant critics, mistaking common features for influence, that Wagner's work must have inspired *The Lord of the Rings*. A familiarity with the medieval sources that inspired both writers would eradicate that error. Theirs was more of a distant sibling relationship: each transformed themes and plot elements from Norse saga and poetry into original and independent works of art.[22]

Tolkien's reaction to Wagner seems to have been the same kind of mixed feeling as he had about Shakespeare and George MacDonald. Each had an ethos close to Tolkien's in some respects, but that very fact makes the fundamental differences in treatment stand out. In Tom Shippey's words, "All, he thought, had got something very important not quite right."[23]

Even fantasy readers with no interest in opera may already be familiar with Wagner's music — they have, if nothing else, probably heard the motif from Siegfried's funeral march repeated over and over in John Boorman's film *Excalibur* — but Wagner's treatment of magic deserves a little attention. Tolkien was very cross when someone compared his Ring with that of the Nibelungs — "Both rings were round, and there the resemblance ceases," he said[24] — but the resemblances do go beyond that. Wagner's Ring does not lend invisibility, but there is a magic helm which does. It appears in the prelude to the *Ring*, *Das Rheingold*, where Alberich the evil dwarf dons the helm, whips his hapless brother Mime, and immediately succumbs to temptation by declaring himself Lord of the Nibelungs. Wagner represented this by directing the singer wearing the helm to leave the stage and sing through a speaking-tube, an unavoidably crude solution. In modern stagings and recordings, more advanced special effects are used to make the singer sound like he is still on stage interacting with the other characters.

A liking for Wagner is quite common among Tolkien fans — there were even Wagner record listening sessions at early Mythopoeic Conferences — but the spirits of their works are actually very different. Wagner's story has a ruthlessness, a scornful joy in destruction, and a resignation to easily-avoided tragic fate, that are alien to Tolkien's deep-rooted senses of pity, sorrow, recovery, and hopeful faith in a more positive fate despite all loss. Tolkien weaves an epic tale of wonder and beauty mixed with danger, while Wagner's *Ring* essentially boils down to a kind of soap opera of the gods, featuring the rise and self-inflicted fall of a bombastic heroic demigod, rather as if *The Lord of the Rings* had been all about Boromir. And the music, rather than hearkening backwards with dignified restraint as

Tolkien's prose does, is constantly pushing at the limits of harmonic practice of the day, and wearing hyper-charged emotions with an openness unlike Tolkien's stylized formality. It is easy to admire Wagner's *Ring*, a masterpiece of its kind, but no sensitive reader would conflate it with Tolkien's.

If Tolkien had mixed feelings about Wagner, he apparently had quite positive feelings about Wagner's great predecessor, the man who, as Wagner himself testified, invented German Romantic opera, Carl Maria von Weber. In an interview, Tolkien said that he "had always been extremely fond" of Weber's music.[25] This is a striking comment. It may be surprising that Tolkien, so uncomfortable with fantasy drama, should have enjoyed such a flamboyantly supernatural operatist. With a musical vocabulary more restrained than Wagner's, but just as daring for its time, and with a far more vivid imagination than Wagner, Weber was one of the first, and one of the best, composers to paint fantasy with musical notes. This can be heard most vividly in the famous Wolf's Glen scene from Act II of his opera *Der Freischütz*. Though it was written in 1821, long before most other composers had set up romantic picture-painting into a guiding principle, the music is stunningly evocative. The opera's plot is sinister and complex: all a listener needs to know to follow this scene is that Caspar, the villain, has gone to a haunted glen in the woods to cast seven magical bullets. In turn they summon a series of unnatural portents, the Wild Hunt, and finally Caspar's master, the devil Samiel. The successive portents become more elaborate both musically and in description: night-birds, a wild boar that "darts wildly across," a hurricane, "four wheels darting fire [that] roll across the stage, the faerie Wild Hunt, and penultimately a "storm of thunder, lightning and hail; flames start from the earth; meteors appear on the hills, &c." The music in turn evolves from trills and woodwind chirps representing the birds, through galloping triplets for the wheels of fire, to a commanding *tutti* theme for the storm and meteors through to Samiel, who at last appears in a sudden hush and final blare of sound.[26]

The major composer who most often reminds listeners of Tolkien is the Finnish master, Jean Sibelius. "It's liquid Tolkien!" Ellen Kushner raved when she first heard Sibelius, and she explains: "Like Tolkien, Sibelius has it all: sweeping grandeur, mystery, magic, and tragedy."[27] Sibelius was a generation older than Tolkien, and wrote most of his music between 1890 and 1925. This is the period when Finland sought and gained its independence from Russia, and Sibelius was an ardent nationalist. What could be more natural, then, than that he should turn for inspiration to Finland's national epic, the *Kalevala*, the same work whose study by Tolkien inspired the language Quenya and large parts of the plot of *The Silmarillion*?

Like Tolkien, Sibelius was a superficially conservative writer, scorned by the avant-garde establishment, whose work, clothed in a welcoming accessibility, was actually more deeply considered and thoroughly transformative than that establishment had any notion of. Like Tolkien's, also, Sibelius's work has a myth-drenched air, which permeates most of the composer's orchestral works, even his abstract symphonies. Of Sibelius's numerous orchestral tone poems based on the *Kalevala*, the best-known are *The Swan of Tuonela* (part of a *Lemminkäinen Suite*, Op. 22) and *Tapiola*, Op. 122. These are basically atmospheric works rather than story-telling ones. For specific narrative content, the listener might turn to *Pohjola's Daughter*, Op. 49. It depicts a mysterious woman who taunts Väinämöinen, one of the saga's heroes, into futile tasks, such as making a boat from her spindle. After a slow, dark opening, the music suddenly picks up with a string *ostinato*, while a series of wind motifs evolve into a broader theme and a first climax in the brass: this music, representing Väinämöinen, is the selection Kushner chose to represent Sibelius on her radio program about Tolkien and music.

Sibelius's major work based on the *Kalevala*, however, is choral; so here one may not only encounter the stories that inspired Tolkien, but at the same time hear the primary-world language, Finnish, that chiefly inspired his elven tongue of Quenya. This work is a symphonic poem in five movements titled *Kullervo*, Op. 7; it tells of the adventures of that one of the heroes of the *Kalevala*. Kullervo is the one who, like Túrin Turambar, mates with a woman who, unknown to him, is his sister. Three of the movements are purely orchestral, but the central and longest one, "Kullervo and His Sister," sets a long dialogue and narration from the *Kalevala* depicting that tragic meeting. The unnamed sister is a feistier and more reluctant companion than Nienor, but the story ends similarly, with Kullervo realizing his misdeed and wishing himself woe. Each section of the seduction scene begins with the narrating chorus singing the same opening words — "Kullervo, Kalervon poika" (Kullervo, son of Kalervo) — to the same music, giving the movement a sense of repetitive structure.

Kullervo is an early work and not always characteristic of Sibelius's mature music, but by size alone it is worthy of note.

But there is another composer who may seem even closer than Sibelius in character to Tolkien: the Englishman Sir Edward Elgar. Like Sibelius, he was a generation older than Tolkien. Those who know only his *Pomp and Circumstance March No. 1*, famous from a few thousand high-school graduations, may think of Elgar as a flag-waving imperialist patriot, but he was not really like that at all. He was in fact remarkably like Tolkien. Beneath his bluff exterior he hid, like Tolkien, a deep vein of melancholy; like Tolkien's, his patriotism was a love of the land and its people, not a jingoistic imperialism; like Tolkien, he came from the West Midlands, from Worcestershire, and always looked on it as his true home; like Tolkien, he was a devout Roman Catholic; like Tolkien, he was a product of the Victorian and Edwardian eras, and felt increasingly out of place in the bustling modern commercial world that dominated after World War I.[28]

Unlike Weber or Sibelius, Elgar was not much of a fantasist — though he did once collaborate on a musical fairy play with Algernon Blackwood — but the somber nobility that pervades much of his work is a perfect match for Tolkien's. Anyone who wants symphonic music for the death of Thorin or the funeral of Théoden, or for the end of *The Lord of the Rings*, where solemn joy, for victory won, mixes with tears of sadness, surely could not do better than the famous "Nimrod" variation from Elgar's *Enigma Variations*, Op. 36. The slow and serious "Nimrod" holds a place in the English national pantheon roughly similar to that which Samuel Barber's *Adagio for Strings* holds for Americans, and its application to Tolkien would honor both creative artists.

The Hobbit and *The Lord of the Rings* are actually works of a great variety of moods, but then so is the *Enigma Variations*. The personality portraits of Elgar's friends in the diverse variations would fit splendidly with the books. The dignified acting of "R.B.T." could depict comfortable hobbit living; the fast piano warm-up exercises of "H.D.S.-P." could be Bilbo running down to the Green Dragon; the serious and feeling conversation, broken up by humor, of "R.P.A." could equally be the tremendous learning and glinting wit of Gandalf; the graceful old home of "W.N." could as easily apply to a pleasant stay in Rivendell; Elgar's galumphing attempt to teach "Troyte" to play the piano might pass for a fast ride on Shadowfax; the flirtatious "Dorabella" could be the whimsical Elves from

The Hobbit singing in the trees; "G.R.S."'s bulldog falling into the River Wye would be perfect for Bilbo struggling to stay on top of his barrel in the River Running; the sober and dedicated cello playing of "B.G.N." might picture Frodo and Sam slowly trudging towards Mordor. Appropriate Tolkien settings could surely be found for the other variations as well. Elgar has it all, and, amazingly, all these diverse portraits are variations on the same theme. A *Lord of the Rings* film that used this for its music could have been a very different work from Peter Jackson's, and a more appealingly Tolkienian one.

Nor need this be the only Elgar work that would fit a Tolkien setting. From his large-scale Catholic oratorio, *The Dream of Gerontius*, Op. 38, setting a poem by John Cardinal Newman on the journey of a man's soul from death to Purgatory,[29] to his Symphony No. 1 in A-flat Major, Op. 55, in which one critic has seen a quest narrative structure specifically comparable to those of *The Hobbit* and *The Lord of the Rings*,[30] Elgar's music is rich in Tolkienian resonance.

A few other composers of Tolkien's time and place deserve mention. Many composers of the generation after Elgar — of Tolkien's own age and a little older — were deeply drawn to the English countryside and culture as Tolkien was, becoming "landscape" composers of a kind that Elgar, for all his love of his country, was not. Ralph Vaughan Williams and Gustav Holst, mentioned above, were not the only composers of this generation to find the collecting, transcribing, and arranging of folk songs to be rewarding. Another was George Butterworth, an Oxford graduate a few years older than Tolkien, best known for an idyllic orchestral piece called *The Banks of Green Willow*. Like Tolkien, Butterworth served as an officer on the Somme, and there Butterworth died, felled by a sniper; he was probably the greatest loss to British music from World War I. Vaughan Williams and Holst, friends of Butterworth who survived the war, were like Tolkien in another way: despite their pastoral associations, they were capable of terrifying depictions of war in their art, Vaughan Williams in some of his later symphonies (the brutal Fourth and nihilistic Sixth) and Holst even more famously in the "Mars" movement of *The Planets*, Op. 32, a dramatic *ostinato* that, though by now clichéd, would go well with the iron-bound disasters of the crawl of Grond in *The Lord of the Rings* or the fall of Gondolin in *The Silmarillion*.

Sir Thomas Armstrong was another English pastoralist composer of this generation, though he was more drawn to setting metaphysical poetry than to transcribing folk song as were Vaughan Williams and his colleagues. But this Oxford music don and, later, principal of the Royal Academy of Music is of special interest as a colleague and personal friend of Tolkien's. He advised Tolkien concerning the performance of Swann's *Road Goes Ever On*, and his love for poetry expressed itself in a very Tolkienian interest in the meaning of words used in the critical vocabulary of both arts, poetry and music.[31]

In 1921, while Tolkien was teaching at Leeds, a young American composer of Swedish ancestry, Howard Hanson, was visiting England when he came across a copy of William Morris's translation of *Beowulf*. The solemn austerity of the poem so struck Hanson that he set the ending as a choral work called *Lament for Beowulf*. This was perhaps the first music since Anglo-Saxon times to be inspired by *Beowulf*, and also perhaps the only modern attempt to set its verses to music. Tolkien might have found Hanson's musical idiom a little severe, but the subject was certainly close to his heart.

Music Inspired by Tolkien

The realm of music inspired by Tolkien is a large and perilous one. One article could not even begin to cover it, and its regions are so varied that no one commentator could be an equally learned guide to all its regions. The definitive discography of Tolkien-inspired music is *The Tolkien Music List*, maintained by Chris Seeman,[32] listing every piece of recorded music he can find that sets Tolkien's poetry, or openly alludes to or was acknowledgely inspired by Tolkien's work. There are no evaluative reviews on this site, but Seeman has reviewed a number of notable popular music albums, particularly for *Beyond Bree*. Besides Ellen Kushner, Amy H. Sturgis and Diane Joy Baker are among the many others who have written on Tolkien-inspired music.[33] Their writings display their opinions and tastes; this article displays mine.

There are many approaches to Tolkien-inspired music. Musical settings of his poetry can be either attempts to hypothesize a subcreationally appropriate music for hobbits and elves, the music that they would have played in reality, whatever "reality" may mean in this context; or it can be just whatever sort of music the poetry as poetry inspires the composer to write, as composers have done with poetry for centuries. Confusion can arise if a setting intended merely as a composer's artistic response to Tolkien is taken as an attempt to make a consistent addition to Tolkien's sub-creation. Donald Swann in particular has received some unjustified criticism on that account, but apart from his anomalous "Namárië," adding to Tolkien's sub-creation is not what he was trying to do.

Alternatively, a composer can create an artistic response to Tolkien's work without using Tolkien's words; and this in turn can be in purely instrumental form, or by writing one's own text and setting that to music, either as a song or as some other form of vocal music. Instrumental music can try to tell a story in music, like a tone poem of the kind perfected by Richard Strauss; it can be a character portrait; or it can be more amorphous and atmospheric. Tolkien-inspired music has been written in all these ways.

And any of these may be in any musical genre imaginable — and they have been. This survey will concentrate on the musical genres most meaningful to this writer: classical orchestral music inspired by Tolkien, and classical and folk settings of Tolkien's poetry. Even that will have to be very selective. But it should begin by saying a little about other forms of Tolkienian music.

Except for strict attempts to create "real" hobbitish and elven music — and sometimes even then — the first thing a listener realizes on hearing *any* Tolkien-inspired music is that, just as with Tolkien-inspired artwork, what you are hearing is not Tolkien. It is an aural image of Tolkien, as filtered through the individual musician's ears. Some composers are aiming at narrowly-defined direct responses to Tolkien's works; others are just using him as a take-off point to travel somewhere else. When Led Zeppelin sings of finding "a girl so fair" in Mordor,[34] this is not setting Tolkien to music, and probably was not intended that way — if it were, one would immediately ask what she is doing there, surely not the question the song intends to pose — it's just using Tolkien as a convenient backdrop to let Led Zeppelin be themselves. This probably explains the startling number of heavy metal and thrash-rock groups on Chris Seeman's list. These bands are not interested in Tolkien in any way that serious Tolkien readers would understand as interested in Tolkien; they just think orcs and Nazgûl are cool.

Middle-earth Minstrel

A novel called *The Armageddon Rag* by George R.R. Martin gives some insight into this mindset without forcing the dubious auditor to listen to the music. It recounts, as a heavy-handed but well-crafted dark fantasy, the mid–1980s reunion of a fictional early heavy-metal band called the Nazgûl, "after the flying baddies in the books," as one of the characters casually puts it,[35] rather similar to an American version of Led Zeppelin. This band supposedly gets its start about 1967, when the first Tolkien craze was at its height: they begin by playing off Tolkien references, with a first album titled *Hot Wind Out of Mordor* and song titles like "Elf Rock" (*à la* Led Zeppelin's real-life "Misty Mountain Hop"), but soon enough they turn to generalized inchoately loud and angry music and lyrics that Martin intends as *echt* Sixties, leaving behind everything Tolkienian but a few relics: the band name and their logo, the Eye of Sauron. There is little evidence in the novel that the band members, or even the author, know much more about Tolkien than that. But there is no sense of a cynical exploitation of Tolkien, either. It is merely necessary that "the whole Tolkien bag," to quote the same character, be lurking around in the background somewhere, along with drugs, sex, and references to obscure television shows, because this ethos expects that it will be there.

Of course, even in the 1960s and 1970s, not all rock and pop musicians inspired by Tolkien were orc-lovers. There really was such a thing as Tolkien flower-children, and this gentle but rather airy side of Tolkienian music may be heard in its purest form in a sequence titled "Songs of the Quendi" on Sally Oldfield's album *Water Bearer*.[36]

Nor is Tolkien-based rock of subsequent years all heavy-metal; far from it. A friend of this writer's who is learned in these matters suggests that the defining characteristic of a neo-progressive rock group is gratuitous Tolkien references.[37] The group that is generally considered to have founded this style in the 1980s, Marillion, is said to have cut the name down from "Silmarillion," either to avoid copyright conflicts or after finding that the full word would not fit on their album cover.[38] A band called Ilúvatar is said to have chosen its name from a copy of *The Silmarillion* that one of its members had picked up at a yard sale, and of which they had not read any more than the first few paragraphs. They just thought the name sounded cool. Their music, my friend tells me, is "amazingly pretentious," but as this history would suggest, it is otherwise unrelated to Tolkien. One neo-prog rock band without a Tolkienian name, Glass

Hammer, is better-known in Tolkien circles for two albums inspired by *The Lord of the Rings*. *Journey of the Dunadan* was a pretentious prog-rock summary of Aragorn's part of the story, with a lighter interlude in the form of a couple of songs as the band imagined might have been sung in the Prancing Pony. This was apparently the most popular part of the album, because Glass Hammer followed it up several years later with an entire album in the persona of an imaginary Middle-earth bar band, vaguely in the electric folk style, complete with crowd noises. Entirely and cheerfully anachronistic, this recording, titled *The Middle-earth Album*, was good casual fun to listen to, enjoyable by anyone who appreciates Tolkien parodies.[39]

In the primary world, the idea of music inspired by Tolkien's works apparently first took on concrete meaning in the early 1960s, before the huge boom of interest in his work, when Tolkien received letters of inquiry from two young British concert-music composers. They could not possibly have been more different from each other. One was a Scotswoman named Thea Musgrave.[40] Nothing came of her proposal for some sort of opera based on *The Lord of the Rings*, which may have been for the best: her compositions are mostly daunting, formidable serialist music, the kind that audiences stay away from in droves, though at least one stage work of hers, an opera of Dickens's *Christmas Carol*, has some effective dramatic power.

The other composer who wrote to Tolkien was an Englishman named Carey Blyton. In 1964 he asked Tolkien for permission to compose an overture based on *The Hobbit*. Tolkien was immensely flattered. "You certainly have my permission," he wrote. "As an author I am honoured to hear that I have inspired a composer. I have long hoped to do so." What flattered Tolkien was the reflection of his work in music, an art he respected but had no pretentions to mastering on his own. "Music gives me great pleasure and sometimes inspiration," he explained, but "I have little musical knowledge."[41] He gave far less polite responses to people who wanted to write sequels to his work, produce inept dramatizations, or misapply his invented names to hydrofoil boats, or to Siamese cats (a breed he detested).

Tolkien plaintively added in his letter to Blyton, "[I hope] also that I might perhaps find the result intelligible to me." He need not have worried. As a composer, Blyton was completely unlike Musgrave, and not at all formidable. He specialized in music for schools, and he is best known for having written incidental music for the BBC television program *Dr. Who* in the 1970s. Many have read Tolkien's letter to Blyton in his published correspondence; fewer know that Blyton actually did go ahead and write his *Hobbit* Overture; and fewer still have ever heard it, but some years ago it was recorded.[42]

Blyton miniaturizes *The Hobbit*, condensing Tolkien's novel into 4½ minutes of charming light orchestral music. After an introductory horn call taking the listener into this miniature kingdom, Bilbo the hobbit is introduced with a jaunty, skipping theme on solo winds and later on cellos. He is then joined by Gandalf the wizard (muted trumpet) and Thorin the dwarf (harp, the instrument he plays in the book). A little traveling music gets them quickly to Gollum (a stiff, creepy theme on oboe and bassoon) and the Ring (a single held chord on trumpet, with cymbals). The plot immediately jumps to Thrór's treasure (a stately brass theme, extended to some length). Smaug, the dragon guarding it, is represented by abrupt *tutti* chords and trombone *glissandi*, and his death should be instantly recognizable in the form of a *pizzicato* string pluck as the fatal arrow is shot, followed by more agonies in the brass and falling *pizzicati* in the strings. The work concludes with an extended happy ending: the treasure theme and the dwarves' traveling music are counterpointed, followed by a reprise of Bilbo's jaunty theme and a simple cadence for a conclusion. It is a colorful little piece reminiscent in musical terms of some of the lighter cartoonish illustrations that artists have provided for the book.

Another composer came into Tolkien's life the year after Blyton, 1965, and became a lasting friend. Donald Swann was a pianist and composer who had become noted for his intelligently witty songs about zoo animals and such, written in collaboration with Michael Flanders, which they performed in a revue show titled "At the Drop of a Hat." But Swann also had a more serious side. He had written an opera based on C.S. Lewis's *Perelandra*, he loved *The Lord of the Rings*, and having set several of Tolkien's poems to music and received Tolkien's permission to do so, he included them in his stage performances and then recorded them as a song cycle titled *The Road Goes Ever On*.[43] With the exception of "Namárië," Swann made no claims to be writing authentic Middle-earth music: these are his artistic interpretations in his style, modern art songs with piano. It is curious, however, that so far as I have heard, no one else, anywhere, has attempted to write Elvish songs that, like Swann's "Namárië," sound like Gregorian chant, despite the clear directive from the author that this is what he thinks Elvish music sounds like.

Swann's song cycle has never gotten quite the attention it deserves, partly because its one recording is in a reserved, fastidious style.[44] It has been performed live at a couple of Mythopoeic Conferences, in much better performances, and been received very well. Swann has actually written a sophisticated art song cycle in which the individual songs are integrated into a larger whole, and are sensitively and expressively arranged.

Of all Tolkien's poems, Swann's title song, "The Road Goes Ever On," is the one that invariably turns up in anyone's collection of Tolkien songs. This is almost literally true: every recorded Tolkien song cycle that I have ever actually heard has a setting of at least one of the several variants of "The Road Goes Ever On." It might not be all that boring to hear them in sequence: they are all different. But there are many other poems for a sampler to choose from. The Tolkien Ensemble, a group from Denmark, has conscientiously recorded a version of every poem from *The Lord of the Rings*, including Bombadil's doggerel. Even excluding their work, most of the poems from both *The Lord of the Rings* and *The Hobbit*, and at least ten of the sixteen in *The Adventures of Tom Bombadil*, have at least one musical setting. After "The Road Goes Ever On," the most popular are "I Sit Beside the Fire and Think," "The Stone Troll," and "In Western Lands," each of which has been set, and recorded, at least five times.

This is actually quite remarkable. Tolkien's poetry has never been rated highly by reviewers of *The Lord of the Rings*.[45] Even today there is a beginners' guide to *The Lord of the Rings* which advises easily-bored readers to skip the poetry, and there is a well-known movie that found room for about thirty seconds of it in its tightly compressed space of ten hours.[46] Tolkien made no claims for his own poetry's quality, for instance constructing an elaborate preface to *The Adventures of Tom Bombadil* excusing the contents as simple hobbit doggerel collected solely for scholarly interest, not for any literary merit.[47] But the very qualities of simplicity and plainness that give his verse a dubious reputation as high-literary poetry are its virtues as song lyrics, a genre of verse with quite different aesthetic needs.

There is a wide variety of settings available, to suit a wide variety of tastes. The most musically sophisticated Tolkien setting I have heard since Swann's, and the most like his, is by a Canadian named James Stark, who accompanies himself on harp; his is an intelligent and thoughtful song cycle with intricate structures and recurring motifs, but lacks variety; all the songs sound like fastidious drawing-room ballads, even the bumptious hobbit songs.[48] The most new-agey setting I know is by Giuseppe Festa, an Italian who sings in his native language. He accompanies himself on guitar, with an ambient orchestra lurking in the background. It is extremely attractive wallpaper music.[49]

The most genuinely hobbitic setting is from The Hobbitons, the singing group of the Dutch Tolkien Society "Unquendor." These gentle-hobbits began belting out their settings of hobbit and goblin songs at top volume during parties at Tolkien conventions, and eventually they preserved them on disc. The Hobbitons are the opposite of James Stark: the more bumptious they get, the better they are.[50]

And the most seriously authentic setting of hobbit songs is by the American folk/early music band Broceliande. As discussed above, an American hillbilly twang creeping in to their setting of "Man in the Moon Stayed Up Too Late" is an appropriate accent. Broceliande's characteristic blend of Anglo-American folk with medieval and Renaissance influences seems a perfect mixture for capturing Tolkien's spirit, especially the spirit of hobbits, though the Elvish songs are also beautiful. And the melodies, many of them penned by the late fantasy author Marion Zimmer Bradley, and sung by her on occasion in the 1960s and 1970s, are both sturdy and delightful.

If Broceliande and the Hobbitons are hobbits in ethos, some other groups are elves. The Tolkien Ensemble, the Danish group, have created some of the most atmospheric Tolkien settings on disc in four albums released over a decade. Two of the albums were made in collaboration with actor Christopher Lee, who recites some non-musical poems and impersonates Treebeard half rhythmically talking and half singing, *à la* Rex Harrison as Professor Higgins. In the course of this project, the Ensemble's composers, Caspar Reiff and Peter Hall, set every poem in *The Lord of the Rings*. A box set re-release arranged all the songs in the order that their words appear in the book.[51]

Like Broceliande's, the Tolkien Ensemble's approach is formed from an effective combination of folk and classical music. The group includes both conservatory students and folk-music performers, and their work mixes the two styles in comfort. The song of Beren and Lúthien as a classical art song sits easily next to hobbit folk music with guitar. Unlike Broceliände's early music approach, the Ensemble's classical orientation is Nordic post-modernist, and their third album has a lot of ruminative string orchestra music reminiscent of Peteris Vasks or Arvo Pärt. An ethereal air of wistfulness pervades all their work, and makes their Elven music shine. They do hobbit songs as well, lightly with guitar with a kind of all-purpose tune that is sturdy enough also to serve surprisingly well for that unpromising material, the rhymes of Bombadil. The meeting of hobbit and elf comes out best in the last track of their third album, in which, as in the book's last chapter, Frodo's walking song meets an Elvish hymn to Elbereth.

A Russian group called Caprice is more classically-oriented still, but if anything it is slightly post-minimalist with a hint of rock. Some consider their two albums, released in France, to be the finest settings of Tolkien yet. I was less impressed with their first album, *Elven Music*, which seemed to me to have fairly weak, overly chromatic melodic lines, too much of the same accompaniment style of harp arpeggios, the same too closely-miked oboe, and the same female voice singing in English with a Russian accent so thick you could use it to protect yourself from Siberian wolves in winter.

Caprice's second album is mostly by the same vocalist, but it is a much more imaginatively arranged work. Despite the generally somber tone, they come up with a setting of "In Western Lands" that sounds incongruously cheerful, but the album's most outstanding track is, so far as I know, the only setting of the poem "Shadow-bride" from *The Adventures of Tom Bombadil*. Although the words are difficult to understand without a text, it is a truly arresting version, presented with creepy rising intensity and concluding with a snarling rendition of the final verse, that makes the poem sound as if it might have been written by Neil Gaiman.[52]

After the songwriters came what perhaps could be called the ambient musicians, pop composers who write mood music perhaps intended to be played in the background as one reads the book. It is usually in the form of vaguely Celtic or new-age, unimaginatively-titled suites with movements depicting places in Middle-earth. The first of these to hit disc was a Swedish rock organist named Bo Hansson in 1972 with *Music Inspired by Lord of the Rings*. At one time it seemed that every Tolkien fan had a copy of this record. This was undoubtedly because it was just about the only one out there, not for the inherent merit of the music, which was evocative but, due to the tinny organ, sounded vaguely seedy.[53]

There have been many others since. The rock keyboardist Rick Wakeman's album *Landscapes of Middle-earth* consists largely of overdubbed synthesizers with a backbeat, while noodling new-age piano music represents the Elven lands and, strangely, Rohan. If it does not seem to fit with Tolkien, there is a good reason: the association is retroactive. Wakeman wrote it with other purposes in mind, and this album is only a repackaging.[54] The appropriately-named David Arkenstone released *Music Inspired by Middle-earth*: at times it sounds more like music inspired by the Middle *East*, mixed with Celtic lounge music *à la* Howard Shore's hobbit music, with rich but static harmonies, and a partiality for bagpipes and harps.[55]

Music from film adaptations of *The Lord of the Rings* is well-known and needs little discussion here. Howard Shore's music for the Peter Jackson films — despite its pseudo–Celtic hobbit music, its use of cheap sequencing instead of harmonic growth to build tension, and its general pedestrian quality — is honest hackwork, imaginatively orchestrated and with some quality to the melodies, and unlike so much recent music for epic films it is not an imitation of the brittle style of John Williams. It strikes this listener as superior to Leonard Rosenman's music for the Ralph Bakshi film, which was a combination of the Colonel Bogey march and the worst of Carl Stalling, as put together by a 1950s-vintage hack Broadway orchestrator.

The music to the BBC radio dramatization of 1981, written by Stephen Oliver, is much more interesting. It is startlingly derivative of modern British classical music of the generation immediately younger than Tolkien, but quite moving in context. The theme music is stodgy — it sounds like the march of the absent-minded professors — and could have been by any number of the followers of Benjamin Britten or William Walton. The vocal music is largely for counter-tenor and boy sopranos, and some of that is straight out of the English choral tradition of which Hubert Parry's World War I era setting of William Blake's *Jerusalem* is the banner work. Oliver's setting of "Bilbo's Last Song" (the only setting of this poem I know of), is particularly successful in the context of the close of the epic drama.[56] Some of Oliver's settings, including "Bilbo's Last Song," are covered on the Hobbitons album, with somewhat mixed results.

With that, this survey returns to classical music, which we left with

Carey Blyton back in 1967. The massive popularity of *The Lord of the Rings* makes it not surprising that Tolkien, the writer who had long hoped to inspire a composer, has inspired many. Tolkien's work has been very popular in the Nordic countries, and Nordic composers, who often tend towards an austere but tonal idiom, have occasionally set Tolkien. Thea Musgrave never composed her speculative *Lord of the Rings* opera, but in the mid 1970s a Swedish composer, Sven-Eric Johanson, did write one. It has never been recorded, but one reviewer of his works describes his vocal style as "modern zany choral tonalism," which does sound promising.[57]

There have been several other Tolkien-based operas. A Mythopoeic Society member, Richard Wunder, was working on an opera of *The Lord of the Rings* at the same time as Johanson's, and some excerpts were performed at early Mythopoeic Conferences. A *Silmarillion*-based opera by Adam C.J. Klein, titled *Leithian*, received a chamber performance in New York in 2006 with the composer, a professional tenor, as Beren, and has received some attention in Tolkien fan circles.[58] Klein's libretto is heavily based on spoken narration; his music mixes modern chromatic tonalism with musical theatre *à la* Andrew Lloyd Webber, and in his "Ainulindalë" an open quotation from J.S. Bach.

After "opera," no title in classical music carries more prestige than that of "symphony," though the word is often used very loosely. A number of Tolkien-inspired works have this word on them. Among others, Howard Shore has given the title of symphony to an orchestral suite of his film music, and Jonathan Peters' home-recorded suite in a similar film-music style also bears the title.[59]

Besides these, at least two genuine symphonies, with more of the thematic development and harmonic counterpoint expected from a concert symphony by the likes of Sibelius or Elgar, have been inspired by *The Lord of the Rings*. One of them is by the man who by the turn of the 21st century had emerged as perhaps the world's leading living symphonist, the Finnish composer Aulis Sallinen. Sallinen, who had already shown an interest in mythic literature by writing an opera inspired by the *Kalevala*, was commissioned in the 1990s for a ballet based on *The Lord of the Rings*. The plan never came off— though some years later he did recycle some older music into a children's ballet on *The Hobbit*— and Sallinen was left with some themes and material that he reshaped into his Symphony No. 7, Op. 71, which he titled "The Dreams of Gandalf."[60] The symphony is an episodic and stylistically eclectic single movement of some 25 minutes which, Sallinen says in the recording's liner notes, "is not a description of the events in the novel but rather the documentation of a reading experience and a literary mood."

The only information I have on specific inspirations is the presence in the work of a Gandalf motif. Musical notes are lettered from A to G, and in German a slightly different system is used that includes an H; so, for instance, a composer whose name uses only letters between A and H — as, for example, Bach — can write his name in musical notes and use it as a theme. J.S. Bach did this, and a number of other composers have also written their own names or other messages in musical notes this way. Sallinen wanted to write the name Gandalf, and as that includes two letters not covered by musical notes, he wrote GADAF instead. The GADAF motif is a striving, rising theme — all the succeeding notes are in the octave above the initial G. It first appears in brass over rolling drums at the very opening of the symphony. Sallinen's musical idiom is more angular and dissonant than Sibelius's, but his work has a similar sweep and wide-scale vision.

The other symphony based on *The Lord of the Rings* is so popular that it has been recorded at least four times since it was composed in 1987, something almost unheard of for a contemporary classical work. It is the Symphony No. 1 for concert band (also arranged for symphony orchestra) by Johan de Meij.[61] Although de Meij is Dutch, his music is very much in the tradition and style of popular British concert band and symphonic music by composers like Gustav Holst and Malcolm Arnold. Like Sallinen, de Meij is more interested in creating a mood than telling a story. Three of his symphony's five movements are character portraits, each opening with a long introduction. His Gandalf is marked by a full, striving theme, and later breaks into a fast ride on Shadowfax. Gollum is depicted with a sinuous soprano saxophone solo over a hopping accompaniment. The finale represents hobbits in general with what is known in British classical music terminology as "The Big Tune." It is a catchy, self-contained melody that is stolidly repeated in both lively and somber colors, but tends to resist development. Another movement (the second in playing order) goes with the three character movements as a portrait of a place, in this case Lothlórien, which, like everyone from Bo Hansson to Enya, de Meij seems to hear as steamy.

But de Meij's remaining movement (the fourth in playing order) does tell a story: it is called "Journey in the Dark," after the chapter telling of the journey through Moria towards the Bridge of Khazad-dûm. This remarkable tone poem, nine minutes long, begins with exceedingly quiet slow tramping with occasional weird sounds in the background, suddenly races into a blazing accelerando when the battle on the Bridge begins, climaxes with a mighty call of the Gandalf theme from the first movement, and then dies into a mournful coda.

The *Middle-earth* suite of the American composer Craig Russell is a very short work in nine tiny movements, written for a student orchestra, aiming in the composer's words to be, "whenever possible, funny or clever."[62] Russell is a music professor at California Polytechnic University who composes in the American nationalist tradition of Aaron Copland and Henry Cowell. His Gimli is an Irish-American Dwarf, and his Gandalf stands out in the open harmonies of Copland's prairie. Russell has fun with Gollum as growling "swallowing" sounds on double bass, and with Shelob as strings clicking their bows *col legno* against a hard surface, giving a creepy, insectoid sound.

Another distinctively American composer inspired by Tolkien is Thomas Peterson, whose massive choral-orchestral work *The Tale of the Rings of Power* has never been commercially recorded, although the score was published with illustrations by Patrick Wynne. Excerpts presented on a promotional tape, which is all I know of it, reveal a massive work consisting of no fewer than 18 vocal or choral movements setting Tolkien poems, linked together by narrators intoning lengthy quotations from *The Lord of the Rings* and *The Silmarillion* to tell the story. In the slow movements, such as Galadriel's hymn, the music is American pastorale, more akin to Howard Hanson or Randall Thompson than Copland, and in the dramatic moments ("Seek for the sword that was broken" and the Ring spell) it is strikingly like modern primitivism from Igor Stravinsky's *Le Sacre du Printemps* and Carl Orff's *Carmina Burana*. Peterson, like Russell, believes in stealing from the best.[63]

One might expect that the more harmonically advanced composers of our time would generally avoid supposedly retrogressive literature like Tolkien's, but as mentioned above, Thea Musgrave showed an interest. Another exception is the Canadian modernist composer Glenn Buhr, whose tone poem *Beren and Lúthien*, from the surprisingly early date of 1984, was one of the first works inspired by *The Silmarillion*.[64] The concluding section of this 20-minute work represents the conflict between Morgoth and Lúthien, as portrayed by timpani and harp respectively. The orchestration is imaginative, and the work as a whole is well-constructed, but its post-tonal harmonic approach leaves it melodically limited. Buhr's Lúthien is no more beautiful than his Morgoth, though she is more lyrical. The Inklings generally did not care for this kind of music. Warren Lewis, who considered himself a connoisseur of classical music, once attended a performance of a modern string quartet which he called "perfectly agonizing ... a very little more would I think have given me a toothache."[65] He might have said the same of Glenn Buhr. Tolkien might have been more circumspect and said merely that it was not akin to his own inspiration. Buhr has also set Aragorn's song of Beren and Lúthien for voice and harp.

Other recent classical composers recommended by Chris Seeman include Daniel McCarthy and Lubomyr Melnyk. McCarthy, who has taught at the Interlochen arts camp and at universities in the American Midwest, has composed more works based on *The Lord of the Rings* and *The Hobbit* than probably any other classical composer of his standing. His works, in a sometimes jazz-influenced chromatic modern idiom but less harsh than Buhr's, include a setting for soprano and tenor of Treebeard's song of the Ent and Entwife, a dark and brooding concert overture for orchestra titled *Towers: Ascent of Orodruin*, a multi-movement *Song of Middle-earth* for percussion ensemble with marimba solo, *Swords of Power* (referring to Orcrist and Glamdring) for two percussionists, *The Call of Boromir* as a duet for horn and marimba, and *Time Out of Mind: Six Tales of Middle-earth* for piano. Several of these have been recorded.[66] Lubomyr Melnyk is a Canadian pianist who specializes in composing and playing works consisting of fast rolling arpeggios that set up standing overtones. His lengthy piano work *Song of Galadriel* is thus perhaps the closest yet to a Tolkien-inspired minimalist composition.[67] Another modern classical work inspired by Tolkien that has come to my attention is an orchestral *Ainulindalë* by Frank Felice. An excerpt on Felice's web site suggests that the depiction of the opening chaos is somewhat more astringent than Felice's usual style of American *Gebrauchsmusik* of the Hanson/Thompson school.[68]

Conclusion

This chapter has described only a small sampling of the tremendously wide variety of music that has been inspired by the works of Tolkien.

Liquid Tolkien (Bratman)

Much more has been written, and much more will come in the future, as Tolkien's deeply inspirational works strike responses in musicians of all kinds and in many places.

Notes

1. Michael White, *The Life and Work of J.R.R. Tolkien* (Indianapolis: Alpha, 2002), 17.
2. E.g., J.R.R. Tolkien, *The Letters of J.R.R. Tolkien* (Boston: Houghton Mifflin, 1981), 173.
3. Tolkien expressed irritation at various forms of jazz, rock 'n' roll, and even operetta impartially. See Christina Scull and Wayne G. Hammond, *The J.R.R. Tolkien Companion & Guide* (Boston: Houghton Mifflin, 2006), 2:617; see also specifically Tolkien, *Letters*, 89, 111, 345.
4. Tolkien, *Letters*, 89.
5. J.R.R. Tolkien, *The Annotated Hobbit*, ed. Douglas A. Anderson, 2nd ed. (Boston: Houghton Mifflin, 2002), 43.
6. It has been suggested that for clarinets we should read crumhorns, but this does not really solve the problem. If Tolkien had meant crumhorn he could have written it; the crumhorn may be related to the clarinet but the sound is totally different; and if prehistoric Dwarves couldn't have gotten clarinets, where would they have found crumhorns and viols?
7. Tom Shippey, *The Road to Middle-earth*, rev. and expanded ed. (Boston: Houghton Mifflin, 2003), 102.
8. Tolkien, *Annotated Hobbit*, 44.
9. J.R.R. Tolkien, *The Lord of the Rings*, 2nd ed. (Boston: Houghton Mifflin, 1965), 1:219.
10. Originally released on an LP, *J.R.R. Tolkien Reads and Sings His The Hobbit and The Fellowship of the Ring*. Caedmon TC 1477, 1975, with liner notes by George Sayer. Now available in a 4-CD set, *The J.R.R. Tolkien Audio Collection*. Caedmon/Harper Audio CD 101(4), 2001, without the liner notes.
11. Cecil Sharp, *Cecil Sharp's Collection of English Folk Songs*, ed. Maud Karpeles (London: Oxford University Press, 1974), 399–402. The researcher seeks in vain if expecting standard or consistent versions of either the words or the music of English folk songs, or consistent pairings between them. Words may be completely rewritten; the same words may be sung to totally different tunes, and one tune applied to several different sets of words.
12. Tolkien, *Letters*, 230.
13. As "Merry Old Inn," Broceliande, *The Starlit Jewel: Songs from J.R.R. Tolkien's The Lord of the Rings & The Hobbit* (Flowinglass Music FM007, 2000).
14. As demonstrated in Cecil Sharp, *English Folk Songs from the Southern Appalachians* (London: Oxford University Press, 1932).
15. Donald Swann, Foreword, in *The Road Goes Ever On* by J.R.R. Tolkien and Donald Swann (Boston: Houghton Mifflin, 1967), vi.
16. Some critics have noted the Gregorian and therefore clerical nature of the Elves, e.g. Bradley J. Birzer, *J.R.R. Tolkien's Sanctifying Myth* (Wilmington, DE.: ISI, 2002), 80.

17. This writer has heard two choral-orchestral depictions of the Ainulindalë in a classical idiom, composed by Adam C.J. Klein and Thomas Peterson as segments of works discussed below. Both use narrators and present a relatively simple version of the musical structure.

18. J.R.R. Tolkien, *The Silmarillion* (Boston: Houghton Mifflin, 1977), 15–17.

19. Tolkien, *Letters*, 145. It is clear here and from his essay "On Fairy-Stories" that Tolkien considered drama an art separate from literature.

20. Tolkien, *Letters*, 350.

21. Warren Lewis, *Brothers and Friends* (San Francisco: Harper and Row, 1982), 145–46.

22. Serenely confident assertions that Tolkien must have directly copied Wagner still find their way into print, even from critics who should know better. One recent example is Alex Ross, "The Ring and the Rings: Wagner vs. Tolkien," *The New Yorker*, December 22, 2003: 22–29.

23. Shippey, 344. The most thorough discussion of Tolkien's difference from Wagner's (and the Nazis') approaches to mythic history is in Christine Chism, "Middle-earth, the Middle Ages, and the Aryan Nation: Myth and History in World War II," in *Tolkien the Medievalist*, ed. Jane Chance (London: Routledge, 2003), 63–92.

24. Tolkien, *Letters*, 306. Contrary to a usual assumption, Tolkien is here discussing not Wagner at all, but a mythological farrago in the mind of a critic.

25. Scull and Hammond, 2:617.

26. Carl Maria von Weber, *Der Freischütz*, vocal score, libretto by Friedrich Kind, translated by Natalia MacFarren (New York: Schirmer, n.d.), 108–12.

27. Ellen Kushner, *The Lord of the Rings*, episode in *Sound & Spirit*, NPR, broadcast week of August 27, 2006.

28. Many biographies and studies of Elgar discuss his personality and character. One specific consideration of "Elgar the Catholic" is by Stephen Hough, in *Elgar: An Anniversary Portrait*, introduction by Nicholas Kenyon (London: Continuum, 2007), 54–69.

29. Gerontius, a Latin name meaning "old man" which Tolkien had perhaps found in Newman's poem, is in *The Lord of the Rings* revealed as the given name of Bilbo's grandfather, The Old Took.

30. J.P.E. Harper-Scott, *Edward Elgar, Modernist* (Cambridge: Cambridge University Press, 2006), 104–6, 174, 195. Harper-Scott goes on to discuss Tolkienian *eucatastrophe* and *dyscatastrophe* in the context of the teleology of large-scale musical compositions by Beethoven and Mahler as well as Elgar, 175–83.

31. For Tolkien's interactions with Armstrong, see Scull and Hammond, 1:496, 647, 721.

32. Chris Seeman, *The Tolkien Music List,* http://www.tolkien-music.com. Seeman's listings are meticulous in their inclusiveness, and include lyrics whenever possible, but descriptive information on recordings tends to be limited. Both here and in his commentary Seeman can be vague about classification. He often applies the term "classical" to music better described as electric folk or folk-influenced pop.

33. Amy H. Sturgis, "Lord of the Rings, Rock On!," http://www.popthought.com/display_column.asp?DAID=282. Diane Joy Baker has published various album reviews in *Mythprint* starting in 1997.

34. Led Zeppelin, "Ramble On," *Led Zeppelin II* (Atlantic 82633, 1969).

35. George R.R. Martin, *The Armageddon Rag* (New York: Pocket, 1985), 45.

36. Sally Oldfield, *Water Bearer* (Chrysalis 1211, 1978).

37. Dan'l Danehy-Oakes, personal communication, undated.
38. "Marillion Biography," http://www.progfreaks.com/Marillion/Biography/Chapter1.htm.
39. Glass Hammer, *Journey of the Dunadan* (Arion Records 7690-51111-120, 1993); *The Middle-earth Album* (Arion Records SR1311, 2001).
40. Scull and Hammond, 1:592.
41. Tolkien, *Letters*, 350.
42. Carey Blyton, *The Hobbit*, from *British Light Overtures 3*, Royal Ballet Sinfonia, dir. Gavin Sutherland (White Line 2140, 2003). Blyton's description of the piece, which is necessary to follow its storyline, is not printed in the liner notes of this recording, but it may be found on Seeman's website at http://www.tolkien-music.com/songs/blyton1.html.
43. Sheet music published as J.R.R. Tolkien and Donald Swann, *The Road Goes Ever On: A Song Cycle* (Boston: Houghton Mifflin, 1967).
44. Donald Swann, *The Road Goes Ever On*, William Elvin (singer) and Donald Swann (piano), originally on LP on J.R.R. Tolkien, *Poems and Songs of Middle-earth*. Caedmon TC 1231, 1967. Re-released on CD inserted into a later edition of Tolkien and Swann, *The Road Goes Ever On* (London: HarperCollins, 2002).
45. Burton Raffel famously stated that "the trilogy's poetry [shows] almost no independent literary merit" (*"The Lord of the Rings* as Literature," in *Tolkien and the Critics*, ed. Neil D. Isaacs and Rose A. Zimbardo [Notre Dame: University of Notre Dame Press, 1968], 231). Mary Quella Kelly, in "The Poetry of Fantasy: Verse in *The Lord of the Rings*," Isaacs and Zimbardo 170–200, treats the verse as purely functional. Later, more sophisticated articles, such as Joe R. Christopher, "Tolkien's Lyric Poetry," in *Tolkien's Legendarium*, ed Verlyn Flieger and Carl F. Hostetter (Westport, CT: Greenwood, 2000), 143–60, discuss mostly poems from outside *The Lord of the Rings*, few of which have been set to music. One notable exception to both — it is in *The Lord of the Rings*, and has been set — discussed by Christopher is Aragorn's *linnod* of Beren and Lúthien.
46. The book is *The Rough Guide to The Lord of the Rings* (London: Rough Guides, 2003), 102. The film needs no identification.
47. J.R.R. Tolkien, *The Adventures of Tom Bombadil and Other Verses from The Red Book* (Boston: Houghton Mifflin, 1962), 7–9.
48. James A. Stark, *Songs of Middle-earth* (Prime Time 9201, 1989).
49. Giuseppe Festa, *Voci dalla Terra di Mezzo* (Pongo Classica 2050, 2000).
50. The Hobbitons, *Songs from Middle-earth* (Dutch Tolkien Society Unquendor STEMRA PR001, 1996).
51. The original four Tolkien Ensemble albums are: *An Evening at Rivendell* (Classico 175, 1997), *A Night in Rivendell* (Classico 275, 2000), *At Dawn in Rivendell* (L.A.G. 067 303–2, 2002), and *Leaving Rivendell* (Classico 675, ca. 2005).
52. Caprice, *Elven Music* (Prikosnovénie PRIK048, 2001); *The Evening of Ilúvatar's Children (Elven Music 2)* (Prikosnovénie PRIK068, 2003).
53. Bo Hansson, *Music Inspired by Lord of the Rings* (Charisma CAS 1059, 1972).
54. Rick Wakeman, *Landscapes of Middle-earth*, accompanying the DVD *J.R.R. Tolkien: Master of the Rings* (Eagle Vision 37685, 2001). The CD label notes, "The titles on this CD have been selected from and previously released on 'The Seven Wonders Of The World' and 'Heritage Suite' performed by Rick Wakeman and the titles have been re-titled for the present compilation."
55. David Arkenstone, *Music Inspired by Middle-earth* (Neo Pacifica NP 3012, 2001).

56. Oliver's music works best in the context of the radio dramatization itself, but may also be heard separately on LP. Stephen Oliver, *Music from the BBC Radio Dramatisation of J.R.R. Tolkien's The Lord of the Rings* (BBC Records REH 415, 1981).

57. Rob Barnett, review of Sven-Eric Johanson, *Fancies* et al., http://www.music web.uk.net/classrev/2003/Sept03/Johanson.htm.

58. Information and audio are available on Klein's website at http://www.adamcj klein.us/adamsopera.html.

59. Jonathan Peters, *Symphony No. 1 "Journey of the Ring"* (Music for the Soul, 2005). The present author reviewed this in *Mythprint* 43:4 (whole no. 289), April 2006, 4.

60. Aulis Sallinen, *Symphony No. 7, Op. 71 "The Dreams of Gandalf"* from *Symphonies 1 & 7*, Staatsphilharmonie Rheinland-Pfalz, dir. Ari Rasilainen (CPO 999 918-2, 2003).

61. The recording at hand is Johan de Meij, *Symphony No. 1 "The Lord of the Rings,"* Koninklijke Militaire Kapel, dir. Pierre Kuijpers (KMK 001, 1989).

62. Craig Russell, *Middle-earth*, San Luis Obispo Symphony, dir. Michael Nowak (Naxos 8.559168, 2003).

63. An NPR promotional radio program on Peterson, *Profile: Thomas Peterson and "The Tale of the Rings of Power,"* was reviewed by the present author in *Mythprint* 27:8 (whole no. 122), August 1990, 5–6, reprinted in *Mythlore* 17:1 (whole no. 63), Autumn 1990, 44–45.

64. Glenn Buhr, *Beren & Lúthien* from *Winter Poems*, Winnipeg Symphony Orchestra, dir. Bramwell Tovey (CBC 5184, 1999).

65. Warren Lewis, diary, 31 January 1936. Marion E. Wade Center, Wheaton, Ill. The quartet he was thus condemning was by Elizabeth Maconchy, not generally considered one of the more avant-garde of British modernists.

66. Information on McCarthy is at his web page, http://dmccarthycomposer.com/.

67. Lubomyr Melnyk, *Song of Galadriel*, Lubomyr Melnyk (piano) (Bandura 19884).

68. Information on Felice is at his web page, http://www.frank-felice.com/.

Works Cited

Arkenstone, David. *Music Inspired by Middle-earth*. Neo Pacifica NP 3012, 2001.

Barnett, Rob. Review of Sven-Eric Johanson, *Fancies* et al. http://www.musicweb.uk. net/classrev/2003/Sept03/Johanson.htm. Available on the Internet Archive, http://web. archive.org

Birzer, Bradley J. *J.R.R. Tolkien's Sanctifying Myth*. Wilmington, DE: ISI, 2002.

Blyton, Carey. *The Hobbit*, from *British Light Overtures 3*, Royal Ballet Sinfonia, dir. Gavin Sutherland. White Line 2140, 2003.

Bratman, David. Review of Jonathan Peters, *Symphony No. 1: Journey of the Ring*. *Mythprint* 43:4 (whole no. 289), April 2006, 4.

_____. Review of *Profile: Thomas Peterson and "The Tale of the Rings of Power."* *Mythprint* 27:8 (whole no. 122), August 1990, 5–6. Reprinted in *Mythlore* 17:1 (whole no. 63), Autumn 1990, 44–45.

Brocelïande, *The Starlit Jewel: Songs from J.R.R. Tolkien's The Lord of the Rings & The Hobbit*. Flowinglass Music FM007, 2000.

Buhr, Glenn. *Beren & Lúthien*, from *Winter Poems*, Winnipeg Symphony Orchestra, dir. Bramwell Tovey. CBC 5184, 1999.

Caprice. *Elven Music.* Prikosnovénié PRIK048, 2001.
_____. *The Evening of Ilúvatar's Children (Elven Music 2).* Prikosnovénié PRIK068, 2003.
Chism, Christine. "Middle-earth, the Middle Ages, and the Aryan Nation: Myth and History in World War II." In *Tolkien the Medievalist*, ed. Jane Chance. London: Routledge, 2003, 63–92.
Christopher, Joe R. "Tolkien's Lyric Poetry." In *Tolkien's Legendarium*, ed Verlyn Flieger and Carl F. Hostetter (Westport, CT: Greenwood, 2000), 143–60.
Felice, Frank. "Frank Felice, Composer." http://www.frank-felice.com/
Festa, Giuseppe. *Voci dalla Terra di Mezzo.* Pongo Classica 2050, 2000.
Glass Hammer. *Journey of the Dunadan.* Arion Records 7690-51111-120, 1993.
_____. *The Middle-earth Album.* Arion Records SR1311, 2001.
Hansson, Bo. *Music Inspired by Lord of the Rings.* Charisma CAS 1059, 1972.
Hobbitons, The. *Songs from Middle-earth.* Dutch Tolkien Society Unquendor STEMRA PR001, 1996.
Hough, Stephen. "Elgar the Catholic." In *Elgar: An Anniversary Portrait*, intro. by Nicholas Kenyon. London: Continuum, 2007, 54–69.
Harper-Scott, J.P.E. *Edward Elgar, Modernist.* Cambridge: Cambridge University Press, 2006.
Kelly, Mary Quella. "The Poetry of Fantasy: Verse in *The Lord of the Rings.*" In *Tolkien and the Critics*, ed. Neil D. Isaacs and Rose A. Zimbardo. Notre Dame, IN: University of Notre Dame Press, 1968, 170–200.
Klein, Adam C.J. "Adam's Opera He Wrote." http://www.adamcjklein.us/adamsopera.html
Kushner, Ellen. "*The Lord of the Rings.*" Episode in *Sound & Spirit*, NPR, broadcast week of August 27, 2006. Available online at http://www.wgbh.org/programs/programDetail.cfm?programid=226
Led Zeppelin. "Ramble On," from *Led Zeppelin II.* Atlantic 82633, 1969.
Lewis, Warren Hamilton. *Brothers and Friends: The Diaries of Major Warren Hamilton Lewis*, ed. Clyde S. Kilby and Marjorie Lamp Mead. San Francisco: Harper and Row, 1982.
_____. Diaries. Marion E. Wade Center, Wheaton, IL.
"Marillion Biography." http://www.progfreaks.com/Marillion/Biography/Chapter1.htm. Available on the Internet Archive, http://web.archive.org
Martin, George R.R. *The Armageddon Rag.* New York: Pocket, 1985.
McCarthy, Daniel. "Daniel William McCarthy, Composer." http://dmccarthycomposer.com/
Meij, Johan de. *Symphony No. 1 "The Lord of the Rings,"* Koninklijke Militaire Kapel, dir. Pierre Kuijpers. KMK 001, 1989.
Melnyk, Lubomyr. *Song of Galadriel*, Lubomyr Melnyk, piano. Bandura, 1984.
Oliver, Stephen. *Music from the BBC Radio Dramatisation of J.R.R. Tolkien's The Lord of the Rings.* BBC Records REH 415, 1981.
Oldfield, Sally. *Water Bearer.* Chrysalis 1211, 1978.
Peters, Jonathan. *Symphony No. 1 "Journey of the Ring."* Music for the Soul, 2005.
Raffel, Burton. "*The Lord of the Rings* as Literature." In *Tolkien and the Critics*, ed. Neil D. Isaacs and Rose A. Zimbardo. Notre Dame, IN: University of Notre Dame Press, 1968, 218–46.
Ross, Alex. "The Ring and the Rings: Wagner vs. Tolkien." *The New Yorker*, December 22, 2003, 22–29

The Rough Guide to The Lord of the Rings. London: Rough Guides, 2003.
Russell, Craig. *Middle-earth*, San Luis Obispo Symphony, dir. Michael Nowak. Naxos 8.559168, 2003.
Sallinen, Aulis. *Symphony No. 7, Op. 71 "The Dreams of Gandalf,"* from *Symphonies 1 & 7*, Staatsphilharmonie Rheinland-Pfalz, dir. Ari Rasilainen. CPO 999 918-2, 2003.
Scull, Christina, and Wayne G. Hammond. *The J.R.R. Tolkien Companion & Guide.* Boston: Houghton Mifflin, 2006. 2 vols.
Seeman, Chris. "The Tolkien Music List." http://www.tolkien-music.com
Sharp, Cecil. *Cecil Sharp's Collection of English Folk Songs*, ed. Maud Karpeles. London: Oxford University Press, 1974.
_____. *English Folk Songs from the Southern Appalachians.* London: Oxford University Press, 1932.
Shippey, Tom. *The Road to Middle-earth.* Rev. and expanded ed. Boston: Houghton Mifflin, 2003.
Stark, James A. *Songs of Middle-earth.* Prime Time 9201, 1989.
Sturgis, Amy H. "Lord of the Rings, Rock On!" http://www.popthought.com/display_column.asp?DAID=282
Swann, Donald. *The Road Goes Ever On*, from J.R.R. Tolkien, *Poems and Songs of Middle-earth*, William Elvin (singer) and Donald Swann (piano). Caedmon TC 1231, 1967. Re-released on CD inserted into a later edition of Tolkien and Swann, *The Road Goes Ever On.* London: HarperCollins, 2002.
Tolkien, J.R.R. *The Adventures of Tom Bombadil and Other Verses from The Red Book.* Boston: Houghton Mifflin, 1962.
_____. *The Annotated Hobbit*, ed. Douglas A. Anderson. 2nd ed. Boston: Houghton Mifflin, 2002.
_____. *The J.R.R. Tolkien Audio Collection.* Caedmon/Harper Audio CD 101(4), 2001.
_____. *J.R.R. Tolkien Reads and Sings His The Hobbit and The Fellowship of the Ring.* Caedmon TC 1477, 1975. Liner notes by George Sayer.
_____. *The Letters of J.R.R. Tolkien: A Selection*, ed. Humphrey Carpenter with the assistance of Christopher Tolkien. Boston: Houghton Mifflin, 1981.
_____. *The Lord of the Rings.* 2nd ed. Boston: Houghton Mifflin, 1965.
_____. *The Silmarillion.* Boston: Houghton Mifflin, 1977.
_____ and Donald Swann. *The Road Goes Ever On: A Song Cycle.* Boston: Houghton Mifflin, 1967.
Tolkien Ensemble, The. *At Dawn in Rivendell*, L.A.G. 067 303-2, 2002.
_____. *An Evening at Rivendell*, Classico 175, 1997.
_____. *Leaving Rivendell*, Classico 675, ca. 2005.
_____. *A Night in Rivendell*, Classico 275, 2000.
Wakeman, Rick. *Landscapes of Middle-earth.* Accompanying the DVD *J.R.R. Tolkien: Master of the Rings.* Eagle Vision 37685, 2001.
Weber, Carl Maria von. *Der Freischütz.* Vocal score. Libretto by Friedrich Kind, translated by Natalia MacFarren. New York: Schirmer, n.d.
White, Michael. *The Life and Work of J.R.R. Tolkien.* Indianapolis: Alpha, 2002.

Performance Art in a Tunnel: A Musical Sub-Creator in the Tradition of Tolkien

Anthony S. Burdge

> *"[Thoth] is the living embodiment of human potential."* — Sarah Kernochan, Director *Thoth*

Introduction: The Creative Spark

As a one-man opera and sub-creator, S.K. Thoth stands amongst those who have inspired and gone before him. His life, philosophy, and what he refers to as his "death dance" are balanced methods that have brought forth a mythological world. There are many disciplines of art, literature, music, and drama that have been of far reaching influence for S.K. Thoth, which as illustrated below will demonstrate how his work is a unique new leaf upon the Great Tree of the creative spirit. This chapter endeavors to explore how S.K. Thoth has utilized the sub-creative methodology of J.R.R. Tolkien and has fashioned that understanding toward his work. It will focus specifically on the evolution of creativity in Thoth's life, and how it has developed his own musical and literary mythological world.

Thoth's work can be experienced via a live prayformance, listening to his Solopera on CD, or watching *Thoth*, the Academy Award winning film based on his life, for which director and co-producer Sarah Kernochan won her second Academy Award for Best Documentary Short Subject, 2002.

There are two recurring terms throughout this chapter that will be utilized, and require some further clarification: Solopera and prayformance. Both terms are derived from and applicable to the work of Thoth. Solopera is a term coined by Thoth to describe his work. It comes from the prefix "solo," meaning the work is performed alone, and "sol" defining sun. "Sol," a homonym for soul merged with "opera," meaning a dramatic performance put to music, and the plural form of "opus," which means work. The solopera is part vocalizing, puzzle, aerobics routine, monologue, language deconstruction, alchemy, theater, healing ritual, sacred dance, all accompanied by solo violin and complex percussive rhythms. According to Thoth, a solopera is much more than art; a solopera is a combination of meditation and prayer, which has led him to the discovery of an inner calm that few ever achieve.

Thoth defines the term prayformance thus:

> I perform and pray simultaneously. The word was a gift. Someone asked me what I was doing and I said I was praying and performing, and he said, "It sounds like you're prayerforming." And it just struck me that that was a wonderful way of describing what I do. I was telling that story to a friend who learned English as a second language, and was very precise in his use of English. He said that to him it didn't sound like I needed the letters "er." I tried saying it in the new way, prayformance, and it worked. I loved the pun. Now I say I put the *ray* in performance [Simmons, 26].

These terms succinctly describe a Thoth performance, which can be equally described as a form of universal prayer. The prayformance contains the objective truths at the core of all religions, completely detached from the ego of a typical performance.

Thoth is New York's own mystical conjurer, urban shaman, berdache, channeler of divine worlds, healer and mythmaker. His artistic power, presence, and purpose encapsulate him as a highly principled artist, with a strong focus on healing both personal and social divisions (Mewbourne 49). Thoth's immense improvisational range of talents is a broad expansion of his training as a classical violinist, which embodies a deep array of operatic vocalizations. The tones of his vocal and instrumental range culminate within and resonate without, the hallowed hall of the Angel Tunnel in the very core of New York City's Central Park. In this space, raw divine energy, channeled by Thoth, cleanses and balances — unhindered by the barriers of modern materialistic consumer thought, culture and society — an audience that will remain ever changed. The Angel Tunnel, the familiar name for the hall beneath Bethesda Fountain Terrace, is a nexus where the progress of Thoth's life, training, work and death dance is fulfilled and realized. According to Thoth, the "death dance" is when a person's being, the "I am," aligns the bliss of its existence or its reason for being with the moment of death of its physical body.

A primary influence, who will remain with Thoth his entire life, has been J.R.R. Tolkien, author of *The Hobbit* and *The Lord of the Rings*. Thoth's first creative spark came from learning that as isolated as he felt as a being, he could experience Tolkien's world fully. Tolkien's Middle-earth transported Thoth into feeling he no longer was within our Primary world. Tolkien's methods of creating a believable secondary world were that of sub-creation (a term coined by Tolkien in his essay "On Fairy Stories"). Sub-creation refers to the subjective tools of the artist which Tolkien attributes the source as being the divine act of creation as used by the Creator in manifesting our primary world. These acts of sub-creation emanate from the same source, regardless of cultural or religious lenses of interpretation. Sound and language, claimed by some to be the origins of Creation itself, is the sub-creative source. Thoth pushes Tolkien's plan for a "creative continuity" to new heights. According to Diana Pavlac Glyer in her work, *The Company They Keep: C.S. Lewis and J.R.R. Tolkien as Writers in Community*, Tolkien stated that his plan was to "leave scope for other minds and hands wielding paint, and music, and drama emphasizing that each individual creative act is a participation in something large, complex and beautiful, as party to a creative continuity" (Glyer 222).

After investigating and studying Tolkien's works, Thoth realized he shared similar thoughts and principles concerning the intricacies of creation with Tolkien. Thoth's first sub-creation — the hero's journey of an anthropomorphic coffee bean — came to him intuitively. Thoth readily admits that when he became so absorbed in this intuitive creation, he felt high, elated: in the realm of epiphany. He sensed becoming limitless, and grabbed anything in order to express it. Tolkien, helping him in a period of isolation, opened Thoth's eyes to the possibility of experiencing and creating alternate realities.

According to the work and vision of Thoth, artists are beings blessed with the divine gift of creativity, who draw inspiration from those who have gone before them. The heroic journey of the artist and the subsequent creation, "Art," or "death dance," is the creative mark left upon the world. Each successive step toward the manifesting of the sub-created world through music or literature is a step in the rhythm of the individual's own death dance. These steps consist of a pulse or release of energy directed in a specific manner toward the expression of the work. Death is the largest release of energy from the physical body, the final step in leaving behind a significant sub-creative impression upon the global community. Tolkien's death dance would be the tales of hobbits, elves and wizards through all the ages of his Middle-earth. This paper need not digress into a discussion of the monumental impression Tolkien's work has left upon the world. Readers of this chapter already have an inkling that Tolkien's creative work has continued to exist beyond the ending of his own physical body.

For artists like Tolkien and Thoth, the creation of a believable secondary world manifested with the means and methods of the primary world is an all-encompassing life's work. The means and methods of achieving such a creation are so varied that they are impractical to categorically list here. Each tool is personal to the artist and should be left to humanity's own individual learning and understanding of the creativity that inspires every artist and their implementation. Tolkien's methodology laid the foundation for us to discover the sub-creative tools possessed by all of humanity. These uniquely structured processes should not be judged right or wrong by an institution, provided that the artist is true to his or her purpose as a sub-creator. The secondary, mythological world are expressions of the artist's own life spark, which reflect universal principles of active, passive and neutral, or that contain the language of past, present and future. It is the harmony of these modes, the open doorways to worlds waiting to be unveiled, which exists in the mind and spirit of the artist. "To be," unlike the dramatic Shakespearean reference, is for Thoth the ultimate balanced state of being, which he has sought for himself. "To be" is a term in union with a divine principal that has a strong focus on healing personal and social divisions. Contained within the artist is the essence and harmonics of Creation. When an awareness of this state of being is realized, then a perfected balance which is outside the realm of cultural, political or religious censure, begins to unfold. The purpose and link to artistic synchronization is that all are meant to unite creative sparks with the Creator and Universe.

As Thoth readily states, he is the culmination of all his ancestors, all people and all cultures brought forth by the utilization of not one dominant energy, but a wholeness achieved by mastery and union of both male and female principles, or yin and yang. Most people do not utilize this union, preferring instead one overt energy over another, without consciously being aware of what they are doing. This lack of awareness thereby leaves worlds, methods and energies dormant and underutilized. In the archaic traditions of healing and storytelling, of paramount central importance to Thoth's work is the hearing and expressing of his ancestral voices. Thoth consistently receives guidance and inspiration from them. By adhering to these principles, Thoth becomes an undeniable authentic voice for transcending socially-constructed polarities. By unifying these ancestral ethnic voices, Thoth becomes a messenger of unity (Mewborne 49).

At the heart of Tolkien's love of story is his equal if not higher love of language. Linguistic patterns affected him emotionally, like color or music (Carpenter 212). As observers of a secondary world, readers must be fully invested in the artistic world they explore, thereby leaving behind all contemporary attachments, egos and insecurities. Thoth consciously lets go of attachments, judgments, and ego with each prayformance, because he feels they block the flow of creative ancestral guidance (Mewborne 48).

A unique quality and recurring theme Thoth finds in the masters who have inspired him — from Tolkien to Bartók, Wagner to Hendrix — is the hearing, seeing or reading of the work. Yet the experience is not as limited to the external enjoyment of the work. The understanding comes internally, as participants within the world, experiencing it in original ways, seeing many layers of interpretation, many angles to understand the work on different levels. Each of these layers within the inspired parts of the sub-creator's world should not dominate one over the other. The artist carefully orchestrates each thematic layer into a unique symphony of mythical tones. The viewpoints of critical interpretation are not the work, nor a sum of their inspired parts.

Western society lives within a realm that prefers comfortable labels and preprogrammed thought processes. So much of what Westerners experience is mediated through technology, from musical recordings to cinema to TV to media, and the Internet. Thoth believes that a society that depends upon technology actually enslaves the will of the people, in turn harboring material desires. This technology is not necessarily an honest measure that the society is necessarily better or more advanced than another.

In fact, it is quite possible that primitive societies are more advanced than those in the Western or "modern" world because of their environmental concerns and shamanic traditions, all of which are capable of supporting sub-creation. In this regard Thoth's work, akin to Tolkien's universal applicability, becomes a refreshing antidote to our preprocessed techno-centric world (Mewborne 48).

Unfortunately, the standards of a technologically-based culture do not provide the tools to fully grasp a created work and world such as those presented by Tolkien or Thoth. The artist's journey takes the initiate beyond the limitations set by society and mass media placed upon creative thought. Attendees at Thoth's prayformances may see certain things they are able to identify with, which help them become enveloped in his secondary sub-created world. Thoth's work envelops a plethora of identifying symbols, yet adheres to none: his unique work and sub-created world illuminates and honors aspects of world culture and myths. The true experience of the sub-created world would not be to become trapped within the minor notes, or to identify with select parts of the whole, but to flow throughout knowing the entirety, which then would not hold the observer back by what is not understood.

In the opinion of this author, this precise element of the entirety of the work, the applicability of the whole versus the deconstruction of a single thread from the tapestry, has been an issue of great debate with Tolkien's work. This debate has originated from a statement from Tolkien's letter that *The Lord of the Rings* is a deeply Catholic work; without thinking so at first, but intentionally in revised drafts (Carpenter 172). This statement stands at the center of a large body of religious fervor bound with analysis and deconstruction of Tolkien's work, which serves to only undermine the whole. The religious strand within the tapestry of Tolkien's epic is mistaken for the whole. Tolkien's comments show that there was no intended message, that his intent was indeed a course in linguistic aesthetic. This exercise is then coupled with observations of nature, and his argument concerning the mortality of man. Tolkien felt at a certain point that he ceased to invent, implying that another force wrote through him: that he was the chosen instrument for the writing of the tales (Carpenter 211–212). The tales of Middle-earth, whether received as a direct communication from the Creator, or filtered through as messages from Tolkien's own ancestral voices, wrote themselves through his mind as sub-creator. This is where

Thoth and Tolkien share methodology. Implementing the tools of storytelling, both artists have transformed themselves into divine messengers for the transmission of stories.

Tolkien realized a clash was present between "literary" technique and the fascination of elaborating in detail an imaginary mythical age, mythical not allegorical (Carpenter 174). The observations of Tolkien's direct critics, those not directly commenting on Tolkien's Catholicism, has led some to believe that he struggled within the confines of his religious framework. These same adherents may also ignore the fact that his theories of sub-creation and entering Faërie can be seen as heretical to the institution of his faith. What does this suggest? Tolkien states, as cited previously, that parts of his work were revealed through him than by him, which would make Tolkien the vessel and messenger of the stories he received and transmitted (Carpenter 189). Furthermore, the stories then become part of Tolkien's imaginative landscape during his writing. The stories become not only the product of his geographical, historical, ethnic knowledge but a product from the direct union with the Creator and the natural world. Is he then communing with his "characters" as they were revealed to him? How would Tolkien know to say that the power of Faërie is, in part, the communion with the natural world unless he himself had experienced it first hand? This is where his faith may have been problematic for him.

If Tolkien intended his work to be a one-to-one distillation of his Catholic religion, he would have had direct references similar to those utilized in C.S. Lewis' *Chronicles of Narnia* or *Space Trilogy*. Tolkien intentionally left out any such allegory (Carpenter 174). Numerous parallel examples of correlations within Tolkien's work have been cited throughout academia, i.e. Lembas as Eucharist, Galadriel as Virgin Mary, Aragorn (or Frodo or Gandalf) as Christ. These examples, in the opinion of this author, do a great disservice to the overall understanding of Tolkien's unique writing. Micheala Baltasar encapsulated this best by stating: "There are no exact links to prove any of these connections true and definite" (Chance 21). The universal truths present in Tolkien's work broaden his mythological world beyond the scope of Lewis' Christian allegory.

The myriad dogmatic analyses of Narnia presents a belief that to know the work of Lewis, one must be familiar with the Christian mindset, and an adherent of that faith. For Thoth, the whole shape of religion has to do with controlling the way someone else perceives the connected energies of all things. If in an institution one can control that perception, then they are able to control the very face of how people build their worlds. Each of the major religions presents itself as the "chosen faith," yet are at each other's proverbial throats. For Tolkien and Thoth, it is the reverse, the opposite of religion's "correct behavior." An individual's interpretation of these works holds greater meaning for their audiences. A standard interpretation for a work does an injustice to an audience outside the focus of that particular interpretive vision. Thoth's work cannot be labeled as one standard or another. Tolkien's own faith may be seen as at the foundation of his work, but it appears he purposefully designed his work to be applicable to people outside of his faith no matter where they live. Perhaps this lends to the worldwide popularity of Tolkien's work. By classifying Tolkien or Thoth's work under a particular interpretive umbrella, we do not lend to a stronger individualized, rewarding understanding of the work. The universal creativity of Tolkien and Thoth instills their audience with the ability to establish wholly new lands of their own devising.

Awakening and Development

Born to an interracial couple during a time of racial turmoil in the 1950s, Stephen Kaufman would later change his name to "Thoth" after graduating from San Francisco State University with a Comparative Literature degree. His reasoning for this was "Thoth was a high priest of ancient Egypt and the deity of scribes, wisdom, communication and mathematics. I took the name because it symbolized an important point in my spiritual development when I transited from Greece (Hermes) to Africa (Thoth)." As a being of mixed ancestral heritage, Thoth found that by accepting who he was, his own heritage and manifested reality, he was then open to receive the gifts of energy from his ancestors. This principle is applicable to all beings. The energy this incorporates emanates throughout knowledge, wisdom, intellect, vision and beliefs. Accepting this has lead Thoth to an interconnectivity of his family line to that of all world nationalities, all beings, and all races, becoming a descendant of the world community.

When Thoth was younger, depressed by the racial oppression his family had endured, a mentor encouraged Thoth to look into mythology as a way to develop the Self. Several years earlier, a statement from Tolkien paralleled Thoth's desire to seek out the mythological in life. In 1951 Tolkien wrote to Milton Waldman explaining that the mythological in stories must echo the essentials spiritual truth (or fault) not depicted in overtly known forms of the "real" world (Carpenter 144). As Thoth absorbed this, he was able to understand Tolkien's example as a way to achieve a better understanding of humanity's problematic experiences, that individuals should set these difficulties into a mythological context thereby allowing the artist to overcome a variety of emotional anxieties. This concept can be seen in Tolkien's scenes of the Dead Marshes in relation to his own war experiences. The harshness of reality helps the artist give way to a myth of his own devising.

In 2001 Thoth was quoted in *The Village Voice* as saying: "What I am doing is myth-making.... Myths offer a reflective way of perceiving the now, because it's difficult for us to see it. It gives us an objective viewpoint" (Andrews 75). At the time, mythology culminated around Thoth's personal identification with the fleet-footed god of communication, Hermes. During the course of studying his African ancestry, S.K. Thoth found Hermes to be the Egyptian "Thoth" and realized he himself bore the same mantle. By adapting these spiritual values, having the inner knowledge from divine storytellers Hermes and Thoth, S.K. Thoth wears the mantel of messenger, which is a divine role for the conveyance of truth through the chosen medium of the artist.

Thoth's mother, Elayne Jones, was born of ancestry from Barbados, Africa, Scotland, and Carib Indian, while his father, George Kaufman, known primarily as a Russian Jew was also from a Romanian gypsy descent. Jones, a Harlem-born Juilliard graduate, originally wished to play the violin, but became a timpanist, a kettle drum player. She performed with the American Symphony Orchestra, and was the first African-American to play on both the New York Philharmonic and the San Francisco Symphonies, which she later left when her son was in his early twenties. She ultimately sued the San Francisco Symphony because of racial discrimination. The energy against the relationship between Thoth's parents during this time of racial turmoil was strong, making their own love and energy together that much stronger. The manifestation of their children through that love made Thoth and his two sisters kind to people in the world, yet this did not ease their individual burdens. Before the Civil Rights movement, memories abound of this time when the family was the focus of racial hatred, bigotry, name calling and threats while in their car, or walking on the street. In this early point in his life, Thoth felt oppressed from these societal demands on his family. These moments of oppression and societal demands upon himself and family sparked Thoth's isolation from the rest of the world. This isolation gestated into an internalized hatred of himself. Unfortunately, due to conflicting work schedules, George and Elayne later separated (this is further elaborated upon in a discussion by Thoth and Elayne Jones in the film *Thoth*). At the age of ten, Thoth was emotionally devastated during an already troubling time from the separation of his parents. Only in recent years has Thoth no longer taken responsibility for his family's dissolution, nor does he internalize the hate-filled messages of a society not inclined to have accountability for their own hateful actions. He has broken the emotional ties to what these messages, found within his own parents' social division, represent. Thoth has immensely changed his internal core reality. Through his self-realizations he has broadened his connectedness to the whole planet via his diverse ancestry (Mewbourne 49).

After several childhood attempts to learn the piano in their basement, his mother asked him what kind of instrument he wished to play. It had occurred to him that either the night before or earlier that day, he had a dream of receiving a violin, and he immediately answered that that was what he wished to play. There was a violin in the family, its origins were unknown to him, and he used that until another was bought for him to play. With his taking up of the violin, Thoth felt that his mother was perhaps, in part, fulfilling a leftover childhood desire. He found the violin to be the most soulful instrument in existence. During this period of oppression and isolation Thoth turned to honing his talents, in understanding his mixed heritage, exploring his love of creative writing and his musical training in the violin. After his first story, the heroic journey of the coffee bean was dismissed and rejected by a school teacher, he began his internal private journey, investing his entire being into the art of sub-creation.

As previously stated, the first creative spark came from learning that as isolated as he felt as a being, he could experience Tolkien's world fully and in so doing, Middle-earth possessed the power to transport him into feeling as if he no longer was within our Primary world. Thoth investigated Tolkien's work further, especially *Leaf by Niggle*, where he found very powerful and healing tools. Not as well known as Tolkien's other works, *Leaf by Niggle* is the tale of a painter who painstakingly paints leaves, and eventually paints a tree attached to these leaves on a large canvas with a world beyond, which he is later able to explore with his neighbor and family. This tale helped Thoth's creative process grow immensely, as it was Tolkien's own commentary about the sub-creative process. Thoth identified with Niggle, a being of mixed vices, virtues and qualities (Carpenter 321). The underlying discourse on Tolkien's creative process in *Leaf by Niggle* fueled Thoth's own journey into the sub-creative act. Being so attracted to this tale, Thoth realized he shared similar thoughts and principles concerning the intricacies of creation with Tolkien. Both artists — constant "nigglers"— also shared a penchant for accuracy and perfection, even in matters that seem unimportant to most. This niggling pushes the process of sub-creation beyond the canvas of the imagination into a world without boundaries, as experienced by Niggle.

Being drawn to Tolkien's different maps, Thoth knew he had to create in his own voice immediately. New landscapes grew and flowered in his mind's eye, his love for Tolkien's stories continued to grow as he discovered the appendices to *The Lord of the Rings*. He fully invested his time and love into Tolkien's chronologies, glossaries and other areas, readily admitting this is where his imagination began to form, his own very imaginative stories spiraled into existence out of this love of Tolkien. He read *The Hobbit* repeatedly. Reading Tolkien was a safe haven compared to being punished for expressing his imagination in school. The story of the coffee bean came before any influence or inspiration from Tolkien: his first sub-creation came to him instinctively.

At this time, he was fully investing himself into the works of musical greats: Bach for improvisation, Yma Sumac for vocal range, Wagner for drama, Ellington for swing, Callas for vocal drama, Hendrix for explosive virtuosity, Ravel for tonal color, Parker for freedom, and Bartók for everything. This would not have begun without his mother. She first put rhythm into his body as she played the drums while carrying him through her pregnancy, which later helped him seek out his own melodic pattern. Being born to a drummer, Thoth admits helped him "find my rhythmic center" (Simmons 25). Of this prenatal development Thoth happily remarked that: "They are now discovering that the womb is a receptor for information before the child comes out into the world." During gestation, Thoth habitually heard these structures of rhythm, and he now realizes that bass is the first connection between not communicating and creating, meaning that when sound is created, rhythm ensues, and language is born.

The Associate Concert Master of the American Symphony Orchestra was Mara Dvonch, a friend of Elayne's who played in various orchestras together with her, and she became his first teacher. Dvonch, born in New York City in 1914, attended the Juilliard School of the Arts, won the Naumberg Prize, and played under Stokowski, Steinberg, Previn and Beecham. Being a rambunctious, energetic child, and learning the basics of the violin from her, Thoth realized that the traditional way of playing the violin was too sedentary for him. He decided that would change. Mara became Concert Master of the Pittsburgh Symphony Orchestra and soon moved. His mother called on another friend, Harry Glickman, to instruct her son. Glickman, also a graduate of Juilliard, was born in Russia and brought to the U.S. as a child. At the age of 14 Glickman had won a scholarship to the Paris Conservatory of Music and was awarded first prize for music in 1924. During his life Glickman, under Arturo Toscanini, was assistant concertmaster for the NBC Orchestra, concertmaster of the Brooklyn Philharmonic, and first violinist of the WQXR String Quartet for 25 years. Glickman was the most influential violin teacher of Thoth's life, and was also a father figure for him, since his own father had been gone for some time. Glickman didn't take many students. Thoth states of Glickman, "Students had to be ready to study with him," which is a testimony to Thoth's own growing talents. Thoth also admitted not to have practiced a lot, but "was still gaining ground." In speaking with Thoth, he can only imagine what it would have been like if he had applied himself more completely:

> I would have been a classical soloist or member of a symphony orchestra and would have never had done this. That would have precluded me from seeking an alternate way of using the instrument. Classical music is so stultifying, it's so difficult to play the violin and to play the music that has been written requires a huge amount of practice to get all the notes right. Once you're doing it, it's very hard to improvise; your whole mindset is geared toward the memorizing of this number that represents this position on the instrument. Rhythm is broken up into a very mathematical formula that one memorizes and repro-

duces in front of an audience. This is basically what classical music is. Whereas, just playing the instrument is about feeling the beat and hearing the sounds and going to the sound without thinking about it. This is what I want to do: I go from here to here, I just do it, but that is not possible without a certain amount of technique. Yet too much technique makes that impossible also; it makes it almost unthinkable. So now I use the fingerboard just to feel around it to express what I want, whereas classical musicians are not like that: everything is numerical and measured.

After graduating from LaGuardia High School of the Arts in Manhattan, Thoth soon moved to San Francisco with his mother after she received an offer to be a part of the symphony of the San Francisco Opera. It was at San Francisco State University where Thoth met violin instructor David Schneider, the least influential of his teachers. Thoth spent the least amount of time studying with him. This was also in response to his growing difficulty and disillusionment with classical music, which seemed very limiting to him. Thoth played a wide range of classical music from Tchaikovsky to Brahms to Mendelssohn to Bach to Mozart, and knew that he was not going to be a soloist (thinking that he was too undisciplined for such a career). Instead, Thoth felt he would play for a symphony, which was what his mother had wanted for him (Simmons 25). During the course of instruction, his instinct was to improvise his music. He grew to feel that "playing music that is basically dead is a very limited way of expressing one's self." In turn he abandoned classical study in favor of "emanating the perfection of the moment" (Andrews 75).

An influential musical counterpoint to Tolkien was Bartók. The Hungarian and pianist was one of the founders of the field of ethnomusicology, and is considered one of the greatest composers of the twentieth century. Both Thoth and Bartók share similar traits in early musical development. Where Thoth admits to first hearing rhythm in the womb, Bartók learned to play the piano early. Like Bartók, Thoth also began his study of music with the piano. Bartók's synthesis of folk music, classicism and modernism, as well as his harmonic, melodious sense coupled with his fondness of asymmetrical dance rhythms inspired Thoth's own early compositions, which were reminiscent of Bartók.

As he passed into his early adult years, Thoth started looking for a method for being more operatic. Since Thoth had never had a vocal coach or formal vocal training, he listened to Wagner and allowed various parts and pieces to groom him vocally. After discovering Wagner, Thoth began to put his mythological worlds into operatic form. Thoth's three-act mythological opera entitled *The Herma: The Life and Land of Nular-in*, based in the Festad — Thoth's sub-created mythological world — was in part inspired by Wagner's *Der Ring Des Nibelungen*. Thoth soon found Wagner's operas disappointing due to their Euro-centric, one-dimensional constructs of patriarchy and heterosexuality. In his own work, Thoth sought to represent his diverse racial, sexual and cultural ancestors in a more expansive, expressive way rather than exclusively or marginally. Through this expansion of expressive creativity the Festad was born.

For those who have never experienced a prayformance in either Central Park or through Thoth's appearances elsewhere, Thoth's vocal range stems from low chanting, to resonating Wagnerian tones, to resounding bass, going beyond gender lines of tenor to a genuine soprano. Thoth is a true adept at vocal sound and tone, which can only be fully appreciated firsthand. Thoth believes tones are sacred. By vibrating himself with tonal sound and projecting his voice so fully from the center of his being, he is liberating himself by removing inner obstructions which keep him from hearing the voices of his ancestors. Thoth speaks about his music theory to Denise Mewbourne in her enlightening work "S.K. Thoth & the Power of Presence":

> Musically, this concern with unified elements manifests itself as his emphasis on "the one note." He says, "This is very important to my philosophy of music. In order to create music, one has to make every note have the fullest expression it can possibly have. If one note can be real, it means more than thousands of notes played. So it's most important to have a connection with how to make that note real." He cites Miles Davis as a master of the truth of one note, and classical musicians as examples of those focused on playing many notes. "If you ask them to improvise around the one note they don't know what to do, because they're so used to playing many notes ... and it doesn't really communicate what's going on with your spirit at the moment. It's not possible with so many notes because one is worried about missing one" [Mewbourne, 49].

It was this one single carrying note that drew the author's attention in 2003 while enjoying an ice cream in Central Park. Over ten minutes passed before the then unfamiliar sound of Thoth was located. Through the magic of his voice, Thoth's sound had radiated outward from the point where he prayformed in the Angel Tunnel, and permeated that entire area of Central Park. The magic of this was done without the use of amplification. Thoth feels that heavy amplification is greedy and power hungry, and is not true to what he wishes to nourish. Thoth prefers to prayform without amplification, and feels that with electronic mediation people hear the sound at slightly different times. The experience becomes fragmented and out of synch, ultimately not allowing true bonding and healing with the audience to take place (Mewbourne 49). Unencumbered by electrical implements, he is then able to change the vibration wherever he passes and not have the hum of an amp during moments of stillness.

The cleansing tones of Thoth's operatic vocal range are in part what draw a myriad of people to his prayformances. These practices come from Thoth absorbing himself in esoteric philosophies, alongside the variety of mythologies he was already studying. From such study, Thoth understood all people and all things emanate from the same source. The outward emanations of Creation, or vibrations from the Creator, manifest in the slow moving particles called physical being. Thoth utilizes, although he is not limited to, archaic singing and ecstatic dancing, which can fine tune humanity's awareness of these vibrations and expand the conscious mind. Upon recognition of this, the artist can influence not only the level of the body's vibratory output, but also healing of the self and of the community. With this knowledge, the artist intuits the necessary healing tones that flow into the creative venture.

Thoth has strongly sought to sub-create a world that is completely "enwombed" acoustically. This is why he further creates tones with the foot drum and violin, which are his main power tools to manifest his music. Power tools, according to Thoth, are everything the "I am" or seat of consciousness uses to increase energy and focus such as: food, diet, vitamins, natural supplements, hallucinogenics, stillness and most importantly our physical body. Food, diet, vitamin and supplements, and the physical body are almost obvious means by which can alter energy. Food and a healthy diet are essential power tools to create a strong physical form. Nutrients in the form of supplements as well as physical activity are just as important as diet in increasing one's energy.

Stillness is the beginning of the artists death dance, the creative venture of life spiraling from within outward. Stillness is often something feared and misunderstood in Western culture of mass marketed, all-consuming noise. Yet stillness is a conscious-altering power tool. When left with the still thoughts of one's own mind, most in our culture find a terror looming. Past hopes and dashed memories come to the forefront of the mind. How many members of society can say that they will be fully content, fully realized beings, and comfortable with themselves if their life was to end tomorrow? Both death and stillness are feared when they should be embraced. If Thoth were to die in the next second, he hopes to be prayforming, singing, dancing and spinning. Yet, the mastery of his craft comes from knowing and accepting death. The death dance is one of the truths of this world, where people are surrounded by the cycles of life, growth and destruction. The sub-creative act is an evolutionary ongoing process and will always be for Thoth, aligned and affected by the cycles of the world as he tunes his being into a living universe. Yet to fully manifest a sub-creation through the moment of death, both for the individual and the world, the artist's intent must be pure. The importance of sub-creation lies with its connectivity to the rhythmic patterns of the planet.

Another power tool mentioned, hallucinogenics, are exceptionally stimulating and should neither be disregarded or taken lightly. Nor should their mention be taken as blanket permission to be used without ritualized purpose or spiritual intent. For millennia, shamans utilized psychoactive plants as communicative tools to interface with the spirit plane. In addition, these plants were integral to the healing rituals identifying and extracting illnesses from a patient. Through the use of natural hallucinogens, the mind's eye can be trained and re-opened from what modernity has denied it. In order to receive a key to extended sight and see the true forms of all things, as beautiful or horrible they may be, plants have been used as an influential interface between brain/mind/body and spirit. These views can then be seen as a divine revelation from a source outside the self, in this case a god within the plant (McKenna, XVIII). An added benefit, perhaps one of the reasons shamans were also myth-makers and story-tellers, is that through this practice, natural hallucinogens illuminate the dark cavernous depths of the creative mind.

It is through the culmination of all of these elements that Thoth's improvisational foundation rapidly blossomed. Thoth grew his hair as a reflection of his desire to express himself more fully, to delve the well expanding before him as defined in his music. His growing dreadlocks, however, became an obstacle in keeping a 9 to 5 job. He soon found himself taking to the streets as a street performer. This honed his sound and talents, shaping his outward appearance along with his growing spirituality.

Thoth began to live the mythology he was building. By adding singing and dancing to his repertoire, he found himself playing in the BART subway system, and on "walkabouts" throughout the parks, and public areas of the San Francisco Bay Area. This allowed him the freedom to experiment with various forms of dress and percussion with his feet and dance techniques. Thoth fell in love with the reverberating sound waves of tunnels throughout the subway system. After a short time with a band, he added the bells and heavy-heeled sandals upon his ankles, as a solo source of his percussive beats. Upon his return to New York, and the dissolution of the band, he found the tunnel facing Bethesda Fountain in Central Park appropriately nicknamed the "Angel Tunnel" because of the "Angel of the Waters" statue that crowns the fountain. Thoth sanctifies the hall as an the angelic violinist. The perfect drum for his prayformance was found in a metal grate in the middle of the tunnel with the accompanying hollow depths below. Using this found instrument, Thoth soon became the percussive soul of the tunnel and park.

Reflecting on his use of the tunnel to Nancy Ruhling in her piece, "Ancient God Plays Central Park" the tunnel taught him how to manifest himself in a theater (Ruhling A53). The metal grates become his drums. Ideally, he would like to find a stage with drums built into the floor so he performs the bass drumbeats with his feet. In an earlier piece written by N.C. Maisak, entitled "Loincloth Maestro" he states that: "The tunnel is a magical place.... It's my temple. It concretizes my work. Everywhere I go, everywhere I play, I'm always looking for a spot like the tunnel." The reverberating rhythmic earthen drumbeat of Thoth's dancing and pounding steps, when he is not spinning or leaping, accompanied by his simultaneous singing and violin playing has made the tunnel, Central Park's emanating, pulsating heart-song. By making enough money to survive and pay for the maintenance of his art entirely through prayforming, and the sale of CDs and DVDs, Thoth has become the living embodiment of human potential. He refuses to allow the values of Western culture to affect his ability to fully manifest his being and art.

In speaking to Thoth about his life and the process of sub-creation, world creation and destruction, a realization has been brought to light that indeed this is the path of true human evolution. Whether it was the dramatic atonality of Bartók, the Flying Dutchman or valkyries of Wagner, the tearing riffs of Hendrix, journeying alongside him still was Tolkien's beautifully woven heroic tales of fellowship, which began animating Thoth's own hero's journey. In a desire to create a world where everyone loves one another, are good to one another and can find their own bliss, Thoth sought to perfect his sub-creative world through neutrality of being. Tolkien had first shown him alternate realities, and that he had the ability to present a created world. Thoth knew that this would be no modest undertaking.

World Creation and Destruction

Thoth continued to develop an awareness that the divine gift was the ability to sub-create — to create and destroy worlds. In order "To be" fully, he had to walk a tightrope, to trust his own vision, because social, cultural and religious boundaries were an illusion. The illusion that money and technology are benchmarks of progress toward human evolution traps a people into believing that an iPod or cell phone is a symbol of power. Equally, the latest trend in media, fashion, celebrity lives, or reality TV trumps the creativity of the writer, musician or artist, thereby instilling a distrust in the artist's own divine visionary abilities. Western society promotes a false vision of material wealth, which is the ultimate fall of humanity. This is most important to Thoth as an artist, and for artists in general, because potential artists, with enormous talent, fail to trust their own vision and stay the course of true creation. For Tolkien, the sub-creative process entailed utilizing the tools given to us by the Creator, which allows each being to create as each is created, to manifest believable secondary worlds through the material of the primary world.

Thoth believes he is manifesting his mythological world in an unusual way, a completely subjective way, which he believes is the reality lived in. Thoth states that when we break out of subjectivity then "death" occurs, and at that point objectivity allows the individual to see all things clearly, because the body is no longer possessed, no longer needed as it slowly dissolves like the ringing of a note. The beginning of this process to fully manifest a universe is stillness. After stillness, Thoth uses spinning and dancing to manifest the sub-created reality within the context of a prayformance.

As a being of mixed heritage, Thoth found that by accepting who he was, his own manifested reality, his own ancestry, then he was open to receive their gifts of energy. This principle is applicable to all beings. This incorporates energy that emanates into realms of knowledge, intellect, vision and spirituality. A pattern of interconnectivity within his family line expands to all world nationalities, all beings, and all races, creating a descendent of the world community. Thoth, with every creative act through prayforming and sub-creation, brings forth his ancestral knowledge and incorporates this wisdom into his everyday life and rituals. A believer that humanity, and all of creation for that matter having emanated from the same source, Thoth found his New York audience with their own various mixed heritages able to identify with him on an ethnic level. "To be" fully, to create as he sought to do with the proper energy, he came to a realization that a balance was necessary and the artist must be one who finds the "Christ," or Messiah of Self. A better measure of evolution and advancement could be how people in society manifest themselves as Christs or messiahs, capable of sub-creating, rather than to the amassing of physical wealth, hierarchical advancement, and other forms of material gain. To become free from technological enslavement, society should look to the spiritual enlightenment of "primitive" societies. The people of primitive societies were endowed with the ability to fully grasp their connectivity to bird, beast and tree. For Tolkien this was the power of Faërie or enchantment, an ability nearer primordial societies than our own (Tolkien 117). Enchantment is lost with the multitude of intrusive distractions by a consumer culture. The enchanted mind or shamanic role is the only counterflow against a world that is fed purely on the

> designs of Madison avenue, of the Pentagon, of the Fortune 500 corporations.... Not to know one's true identity is to be a mad, disensouled thing—a golem. And, indeed this image, sickeningly Orwellian, applies to the mass of human beings now living in the high-tech industrial democracies. Their authenticity lies in their ability to obey and follow mass style changes that are conveyed through the media. Immersed in junk food, trash media, and cryptofascist politics, they are condemned to toxic lives of low awareness. Sedated by the prescribed daily television fix they are a living dead lost to all but the act of consuming.... The public has no history and no future, the public lives

in a golden moment created by a credit system which binds them ineluctably to a web of illusions that is never critiqued. This is the ultimate consequence of having broken off the symbiotic relationship with the Gaian matrix of the planet. This is the consequence of lack of partnership; this is the legacy of imbalance between the sexes; this is the terminal phase of a long descent into meaninglessness and toxic existential confusion.... This isn't just metaphor; it is really happening to us [McKenna, 254–265].

Thoth continues this flow against the toxic vision presented to us by the government and media by helping his audience find tools to manifest sub-created worlds. In this manner, there can be an awakening to a new awareness after years of having been subjected to the false and artificial motivations of the Western World. Western society can then begin to live a highly renewed sense of connection to the greater world and universe.

With this perspective, the artist is able to move any type of creative energy, regardless of its polarity. Generally people stand on one side or the other of polar opposites, whether it is due to cultural, political or religious conditioning. The mainstream majority generally does not realize that they are moving energy of the reverse spectrum to their intent. If the initiate stays balanced, then the energy travels along with the focused intent; this allows people to move energy away from themselves thereby transforming energy. Thoth's audience interacts in this process during a prayformance as the energy is reflected through their own feelings. Thoth's neutral energy has a positive effect that is very helpful and healing to each within the audience.

Thoth finds the hermaphrodite a perfect metaphor of balance for all creative beings and his personal truth. In order to fulfill the creative act a balance of both masculine and feminine principles is necessary. How would it be possible to create any world without realizing the creator as a Male and Female being, and balancing these archetypes? Thoth does not comprehend the notion of a singularly male god or a male dominant creator. Similarly, as in the case of procreation, it takes both male and female to create life; and as beings within a divine construct, the Creator then must utilize both of these characteristics to bring forth the world and Creation, which then goes beyond religious principles. Utilizing positive and negative polarities, the petitioner connects to the All. Tolkien clearly expresses that the sub-creator, and all living beings, are refracted tones of light fractured from brilliance of the Creator (Tolkien 144).

These concepts clearly expressed by Thoth and Tolkien are akin to a quote by William Blake utilized most expressly by Aldous Huxley, "If the doors of perception were cleansed every thing would appear to man as it is, infinite" (Huxley 1954).

In the same vein as a hermaphrodite, is the "berdache," an anthropological term, which represents individuals often viewed as two-spirits (male/female) inhabiting a single body. There has been some debate over the validity of the term "berdache" because of the etymological connection with the Persian term "bardaj" which was used in reference to a male prostitute or catamite. The dress of the berdache is generally a mixture of male and female clothing, and they have distinct gender and social roles within a Native American tribe. Rather than being shunned or hated, the berdache was often a powerful and valued member of the community. He or she was of a third or perhaps even a fourth distinctly different gender, free from the ordinary confines of a strictly male or strictly female gender box. Many of them, perceived as warriors, held strong mystical powers and were active healers, medicine people, fortune-tellers, astronomers, divine messengers and leaders (whether as a chieftain or matron). This minor detail of a berdache enlightens further unto the role of Thoth in society. He has many of these attributes, yet the term "berdache" is but a term to describe a particular being, such as the term shaman.

Visionary artist Alex Grey once described Thoth as "an urban shaman," a loving and respectable compliment, but unfortunately the term "shaman" has changed greatly in Western society, being as cliché as the word/concept of "heaven," and is no longer recognized as it once was. One of the first places one should look for signs of modern shamanism is in the artistic sphere, which for the artist extends not only to his work, but also to his very life. Through manipulation of the physical medium, the artist seeks to express his personal vision of reality — a vision arising from the roots of the unconscious and not dependent upon public consensus; in fact, often actively opposed to it (McKenna 18).

Up until his death in 2000, Terence McKenna was the foremost visionary scholar who re-ignited the role of the shaman as a symbol of change and return toward an archaic understanding of this important term. McKenna's revival of archaic forms of being teaches humanity to reject the designer states of consciousness programmed by big business and know that by returning to the role of shaman humans can break this industrial web of illusion (McKenna 254). By restating the role of shaman through the eyes of McKenna, the importance of Thoth's role in society can be seen:

> A reverence for and an immersion in the powers of language and communication are the basis of the shamanic path ... this is why the shaman is the remote ancestor of the poet and artist. Our need to feel part of the world seems to demand that we express ourselves through creative activity. The ultimate wellsprings of this creativity are hidden in the mystery of language....
>
> A shaman is one who has attained a vision of the beginnings and the endings of all things and who can communicate that vision ... the shaman is a specialist in the sacred, able to abandon his body and undertake cosmic journeys "in the spirit" (in trance) ... for the supreme goal of the shaman is to abandon his body and rise to heaven or descend into hell ... at its fullest shamanism ... is a dynamic connection into the totality of life on the planet [McKenna 7, 59].

Yet this is a lens of definition, a glimpse of insight from an authority on the subject, but Thoth is not limited by it. Thoth embodies a type of shamanic connection to creation, and his work peers into the mystery of language and embodies shamanic qualities and traditions. Whether it is through the language of the Festad, or ecstatic spinning and dancing as he plays the violin communicating scenes from his mythological world, Thoth is able to channel vital earth and cosmic-based energies into the community. With this energy Thoth is able to heal through his work as a shaman, yet he should be perceived as one who is "fully being," and cannot be classified wholly under the shamanic title.

His statement "I heal through divine prayformance" echoes this sentiment. Thoth prayforms as a healing for himself; if he did not, he would not "Be." He prayforms as a healing for the very much involved audience as well, although he doesn't make this claim himself. He allows them to discover this for themselves, taking great pains through humility not to prompt anyone into a pre-determined end result of his work.

Thoth cannot be classified, or limited to either shaman or berdache, but through the tools of these offices he becomes an intermediary, and technician of the sacred, between the community and the numinous archetypal symbols of the collective unconscious. He has exponentially broadened the methodology of both these roles, bringing one of the most archaic of religious practices into a new context. Both the shaman and the berdache understood that to heal one's self, and the community around them, all types of energies were utilized, not just the limited one-sided patriarchal force that dominates our present culture. Thoth has undergone a radical change from his earlier roots, through symbolic death and resurrection, healing himself through continuously prayforming and sub-creating. In turn he provides aid for those attending a prayformance. Much of this is lost on the mundane materialistic Western culture, as are the rituals of ancient tribal traditions and their esoteric practices, medicines, healing, and understanding of the connectivity of all things. Western humans have lost their sense of unity with the cosmos and with the transcendent mystery within themselves. From the point of view of religious symbolism, this preoccupation of modern humanity with its historical and existential situation springs from an unconscious sense of its impending end (McKenna 17). If this were grasped by Western society, the sub-creating rituals would lend incredible information and assistance to the entire world.

To fully express one's own Truth a great work takes a long time, if not a lifetime to perfect. Thoth stabilizes the principles of balance within his creative world. Physically, he uses both hands, both sides of his physical being to further his total balance. This can be seen in the numerous aspects of his daily life, from the smallest task — eating, shaving, signing CDs with both hands to create a mirror image of the message — to the larger aspects such having the world's only double chin rest for his violin, which allows him to prayform from both sides of the instrument. One of the technical origins of this device, aside from Thoth's neutral approach, was discussed with Michael Simmons in the fall of 2002 for *Fiddler Magazine*:

> At first I found it difficult to play violin and sing. When I was growing up, my teacher never let me use a shoulder rest, so I never learned to hold the violin tightly under my chin, which helped. Not using a shoulder rest gave me the freedom to explore other ways of holding he violin and now I can play the violin every which way, and I can play even when I'm singing and dancing. I can even play it left-handed. I begin my prayformance playing left-handed and switch to right-handed as the piece progresses.... My soloperas are both composed and improvised. Each of the characters has a motif, a brief phrase, and then I improvise upon those motifs. When you listen to the Soloperas, you immediately recognize Caguma and Nular-in from their basic motifs, but they change slightly every time I play [Simmons 25–26].

This all served to educate him on both the masculine and feminine spiritual aspects of his journey.

All of Thoth's favorite influential artists embarked on their own journeys as they perfected their work. Wagner spent thirty years on his Ring cycle. Tolkien labored for over fifteen years on the published version of *The Lord of the Rings* alone. Any great work needs such fine-tuning, for it is in actuality a reflection of the artist's life. Tolkien's *Rings* epic was completely his own and had ties to his own ancestral heritage, archetypes, languages, ancient people and stories. Thoth found Tolkien had the most completion of any creative world that he knew, which he found stimulating. Creating his own maps through the inspiration of Tolkien's, he soon followed this with the creation of his own world. He recognized the importance of the cycles of our primary world, yet he marveled at how Tolkien utilized them. The creative cycle will always be the same for Thoth, to see how things are affected by cycles. These cycles cause change, even for the so-called changeless, because these cycles sail across the ocean into a different cycle. An example of this would be Tolkien's elves, that see great change around them and must in the end sail across the ocean, for their time has come to an end. What would later become the world of the Festad grew from these cycles, life began within the image of crystal, as emanated sound, and ultimately as the manifested language of Thoth's secondary world through sound and tone. This beautiful and pristine crystal begins as their Eden, their bliss, their All. From their first gestation inside the crystal, religion or a cyclical term of it is present. Thoth believes people behave in such cyclical terms as well; they are afraid and they behave in a measure prescribed by this belief to overcome their fears.

With this understanding, Thoth is bringing into existence a sub-created world he calls "Festad." Translated roughly as "Dreamland," the Festad was born from Anya and populated by the Mir who emerge from her crystallized being. It grows, flourishes and eventually decays over a period of four ages. The Mir reflect racial, cultural and sexual diversity. Eventually a Mir named Nular-in journeys, spins a death dance and destroys the world, making way for a new world to come into existence. In tribal cultures, the death dance takes various cultural forms according to a particular spiritual practice. Opening the door to Gurdjeiff's "high octave," Thoth floods his every cell with the ability to bring into existence mythical dimensions willed thru his act of the death dance. In discussing the changing of ages, worlds, during the course of our planet's life, Daniel Pinchbeck defines this process with blinding clarity:

> The process of transition from one world to another could be one of simultaneous creation and destruction. The "opening of a world" might be an exquisitely timed process, like the stage of fetal development, but taking place within the psyche. It might even be necessary that this process remain shrouded in mystery until its final stage.... Such a shift would not be the "end of the world," but the end of a world, and the opening of the next [Pinchbeck, 15].

The Festad's ultimate hero/ine Nular-in, learns from mentor, Caguma, and other guides and teachers the divine gifts of world creation and destruction, which allow him/her to affect a shift in the planetary age and destroy the old. The Festad is Thoth's sub-creation, as Middle-earth is Tolkien's, each work containing just enough information and tools for the participant to learn and begin the process of sub-creating.

The Land of Ma is the place where the people are born within the crystal. Yet, Thoth's world is not Utopian. Once people of his world emerge, their troubles soon begin. All things begin to change, they soon begin to break apart and separate. The Land of Ma becomes their religion and because there no longer is a Land of Ma, they become cultists, the Land of Ma people, or the Ma. What has happened is a twist in focus, femininity, religion and language and Ma becomes a control. The inhabitants of the Festad soon accept their place, many lose the ability to reason, many unify with a dictator, and warring amongst the people ensue. Similar to our society, they too must go through this cycle of living and decay, when nearing death they must manifest their sub-creations and will of being. To some in the Judeo-Christian world this stage is called "heaven." All have the opportunity to live well, and take part in public service, "To Be" fully, yet not to gain from it. To fully manifest the sub-creation through death, both for one's self and the world, the moment when one's intent is pure, to maximize one's energy, one must perfect this moment through life by knowing the evil behaviors of the world and life. Here, true to the Primary world, is an example of evolutionary cycles: life, death, rebirth and the journey toward union. The importance of this method lies in actively connecting to the rhythmic patterns of the world, which allows the audience a sense of connected familiarity. This story, the basis of Thoth's sol-opera, is the last age of the Festad, where Nular-in learns what tools are necessary to reunify their people.

Middle-earth Minstrel

All of Thoth's first improvised mood music, the early sounds of the Festad, later became the CD *The Tone Poems of the Festad*. At the same time, he began to write in a Milton-esque heroic pentameter. Yet this was not his own style, he just tended to admire it above other methods. Thoth felt as though he were enmeshed within a complete Homeric archetype, the whole feeling of being on a hero's journey. Many great epics being expressed in the pentameter, Thoth found it magnificent and was compelled to write in this mode, but chose not to adopt it as his own singular style. For him, his work grew beyond any one stylistic pattern of expression, becoming the sounds, the music itself, and hearing what he thought as the emotion and feeling of what the Festad was. He did not want to write the music, as concretely as Milton wrote "Paradise Lost" or as Wagner composed his operas, for fear of losing the essence of feeling behind the journey. When committing to a style such as the heroic pentameter, the artist becomes too bound with the style, the formula, the method and not the feeling. The myths and stories of the Festad are first sounded out acoustically, practiced, and expanded upon. This method allowed the sound to flourish, emanate and expand beyond the original tonal vision. Each bit of the language is born of sound, becoming written form from its energy, which the created world then manifested. For those familiar with science fiction or generic fantasy tales, the languages contained within them are superficial manifestations of what may sound good to their creators. Thoth finds it particularly irritating that the creators of these stories are very good at everything else, yet have no criteria or ready connection for the establishment of their world's language. Tolkien spent his entire life niggling and tweaking his languages, perfecting them, for this should always be the process of language. The language of the Festad, which Thoth sings in during each prayformance, is also a manifested runic system of 252 characters. This language can be read and written in a multitude of directions, whether it is any one of the compass points or spirally. Thoth's own balance of thought, Self and Being, has allowed the language of the Festad to flourish.

The creative process is a process ongoing throughout life. Tolkien labored until the end of his days on his epic *The Silmarillion*, which his son later published posthumously. Tolkien's *Silmarillion* introduces his creation myth and its own pantheon of Creator and gods. Eru Ilúvatar and the Ainur are comparable to many Judeo-Christian, ancient Near Eastern and Greek creation myths. Within the world of Thoth, Anya gives life to the Festad. Anya is the masculine and feminine deity who contains the language in its most pure of forms, known as Mir, cited earlier as the Ma people in a previous incarnation of the myth. It is important for Anya, the people (beings well-balanced in the masculine and feminine principles) and the language to maintain the context of male and female in its pure form, for in this purity it can be written with both hands, and read in various modes. It is only through time that the people veer off, splinter and separate, migrating to various lands within the Festad, which in time they devolve into focusing on the chosen one-sided tool of their land and their perceptions, and their theories all become one-sided, dominant over each other.

The language within the creation myth, when Anya becomes the Ma Crystal and she spirals out of a pyramid, is then based from these three pyramids spiraling within one another forming a crystalline whole. The three pyramids, representing the interconnectivity of past, present and future, also encompass primarily the concepts of active, passive and neutral. The all-encompassing circle of neutrality spins about the pyramids, embracing the active and passive principles as they spiral within it. The spiral of these pyramids connects to the notion of the DNA strand, the spiraling of birds, and the golden mean. The pyramids and their spiraling are the template of these characters as they emerge from Anya. Looking downward into the pyramids as they spiral, the language is seen from a three-dimensional perspective. One can then travel from base to top, downward, around the base, back up the spiral forming each runic character. As a language that can be multidimensional, as well as linear in aspect, one must be able to dance the paths that are formed traversing the letters as well. A curvaceous language represents a loss of the advantages of an organically-based cuneiform language. All languages originate from cuneiform, yet become more technologically-based rather than organically-based and as technology increases, our language becomes more problematic. As Thoth states:

> We have technology to do all of these things for us and we lose the simplicity of the line. Now we have languages, and writing systems, that are less direct. Once you begin doing curves with a stone implement it becomes harder to do than lines. It is also true to dance curves, yet it is more difficult because a curve is less precise. With cuneiform you can go from point-to-point, from each point you have the meaning of the line.

Thoth hopes that this language is a more correct and direct method of cuneiform, where it is the more primitive feature for a future yet to be revealed. This principle is key for Anya to dance the spiral to create the Festad and its people and language. "It all must be danceable." It is important to look upon these principles to see that all the encompassing parts flow together, never becoming one of the transient parts and seeing all sides. As Anya dances, beings begin to emerge, the first is Ma the epitome of the feminine. As she grows more distant from the later generations, she becomes the goddess of motherhood. Thoth compares this to the Greco-Roman gods where the male leadership principle, embodied in Zeus, Achilles, and Odysseus may have indeed been a person at one time. Over time, that person becomes more abstract, a symbol and a portion of a language, which is what occurs with the Mir: they become the abstracted gods of the Festad and its language. As Thoth states:

> Within the language there is not contained the word "the," which our society utilizes to indicate individuality. The first character, if one is speaking of the feminine, will be the first sound, or the last sound on a line of sounds. All the first characters get that position, then the first character is connected to the second and that second one tells us about the sound and it can be in verb form. Up until this point everything "is," then emotions, in the sense of thought begin to put them together. By joining the singular Ma principle with another the term, Ma produces feminine femininity.

As Nular-in has learned from his teachers, Caguma and others, obtaining internal and external power tools learning how to "be fully," he is able to construct a new world for his people. This is not a small undertaking, for Nular-in or the sub-creator, to reconnect the fragments of language, myth, energy and primitive environmental understanding and connectivity. The vision of this new world will unify earlier principles with an understanding that future generations may benefit from their long dormant capabilities.

The Future for Thoth

In speaking to Thoth about his life and the process of sub-creation, world creation and destruction, a realization has been brought to light that indeed this is the path of true human evolution. It would be exciting to see Thoth bring his insights into the lecture format, where participants can bring their sub-created worlds and find help creating rituals to manifest them. Through this course of learning the sub-creative process, participants would be able to learn to trust their own visions and goals, to stop the judgments of society from limiting their arts, to stay the course, Be fully, and know that everything but their sub-creation is illusion. By taking part in a course on prayformance, world creation, destruction, and sub-creation, participants could bring tools they have learned, and Thoth would assist in the first dance of that creation, giving some power tools to teach how to better manifest their sub-created worlds.

With the insights from Tolkien and Thoth's methodology, power tools of sub-creation, divine gifts of energy and ancestral messages, how can individuals allow their own minds or society's markets to label these works as fiction or fantasy? If these worlds reflect and mirror a larger celestial fabric within humanity's physical being and relate to a Creator on a microcosmic scale, then they are indeed worlds waiting to be opened and should not be bordered by disbelief from a blind society.

Note: Anthony S. Burdge would like to thank Jessica Burke for her assistance.

Works Cited

Chance, Jane, ed. *Tolkien and the Invention of Myth*. Lexington: University Press of Kentucky, 2004.
Glyer, Diana Pavlac. *The Company They Keep: C.S. Lewis and J.R.R Tolkien as Writers in Community*. Ohio: University of Kent State Press, 2007.
Hamlin, Jesse. "Race Matters: Overcoming the Hidden Taboos of Crossing the Color Line." *San Francisco Chronicle*, February 19, 2006, D-1.
Hasten, Lauren Wells. "In Search of the 'Berdache': Multiple Genders and Other Myths." *Digital Anthropologist*. Spring 1998. Columbia University, .
Huxley, Aldous. *The Doors of Perception*. New York: Perennial, 1990.
Maisak, N.C. "Loincloth Maestro." *New York Post*, October 2001, 65.
Mewbourne, Denise. "S.K. Thoth and the Power of Presence." *Tea Party Magazine*. Oakland, CA, 47–49, 56.
McKenna, Terence. *The Archaic Revival: Speculations on Psychedelic Mushrooms, the Amazon, Virtual Reality, UFOs, Evolution, Shamanism, the Rebirth of the Goddess, and the End of History*. San Francisco: HarperCollins, 1991.
_____. *Food of the Gods: The Search for the Original Tree of Knowledge — A Radical History of Plants, Drugs, and Human Evolution*. New York: Bantam, 1992.
_____, and Dennis McKenna. *The Invisible Landscape: Mind, Hallucinogens and the I Ching*. San Francisco: HarperCollins, 1975.

Phelan, Sarah. "A Loin in Winter." *Metro Santa Cruz*. San Francisco, CA, April 2002, 7–9.

Pinchbeck, Daniel. *2012: The Return of Quetzalcoatl*. New York: Penguin, 2006.

Ruhling, Nancy. "Ancient God Plays Central Park." *New York Newsday*, December 1, 2000, A-53.

Simmons, Michael. "Thoth: Fiddle Tunes from a Mythological Land." *Fiddle Magazine* (Winter 2002/03): 25–27.

Thoth, S.K. Interviews with author, July and September 2006.

Thoth. Dir. Sarah Kernochan. Direct Cinema, 2002.

Tolkien, J.R.R. *The Letters of J.R.R. Tolkien*. Ed. Humphrey Carpenter. Boston: Houghton Mifflin, 2000.

———. *Smith of Wootton Major*. Extended edition. Ed. Verlyn Flieger. London: HarperCollins, 2005.

Contributors

Amy M. Amendt-Raduege is a doctoral candidate in the Department of English at Marquette University. Her dissertation, "The Bitter and the Sweet," focuses on death and dying in *The Lord of the Rings*.

David Bratman edited *The Masques of Amen House* by Charles Williams, Tolkien's fellow Inkling, published together with "Music for the Masques" by Hubert J. Foss (Mythopoeic, 2000). He is a concert reviewer for San Francisco Classical Voice (*www.sfcv.org*) and has written many articles on Tolkien and the Inklings, including the bio-bibliographical appendix to *The Company They Keep: C.S. Lewis and J.R.R. Tolkien as Writers in Community* by Diana Pavlac Glyer (Kent State University Press, 2007) and the annual review of "The Year's Work in Tolkien Studies" in the annual review *Tolkien Studies*.

Anthony S. Burdge, founder and chairman of the Northeast Tolkien Society, is an independent scholar whose studies range from Native American myth and culture shamanism to the ethnobotanical principles of spiritual transformation, Norse mythology, medieval literature, and Tolkien studies. He is a contributor to *The Oxford Encyclopedia of Children's Literature* (2006) and *The J.R.R. Tolkien Encyclopedia* (Routledge, 2006). His research entails the early Native American people and fairy stories of the New York City area for a historical fiction publication, developing a full length work on S.K. Thoth, and creating a collection dedicated to shamanistic explorer Terence McKenna.

Bradford Lee Eden is associate university librarian for technical services and scholarly communication at the University of California, Santa Barbara. He is editor of *OCLC Systems & Services: Digital Library Perspectives International* and *The Bottom Line: Managing Library Finances*, and is associate editor of *Library Hi Tech* and *The Journal of Film Music*. He has master's and Ph.D. degrees in musicology, as well as an M.S. in library science. He publishes in

Contributors

the areas of metadata, librarianship, medieval music and liturgy, and J.R.R. Tolkien, including his chapter in *Tolkien the Medievalist* (Routledge, 2004).

Deanna Delmar Evans holds a Ph.D. from Case Western Reserve University and is professor emerita of English at Bemidji State University, Minnesota. She has published articles in *Studies in Scottish Literature, Neophilologus, Magistra: A Journal of Women's Spirituality in History, Old English Newsletter, Medieval Feminist Newsletter, Minnesota English Journal,* and *Proceedings of the Medieval Association of the Midwest,* as well as in book collections, including *The European Sun* and *Woman and the Feminine in Medieval and Early Modern Scottish Writing.* She wrote a biography of William Dunbar for the *Dictionary of Literary Biography* and also for *The Companion to Catholic Literature.*

Jason Fisher is an independent scholar specializing primarily in J.R.R. Tolkien and Germanic philology (including Old English and Old Norse). Some of his recent work includes entries in *The J.R.R. Tolkien Encyclopedia: Scholarship and Critical Assessment* (Routledge, 2006) as well as chapters in *Tolkien and Modernity* (Walking Tree, 2006), *The Silmarillion: Thirty Years On* (Walking Tree, 2007), and *Truths Breathed Through Silver: The Inklings' Moral and Mythopoeic Legacy* (Cambridge Scholars, 2008). He has also published articles and book reviews in *Tolkien Studies, Mythlore, North Wind,* and *Renaissance,* and he has presented papers on Tolkien and the Inklings in a variety of academic settings and conferences.

John R. Holmes has been teaching Old English, phonology, and Tolkien at Franciscan University of Steubenville (Ohio) ever since he completed his Ph.D. in unrelated topics at Kent State University in 1985. He has twice taught a summer tutorial on Tolkien and Old English at the Centre for Medieval and Renaissance Studies, Oxford.

Keith W. Jensen is an instructor of humanities at William Rainey Harper College in Palatine, Illinois, and teaches courses in early and modern Western culture, the Middle East, classical mythology, and Tolkien. His research interests include the study of the human body and its representation in Western art, literature, music, and philosophy; theories of myth in reading Classical epic, drama, and their modern counterparts; and the use of free will and religion in Tolkien's *Silmarillion* and *The Lord of the Rings.* He is chair of the college's Humanities Department.

Darielle Richards is the director of Inner Garden Healing Arts in Salem, Oregon, where she practices energy medicine, tending the deep stories that inform our lives. She received her doctorate in mythological studies and depth psychology from Pacifica Graduate Institute. After 25 years of teaching, her research centers on the mythic imagination and the creative process of J.R.R. Tolkien, as well as the tradition of the Magus beginning with early Greek and Persian eras.

Amy H. Sturgis earned her Ph.D. in intellectual history from Vanderbilt University and teaches interdisciplinary studies at Belmont University. She is the author of four books and the editor of four books. With multiple book chapters and articles to her credit, Sturgis routinely speaks at universities, conferences, and genre conventions across North America. In 2006, she received the Imperishable Flame Award for Tolkien/Inklings Scholarship.

Peter Wilkin completed his bachelor of arts (honors) at the University of Sydney in 2007, having written his honors thesis on Tolkien's treatment of the Fall of Man in *The Notion Club Papers*. He is undertaking research into Platonic influences on Tolkien's *legendarium*, especially in regards to the Númenor story.

Index

Adventures of Tom Bombadil 32, 40–41, 47, 127, 130, 157, 159
"Ainulindalë" 3, 5, 7, 17, 50, 96, 102–105, 143–145, 161, 164, 166; *see also* Music of the Ainur
Alliteration 7–9, 11–12, 15–16, 19–21, 77, 144
Anglo-Saxon 4, 7–10, 12–15, 17, 19–20, 23, 51, 66, 116–117, 119, 144, 152
Arkenstone, David 128, 160
Armstrong, Thomas 151
Augustine, St. 44, 86, 102–103, 111
Avens, Robert 68

Bach, Johann Sebastian 161–162, 181, 183
Bachelard, Gaston 70
Baggins, Bilbo 47, 49, 56, 59, 83, 122, 127, 129, 132–134, 137, 150–151, 156, 160, 166
Baggins, Frodo 47, 49, 52, 56–59, 114, 119, 121–123, 127, 129, 132, 135–136, 151, 159, 177
Bamford, Christopher 63
Bard 2, 8, 71, 115–116, 144
Bartók, Belá 175, 181, 183, 188
Battle of Maldon 1–2, 7, 9, 15, 28
Beowulf 7, 9–10, 13, 15–16, 18–20, 22, 29, 34–35, 38, 41–42, 44, 64, 78, 115–118, 152
Blind Guardian (band) 134
Blyton, Carey 146, 155–156, 161
Bombadil, Tom 23, 31–33, 40–42, 47, 71, 127, 130–131
Brobdingnagian Bards (band) 136
Broceliande (band) 142, 158–159
Buhr, Glenn 163–164
Butterworth, George 151

Caldecott, Stratford 3
Callas, Maria 181
Campbell, Joseph 5, 64, 68
Caprice (band) 131, 159
Carpenter, Humphrey 4, 64, 66, 75, 82, 95, 97, 107, 175–177, 179, 181
Catley, Bob 134
Chant 7–9, 19, 127, 143–144, 157, 184
Chopin, Frédéric 141
Cicero 36
Coleridge, Samuel Taylor 63
Consonance 104
Cottage of Lost Play 4, 47, 51, 59
Cynewulf 9, 117, 120

Dissonance 5, 102–108, 111

Eärendel 48, 66, 97–98, 122
Elegy 5, 7–8, 15–16, 19, 116, 118–120, 122
Elgar, Edward 150–151, 161
Ellington, Duke 181
Ents 4, 8, 18–19, 23, 65, 120, 122, 144
Eriol 4, 47, 51, 56, 59
Exeter Book 15, 116

Felice, Frank 164
The Fellowship (band) 137
Festa, Giuseppe 131
Festad 184, 192, 194–198
Flieger, Verlyn 4, 23, 58, 67, 75, 105–106, 167
Franke, William 70

Gabrieli, Giovanni 144
Gamgee, Sam 26–27, 44, 49–53, 57,

Index

59, 114, 119, 121–123, 127, 129, 132, 135, 136, 141–142, 151
Glass Hammer (band) 136, 154–155
Gondor 16, 29, 49, 53, 119–120, 129, 134, 136
Great Luke Ski 132
Grimsditch, Andi 131

Handel, George Frideric 145
Hanson, Howard 152, 161, 163–164
Hansson, Bo 159, 162
Harvey, David 4
Heliand 9
Hendrix, Jimi 175, 181, 188
Henry, Kevin 134
Hildebrandslied 9
Hobbitons (band) 130, 158, 160
Hobbits (band) 137
Holst, Gustav 142, 151, 162
Horvath, Alan 135
Hymn 20, 48–49, 159, 163

Inklings 62–63, 107, 164

Jackson, Peter 128–129, 132, 137, 142, 146, 151, 160
Johanson, Sven-Eric 160
Jung, C. J. 62, 66–68, 70

Kalevala 86, 149, 161
Klein, Adam C.J. 160
Knight, Gareth 62
Kreeft, Peter 27

Lay(s) 5, 12, 76–81, 96–97
Leaf by Niggle 69, 181
Led Zeppelin (band) 128, 132, 153–4
Legendarium 5, 15–16, 47, 59, 140, 144–145
Levertov, Denise 68
Lewis, C.S. 26, 33, 38, 78, 146, 156, 173, 177,
Lewis, Warren 164, 168

Marillion (band) 154
McCarthy, Daniel 164
Meij, Johan de 128, 162
Melkor 22, 52, 77, 102–106, 108, 111, 145; *see also* Morgoth
Melnyk, Lubomyr 164

Mendelssohn, Felix 146
Middle English 4, 9, 11–15, 27–29, 34, 75–78, 82
Monteverdi, Claudio 144
Morgoth 23, 54–56, 58–59, 77, 80–81, 83–84, 97, 107–111, 143, 163–164; *see also* Melkor
Morris, William 87–88, 90, 93–94, 152
Mostly Autumn (band) 135
Mozart, Amadeus 27, 70, 145, 183
Murray, Robert 26, 31, 33
Musgrave, Thea 155, 161, 163
Music, martial 15, 17
Music of the Ainur 17, 50–51, 98, 106; *see also* "Ainulindalë"
Musical instruments, Anglo-Saxon 10

"Namárië" (song) 127, 143, 153, 156–157
Nimoy, Leonard 132
Notion Club Papers 4, 47, 59

Old English 1, 7–16, 19–22, 28–29, 32–35, 38, 41–44, 57, 66, 78, 141
Old Norse 9, 17, 20, 32
Oldfield, Sally 154
Oliver, Stephen 129, 160, 168
Oromë 4, 7, 16–18, 20, 22–23, 57

Palestrina, Giovanni 144
Parker, Charlie 181
Peters, Jonathan 161
Peterson, Thomas 163
Philology 4, 26–28, 43, 75, 86, 98–99
Phonology 4, 27–28, 36, 40, 42
Plotinus 63, 86, 97
Prokofiev, Serge 145
Prosody 34, 86
Prayformance 171–172, 175–176, 184–185, 187, 189–190, 192–193, 196, 199

Quenya 7, 16–18, 22, 149

Raine, Kathleen 62
Ravel, Maurice 181
Rhythm 4, 27, 32–37, 41–42, 64, 131, 158, 172, 174, 181–183, 186–187, 195
"The Road Goes Ever On" (poem) 49

Index

The Road Goes Ever On (song cycle) 127, 130, 143, 152, 156–157
Rohirrim 7, 12–13, 15–18, 119–120, 144
Roseman, Leonard 133
Rush (band) 131
Russell, Craig 163

Sallinen, Aulis 161–162
Sardello, Robert 68
Sauron 19, 53, 56, 58, 107, 114, 121–122, 135–136, 143, 154
Sayer, George 141, 143
Scop 8–10, 17, 20, 115–117
Seeman, Chris 152–153, 164
Segal, Charles 83
Shakespeare, William 9, 145, 147, 174
Shippey, Tom 9, 12–13, 20–22, 27, 33, 37–38, 75–76, 78–80, 83, 119, 141, 147, 166
Shore, Howard 129, 135, 142, 146, 160–161
Sibelius, Jean 148–150, 161–162
The Silmarillion 2–3, 5, 18, 22, 48, 50, 52, 55–56, 59, 67, 77, 80, 96–98, 102, 106, 112, 127, 134–135, 143, 149, 151, 154, 161, 163, 196
Silmarils 107, 134
Sindarin 7, 18, 48, 135
Sir Orfeo 4, 11, 76–83
Solopera 171–172, 193, 195
Stark, James 130, 157–158
Sub-creation 40, 57, 126, 128, 132–135, 153, 173, 176–177, 181, 186–187, 189, 195, 198–199
Swann, Donald 123, 127, 143, 152,–153, 156–158

Swinburne, Algernon Charles 85, 87–88, 90–93

Tennyson, Alfred 85–91
Tolkien, Christopher 20–21, 67, 69–70, 77
Tolkien Ensemble (band) 130–132, 157–159, 164
Túrin 77, 97–98, 107, 109–111, 149

Unwin, Rayner 64
Unwin, Stanley 59, 64

Valar 16–18, 22–23, 54, 56, 59, 96–97, 106
Valinor 16, 48–49, 51–54, 56–59, 107, 143
Vaughn Williams, Ralph 142, 151
Verdi, Giuseppe 145
Vespasian Psalter 14–15
Vivaldi, Antonio 145

Wagner, Richard 86, 146–148, 175, 181, 183–184, 188, 194, 196
Wakeman, Rick 160
Waldman, Milton 54–55, 145, 179
Weber, Carl Maria von 148, 150
Wilhelm, Richard 68
Wordsworth, William 63, 65
Woses 4, 8, 18,
Wunder, Richard 160

Yarbrough, Glenn 128, 133

www.ingramcontent.com/pod-product-compliance
Ingram Content Group UK Ltd.
Pitfield, Milton Keynes, MK11 3LW, UK
UKHW041918140426
5217IPUK00013B/219